Charmed by His Love

Janet Chapman

JOVE BOOKS, NEW YORK

THE BERKLEY PUBLISHING GROUP
Published by the Penguin Group
Penguin Group (USA) Inc.
375 Hudson Street, New York, New York 10014, USA
Penguin Group (Canada), 90 Eglinton Avenue East, Suite 700, Toronto, Ontario M4P 2Y3, Canada
(a division of Pearson Penguin Canada Inc.) • Penguin Books Ltd., 80 Strand, London WC2R 0RL,
England • Penguin Group Ireland, 25 St. Stephen's Green, Dublin 2, Ireland (a division of Penguin
Books Ltd.) • Penguin Group (Australia), 250 Camberwell Road, Camberwell, Victoria 3124, Australia
(a division of Pearson Australia Group Pty. Ltd.) • Penguin Books India Pvt. Ltd., 11 Community
Centre, Panchsheel Park, New Delhi—110 017, India • Penguin Group (NZ), 67 Apollo Drive,
Rosedale, Auckland 0632, New Zealand (a division of Pearson New Zealand Ltd.) • Penguin Books
(South Africa) (Pty.) Ltd., 24 Sturdee Avenue, Rosebank, Johannesburg 2196, South Africa

Penguin Books Ltd., Registered Offices: 80 Strand, London WC2R 0RL, England

CHARMED BY HIS LOVE

A Jove Book / published by arrangement with the author

PUBLISHING HISTORY
Jove mass-market edition / June 2012

Copyright © 2012 by Janet Chapman.
Excerpt from *Courting Carolina* copyright © 2012 by Janet Chapman.
Cover art by Jim Griffin.
Cover handlettering by Ron Zinn.
Cover design by George Long.

ISBN: 978-0-515-15090-2

JOVE®
Jove Books are published by The Berkley Publishing Group,
a division of Penguin Group (USA) Inc.,
375 Hudson Street, New York, New York 10014.
JOVE® is a registered trademark of Penguin Group (USA) Inc.
The "J" design is a trademark of Penguin Group (USA) Inc.

PRINTED IN THE UNITED STATES OF AMERICA

10   9   8   7   6   5   4   3   2   1

ALWAYS LEARNING   **PEARSON**

Jove titles by Janet Chapman

HIGHLANDER FOR THE HOLIDAYS
SPELLBOUND FALLS
CHARMED BY HIS LOVE

Any similarities between Duncan MacKeage and my own driven, never-say-die, magical hero are, of course, purely coincidental. You're still standing guard at the gate of my dreams, husband, and you still rock my world!

Chapter One

Peg Thompson slid open the side door of her minivan and gave the four children inside her well-perfected, I-mean-business scowl. "Okay, you clean and handsome little human beings, your challenge for the day is to *stay* clean and handsome until *after* the wedding. And when we come back here for the reception, you will change into your play clothes *before* you go near any food. Got that?" Peg paused for effect, stifling a smile when every last one of them vigorously nodded. "So that means until we leave for church you will stay away from mud puddles, melting piles of snow, and the lake." She lost her scowl when her gaze landed on her youngest son. "And nobody goes near the scientific equipment on the beach, or any of the scientists. Charlotte, you're in charge of Jacob, and Isabel, you're in charge of Peter." She held up her hand when both girls started to protest. "This is Miss Olivia's special day, and as her bridesmaid I have to help her get ready. So could you all please just cooperate with me this morning?"

"But *Mommm*," Charlotte protested anyway. "I need to help Sophie. Today's special for her, too. She's going to be the maid of honor and she's getting a new *dad*."

"And Henry needs me," Isabel chimed in, not about to

be out-whined. "I have to make sure he looks all handsome because he's getting a new *mom* today."

Peg was fairly certain the last thing Henry wanted was Isabel's help, considering the girl had blatantly been stalking the poor boy for the last two weeks. "Henry's grammy and auntie Caro are making sure he's all handsome. And besides, as the best man he'll be busy helping his dad get ready. Now, are there any questions or comments or concerns before I turn you loose on Inglenook?"

Jacob, bless his little heart, actually raised his hand. "Do I come get you if I see that scary man?" he asked, giving a shudder as he shrank back into his booster seat.

"Not today, big man," Peg said with an encouraging smile. "This morning we need to stay focused on Mac and Olivia's wedding. But first thing Monday morning, you and I are going to find the man who scolded you, and after you bravely tell him you're sorry for climbing on his submarine and that you won't ever do it again, you will see that you don't have to be afraid of him."

And then I'm going to send you away, Peg silently added, *and give the bastard hell for scaring two years off your tender little heart.*

"So okay," she said as she stepped aside and waved them out of their seats. "Be good this morning, and by noon you can all turn back into the noisy, disheveled little heathens that I know and love."

"I'm not changing out of my party clothes until after the reception," six-year-old Isabel said as she jumped out of the van and smoothed down the front of her dress. She squinted up at Peg. "And don't forget to take a picture of me dancing with Henry so I can bring it to school. Rhonda Beekman is telling everyone that I made up my new boyfriend."

"Trust me," Peg drawled, "if you get Henry to dance with you, I will definitely take your picture."

"Mom," eight-year-old Charlotte said as she helped Peter get his booster seat belt untangled. "Does Sophie have to change her last name to Oceanus, too?"

"Nope. She'll remain Sophie Baldwin until *she* gets married, unless she decides to keep her maiden name."

"I'm going to change my name to Oceanus when I marry

Henry," Isabel said as she fussed with the bow on her dress. She held out her hand. "Come on, Peter. Let's go sit in the gazebo and see if we can spot any whales."

Not about to be caught dead holding his sister's hand, Peter jumped from the van and bolted toward the pine-studded peninsula that jutted out between Whisper Lake and the new Bottomless Sea. "You can watch for whales," he called over his shoulder. "But I'm watching for sharks!"

Peg pulled Jacob out of his seat to look him in the eye. "Be brave, my big man," she whispered. "I won't let anyone hurt you. But you have to help me by not going near the science equipment, okay? You can see everything the scientists are doing from the gazebo. And if you behave for Charlotte, I'll buy you a book about ocean creatures."

"Of my very own?" Jacob asked. "I won't have to share it with Pete?"

Peg gave him a quick hug and swung him out of the van. "It'll be all yours. Together we'll write your name on the inside, and if Peter wants to look at it he'll have to ask your permission. Now go on," she said, giving him a nudge to follow his siblings. "And you all stay clean!" she called after them.

"Mom, where's Miss Olivia going with that toilet plunger?" Charlotte asked. "Shouldn't she be getting ready for her wedding?"

Peg looked at where her eldest daughter was pointing. "Oh, good Lord," she muttered, gesturing for Charlotte to go after her brothers and sister. "Keep an eye on everyone for me, okay, while I go see what Olivia's up to."

Peg headed off knowing *exactly* what her friend was up to. Why else would Olivia be micromanaging her little kingdom of aging cabins today of all days, if not to keep her mind off the fact that she was about to marry one of the richest, handsomest, scariest men on the planet?

"And just what do you think you're doing?" Peg asked, cutting her off.

Olivia blinked in surprise, then held up the plunger. "The toilet in cabin three is overflowing and I have to go fix it."

Peg snatched the plunger out of her hand. "Why isn't one of your *employees* saving our mad scientists?"

Olivia brushed at nothing on the front of her old sweatshirt, and Peg couldn't help but notice her friend's hands were trembling slightly. "Um, our cook has everyone helping him get ready for the reception." Olivia grabbed her arm. "My God, Peg, I swear a small army of guests crawled out of the woodwork. How in hell can everyone drop whatever they're doing to come to a wedding on only a week's notice?" She leaned closer. "I think several of the people Mac's father invited are royalty," she whispered. "And I heard one of them address Titus as 'Your Royal Highness.'" Her hand on Peg's arm tightened. "Will you please tell me what in hell I'm *doing*?"

Peg wrapped an arm around Olivia and started toward the small cottage nestled in the woods a short distance from the main lodge. "What you're doing is marrying Mac, who I happen to know loves you to pieces." She gave her friend a squeeze. "This will all be over tonight, Olivia. Your small army of guests will crawl back into the woodwork, and tomorrow morning you're going to wake up the happiest woman on the planet. All you need to remember is that you're not marrying Mac's father or his royal friends; you're marrying the man of your dreams."

Olivia stopped walking. "But you know everyone in town is going to think I'm only marrying Mac because he's rich, especially when word gets out that he purchased most of the timberland surrounding Bottomless. And when they find out we're building a huge resort that will turn Spellbound Falls into a world-class tourist destination, all hell's going to break loose."

"Which is exactly what this forgotten town needs," Peg said, starting them walking again. "Not only is Mac a genius but his timing's not bad, either, since that freaky earthquake turned Bottomless into an inland sea. Hell, I actually own oceanfront property now because those shifting mountains cut an honest to God *fiord* right past my house and flooded my gravel pit."

"Ohmigod," Olivia gasped, stopping to grab Peg's arm again. "Why didn't you tell me? Was your house damaged?"

"I did tell you. But you've been a tad preoccupied lately, what with helping your ex-in-laws pack, dealing with a bunch of mad scientists trying to figure out exactly what went on here last week, and planning a wedding that's taking place in *three hours.*" Peg started her moving again. "So you go take a hot bubble bath while I go fix that toilet, and I'll be back in time to help you dress and put up your hair."

"But—"

"No *but*s! You're getting married today if I have to drag you down the aisle myself. And then you're going to smile and nod your way through the reception, and tonight you're going to begin living happily ever after in the arms of your sexy husband." Peg started walking backward, only to stop and point the plunger at Olivia. "And you stay away from the groom! He can't see the bride until you're walking down the aisle looking all radiant and beautiful, so he'll realize he's the luckiest man on the planet."

Olivia took a deep breath, threw back her shoulders, and broke into a radiant smile. "Thank you for reminding me that he's the lucky one." She canted her head. "Can you tell me how we've lived in the same town for nearly twelve years and only became best friends two weeks ago?"

"That's easy; you were too busy managing Inglenook for your ex-in-laws, and I was too busy making babies."

Olivia's eyes turned pained. "You will find love again, Peg." She smiled sheepishly, shrugging her shoulders. "Heck, if it can happen to me, it can happen to you, too. You've been a widow over three years, so please don't make the same mistake I did by giving up on love. You just have to start believing in magic again."

Peg laughed and started walking backward. "I'm afraid it'll take more than magic to find a man who'd be interested in a woman with four young children." She shook her head. "And then I'm not sure I'd be interested in anyone crazy enough to date me." She stopped walking and pointed the plunger again. "Now quit stalling and go turn yourself into a beautiful and deliriously happy bride."

That said, Peg pivoted and started jogging away before Olivia decided that she should be deliriously happy in love, too—which was the last thing Peg needed. She was fully resigned to the fact that she would remain a widow until the day she died, considering she'd learned the hard way that her family's curse was more than just some funky old legend. It was bad enough living with the guilt that she was in some arcane way responsible for Billy's death; she wasn't about to kill off a second husband like her mother and aunt had.

And just what was she supposed to tell Charlotte and Isabel when they each came to her and announced they'd found the man of their dreams? *Well sure, sweetie, go ahead and marry the poor schmuck, if you don't mind that he won't live long enough to see his children graduate from elementary school.* Because any man who married any of the women in her family never made it past his thirtieth birthday. And even when Peg's mom and aunt had waited until they were into their forties to remarry, they'd both lost their second husbands in freak accidents.

Peg often wondered what wicked sin the first black widow had committed to have placed such a horrible curse on five generations of female descendents—even as she continued to wonder what it would take to break it.

Heck, she'd actually thought *she* had broken the curse the day she'd slid Billy's thirtieth birthday cake in the oven just hours before the surprise party she'd planned for him. Only the kitchen had filled with smoke as she'd stood staring at Billy's boss and another coworker, utterly insensate from their news that her husband was dead.

"Mom, wait up!"

Peg turned to see Charlotte and Peter running toward her. She immediately looked at the gazebo, and sighed in relief when she saw Isabel and Jacob sitting quietly watching the beach.

"Can Peter and I go to the barn?" Charlotte asked. "Sophie said most of the horses are leaving tomorrow because Inglenook's not going to have any campers this summer, and Isabel promised to watch Jacob, and I won't let Peter go in the stalls. We just want to give them each a pat good-bye."

Peg looked toward the barn. "I don't think Sam's around." She looked back at her daughter and eldest twin son. "You remember that Olivia told us Sam is her father, so he's probably busy getting ready to walk her down the aisle."

"And Mr. Ezra is her grandfather," Peter added with a semitoothless grin. He suddenly frowned. "Only how come Miss Olivia didn't know he was her grandfather? She saw him at his store in town all the time."

Peg ruffled his hair. "It's a confusing story. And the important thing is that Olivia and Sam and Ezra are finally together now."

"So can we go see the horses?" Peter asked. "I promise not to let them drool on my shirt, and we'll go right back to the gazebo after."

"Only if you also promise not to go in their stalls." Peg started walking toward cabin three again. "And thank you for asking."

"Mom!" Jacob shouted from the gazebo where he was standing on a bench. "Isabel thinks she just saw a whale blow! Only I missed it 'cause I was watching the beach. It looks like they're gonna take out the submarine. Can we sit on that rock over there to see better?" he asked, pointing toward the boulder on the shoreline. He lowered his voice as she approached. "I promise I won't talk to any of the scientists."

Peg eyed the large, flat rock jutting out into the new Bottomless Sea. She wasn't worried the kid would drown since the water wasn't deep and Jacob swam better than most fish, and she really didn't want to squelch his enthusiasm, considering his traumatic run-in with one of the scientists yesterday. Besides, what could be more entertaining for three hours than to watch a tiny two-man sub being launched?

"Okay, but you don't go any closer than the boulder, got that?"

"I got it!" Jacob shouted, jumping off the bench and running down the gazebo steps. "Come on, Isabel. I'll help you climb up the rock."

"Mommm," her daughter whined, giving Peg a rather impressive scowl. "I can't climb a rock in my party dress."

"Then sit on the log next to it," Peg suggested, once again heading off on her mission. God, she hoped the bastard who'd scared Jacob was staying in cabin three, because if he was, she intended to use his *head* for a plunger.

Since when was some stupid submarine more precious than the tender heart of a young child? For crying out loud, Jacob was four! Well, he'd be five in a couple of months, but her younger son was way behind his boisterous twin brother in many aspects. Peter was her daredevil, where Jacob was a sensitive soul.

But thanks to the family curse, her sons didn't have a whole bunch of males to emulate, now did they? Well, except for her father-in-law and Billy's older brother. Only Peg figured she had more testosterone than the two of them put together.

Honest to God, Clive Thompson sent his wife to investigate anything that went bump in the night, and his idea of sports was putting on an engineer's hat and playing with toy trains. As for her husband's hulk of a brother, Galen . . . well, everyone knew Arlene wore the pants in that family. And damn if the one time Peg had called Galen to come check out a strange vehicle in her gravel pit if Arlene hadn't shown up instead.

At least her sister-in-law had brought along a shotgun.

Peg knocked on cabin three's door, then walked inside when nobody answered, only to nearly trip over a pile of diving . . . stuff. "Be careful of that gear," a voice said from somewhere inside another pile of stuff on the couch. "It's expensive."

Peg picked her way through the clutter, but stopped at the couch to peer over the guy's shoulder. "Hey, is that a map of Bottomless?"

He kept hitting keys on his laptop, although he did give a nod.

Peg leaned closer, squinting at the screen. "Are all those numbers depths? Is Bottomless really eighteen hundred feet deep now, there in the middle?" Peg was so fascinated, she couldn't stop asking questions. "But everyone knows the deepest basin has always been four hundred feet, so does that mean the earthquake really did split open the bottom of the lake like they said on the news? And is there really an underground saltwater river running up here all the way from the Gulf of Maine?"

Again nothing, except for a grunt when she impatiently nudged his shoulder.

Peg sighed and headed toward the bathroom, only to stop and stare in dismay at the mess. Jeesh, these guys hadn't even had the combined brainpower to turn off the valve at the base of the toilet. Heck, Peter and Jacob knew enough to shut off the water, and they weren't even in school yet. She bent down to reach the valve, glad that she had enough brains to bring her bridesmaid dress instead of wearing it this morning.

"We're going to need more towels," she heard from behind her.

Wow, a whole sentence. Peg looked over her shoulder to find that the guy might be talking to her, but it was her three-pregnancy-wide backside he was looking at.

She immediately turned to face him. "You guys aren't getting any more towels until you round up the ones you've been lugging onto your boats. And here," she said, thrusting the plunger toward him. "I'll just leave this with you, since you must know more than I do about the physics of suction."

The guy—who appeared to be barely twenty—eyed the plunger as if he didn't have a clue what it was.

"Oh, you've gotta be kidding me." Peg pulled him over to the toilet. "Okay, watch and learn, because there's going to be a pop quiz later." She shot him a brilliant smile. "And if you pass, I will *give* you this fascinating tool, and then you can show all your cabinmates how it works."

"I haven't got time to mess around with some toilet," he said, turning to leave. "We're about to launch the submersible and I'm piloting it today."

Her heart skipping a beat that she may have just found Jacob's scary man, Peg grabbed the back of his shirt and pulled him back around. "Then they won't launch until you get there, will they?" She slapped the plunger against his chest. "Consider this training for when you're eighteen hundred feet underwater and your Porta-Potty clogs." She pulled him over to the toilet. "See, I'm really doing you a favor."

The guy actually shoved the *handle* of the plunger into the bowl of clear water—which made Peg suspect it was probably a washcloth plugging the toilet. "You're a rather bossy broad," he muttered, sloshing water all over the place.

Peg closed her eyes to count to ten, but only made it to five. "You try being a single parent without being bossy." She grabbed the plunger, turned it around, and slapped it back in his hand. "That's the business end."

He blinked at her. "But it's too big to fit down the hole," he said, utterly sincere as he held it up for her to see.

Really? Honest to God *really*? Peg took hold of his hand and guided the plunger down into the bowl. "Speaking of children," she said, keeping her tone neutral, "I bet when you were a kid you were fascinated by little submarines, weren't you? And some nice scientist must have showed you all around one, and you got so excited that you decided you were going to drive them when you grew up." She stopped plunging to give him another brilliant smile. "And because of that nice man, now you do."

The guy straightened, getting a faraway look in his eyes. "I was eight when my dad took me down to the pier where they were loading a four-man submersible onto a ship. One of the crew snuck us onboard and even let me climb inside it. That is, until Claude caught us." He shrugged. "But we left with a snorkel and mask, and the crewman told me to come back when I got out of college." He smiled, nodding toward the window. "I've been interning with Claude for over a year now."

"So if you were to see a little kid admiring your little submarine out there," she said conversationally, "would you show him around and feed his enthusiasm, or would you scare the bejeezus out of him by threatening to use him for shark bait?"

The guy's smile disappeared, replaced by confusion. "Oh, you must have met Claude," he said with a shrug. "He hasn't got much use for kids. And the submersible has some pretty expensive equipment and delicate instruments. Why? You mentioned being a single mom; you want me to give your kid a tour?" His gaze lowered and then lingered a tad too long on her chest before he shot her an utterly male grin. "If you let me take you to dinner tonight, I could give *you* an in-depth tour of the equipment."

Wow; she hadn't seen that one coming.

"I . . . um . . . I don't date." Peg swiped the plunger from him and drove it into the toilet bowl. "Mostly because I can't find anyone to babysit my *four* kids."

He took a step back, although Peg didn't know if it was because she was splashing water all over the place or because *she* had just scared the bejeezus out of *him*. "Four?" he choked out, taking another step back.

"Yup. All under the age of nine. There, that took care of that little problem," she said over the sucking sound of the toilet unclogging. She set the plunger beside the tank and washed her hands in the sink, but not seeing any towels, she wiped them on her pants as she turned to face him. "Now, if you can find out where all the towels are hiding, I'll give you an in-depth tour of our laundry facility," she said on her way past him. She stopped in the doorway. "What's Claude look like, anyway?"

"Hey, you aren't going to tattle on me, are you? I mean, jeeze, I was only asking you out to dinner."

"And I thank you for that." She shrugged. "I just want to keep all you guys straight, since you're going to be here all summer exploring Spellbound Falls's freaky new tourist attraction. Is Claude the boss of your little operation?"

He nodded, looking relieved—which told Peg that *Claude* was her target.

"He's fortyish," Mr. Romeo said, "a good three inches taller than me, athletic build, short dark hair." He shook his head. "You might want to leave your bossy-mama attitude at home when you're around him, though. Not only is Claude not into kids, but on a good day he barely tolerates women. And on a bad day I've actually seen him throw them overboard."

"Thanks for the heads-up," Peg said, picking her way through the cluttered cabin.

"Wait. About Bottomless," he said, making her stop at the door. "Have you lived around here long?"

"All my life."

"So you were here when the earthquake hit last week?"

"Yup."

"It must have been pretty scary when those mountains split apart," he said, pointing toward the window. He shook his head as he looked around the cabin. "The fiord the earthquake created is twelve miles long and over two thousand feet deep, but after talking to the geologists staying in cabin seven, none of us can figure out why nothing was damaged. Hell, we arrived within two days of the event and we didn't even see a broken window. All the buildings in Spellbound Falls and here at Inglenook seem to be perfectly intact."

Peg snorted. "The ground did a lot of shaking, and when Bottomless split open and the ice covering it caved in, it made one heck of a deafening *boom*. It's a miracle none of the structures were damaged. As for that new fiord, it cut right along my eastern property line and flooded a large part of my old gravel pit. So tell me, have you guys been able to come up with an explanation for what happened? Because honestly, people in town are really rattled and are calling it *magic*." She snorted. "And some are afraid to even go in a boat now, claiming Bottomless is cursed or something."

"Sorry, we're as baffled as anyone." He picked up his laptop and followed her out of the cabin. "The geologists can't figure it out, either, swearing there wasn't one warning sign of an impending earthquake. But what has us oceanographers really baffled is that the subterranean river actually became a navigable passageway from the Gulf of Maine to the St. Lawrence Seaway. The underground river surfaced in seven lakes; six here in Maine and one in Canada." He stopped at the bottom of the stairs to face her. "Each of them appearing almost deliberately spaced so that ocean mammals can come up for air."

"Does that mean there really could be whales in Bottomless?"

He nodded, gesturing toward the lake. "One of our crew swears he spotted the biggest sperm whale he's ever seen the very first day we were here, and yesterday a pod of harbor porpoises thought our submersible was a fun little toy to play with. A wide variety of saltwater creatures are already calling Bottomless home, including crustaceans that got sucked in with the river's initial surge." He grinned. "Tell your kids to keep an eye on that new fiord running past your house and they'll probably spot anything from whales to harbor seals to sharks, and your flooded pit will probably become a sheltered cove for all sorts of tiny sea creatures."

"Sharks! Does that mean we can't swim in Bottomless anymore?"

He shrugged away her concern. "They shouldn't bother you any more than they would ocean swimmers. But I'd keep your kids in the protected coves."

Peg turned away to hide her shudder. "Thanks for the heads-up," she said with a wave over her shoulder.

"Hey, what's your name?"

She turned and walked back to him with a sheepish smile. "Sorry about that. It's Peg." She held out her hand. "But I also answer to Peggy or Margaret or *Mommm*."

"Steve," he said, shaking her hand. He looked toward the beach then back at her. "So, Peg, how about I give your kids a tour of the submersible the next time Claude goes to town . . . say, in exchange for more towels?" he added with a grin.

"Deal. And as an added bonus for being such a nice guy, I'll even steal some towels from the geologists for you."

He stepped closer. "Hell, for more towels I'll sneak your kids a *ride*. Claude said something about driving down to Turtleback Station this afternoon."

"Sorry," Peg said with a shake of her head. "I'm making sure my friend gets married this afternoon." She waved toward the main lodge. "I don't know if you happened to notice all of the fuss, but there's a wedding going on here today."

"Oh yeah, that's right. I heard something about the new owners getting married. Don't worry, then. Claude's supposed to meet some oceanographers at the airport in Bangor on Tuesday, and I'll round up a couple of buddies and we'll at least get your kids out on our boat. They can watch the screen of our unmanned rover as it follows the subterranean river north." Steve paused, canting his head. "You sure you don't date? Because it just so happens I like kids."

Peg laughed and started walking backward. "Are you trying to get me arrested for compromising a minor?"

"Hey, I swear I'm legal." He sighed and waved her away. "Never mind. I just finally moved out of my parents' house, so I'm really not up to dealing with another bossy mother. I'll see you around, then," he ended, turning and jogging down the path toward the beach.

Peg headed for Olivia's cottage, a tad disturbed at how bummed she was that Steve had given up so easily.

Chapter Two

Peg rounded a curve in the peninsula's winding lane and gasped in surprise when she spotted the strange man striding across the parking lot with Jacob thrown over his shoulder. Even from this distance she could see the sheer terror in her son's eyes as Isabel skipped backward in front of them, trying to get the man to stop. Peg started running even as she sized up her adversary: tall, athletic build, short dark hair. Yeah, well, instead of traumatizing defenseless little children, Claude the mad scientist was about to find himself on the receiving end of a healthy dose of fear.

"I swear I'll kick you if you don't put him down, mister," Peg heard Isabel threaten. "He wasn't hurting your stupid machine none. He's just a baby!" And then the six-year-old actually did kick out when the guy didn't stop, only to stumble backward as he merely sidestepped around her. "Charlotte! Peter!" Isabel screamed as she scrambled in front of him again. "Come help me save Jacob from the scary man!"

Alarmed that the guy would go after her daughter when she saw him hesitate, Peg didn't even stop to think and lunged onto his back. "Put him down!" she shouted, wrapping her arm around the bastard's neck as she tried to pull Jacob off his shoulder with her other hand. "Or I swear I'll rip out your eyes!"

The guy gave his own shout of surprise and suddenly dropped like a stone when Peter slammed into his right knee. "You leave my brother alone, you scary bastard!" Peter shouted as he rolled out of the way, dragging Jacob with him.

Peg reared up to avoid Charlotte's foot swinging toward the guy's ribs, although she didn't dare loosen her grip or take her weight off him, fearing he'd lash out at her children. He suddenly curled into the fetal position with a grunt when Peter landed on him beside her.

"Get away from him!" she screamed over her shouting children, trying to push them off when they all started pummeling him. "Run to the—" Peg gave a startled yelp when an arm came around her waist and suddenly lifted her away.

"Sweet Zeus," Mac muttered, dragging her up against his chest as he took several steps back. "You will calm down, Peg, and control your children," he quietly commanded even as he tightened his grip against her struggles.

"Ohmigod, Jacob, come here!" she cried, holding out her arms. Jacob and Isabel threw themselves at her, actually making Mac step back when he didn't let her go. "You're okay, Jacob. You're safe now," she whispered, squeezing both trembling children. "You're a brave girl, Isabel, and a good sister."

Charlotte called out, and Peg saw the girl pull away from Mac's father just as he also released Peter. Both children ran to her, giving the bastard rising to his hands and knees a wide berth. Peg took a shuddering breath, trying to get her emotions under control. "You can let me go," she told Mac over the pounding in her chest. Holy hell, she couldn't believe they'd all just attacked the giant!

Mac hesitated, then relaxed his hold, letting her slip free to protectively hug all four of her children. "Mind telling me what incited this little riot?" he asked the man who was now standing and wiping his bleeding cheek with the back of his hand.

The guy gestured toward the lower parking lot. "I was taking the boy to find his parents, because I caught him inside my excavator not five minutes after I'd just pulled him off it and told him to go play someplace else." He shrugged. "I figured his mother or father could explain how dangerous earth-moving equipment is, since he didn't seem to want to listen to me." He suddenly stiffened, his gaze darting from Jacob to Peter and then to Peg. "They're twins." His eyes narrowed on the boys again. "Identical."

Pushing her children behind her, Peg stepped toward him. "I don't care if they're sextuplets and were *driving* your exca-vator or stupid submarine." She pointed an unsteady finger at him. "You have no business manhandling my kids. And if you ever touch one of them again, I swear to God I'll—"

"Take it easy, mama bear," Mac said, dragging her back against him again. "He was only concerned for Jacob's safety. As well as yours, apparently," Mac said quietly next to her ear. "Did you not notice he didn't defend himself when you and your children were attacking him? Duncan's intentions were good."

Peg stilled, a feeling of dread clenching her stomach. "D-Duncan?" she whispered, craning to look at Mac. "He . . . he's not Claude, the scientist?" She lifted her hands to cover her face. "Ohmigod, I thought he was the guy who scolded Jacob for climbing on the submarine yesterday."

She peeked through her fingers at the man she and her kids had just attacked, horror washing through her when she saw the blood on his cheek and scratches on his neck. "Ohmigod, I'm *sorry,*" she cried, jerking away from Mac and rushing to her children. Even though he was over half as tall as she was, Peg picked up Jacob and set him on her hip as she herded the others ahead of her, wanting to flee the scene of their crime before she burst into tears. "C-come on, guys," she whispered roughly, her heart pounding so hard it hurt. "Let's go to the van."

Mac's father plucked Jacob out of her arms and settled him against his chest, giving the boy a warm smile as he smoothed down his hair. "That was quite a battle you waged, young Mr. Thompson," Titus Oceanus said jovially, shooting Peg a wink as he took over herding her children away when Mac pulled her to a stop. "I'll have to remember to call on you young people if I ever find myself in a scary situation," Titus contin-ued, his voice trailing off as he redirected them toward the main lodge.

Damn. Why couldn't Mac let her slink away like the hu-
miliated idiot she was?

"It will be easier to face him now rather than later," Mac
said, giving her trembling hand a squeeze as he led her back
to the scene of her crime. "Duncan's a good man, Peg, and
you're going to be seeing a lot of him in the next couple of
years."

Wonderful. How pleasant for the *both* of them.

"Duncan," Mac said as he stopped in front of the battered
and bleeding giant. "This beautiful, protective mama bear is
Peg Thompson."

God, she wished he'd quit calling her that.

"She's not only Olivia's good friend, but Peg is in charge of
keeping the chaos to a minimum here at Inglenook." He
chuckled. "That is, when she's not creating it. Peg, this is Duncan MacKeage. First thing Monday morning, he and his crew
are going to start building a road up the mountain to the site
of our new resort."

MacKeage. MacKeage. Why did that name sound familiar
to her?

All Peg could do was stare at the hand her victim was holding out to her, feeling her cheeks fill with heat when she saw
the blood on it. Which he obviously only just noticed, since he
suddenly wiped his hand on his pants, then held it out again.

Peg finally found the nerve to reach out, saw his blood on
her hand, and immediately tucked both her hands behind her
back. "I'm sorry," she whispered, unable to lift her gaze above
the second button on his shirt—which she noticed was missing. "We . . . I thought you were the man who scared Jacob
yesterday. He had nightmares all night and I barely got him
back here today."

He dropped his hand to his side. "I'm the one who needs to
apologize, Mrs. Thompson, as I believe you're correct that I
shouldn't have touched your son." She saw him shift his
weight to one leg and noticed the dirt on his pants and small
tear on one knee. "I assumed he was the boy I'd just told to get
off the excavator. And having a large family of young cousins,
I thought nothing of lugging him off in search of his mother
or father." He held out his hand again. "So I guess I deserved
that thrashing."

Damn. She was going to have to touch him or risk looking petty. Mac nudged her with his elbow. After wiping her fingers on her pants, Peg finally reached out, and then watched her hand disappear when Duncan MacKeage gently folded his long, calloused fingers around it.

Oh yeah; she had been a raving lunatic to attack this giant of a man. Not that she wouldn't do it again if she thought her kids were being threatened.

Okay, maybe she *was* a protective mama bear.

It seemed he had no intention of giving back her hand until she said something. But what? *Nice to meet you? I look forward to bumping into you again? Have we met before? Because I'm sure I know someone named MacKeage.*

Damn. She should at least look him in the eye when she apologized—again.

But Peg figured the first three times hadn't counted, since she'd mostly been sorry that she'd made a complete fool of herself trying to gouge out his eyes with her *bear* hands. But looking any higher than that missing shirt button was beyond her. "I'm sorry!" she cried, jerking her hand from his and bolting for the main lodge, her face blistering with shame when she heard Mac's heavy sigh.

Duncan stood leaning against the wall of Inglenook's crowded dining hall, shifting his weight off his wrenched knee as he took another sip of the foulest kick-in-the-ass ale he'd ever had the misfortune to taste, even as he wondered if Mac was trying to impress his guests by serving the rotgut or was making sure they never darkened his doorstep again. He did have to admit the ancient mead certainly took some of the sting out of the claw marks on his neck, although it did nothing to soothe his dented pride at being blindsided by a mere slip of a woman and her kids.

Hell, if Mac and Titus hadn't intervened, he'd probably still be getting pummeled.

Duncan slid his gaze to the bridesmaid sitting at one of the side tables with her four perfectly behaved children, and watched another poor chump looking for a dance walk away empty-handed. Peg Thompson appeared to be a study of innate grace, quiet poise, and an understated beauty of wavy blond hair framing a delicate face and dark blue eyes—which was one hell of a disguise, he'd discovered this morning. He couldn't remember the last time a woman had left her mark on him, much less taken him by surprise, which perversely made him wonder what the hellcat was like in bed.

She was a local woman and a widow, raising her four children single-handedly for the last three years, Mac had told Duncan just before leaving him standing in the parking lot bleeding all over his good shirt. After, that is, Mac had subtly explained that he also felt quite protective of his wife's friend. A warning Duncan didn't take lightly, considering Maximilian Oceanus had the power to move mountains, create inland seas, and alter the very fabric of life for anyone foolish enough to piss him off.

But having been raised with the magic, Duncan wasn't inclined to let the powerful wizard intimidate him overly much. He was a MacKeage, after all, born into a clan of twelfth-century highland warriors brought to modern-day Maine by a bumbling and now—thank God—powerless old drùidh.

And since his father, Callum, was one of the original five displaced warriors, not only had Duncan been raised to respect the magic, he'd been taught from birth not to fear it, either. In fact, the sons and daughters and now the grandchildren of the original MacKeage and MacBain time-travelers had learned to use the magic to their advantage even while discovering many of them had some rather unique gifts of their own.

Hell, his cousin, Winter, was an actual drùidh married to Matt Gregor, also known as Cùram de Gairn, who was one of the most powerful magic-makers ever to exist. And Robbie MacBain, another cousin whose father had also come from twelfth-century Scotland, was Guardian of their clans and could actually travel through time at will. In fact, all his MacKeage and MacBain and Gregor cousins, whose numbers were increasing exponentially with each passing year, had varying degrees of magical powers. For some it might only be the ability to light a candle with their finger, whereas others could heal, control the power of mountains, and even shapeshift.

Duncan had spent the last thirty-five years wondering what

his particular gift was. Not that he was in any hurry to find out, having several childhood scars from when more than one cousin's attempts to work the magic had backfired.

That's why what had happened here last week wasn't the least bit of a mystery to the clans, just an unpleasant shock to realize that Maximilian Oceanus had decided to make his home in Maine when the wizard had started rearranging the mountains and lakes to satisfy his desire to be near salt water and the woman he loved.

Duncan sure as hell wasn't complaining, since he was ben-efiting financially. Mac was building his bride a fancy resort up on one of the mountains he'd moved and had hired Mac-Keage Construction to do a little earth-moving of its own by building the road and prepping the resort site. Duncan figured the project would keep his fifteen-man crew and machinery working for at least two years.

And in this economy, that was *true* magic.

Spellbound Falls and Turtleback Station would certainly reap the rewards of Mac's epic stunt, since there wasn't much else around to bolster people's standard of living. Not only would the resort keep the locals employed, but stores and res-taurants and artisan shops would soon follow the influx of tourists.

It would be much like what the MacKeage family busi-ness, TarStone Mountain Ski Resort, had done for Pine Creek, which was another small town about a hundred miles south as the crow flies. Only it was too bad Mac hadn't parted a few more mountains to make a direct route from Pine Creek to Spellbound, so Duncan wouldn't have to build a temporary camp for his crew to stay at through the week. As it was now, they had to drive halfway to Bangor before turning north and west again, making it a three-hour trip.

Then again, maybe Mac didn't want a direct route, since the clans had recently learned the wizard was actually allergic to the energy the drùidhs he commanded gave off. And that had everyone wondering why Mac had decided to live so close to Matt and Winter Gregor, who were two of the most power-ful drùidhs on earth.

Apparently the wizard's love for Olivia was greater than his desire to breathe.

Not that Duncan really cared why Mac was here; only that the money in his reputed bottomless satchel was green.

"Have ye recovered from your trouncing this morning, MacKeage?" Kenzie Gregor asked. He looked toward the Thompson family sitting quietly at their table and chuckled. "I can see why ye were so soundly defeated, as together the five of them must outweigh you by at least two stone."

Wonderful; help a man rebuild his home after it was nearly destroyed by a demonic coastal storm, and the guy felt the need to get in a shot of his own. But then, Kenzie was an eleventh-century highlander who'd only arrived in this time a few years ago, so Duncan figured the warrior didn't know better than to poke fun at a MacKeage. Kenzie might have his drùidh brother Matt to back him up, but the sheer number of MacKeages was usually enough to keep even good-natured ribbing to a minimum.

"If you're needing a lesson on defending yourself," William Killkenny said as he walked up, a large tankard of mead in the ninth-century Irishman's fist, "we could go find a clearing in the woods. I have my sword in the truck, and I'm more than willing to show another one of you moderns the art of proper fighting." He looked toward the Thompson table, then back at Duncan and shook his head. "It pains me to see a man defeated by a wee slip of a woman and a few bairns."

"I think Duncan is probably more in need of dance lessons," Trace Huntsman said, joining the group. "Have I taught you nothing of modern warfare, Killkenny?" Trace slapped Duncan on the shoulder even as he eyed William, making Duncan shift his weight back onto his wrenched knee. "Our friend here knows the only way he's going to defeat the Thompson army is to lure their leader over to his side. And women today prefer a little wooing to feeling the flat of a sword on their backsides."

William arched a brow. "Then someone should have explained that to his cousin, don't ye think? Hamish kidnapped Susan Wakely right out of Kenzie's dooryard in broad daylight, and rumor has it he wouldn't let the woman leave the mountain cabin he took her to until she agreed to marry him."

Trace gave Duncan a slow grin. "So I guess it's true that you first-generation MacKeages inherited many of your fathers' bad habits?" He shook his head. "You do know you're giving us moderns a bad reputation with women, don't you?" He nodded toward the Thompson table. "Maybe you should go ask her to dance and show these two throwbacks a better way to win the battle of the sexes."

"And let her trounce me twice in one day?" Duncan gestured in Peg's direction. "I believe that's bachelor number five walking away now, looking more shell-shocked than I was this morning."

"Sweet Christ," William muttered. "The woman just refused to dance with a fourteenth-century king of Prussia."

"Who in hell are all these people?" Duncan asked, looking around Inglenook's crowded dining hall.

"Friends of Titus, mostly," William said, "who aren't about to incur old man Oceanus's wrath by not showing up to his only son's wedding."

"I can't believe he dared to put time-travelers in the same room with modern locals," Trace said, also glancing around.

"And serve liquor," Duncan added, just before taking another sip of mead—because he really needed another good kick-in-the-ass. His knee was throbbing, the scratches on his neck were burning under his collar, and social gatherings weren't exactly his idea of a good time. But like most everyone else here today—the small party from Midnight Bay plaguing him now likely the only exception—Duncan wasn't about to insult the younger Oceanus, either, considering Mac was his meal ticket for the next two years.

"Uh-oh, your target is on the move," William said, his gaze following Peg Thompson and her ambushing children as they headed for the buffet table. He nudged Duncan. "Now's your chance to show us how it's done, MacKeage. Go strike up a conversation with the lass."

"Maybe you could offer to let her children sit in your earth-moving machine," Kenzie suggested. "That would show her ye don't have any hard feelings."

"Kids and heavy equipment are a dangerous mix," Duncan growled, glaring at the three of them. "Don't you gentlemen have wives and a girlfriend you should be pestering?" He elbowed William. "Isn't that Maddy dancing with the king of Prussia?"

"Oh, Christ," William muttered, striding off to go reclaim his woman.

Kenzie also rushed off with a muttered curse when he saw his wife, Eve, start to breastfeed their young infant son under a blanket thrown over her shoulder.

Trace Huntsman, however, didn't appear to be in any hurry to leave. "If it's any consolation," Trace said, "Peg Thompson was more rattled by this morning's attack than you were. Maddy and Eve and my girlfriend, Fiona, were there when Peg came to Olivia's cottage. Fiona told me it took the four of them over twenty minutes to calm her down." He shot Duncan a grin. "The women all promised Peg they would have done the exact same thing if they'd caught a stranger manhandling their child. Can I ask what you were thinking?"

"I wasn't thinking," Duncan said. "I manhandle dozens of children every time my family gets together. Everyone looks out for everyone's kids, making sure the little heathens don't kill themselves or each other. Hell, that's the definition of *clan.*"

Duncan tugged his collar away from his neck as he eyed the widow Thompson leading her gaggle of children back to their table, each trying to reach it without spilling their plates of food. He sighed, figuring he probably better apologize to her again, seeing how she owned the only working gravel pit in the area.

Just as soon as Mac had hired him to do the resort's site work, Duncan had started calling around to find the closest gravel pit to Spellbound Falls. He would eventually dig his own pit farther up the mountain, but he needed immediate access to gravel to start building the road. Duncan had been relieved to discover that the Thompson pit was just a mile from where the resort road would start, and that it had a horse-back of good bank run gravel. Only he'd also learned Bill Thompson had been killed in a construction accident three years ago.

Which is why a feather could have knocked him over this morning as he'd stood beside his truck in the parking lot changing his shirt, when he'd finally put two and two together and realized he'd just pissed off the person he wanted to buy gravel from. Assuming she'd even sell to him now. And then even if she did, he'd likely be paying an arm and a leg for every last rock and grain of sand.

"Which branch of the military were you in?" Trace asked.

Duncan looked down at himself in surprise. "Funny; I could have sworn I left my uniform in Iraq."

Trace chuckled. "You forgot to leave that guarded look with it." He shrugged. "It's common knowledge that every Mac-Keage and MacBain serves a stint in the military." He suddenly frowned. "Only I've never heard it said that any of the women in your families have served."

"And they won't as long as Greylen MacKeage and Michael MacBain are still lairds of our clans," Duncan said with a grin. "It'll take a few more generations before we let our women deliberately put themselves in harm's way."

Trace shook his head. "You really are all throwbacks. You must have a hell of a time finding wives. Or is that why some of you resort to kidnapping?"

Duncan decided he liked Trace Huntsman. "There's no 're-sorting' to it; we're merely continuing a family tradition that actually seems to work more often than it backfires. And besides, it beats the hell out of wasting time dating a woman for two or three years once we've found the right one."

"You don't think the woman might like to make sure *you're* the right one before she finds herself walking down the aisle, wondering how she got there?"

Duncan shifted his weight off his knee with a shrug. "Not according to my father. Dad claims time is the enemy when it comes to courting; that if a man takes too long wooing a woman, then he might as well hand her his manhood on a platter."

Trace eyed him suspiciously. "Are you serious?"

"Tell me, Huntsman; how's courting Fiona been working for you?"

"We're not talking about me," he growled. "We're talking about you MacKeages and your habit of scaring women into marrying you."

"I did notice you managed to get an engagement ring on her finger," Duncan pressed on. "So when's the wedding?"

Trace relaxed back on his hips and folded his arms over his

chest with a heavy sigh. "You don't happen to have an available cabin in Pine Creek, do you?"

Duncan slapped Trace on the back and started them toward the refreshment table. "Considering Fiona is Matt Gregor's baby sister, I think you might want to look for a cabin a little farther away. Hell, everyone within twenty miles of Pine Creek heard Matt's roar when he learned she was openly living with you without benefit of marriage."

Trace stopped in front of the large bowl of dark ale and glared at Duncan. "A fact that has brought us full circle back to women being warriors. The only reason I'm still alive is because Fiona puts the fear of God into her brothers if they so much as frown at me." He looked at Peg Thompson, then back at Duncan—specifically at the scratch on his cheek. "Trust me; the strong-arm approach won't work on any woman who can handle children. Not if a man values his hide."

Duncan refilled his tankard. "Which is exactly why I'm still a bachelor," he said, just before gulping down his third kick-in-the-ass like a true highlander.

Chapter Three

Peg stared out the windshield of her van at Inglenook's main lodge, so disheartened that she couldn't quit sobbing. She had finally found a job that paid enough that she'd finally be able to put a roof that didn't leak over her children's head, yet here she was trying to pull herself together long enough to quit. She couldn't even give a two-week notice, since the reason she was quitting was that she couldn't find affordable daycare for the twins. After Jacob's traumatizing incident Friday and her shameful behavior Saturday, Peg had spent two sleepless nights and all day Sunday wrestling with her decision to give her notice first thing Monday morning.

And now it was Monday. And after a third sleepless night, she still couldn't see any way around it, since Olivia had hired her when Inglenook had been a family camp that offered programs to keep her children occupied all day. Only a little over a week ago that camp had closed when Olivia's ex-in-laws had sold the property to Mac and that freaky earthquake had turned Bottomless Lake into the ninth wonder of the world.

She still had a job because a small army of scientists had replaced the campers, but now there weren't any organized activities for her children. And that meant this was no longer a safe environment for the twins, and she couldn't in good conscience draw a salary when she'd have to spend her time watching out for them instead of working. And besides, she really wasn't needed anymore, since several of Inglenook's original staff from town were looking after the scientists renting the cabins.

Dammit to hell, she needed this job!

What she didn't need was to look out her kitchen window every morning at her flooded gravel pit, especially now that she actually had a chance to make money off it. Duncan MacKeage had come to see her yesterday, but not finding her home, he'd left his card tucked in her door with a note on the back saying he wanted to speak to her about buying gravel for Mac and Olivia's resort road. Except most of the pit was underwater thanks to that stupid fiord, and the Land Use Regulatory Commission was pretty strict about disturbing ground near a lake.

Peg wiped her eyes for the hundredth time since she'd left Peter and Jacob with Billy's mom, and tried to take a deep, steadying breath. Only she wasn't surprised when she failed yet again, considering she hadn't taken a full breath since Billy had died. Damn, she was tired of holding it all together all by herself. She'd been fresh out of high school when she'd signed on for happily-ever-after, never dreaming she'd end up sleeping in an empty bed every night and raising four children all by herself.

Not that she'd give one of them up, not even for all the money in the world. Because what good was having gobs of money if she didn't have kids to take to the Drunken Moose for Vanetta's infamous cinnamon buns? Or to dress in beautiful clothes that didn't come from the thrift shop? And what good was being able to stop driving all the way to Millinocket to spend her food stamps so no one in town would know how desperate she was, if she didn't have children to worry about being—

Peg gave a startled yelp when the passenger door opened and Olivia slid into the opposite seat.

"Sorry," her friend murmured, folding her hands on her lap and staring out the windshield. "I just wanted to see what you found so fascinating that you've been sitting out here for over ten minutes staring at the lodge."

Peg buried her face in her hands and burst into tears.

"Hey!" Olivia cried, turning Peg to face her. "Have you been out here crying all this time? Peggy!" she growled, giving her a shake. "What's wrong?"

"I . . . I have to quit my job."

Olivia reared back in surprise. "Why?" She gasped. "Is this about that little incident on Saturday? Because really, you had every right to go after Duncan MacKeage like you did."

"It wasn't a *little* incident; it was a violent and utterly embarrassing attack." Peg held up her hand to stop Olivia from responding. "It was also a rude awakening. I can't work here now that Inglenook doesn't have programs for Peter and Jacob, or for Charlotte and Isabel once school gets out. I can't keep asking the girls to watch the boys, because that's not fair to any of them, and I can't watch them and do my job at the same time."

"Then we'll come up with another plan."

Peg shook her head. "I spent all weekend trying to figure something out, and the only solution I came up with is for me to quit." She grasped Olivia's hand. "And you don't really need me anymore. You have enough staff to look after the scientists."

Olivia reversed their grip, giving Peg's hand a squeeze. "But you know I have to take Sophie to California so she can donate bone marrow to little Riley, and I was counting on *you* to look after Inglenook for me." She blew out a sigh. "Because Mac's decided we're making a road trip out of it instead of flying. He wants Henry and Sophie to start feeling like the four of us are a real family."

"That's wonderful," Peg said more brightly than she was feeling.

Olivia pointed to the right of the lodge. "Do you see the nose of that . . . that *bus* sticking out past the side of the garage? That's my wedding present from Mac, and for the next two months it's going to be my home." She leaned closer. "I swear it cost more than a house. Hell, half the walls slide out on either side, making it twice as wide when we're parked for the night. And it has granite countertops and marble floors, two bathrooms, a washer and dryer, and three televisions. Three! Why would anyone need three televisions—all hooked up to satellite, I might add—in an RV?"

"Oh, Olivia, that's wonderful. You're going to see America."

"I can't live in a bus for two months! I'll go nuts."

"But it's every mother's dream to take her children on a road trip across America. Think of all Henry and Sophie will experience." Peg gave what she hoped was a cheeky smile. "And I can't imagine a better way to stay up close and personal with your sexy new husband."

"Are you insane?" Olivia whispered, looking horrified. "If I don't kill Mac before we reach the Mississippi River, I'll probably shove him into the Grand Canyon." She sighed again, shaking her head. "I know it's going to be an exciting adventure, but I really don't want to leave Inglenook that long." She leaned back against her door, waving at the windshield. "I just finally got this place all to myself; why in hell would I want to leave it for two whole months?"

"Maybe because the farthest you've been from Spellbound Falls in over eleven years is Bangor?" Peg pointed at her friend, shooting Olivia her I-mean-business scowl. "The day after school gets out you are leaving in that RV if I have to tie you to the roof."

"Actually, we're leaving this Saturday. I'm pulling Sophie out of school early because Riley's transplant is scheduled for three weeks from now—which is why you can't quit. I need you here to hold down the fort so I actually have a home to return to." She went very still. "Wait, I know; we can hire someone to watch your kids. There are plenty of women around who'd love a job, and with your being right here you won't have to worry about what your little tribe of heathens might be up to."

Peg was shaking her head before Olivia even finished. "Too much of my salary would have to go toward a babysitter to make it worthwhile."

"I'll pay her salary."

Peg glared at her. "Nothing's changed from two weeks ago when I stormed up here to tell you that I'm not a charity case. I'm not drawing a full salary and getting free daycare just because *you* can afford it." Feeling her face flush with . . . with . . . dammit, she wasn't a charity case! Peg reached down and started the engine. "I've done what I came here to do, so please get out of my van."

"Peg," Olivia whispered.

Peg pulled her seat belt across her lap and snapped it shut. "You can put my paycheck in the mail."

Silence filled the van but for the uneven rattle of its engine, until Olivia quietly got out and softly closed the door. Peg slowly pulled onto Inglenook's main lane then pressed down on the accelerator, pretending not to see Duncan MacKeage waving at her as he left Mac in the parking lot and started running to intercept the van—only to have to jump out of the way when she sped past him in a blur of blinding tears.

Duncan stood with his feet planted and his hands on his hips, scowling at Peg Thompson fleeing from him. "What in hell is up with that woman?" he growled when Mac walked over. He pointed at the cloud of dust trailing in her wake. "If that's your idea of a good friend, Oceanus, I'd hate to meet your enemies."

Instead of answering, Mac arched a brow at Olivia as she walked toward them. "Mind telling me what that was all about?"

"Peg quit her job," Olivia told him, though she was glaring at Duncan.

"Because of me?" Duncan asked in surprise.

Olivia turned her glare on Mac. "Fix this," she said, gesturing toward the knoll. "She needs this job even more than I need her."

"Then why did she quit?" Mac asked.

"Because she can't afford daycare for the twins." Olivia went back to glaring at Duncan. "After what happened Saturday, Peg doesn't dare bring her children to work with her anymore." She looked back at Mac. "So fix this."

"How?"

"I don't care how." She stepped in the shadow of her husband, out of Duncan's line of sight. "Pull a rabbit out of your hat or something," he heard her whisper tightly. "Better yet, pull out a nanny. Because I'm not getting on that bus until you fix this."

Duncan smiled, realizing Olivia was asking her husband to use his magic. And even though she was upset and obviously desperate, she was also acutely aware that she had an audience.

"You don't have to whisper, wife," Mac said. "Duncan knows who I am. All the MacKeages and MacBains and Gregors do."

"Then *fix this*," she growled loudly.

"I'm sorry," Mac said, slowly shaking his head. "It's not my place to interfere in people's lives."

Duncan didn't quite manage to stifle his snort.

After glaring over his shoulder at him, Mac looked back at his wife. "Peg's journey is one *she* must walk, Olivia. And for me to magically clear the obstacles in her path would in essence be robbing your friend of her free will. It's the trials and tribulations people overcome and how they deal with the ones they can't that define a person." Mac smiled tenderly. "Just as you are empowering Sophie by letting her save her half brother's life, you must also allow Peg to empower herself."

"Yeah, well, that may be how they do things in mythological Atlantis, but in Maine we *help* each other through our trials and tribulations." She stepped around Mac and went back to glaring at Duncan. "So *you* fix this."

"Me? Why should I be expected to fix something I didn't break? She's your friend; you fix it."

"I can't," Olivia snapped, pivoting away. "Because I have to go spend the next two months in a bus with my 'divine agent of human affairs' theurgist husband, who can turn an entire state upside down but apparently can't help my friend find daycare."

Duncan actually took a step back when Mac turned on him. "By the gods, MacKeage," the wizard said quietly—which sure as hell contradicted the wild look in his eyes. "I have no intention of traveling across this country and back with an angry wife. So fix this, dammit."

"But I didn't *break it*. I only just met Peg Thompson two days ago."

Mac glanced at Olivia stomping up the stairs to the lodge, then turned back to Duncan with a heavy sigh and scrubbed his face with his hands. He dropped them, the wild look having been replaced by desperation. "Then help me fix it."

Holy hell; the wizard was asking him—a mere mortal—for help?

"Only we have to find a way that doesn't involve the magic," Mac continued. He folded his arms over his chest, looking thoughtful. "It's my guess that Olivia is mostly concerned that Peg needs the income, as Olivia's father, Sam, is more than capable of looking after Inglenook while we're gone. So I believe if we can find some way for Peg to earn a decent living and still look after her children, then my wife won't spend the next two months glaring at *me*."

"Well, hell; if that's all you need, then consider it fixed," Duncan drawled. "Peg Thompson owns a gravel pit, and I've just spent the last two days trying to talk to her about hauling out of it until I get far enough up the mountain to open my own pit. The money I'll pay her this spring for stumpage would be more than she could earn in two years. And the best thing is she won't have to lift a finger other than to cash the checks." He frowned. "Assuming that horseback of gravel continues running west. When I was there yesterday, I noticed most of the pit was flooded with *seawater*."

Mac stared at him, clearly nonplussed, and then shook his head. "I specifically cut the fiord along Peg's land so she would end up with valuable oceanfront property." He grinned. "I felt the pit would make a good marina."

Duncan turned to head for his pickup. "So much for not interfering in people's lives," he muttered.

"Where are you going?" Mac asked. "I thought we were hiking up the mountain to decide where to position the road."

Duncan stopped and looked back. "It'll have to be this afternoon. Right now I need to go place myself in front of the widow Thompson so she can take another shot at me." He headed for his truck again. "Because with a little more practice, I'm hoping she can finally finish me off and move on to her next victim."

"MacKeage."

Duncan stopped.

"I believe you'll find that vein of gravel takes a sharp turn north rather than continuing west." Mac hesitated and then stepped toward him, his brilliant green eyes turning intense.

"And I would consider it a personal favor if you kept an eye on Peg and her children for me while I'm gone."

Duncan stared at Mac in silence for several heartbeats, uncertain if he was being given an imperial dictate or if the powerful wizard was actually asking. He finally nodded and slowly walked away, wondering how he was supposed to keep an eye on a woman he couldn't even get near, much less one who recklessly attacked a man nearly twice her size.

Duncan pulled his truck up behind the tired-looking minivan and shut off the engine as he stared at Peg Thompson's house, which appeared to be in rougher shape than her transportation. Although the dooryard was neat to a fault, time and weather and basic neglect had obviously taken a toll on the double-wide mobile home, and he was surprised it hadn't collapsed under the weight of this past year's record snowfall.

He climbed out of his truck and carefully looked around like he had yesterday, half expecting to be ambushed again if not by a small tribe of heathens then at least by a dog. But just like yesterday, he was greeted by silence. Which was baffling, since practically every house in Maine—especially if it sat back in the woods and was full of kids—had one or even several dogs in residence to discourage coyote and bear and all manner of uninvited visitors, including two-legged. Only the Thompsons didn't even seem to have a cat, judging by the squirrels coming and going through the various holes in the eave of the house.

He took the porch stairs in one stride—mostly in fear the steps wouldn't support his weight—and knocked on the storm door that was missing its top pane of glass. Oh yeah, Peg Thompson would definitely sell him gravel.

Maybe he'd offer to have his crew do some minor repairs on the house when he negotiated the price per yard, as well as point out that she'd have a working gravel pit again after he cleared off the timber and topsoil to expand it. That way he'd not only be sweetening the pot to get access to the gravel he needed, but Mac would see that he really was looking out for Peg. It was a win-win for everyone, including Olivia Oceanus.

And having a wizard's wife beholden to him was definitely a good thing.

Hell, had he fixed their little problem or what?

Except once again it appeared no one was home, so he couldn't actually execute the fix. Duncan turned and frowned at the minivan. He could hear an occasional tick coming from the engine as it cooled, and he was pretty sure the van wasn't an identical twin. So where in hell was she?

Again avoiding the porch steps, he headed around the side of the house, figuring he might as well check out the north end of the pit while he was here. Only he hadn't made it halfway there before a gunshot suddenly cracked through the air.

Holy hell, now she was *shooting* at him?

Duncan dropped to the ground and rolled behind a rock, then eyed the woods for movement where the shot had come from as he tried to rein in his temper. Protecting her children was one thing, and nearly running him down because she was upset about quitting her job was another, but shooting at him was outright hostile—not to mention certifiably insane.

God dammit, he was pressing charges!

There; just inside the tree line, he could just make out her silhouette. She slowly stepped into a stand of older trees and Duncan saw she had a rifle up to her shoulder to shoot again, her focus trained ahead of her. He took a calming breath even as he frowned. The woman hadn't been shooting at him, but was hunting something. Only problem being, it wasn't open season on anything. Unless she was after a coyote that had been hanging around, worried it might be getting too close to her kids.

His respect for Peg Thompson went up a notch. Apparently the lady didn't discriminate between two- and four-legged threats, but simply went after each with equal fierceness. Yeah, well, the protective mama bear was about to be on the receiving end of an ambush. Duncan rose to his feet and silently worked his way to where she'd disappeared, tamping down a twinge of guilt for turning the tables on her. But then, giving her a good scare might actually make her *think* before she attacked another man nearly twice her size.

He stopped just inside the woods to let his eyes adjust to the shadows the strengthening April sun cast against the pine and spruce, and slowed his breathing to listen for movement. Only instead of hearing a branch snap or leaves rustle, he heard . . . Aw, hell, the woman was sobbing again. Duncan silently moved closer, stopping behind a large tree when he saw her kneeling beside the fallen deer.

"I'm sorry. I know it was a r-rotten trick to lure you here with alfalfa pellets," she sobbed as she held the knife poised over it. "But twelve dollars for a bag of feed is a heck of a lot cheaper than a hundred pounds of beef. I'm *sorry*," she cried, plunging the knife toward the deer's neck—only to drive it into the ground because she was shaking so badly. Duncan suspected she couldn't see very well, either, since she was crying so hard. He watched her wipe her eyes with the sleeve of her sweatshirt, then raise the knife as she sucked in a shuddering breath, apparently steeling herself to have another go at the deer.

He stepped forward and caught her wrist, ignoring her shriek of surprise as he used his grip to pull her off balance when she spun toward him. "Take it easy, mama bear," he said, capturing her other swinging fist, then deftly sidestepping when she tried to kick him. "I'm not the enemy."

"Let me go!" she cried, tugging against his grip.

"Not while you're still holding a sharp object."

She immediately opened her hand and Duncan plucked the knife away, stifling a smile when she lunged at the rifle, then cried out in frustration when she discovered his boot was holding it down. He picked up the rifle as she jumped to her feet and backed away with her hands balled into fists at her sides.

"You scared the daylights out of me!"

"Yeah, ambushes have a tendency to do that to a person," he drawled, sliding the knife in his belt at his back. He looked down at the deer between them, then arched a brow at her. "You do know you're about six months shy of deer season, don't you?"

Her face went from blistering red to nearly white even as her chin lifted defiantly.

"And they probably heard that gunshot clear into town," he continued when she remained mute. He canted his head. "Then again, maybe you aren't worried about the hefty fine for poaching because you're sleeping with the local game warden."

She gave him a thunderous glare and pivoted on her heel and walked away.

Duncan dropped his head with a muttered curse, wondering what he was doing antagonizing her. But dammit, he was still angry from thinking she'd been shooting at him. His stint in the military had ended over five years ago, but some instincts—say, the instinct to survive—didn't go away when a man took off his uniform.

He sighed to expel the last of his anger, and watched Peg Thompson skirting her flooded gravel pit on her way to her house. "Bring back some plastic bags and any bins you might have," he called after her. "And a hacksaw," he added when she stopped and simply stared at him in silence. "You want to stand there and think it to death," he continued, "or let me help you get this guy cut up before school gets out?"

She continued staring for several more seconds, then turned and started running. Duncan dropped to his knees with a snort and pulled the knife out of his belt. He hoped like hell she *was* sleeping with the game warden, because if he got caught butchering an illegal deer, he was taking the hefty fine out of her first check. And then he intended to take being labeled a poacher out of the contrary woman's decidedly feminine hide.

Chapter Four

‗‗‗‗‗‗

Peg slammed into her house and immediately ran into the bathroom and threw up, then collapsed onto the edge of the tub to hug herself. She didn't know which had rattled her more, that Duncan MacKeage had scared the daylights out of her or that he'd caught her poaching. Low-life criminals shot deer out of season, and if Duncan didn't turn her in to the authorities he would at least run back to Inglenook and tell Mac and Olivia that he now had proof she was crazy.

Except he'd told her to get some bins and a saw, so did that mean he was going to become an accomplice to her crime? Or was he just being nice to get her gravel?

Only she didn't have any gravel to sell him, did she, since that stupid earthquake had flooded her pit with seawater. For the love of God, there were actual *tides*.

Peg stood up and stepped over to the sink to splash water on her face and rinse out her mouth. Why in hell did she keep thinking she should know someone named MacKeage from Pine Creek?

She'd been to TarStone Mountain Ski Resort in Pine Creek—twice, actually. Once over February vacation her senior year, when their high school basketball team had been so bad they hadn't even made it to the tournament, and all the

seniors had decided to go skiing as a consolation prize. And
she and Billy had honeymooned at TarStone, which they'd
been able to afford only because it had been off-season.

Peg walked to the kitchen, deciding she must have heard
the name MacKeage on one of her trips. And she did recall a
good number of people at the resort and in town spoke with a
slight Scottish brogue like Duncan's, and that she and her girl-
friends had found it quite sexy—although Billy hadn't been
amused when she'd asked him to please roll his *R*s on their
honeymoon.

Peg picked up her pace when the cuckoo clock her in-laws
had given them for a wedding present announced she only had
four hours before she had to catch the school bus in town on
her way to her mother-in-law's to pick up the boys. She dug
through the pantry for a couple of bins and grabbed the box of
freezer bags she'd bought specifically for the deer. Setting the
bags in the bin, she added a large cleaver—because she didn't
have time to hunt through the garage for a hacksaw—then
tossed in several hand towels and a bar of soap before she
rushed back out the door.

She stopped on the deck at the sight of the large pickup
sitting behind her van, and drew in a shuddering breath. She'd
never seen it before, but if it were red instead of dark green, it
could have been an identical twin to her late husband's truck.
Billy's pickup had also worn several layers of mud and road
dust and a company emblem on the door, its cargo bed crowded
with a diesel fuel tank and large toolbox. Except their emblem
had said *Thompson Construction* instead of *MacKeage*.

The pickup had been the first thing she'd sold after Billy
had been killed, so her heart would stop lurching every time
she'd drive in the yard before she remembered he wasn't home.
But it had been when she'd caught Isabel—who'd only been
three at the time—glaring up at the driver's door with fat tears
streaming down her cheeks as she'd shouted to her daddy to
come home now that the sheer force of Billy's death had
brought Peg to her knees.

She repositioned the bins on her hip, carefully walked down
her rickety old stairs, and ran along the shoreline and up the
steep bank to the woods. She came to a stop and took a calming breath when she saw Duncan kneeling beside the deer, his

jacket off and his sleeves rolled up as he expertly dealt with the animal.

"You don't have to do this," she said, setting down the equipment and kneeling across from him. She held out her hand. "I can take over now."

He rolled the already skinned animal over and began butchering it with obvious experience. "Thanks, but I prefer you unarmed."

Peg ducked her head, figuring he deserved a couple of cheap shots after what she and her kids had done to him. Good Lord, those were *her* claw marks on his neck, and she hadn't missed that he'd been limping at the wedding. "I'm sorry we attacked you the other day," she whispered. "And first chance we get, my children will apologize to you, too. They . . . We're more civilized than that."

He sat back on his heels, his steady green eyes darkening with concern. "You also might want to have a talk with them about confronting strange men, because the next guy might actually retaliate."

Peg felt her cheeks heat again. "Don't worry; they got the lecture of their lives that night. The card you left in my door mentioned you want to buy gravel," she said, deciding it was time to change the subject. She gestured toward the pit. "But as you can see, it's underwater."

He used the knife to point at the far end of the pit. "Do you own the land to the north? How far back?" he asked when she nodded.

"I have a hundred and eighty-four acres, almost all of it running up that hillside." She shook her head. "But the horseback runs east to west, and my land stops three hundred yards in the woods to the west of the pit."

He went back to butchering the deer. "Would you mind if I brought over my excavator tomorrow and dug a few test holes to the north? There's a good chance that vein of gravel runs up the hillside as well."

Peg's heart started pounding with excitement. Oh God, it would be the answer to her prayers if it did. That is, until she remembered she now owned lakefront property. "It doesn't matter which direction it runs," she said, her shoulders slumping. "The Land Use Regulatory Commission will never let you expand the pit because of the fiord." She snorted and opened the box of freezer bags. "Up until last week, I lived nearly two miles from the lake."

"Let me deal with LURC and getting the permits," he said, holding out several steaks and nodding for her to open one of the bags. "I'll find a way to meet the required setbacks." He arched a brow. "Assuming we can settle on a price."

Peg set the steaks in the bin and grabbed another bag, her heart pounding again. "I guess that would depend on how many yards you're looking to buy."

His eyes suddenly lit with amusement. "Thirty wheeler loads a day, five days a week for at least two months—or maybe even well into summer if I have to go all the way up the mountain before I find decent gravel on Mac's land. And I was thinking two dollars a yard is a fair price for everyone concerned."

Peg jumped to her feet and actually stumbled backward. Two dollars a yard! And with twelve yards in a wheeler, times thirty trips a day . . . Holy hell, that was seven hundred and twenty dollars a day!

She suddenly stiffened, crumpling the plastic bag in her fist. "Do you think I just crawled out from under a rock, or that because I'm a woman I don't know what gravel costs? I'm not letting you pay me two dollars a yard!"

Duncan MacKeage also stood up, his amusement gone. "Two fifty then, but not a penny more."

"No!" Peg said on a gasp, taking a step back—until she realized what she was doing and stepped forward and pointed toward her house. "You can just get in your truck and drive back to Inglenook, Mr. MacKeage, and tell Olivia that I don't appreciate being played for a fool!"

"What in hell are you talking about? Two-fifty a yard is a damn fair offer. And what's Olivia got to do with this, anyway?" He thumped his chest. "I'm the one signing the checks, not the Oceanuses, so it's my profit you're trying to gouge."

"Then I'll tell *you* the same thing I told Olivia; I am not a charity case!" she all but shouted, bolting for the house.

"Oh, no you don't," he muttered, catching her within three strides. He turned her around to face him, his hands on her arms tightening against her struggles. "Peg, listen to me," he said calmly. "I think we have our wires crossed." He relaxed his grip when she stilled, but didn't let her go. "What's *your* idea of a fair price?"

"There isn't anyone in a hundred miles of here who would pay more than a dollar for stumpage." She started struggling again when he smiled. "So if Olivia told you to offer me two fifty, you can just go back and tell her that I don't want or *need* her charity."

"Aw, Peg," he said, letting her go and stepping away. "I don't think Olivia even knows I want to buy gravel from you."

Peg balled her hands into fists to counter the tingling in her arms from where he'd held her. "Then why did you offer me twice the going rate?"

"Because the *going rate* just rose in direct proportion to your pit's proximity to the new Bottomless Sea, or don't you realize the building boom that's going to follow that underground saltwater river here? Hell, a year from now you'll be kicking yourself for selling me gravel for only two bucks a yard."

"Two *fifty*," Peg quickly corrected, her heart pounding with excitement again.

"God dammit, you were expecting to get a dollar." He stepped toward her. "Two dollars even, and I'll throw in a couple of days' labor from my crew to make some minor repairs on your house."

She had to crane her neck to look him in the eye because he was so close, and she shook her head. "Two twenty-five a yard and I get the logs from the hillside. And I want them neatly stacked in my driveway so I can have a portable sawmill come cut them into lumber." She shot him a tight smile. "You can have the pulpwood."

He folded his arms over his chest, his eyes narrowing. "I've already worked out my deal with the logger I've hired to clear the road up the mountain."

"Then renegotiate with him. I want those sawlogs."

"Okay, if you'll settle on two dollars a yard."

Peg pointed at the hillside. "That gravel is all that's standing between me and prostitution," she growled, only to cover her mouth with a gasp when his jaw slackened. "Destitution!

It's all that's standing between me and *destitution*!" she cried, splaying her hands to cover her blistering face.

"Okay, then," he said, sounding like he was fighting back laughter, "for the sake of men everywhere, I'll give you two twenty-five a yard for the gravel, along with any logs we cut on your land." She jumped in surprise when he lowered her hands and held them in his. "And I'll do some repairs on your house," he continued, the amusement in his eyes contradicting his serious tone, "for your promise not to attack me again—or any of my crew."

Peg was tempted to give her promise *after* she kicked the laughing jerk.

Apparently he was a mind reader, because he suddenly let her go and stepped back, then held out his right hand. "Deal?" Only just as she started to reach out, he pulled it back. "With exclusive rights to your gravel," he added, all trace of amusement gone. "If I'm going through the trouble of expanding your pit, I want to be the only one hauling out of it."

Hell, for two dollars and twenty-five cents a yard he could camp out in her pit for all she cared. She extended her hand. "Deal."

He shook it, then swapped it to his left hand and started leading her back up the knoll. "We'll get the deer in your freezer, and then I have a purchase agreement in my truck that I need you to sign."

"Um . . . don't take this the wrong way, okay?" she said, moving to the other side of the deer and kneeling beside the bin once he let her go. "But am I supposed to keep track of how many loads you haul?" She felt her face redden at his intense stare. "I . . . My husband never sold stumpage because he wanted the full price he got by hauling the gravel himself, so I'm not really sure how this works." She shrugged. "I've only sold an odd load here and there in the last three years, when someone needed to patch a camp road or fix their driveway."

He knelt down with a heavy sigh. "I know you don't know anything about me, but even if you weren't a personal friend of Mac and Olivia's, I value my reputation as an honest businessman a hell of a lot more than a few stolen loads of dirt. I'll keep track of every load that leaves your pit and personally deliver you a tally slip and a check every Friday afternoon. And when I'm done hauling I'll make sure your pit is safe, so you won't have to worry about any steep banks caving in on your children."

Peg dropped her gaze. "Thank you," she said, pulling another bag out of the box.

"Don't take this the wrong way, okay?" he said, amusement in his voice again. "But can you tell me what precipitated your family's little attack on Saturday? I got the impression you all thought I was some man who had scared your son."

"Jacob—he's the younger of the twins—had a run-in with one of the scientists the day before, and it was all I could do to get him back to Inglenook that morning. From what Jacob told me, the guy caught him trying to climb up on the submarine and pulled him off and started dragging him toward the lake, saying he was going to use him for shark bait. Jacob's only four, and the poor kid believed the bastard."

Duncan stopped cutting, the look in his eyes making Peg lean back. "That morning you said you thought I was Claude; is he the bastard?"

"I . . . I'm not sure. But one of the interns told me Claude doesn't have much use for kids. Or women," she said with a smile, hoping to get that look out of his eyes. She reached out and touched his arm when she saw his jaw tighten. "It doesn't matter anymore, Duncan. Jacob's not going back to Inglenook while the scientists are there."

He started cutting steaks off the deer again, rather aggressively, she noticed. "You're not afraid that keeping him away from Inglenook might only make it worse? Kids have a tendency to build things up in their minds if they're left to fester, so shouldn't Jacob face his scary man and see he's nothing more than a bully?"

"Do you have children?"

He grinned tightly. "Not that I know of."

Peg sighed as she set the bag in the bin, wondering how Duncan was still a bachelor well into his thirties . . . unless he was married.

He held out his hand. "I need the saw."

Janet Chapman

Nope, no ring. But then, Billy hadn't worn a wedding band, either, because they were dangerous around machinery. "This will have to do," she said, handing him the cleaver, "because it would take me at least an hour to find a hacksaw in the pile of tools in the garage."

She watched his face darken slightly as he started prying on a shoulder socket. "Mac told me your husband was killed in a construction accident three years ago," he said quietly as he worked. "I recall hearing a few years back about an excavator rolling into a river some thirty miles from here." He stopped to look at her. "Was that him?"

She nodded. "Billy was trying to free up an ice jam that had wedged against a bridge and was causing the river to flood the town above it, when the ground gave way under his excavator. It . . . it took them two days to find his body."

He went to work on the deer again. "I'm sorry. I can't even begin to imagine what it's like to send someone you love off to work in the morning and not have him ever come home again. What are ye planning to do with the sawlogs?"

Peg blinked at the sudden change in subject, then held open another bag for the pieces of stew meat he was cutting off the bone. "Billy started building us a new house back over that knoll about two months after the twins were born," she said, nodding behind her. "It was all framed up and weather-tight, and he'd just started on the interior when he died." She smiled sadly when Duncan sat back on his heels. "It was his idea to cut the pine growing on the hillside and have it sawed into lumber, then planed into tongue-and-groove knotty pine for the interior walls."

"That's why you want the logs? You plan to hire someone to finish the house?"

"No, I intend to finish it."

His eyes widened in surprise. "All by yourself?"

She sat up a little straighter. "I'll have you know that I've run all the electrical wiring and roughed in the plumbing over the last three years, and just last month I finished insulating the attic." She smiled again, this time smugly. "And thanks to your buying my gravel, I'll have the house ready for us to move into by this fall."

"All by *yourself*?" he repeated.

Peg stopped smiling. "Of course not. I have a small army of gnomes who cut the boards and hand them to me, a bunch of fairies who run the wires up through the rafters because I'm afraid of heights, and an entire crew of elves that come in every night to clean up the mess we made that day."

He went back to work on the deer—again rather aggressively.

"Construction's not exactly rocket science," she muttered, picking up the smaller knife and slicing steaks off the ribs once he pulled the front shoulder free. "And the kids help—even Peter and Jacob." She stopped cutting to glare at him. "Or don't you think women are capable of doing more than keeping house and raising babies?"

He set down the cleaver and stood up. "I think," he said ever so softly, "that I'd better go check out that hillside before I have to meet Mac to hike the mountain. I'll bring over the agreement for you to sign tomorrow morning," he finished, reaching down to grab his jacket before turning away.

"Duncan."

He stopped and turned back to her.

"Thank you for helping me," she said, gesturing at the deer, "and for giving me a fair price for my gravel."

He merely nodded, then turned and headed down the knoll.

Peg rested her fists on her knees, watching him stop at the edge of the water and wash his hands. He then rolled down his sleeves, slid on his jacket, and made his way around the flooded pit before finally disappearing into the trees on the hillside.

She dropped her gaze to the half-butchered deer and sighed, wondering what had possessed her to turn hostile. Why should she care if the man had looked incredulous and then suddenly angry when she'd told him she was finishing the house Billy had started for his family? She was proud of what she'd accomplished, dammit, and Duncan had no business assuming she couldn't put a roof over her children's heads *all by herself.*

"Yeah, well," she muttered, driving the knife into the meat, "you men aren't all you think you're cracked up to be, either. Everyone loves a hero except for the wife and kids he leaves behind when he gets himself killed trying to save a bunch of stupid buildings in some stupid town."

Which was another reason she was staying a widow—even if it meant sleeping in an empty bed for the rest of her life—because she'd be damned if she was going to let her children get their tender little hearts broken again.

Chapter Five

"Here's an idea," Duncan said as he stopped to wait for Mac to come up beside him. "Why don't you ask Olivia's father to keep an eye on Peg Thompson and her children while you're gone? Sam seems like the sort of man who relishes a challenge."

Mac's eyes lit with interest. "What did she do this time?"

Duncan headed up the mountain again. "Do you know she owns a high-power rifle and apparently isn't afraid to use it?"

Mac pulled him to a stop. "Peg shot at you?"

"No," he growled as he started walking again. "She shot a deer." He tapped his finger to his forehead. "Smack dead center between the eyes. The damn animal was dead before it even hit the ground."

"Why? Is hunting season not usually in the fall?"

"I gathered from what Peg told the deer as she sobbed all over it that a bag of feed is a hell of a lot cheaper than a hundred pounds of beef." Duncan deliberately slowed his pace when he realized he was getting angry all over again. "Apparently the woman's so desperate that she's willing to risk jacking deer out of season." He frowned over his shoulder. "Did you know she's been finishing off the house her husband started building before he died? All by herself?"

Mac pulled them to a stop when they reached an open ledge and shot him a grin. "Are you that much of your father's son, Duncan, that you believe the house is going to collapse because a woman is building it?"

"She's climbing ladders and messing with electricity and plumbing torches *all by herself.* She could fall and break her neck or set her clothes on fire, and her kids would be the ones to find her."

Mac gestured dismissively. "Since the beginning of time, widows have been doing whatever is necessary to provide for their children."

Duncan turned away, striding to the center of the ledge as he remembered Peg inserting *prostitution* for *destitution.* "Yeah, well, I don't want her breaking her neck on my watch." He shot Mac a glare. "Because the last thing I need is to find myself trying to explain what happened to a pissed-off theurgist at her funeral."

Mac arched a brow. "Is it Peg's neck you are worried about or yours?"

"That woman is reckless and stubborn and too damned proud; and from what I've seen so far, those are her *good* qualities."

"Then you, my friend, are either blind or dead. Peg's beauty and courage and generous heart clearly outshine her more . . . spirited qualities." Mac folded his arms on his chest, his silent regard causing the fine hairs on Duncan's neck to stir in alarm. "You're attracted to her," the wizard said quietly.

"I just met her."

"And that scares you."

"I am *not* afraid of Peg Thompson."

"No, you're afraid of your attraction to her."

Knowing he wasn't going to win this crazy argument, Duncan tried anyway. "I'm a thirty-five-year-old red-blooded male who's been attracted to more women than I can count, so what makes you think Peg is different?"

"You tell me." Mac's eyes filled with amusement. "You're the one who's angry at her for building a house *all by herself.*" He eyed him speculatively again. "Might it have something to do with the fact that you're a first-generation Maine highlander who finds it difficult to have one foot in his father's world and the other in this one?"

"Both of my feet are firmly planted in *this* time—including my attitude toward women. I didn't ask to be born a Mac-Keage, and I sure as hell don't intend to perpetuate a bunch of antiquated traditions. There are enough magic-makers running around these woods already, so Laird Greylen is going to have to rebuild his clan without my help."

"Ah, I see. It's not the antiquated traditions you are opposed to so much as the magic. Tell me, Duncan, what's your particular gift?"

"I was hiding behind the door when Providence was handing out gifts." He turned away to look down at the new Bottomless Sea. "Which is fine by me; I really don't need to start fires without matches, or talk to animals, or travel through time."

"Have you even tried?" Mac asked quietly.

Duncan snorted. "I quit trying when I was eight." He gestured at the mountain they'd just hiked up and shot a grin over his shoulder. "I'm one hell of an earth mover, though. I figure the road should at least be passable by the time you get back from California, although it's going to take all summer to finish the five larger bridges if you keep insisting they be made of stone." He turned to face him. "But I still say you should let me build them out of rough-hewn timber if you really want to give your resort guests a true Maine experience."

Duncan widened his grin when Mac's eyes narrowed at his changing the subject. But he'd be damned if he understood how the wizard had decided he was attracted to Peg, much less that he didn't much care for the magic—even as he wondered which topic was more frightening.

Mac took off his jacket. "Here's an idea," he said with an equally frightening smile. "I'll fight you for the bridges."

Duncan went still but for the fine hairs on his neck rising again. "Excuse me?"

"We'll use swords." The wizard arched a brow. "You are the reigning champion of the highland summer games down on the coast, are you not?"

"How in hell do you know that?"

"And since I'm about to spend the next two months driving a lumbering house across the country and back with only my wife and children for company, I believe I'm up for a rousing battle before I leave. In fact, it might be nice if we met up here a couple more times this week to break a sweat together, as I haven't faced a worthy opponent since I left Midnight Bay."

Yeah, right; like he was going to match swords with a wizard.

"No magic," Mac assured him. "Only mortal brain and brawn . . . and skill."

"Sorry," Duncan drawled, "but considering I came here to *build a road*, I didn't think to bring my sword."

Mac gestured to his left. "No problem; I brought one for you."

Duncan stiffened again when he saw the two swords leaning against a stunted old pine tree growing out of the ledge.

"I believe you'll find the grip will fit your hand," Mac said, walking over and picking up one of the swords. He slid it out of its sheath, then turned and held it out to Duncan. "Just as it did your father's."

Duncan slowly reached for the ancient-looking weapon, only to feel a powerful surge of energy sweep through him when he closed his left fist around the hilt. He snapped his head up. "My father's sword was nearly nine hundred years old when he and the others came to this time over forty years ago, and was sold for a small fortune."

Mac nodded. "Yes, I believe it was purchased by an anonymous bidder at an auction house in Edinburgh."

"And old Uncle Ian's sword?" Duncan asked, staring down at the one in his hand. "It was decided at the time that Greylen and Morgan should keep their weapons as they were the youngest of the four warriors, but Greylen needed the money from the sale of Ian's and Dad's to buy TarStone Mountain."

"Old Ian found his beloved weapon hanging in his hut when Robbie MacBain took him back to his original time several years ago."

Duncan lifted his father's sword so that the sunlight reflected off the tarnished and pitted steel, pulling in a deep breath at how perfectly balanced and how . . . right it felt in his hand. "All the time I was growing up, Dad complained that his left palm constantly itched to wield a true and proper weapon again. When he comes to visit me at the work site, can he see this? Will you let him hold it again?"

"That privilege is yours, Duncan, as is the sword. It's my gift to you."

He snapped his gaze to Mac again. "Why?"

The wizard tossed his jacket down beside the tree, then began unbuttoning his shirt. "Because it belongs in a Mac-Keage's hand, not hanging on some collector's wall gathering dust."

"But it's worth a small fortune."

"A weapon's worth is in the man who wields it." Mac tossed down his shirt and unsheathed the other sword, then turned to Duncan with a frown. "Are you not going to strip off?" He grinned. "Or are you feeling the need to keep a little cloth between my blade and your flesh?"

"You expect me to be a worthy opponent against your thousands of years of experience?"

Mac stood the tip of his sword on the ledge between his feet and rested his hands on the hilt. "I was under the impression MacKeage fathers raised warriors."

"Really? I prefer to think they raised us not to be fools," Duncan muttered even as he leaned his sword against the tree—because dammit to hell, it appeared he was going to have to battle the bastard. He shed his jacket, unbuttoned his shirt and shrugged it off, then picked up the sword and turned to Mac with a heavy sigh. "So, about those bridges; are you saying that if I draw first blood, we build them my way?"

Mac palmed his sword and touched it to his forehead with a slight bow, then planted his feet as he gripped his lethal and far older weapon in both hands. His grin turned feral again with his nod. "If you manage to spill *any* of my blood, then you may build your timber bridges. But if I draw first blood, you will make damned sure Peg Thompson doesn't break her beautiful neck on your watch."

Since he figured he was damned either way, Duncan swung his weapon in a swift arc as he lunged into Mac's defensive strike, his MacKeage war cry rising above the loud, echoing peal of their clashing swords.

* * *

"Is there a reason I left a nice warm bed at two A.M.—which happened to be occupied by an even warmer woman, I might point out—to spend three hours running a gauntlet of road-stupid moose to get here before the sun comes up, only to find you still in bed . . . Boss?"

"Ye nudge me again, and you're going to wish you'd hit one of those moose instead of my fist," Duncan growled without opening his eyes—partly because one of them was swollen shut, but mostly because he didn't want his nephew's face to be the first thing he saw this morning.

"I figure we have about an hour before it gets above freezing and the road postings go back into effect," Alec said, his voice wisely moving away. "Or is it your intention to be on a first-name basis with the local deputy sheriff before we've even hauled our first load?"

Duncan opened the one eye he could and immediately closed it again when Inglenook's otherwise empty dorm suddenly flooded with light. He then tried to push back the blanket only to discover his arms didn't want to move—along with every other muscle in his body except his mouth. "What time is it?"

"Half an hour before sunrise," Alec said, his voice moving closer. "What in hell happened to you? Christ, ye look like you tangled with a bear."

Duncan snorted, then immediately groaned in pain, but he did manage to open both eyes. "I tangled with our new resident theurgist."

"Why?" Alec asked, looking around as if he expected Mac to materialize. "What in hell did ye do to piss him off?"

"He wasn't pissed off; he merely wanted some sport." Duncan snorted again, this time using the pain to lever himself into a sitting position, then immediately hung his head in his hands with a curse. "Only problem is, Mac's idea of sport involves swords. And not the dull ones we use at the summer games, either, but real weapons designed to draw blood. Some of it mine," he muttered, straightening enough to run a hand over his torso. "Christ, I think one of my ribs is cracked." He waved at the bed beside him. "Look under my pants."

Alec lifted the pants but dropped them on the floor in surprise, then reached down and slid the sword halfway out of its sheath. "This isn't your sword. It looks authentic, like . . . like Dad's."

"It's my father's," Duncan whispered. "Mac gave it to me."

"But I thought Callum and old Uncle Ian's swords were sold at auction forty years ago, along with several daggers."

"They were bought by an anonymous bidder named Maximilian Oceanus."

Alec squinted down at it. "That's definitely fresh blood." He straightened, arching a brow as he slid it back into its sheath and set it on the bed. "Mac's?"

Duncan swung his legs off the side of the bed, then hung his throbbing head in his hands again. "I might have lost the battle, but I did manage to spill a few drops of imperial blood, and the bastard's also going to be a little slow getting out of bed this morning." He lifted his head and grinned. "So I guess we're building timber bridges, since that was our wager."

"And for the buckets of your blood that he spilled, what did Mac get?"

Duncan lost his grin. "He gets me keeping an eye on a widow and her four little heathens for the next two months."

"Then you got the best of him after all. You actually like little heathens, and I've yet to meet a woman who didn't fall all over herself trying to get your attention."

"Oh, Peg Thompson got my attention, all right." Duncan ran a finger over the claw marks on his neck. "These are from her, not Mac. And yesterday, after nearly running me down with her minivan, I went to her house and thought she was shooting at me only to walk up on a deer that she'd nailed right between the eyes."

Alec folded his arms with a grin. "Does that mean my summer job comes with hazard pay?" His expression suddenly perked up. "No, never mind; I'll settle for fringe benefits. How about if I keep an eye on the obviously discerning widow, since she doesn't seem all that enamored with you? Is she as pretty as she is lethal?"

Duncan sprang to his feet before he remembered it was going to hurt, his snarl all the more threatening for his pain. "I even catch you talking to Peg and you're going to find yourself limping all the way back to TarStone Mountain."

Alec lifted his hands in supplication—although he was still

grinning. "A tad protective, aren't you, considering ye don't seem all that enamored with the widow Thompson yourself."

"And pass the word along to the crew; the woman is off-limits."

"Including you?"

"*Especially* me," Duncan hissed as he bent down to swipe his pants off the floor. "Unhook the bulldozer you brought and hook your wheeler up to the excavator," he said, carefully slipping into his pants. Christ, he hurt. And the worst part was that he'd agreed to meet Mac up on the mountain for another round tomorrow. "Did you happen to notice any lights on in the dining hall?" he asked as Alec headed for the door. "It's the building behind this one."

"Sorry, all its windows are dark."

Duncan slid on his shirt, gritting his teeth against the pain. Damn, either he'd gotten out of shape over the winter or skiing required completely different muscles than sword fighting. "Wait. You got any coffee left in your thermos?"

"Not enough to cure what's ailing you this morning. I do believe I packed a fifth of liquid gold in my duffel bag, though."

Duncan waved him away with a snort. "Sure, why not? A shot of Scotch sure as hell can't hurt. Warm my truck up while you're at it, would you?"

"Anything else? Ye want me to crush some aspirin to put in the Scotch, or dab ointment on your boo-boos, or give you a massage . . . Boss?"

Duncan stopped looking for his boots and picked up the sword, then took a threatening step toward him. "It's not getting any colder outside, and I'm not so sore that I can't still outrun you."

"Hell, if I'd wanted this kind of abuse I'd have stayed in my nice, warm, occupied bed," Alec said with a chuckle, heading outside.

Duncan closed his eyes on a curse, feeling a really long day coming on.

And if he'd had any idea how true that was going to be he would have crawled right back in bed, because damn if they didn't pass Peg's tired old minivan half an hour later sitting on the side of the road with its hood up about two miles from her house.

"Keep going," Duncan said into his radio mike when the trailer brake lights came on ahead of him. "But keep an eye out for a woman and four kids walking."

"Our merry widow?" Alec responded way too cheerily.

"If they haven't made it home yet, I'm putting her in the excavator and the little heathens in the truck with you."

"Since when are you afraid of women?" Alec returned, the radio doing nothing to disguise his laughter.

"Since I saw this particular woman shoot a deer right between its eyes," Duncan said, a bit startled to hear the laughter in his own voice. Although it might only be the three aspirin and healthy swig of Scotch making him smile. Damn, he had a thing for stubborn, too-proud women—which usually meant trouble for any stubborn, too-proud man foolish enough to find himself attracted to one of them.

"There they are," Alec said, just as the trailer brake lights came on again.

Duncan keyed the mike. "Swing past them and stop. But stay in the lane," he added. "The road shoulders are still soft."

"Whoa, maybe I will risk limping back to TarStone."

"Alec," Duncan hissed in warning as the excavator slid into the oncoming lane, allowing his own headlights to land on Peg and her four children standing out of the way clear across the ditch.

"I'm just saying," Alec continued as he pulled back into his lane and came to a stop. "I don't have a problem with deer-shooting women."

Duncan tossed down his mike and got out of his truck, watching Peg help one of the twins back across the ditch before gathering all four children around her.

"Do you know what's wrong with the van?" he asked, stopping two paces away when one of the boys scooted behind her.

"It might be the alternator." She lifted a hand to her eyes against the glare of his headlights and he heard her sigh. "Or it could only be out of gas, because I think the fuel gauge might have quit working last week."

"Peg, this is my nephew, Alec MacKeage," he said when Alec walked back to them. "He's going to be helping me build Mac's road this summer."

"My pleasure, Peg," Alec said with a smile. He squatted

down. "And who are you?" he asked, extending his hand to the twin Duncan assumed was *not* Jacob, since he wasn't the one hiding behind his mother.

"I'm Pete," the boy said, lisping through a missing front tooth as he shook Alec's hand. He gestured over his shoulder. "And that's my brother, Repeat, and Charlotte and Isabel. Will you give me a ride in your evascator?"

"Well, Pete, I do believe the boss won't let anyone near the equipment unless they're at least twenty-five years old," Alec said, standing up and ruffling Pete's hair. "Heck, he only let me start driving it last year, and I'm thirty!"

Pete shot Duncan the evil eye, then looked up at his mom. "We could ride the school bus to town and still go to the Drunken Moose for cimminin buns. And we'll bring a jug with us for some gas. Repeat and I can take turns carrying it back to the van."

"How about if Alec and I take you home," Duncan offered, giving the kid a warm smile, "and once we get the van running, your mom can take you to the Drunken Moose for cinnamon buns? How does that sound, Pete?"

All he got for answer was another evil eye—which ended abruptly when Peg gave the boy a nudge. "Um . . . if you're headed our way, we'd appreciate that ride," she told Duncan. "But you don't have to deal with my van. I have gas at home."

"And if it's the alternator?"

"I can have my brother-in-law, Galen, tow it home."

"He owns a tow truck?"

She blinked at him, then began herding her children toward his pickup. "No, he owns a rope," she said over her shoulder way too cheerily.

Alec gave a quiet chuckle, slapping Duncan on the back. "Oh man, are you in dark blue–eyed, sassy-mouthed trouble."

"Turn right about a mile and a half up the road," Duncan told him as he limped toward his pickup, only to break into a painful jog when he remembered there was a sword lying on the backseat. "Wait up," he said across the hood on his way by. "I need to make room for everyone."

Peg left her girls and one of the boys standing on the passenger side and walked around the front with the other boy in tow. Duncan opened the rear door and grabbed the sword, and

had started to slide it behind the backseat when the opposite
door opened and the older girl stumbled back with a gasp just
as a shout of excitement came from beside her.

"That's a sword!" the boy—he was pretty sure it was
Pete—cried. "Is it real? How come you got it?"

Duncan closed his eyes on a silent curse and backed out
of the truck holding the sword, causing the twin holding
Peg's hand to scurry behind her again. Oh yeah, it was already
a long day, and the sun was only just now peeking over the
horizon.

"I have it because every summer my family goes to something called the highland games down on the coast and we . . ."
He smiled through the truck at the boy, feeling the back of his
neck heat up. "Well, we all spend the weekend pretending
we're highlanders living centuries ago." He slid the sword behind the seat, then grabbed his duffel bag and straightened.
Smiling again to cover his grimace when his muscles protested, he tossed the bag in the cargo bed—only to jump back
when he turned and nearly bumped into Peg, who was gaping
at him in the rising sun.

"What?" he asked, looking down at himself. He touched
his cheekbone when he remembered his bruise. "This? Oh,
I . . . um, I fell when I was hiking the mountain with Mac
yesterday."

"Peter, get out of the truck," Peg said, backing away. She
gestured for her daughters to do the same. "Charlotte, take
Peter's hand and start walking home," she instructed. "Here,
Isabel, you take Jacob."

"Wait," Duncan said, grabbing her sleeve. "I'm going to
give you a ride."

She checked to make sure her children were out of earshot,
then turned on him, her nose wrinkling as she pulled out of
his grip. "Thank you, but I have no intention of putting my
children in a truck being driven by someone who smells like
a distillery."

"What? Hey, I'm not drunk."

"No, you're obviously hungover."

"I *fell*."

"Because you were *drunk*."

"No, I wasn't. I just . . . fell." He blew out a sigh—which

made her wrinkle her nose again and start walking backward. "Okay, look, I'll admit that I had a small swig of Scotch this morning, but only one sip just to make my muscles stop screaming." Too bad it wasn't doing a damn thing for his pounding head at the moment. Duncan looked up the road to see Alec's taillights disappearing around a curve, then looked back at Peg, who was halfway to her children. "Dammit, quit walking away from me." He opened his driver's door. "Okay, then, *you* drive."

She stopped and turned to him. "Only if you ride in the cargo bed."

"What!"

"That's the only way I'm putting my kids in your truck."

Christ, she was contrary. "God dammit," he growled under his breath, turning and limping to the rear of the truck. "I didn't do one damn thing to deserve this. Not one goddamned thing," he muttered, hoisting himself onto the bumper and practically falling over the tailgate into the cargo bed.

"Come on, guys, we're riding," Peg called out, running to the driver's door with her children scrambling after her.

Duncan settled against his duffel bag and turned up the collar on his jacket, grinning tightly at the little heathen kneeling on the backseat giving him the evil eye. Forget the long day; it was going to be a damn long two months.

Chapter Six

Peg sat at the picnic table the boys had helped her drag down next to the beach and watched them alternating between using sticks to fling seaweed back into the water and stopping to watch the equipment working on the hillside across their . . . new cove. She in turn was alternating between keeping an eye on them and studying her copy of the agreement she had just signed with MacKeage Construction.

It was all happening so fast, it didn't seem real. Yesterday she'd been desperate enough to shoot a deer out of season, and today she was on the verge of being able to buy the rest of the materials to finish her house and also upgrade to a newer used van. And she would still have enough money left over to finally stop feeling like she was one second away from . . . *prostitution*, she thought with a grimace.

Of all the crazy things to have said! When she'd climbed into her lonely bed last night, Peg hadn't been able to stop remembering the look on Duncan's face when she'd mixed up *destitution* and *prostitution*. His jaw may have gone slack, but she hadn't missed the unholy gleam in his sharp green eyes that had immediately followed. She'd spent all night being hot and bothered by that gleam, and it had been all she could do to face him this morning without blushing to high heaven.

That is, until she'd gotten a good look at his face and smelled his breath.

Peg lifted her gaze to the excavator digging another test hole and saw Duncan standing off to the side talking to the logger he'd contracted. Oh, she hoped there was gravel up there, because if there was, then a good many of her troubles would be over. But if that horseback continued running west, all of those big fat checks would be going to her neighbors every Friday afternoon—assuming the Dearborn brothers were willing to give up growing pot on their land to sell the gravel beneath it.

She'd had a couple of go-rounds with the two old coots who'd bought the rickety old shack a quarter mile up the road last spring. They'd started out neighborly enough, but not five months after they'd moved in, Evan and Carl had knocked on her door and accused Peg of sneaking over and stealing buds off their maturing plants—which had made her laugh so hard when they'd left that tears had streamed down her cheeks. But she sure as hell hadn't been laughing a week later when she'd discovered the two idiots had set booby traps all through the woods around their illegal crop.

Afraid the twins would get maimed—because what did little boys know about property lines when they were stalking squirrels with imaginary guns?—Peg had waited until she saw the brothers go into town one morning and marched over and smashed their traps to smithereens. Then she'd cut down one of their pot plants and left it wilting on their doorstep, along with a note saying that she'd turn them in if they didn't start growing their crop away from her property line.

Surprisingly, they'd both come over that evening and apologized. They certainly hadn't meant to endanger her children, they'd assured her, but had only wanted to catch whoever had been raiding their . . . garden. Then, after saying they admired her spunk at how she'd gone about getting her point across, the older brother, Evan, had asked her out to dinner at the Drunken Moose. Only problem was, besides missing more teeth than he had left and smelling like a skunk and desperately needing a haircut, Evan was old enough to be her grandfather.

Peg had politely turned him down and waited until they'd

reached the woods before she'd shuddered all over, then started laughing so hard that she'd cried again.

"Mom! Did you see that?" Jacob shouted, pointing at the hillside. "They just cut down a big tree and I felt the ground shake when it landed. Did you feel it, too?"

"I'm pretty sure I felt something," she called back, returning his huge smile only to frown up at the woods the moment he turned away to watch again.

What were they doing cutting trees already? Good Lord, not ten minutes after Duncan and Alec had started digging holes this morning, a virtual convoy of three tractor-trailer log carriers, several different styles of tree harvesters, a pulp loader, and who knew what else had arrived, and were now lining the road in both directions of her house. She'd assumed they were here to clear the timber off the road Duncan was building up the mountain, which is why she'd been surprised when one of the harvesters had been driven around her old pit and up onto the hillside.

Peter and Jacob had been so excited by all the activity and huge machinery, Peg had promised to sit outside with them to watch, if they in turn promised to stay on the beach and at least try to keep their sneakers dry. They'd both nodded vigorously at the double joys of not only watching big machinery working but also beachcombing for the jellyfish and crabs and snails that were now calling their flooded gravel pit home. For the love of God, the air actually smelled *salty*.

Peg frowned again when she saw another large pine tree topple to the ground, wondering if Duncan wasn't getting ahead of himself. After he'd introduced the owner of the logging convoy as his cousin Robbie MacBain, also of Pine Creek, Peg had asked Duncan why he was cutting trees before he even knew what was under them. He'd suddenly gotten one of those unholy gleams in his eyes and said that if she was willing to drop her price to one seventy-five a yard, he'd pay her even if all he found was sand. And, he'd added, that gleam intensifying, he would also have his crew finish her house.

Knowing he somehow *knew* there was gravel on that hillside, Peg had smiled sweetly despite being aware of Mr. MacBain's amused interest and told Duncan that if he cut all her trees and didn't find any gravel—at two twenty-five a yard—then he was replanting every last one of them *and* finishing her house.

Peg looked down at the purchase agreement again and pulled in a shuddering breath at the realization that she was holding the answer to her prayers. Too bad the angel who'd brought it was an overconfident, drop-dead handsome giant with broad shoulders all but begging a tired, lonely widow to lean on them.

Duncan was also a study of contradictions. For all of his gruffness—as well as his habit of cussing under his breath— there appeared to be a true gentleman lurking behind those rugged good looks. Because honestly? She didn't know any man who wouldn't have defended himself when she and her children had attacked him. Then, after nearly running him down with her van, Duncan had helped her butcher an illegal deer. And this morning he'd loaned her his truck to take the kids to the Drunken Moose as she'd originally planned, and even to drive Charlotte and Isabel to school in Turtleback Station—which was seventy miles round trip—because they'd missed the bus.

And if that weren't enough proof there was a good man inside the battered, Scotch-sipping grouch, Peg had returned home to find her van parked in her dooryard, making her doubly glad that she'd brought back a half-dozen cinnamon buns for him and Alec as thanks, which both men had wolfed down without even tasting.

"Uncle Galen's here!" Peter shouted, running up the beach brandishing a stick full of seaweed, Jacob in hot pursuit.

Peg heard Galen's old pickup rattle to a stop and glanced over her shoulder to see no less than five more pickups pull into the driveway behind him. She quickly folded her agreement with Duncan and tucked it under her sweatshirt inside her bra, then stood up just in time to be pulled into a bear of a hug.

"Hey, sissy sister, what are you doing with all this machinery cluttering up your road and property?" he murmured, squeezing Peg until she squeaked.

Galen had started calling her *sissy sister* the day she'd married his baby brother, only he'd switched to *porky Peg* by the end of her last pregnancy—which no one had realized was twins until Jacob had made his appearance two minutes after Peter. But Galen had thankfully gone back to calling her *sissy sister* once she'd given birth and *almost* gotten her figure back.

"Hey, Pete and Repeat," he said with a laugh, scooping both boys up in his beefy arms to give them each a noisy kiss on their cheeks, which both boys immediately rubbed off on their shoulders before returning the kiss, as was their ritual. Galen turned to face the shoreline. "You hoodlums seen any sharks in your new swimming hole?"

They both shook their heads. "But Isabel says she seen a whale blow when we was at Inglenook last Saturday," Jacob said. "Only I missed it because I was watching the little submarine."

"I got some snails," Peter chimed in, reaching in his jacket pocket and pulling out a tiny fistful of wilted snails, which he then held up under Galen's nose.

"Oh, those look fat and juicy," Galen said, fighting his smile with a serious nod. "I think you should have your mom cook them for you for supper tonight."

Peg gave an involuntary shudder, not only because Peter looked positively taken by the idea, but because she was wondering what other creatures she was going to find when she did the laundry. Angleworms and the occasional frog she could handle, but creepy crawly sea critters were another thing.

"And I hear a person can make soup out of jellyfish," Galen continued, setting down the boys and giving them a nudge toward the beach. "See if you can't find some that's washed up on shore. You're going to need at least a bucketful according to the recipe I found in the *Farmers' Almanac*."

"Thank you for that," Peg muttered when the boys took off in search of dead jellyfish. She eyed the other men getting out of their trucks, recognizing most of them. "What are you doing here, Galen? I called you when I got home and told you the van was only out of gas."

"We've come to meet our new bosses," he said, looking toward the hillside.

"You're going to work for Duncan? All of you?"

"We're working for MacBain Logging until he clears out of here and MacKeage starts the roadwork," he said with a nod, still watching the hillside. He finally turned to her. "Apparently both men are smart enough to know they can't pull into a town with their crew and machinery and not put a good number of the locals on their payrolls." He grinned. "It's the polite thing to do."

"It's also damn cheap insurance," one of the other men said with a snicker—Jonas, Peg thought his name was, from Turtleback Station.

Galen grabbed the sleeve of her sweatshirt and led her away from the men, finally stopping to stand with his back to them. "You don't worry about nothing, Peg," he said softly. "I'll make sure MacKeage gives you a good price for your gravel. Any notion he might have about taking advantage of a woman will be gone once he finds himself dealing with me. You're not selling him one pebble for less than a buck fifty a yard." He held up his hand when she tried to speak. "I know that sounds like highway robbery for stumpage in this area, but word in town is the guy who married Livy Baldwin, Mac somebody, has some mighty deep pockets. They're saying he's bought most the land around here and is planning to build a fancy resort up on that mountain overlooking Bottomless. So you being a softhearted woman and all, I'll just make sure no one takes advantage of you."

"But—"

"And I'm gonna find you someone to sit in a chair and count every truck that leaves your pit," he continued. "MacKeage might be a Mainer, but he's here for a year or two, then he's gone." He patted her arm, then muttered something and pulled her into another bear of a hug. "You just leave things up to me, sissy sister, and you'll finally be able to hire someone to finish that house Billy started for you and the kids."

Damn. The last thing she wanted was Galen sticking his nose in her business. The guy meant well, but he had about as much business sense as Peter's snails. Hell, when Galen and his dad, Clive, had tried to work on the house after Billy died, it had taken her two weeks to unravel all the electrical wires they'd run. And to save her sanity without hurting their feelings, Peg had told them the idea of moving into the house without Billy was too painful for her, anyway. The Thompson men were hard workers, but they often worked in circles.

She had definitely gotten the pick of the litter—or else Billy had been adopted.

"Is there a problem?" Duncan asked from right beside them, making Peg jump and Galen step back in surprise.

Galen recovered quickly and thrust out his hand. "Galen Thompson, Peg's brother-in-law, Mr. . . . ?"

"Duncan MacKeage," Duncan said, giving his hand a quick shake, then turning to Peg. "Is everything okay?"

Peg barely had time to nod before Galen stepped between them. Good Lord, she'd always thought the Thompson men were hulks, but seeing Galen standing toe-to-toe with Duncan . . . well, there must be something in the drinking water in Pine Creek, because Duncan and Alec and Robbie MacBain were nothing short of giants.

"It appears to me that you've gotten ahead of yourself, Mr. MacKeage," Galen said, gesturing at the hillside. "You seem to be expanding Peg's pit before you've even settled on a price."

Duncan's gaze slid briefly to her, but it was long enough for Peg to give a barely perceptible shake of her head, hoping to God that Duncan was astute. "Well, Mr. Thompson," he said, giving his attention back to Galen, "I prefer to know exactly what I'm buying before I throw out any prices." He also gestured toward the hillside. "That's why I'm digging a few test holes today."

"Last I knew it don't require cutting trees to dig a couple of holes."

Duncan shrugged. "Peg mentioned wanting the pine for . . . something," he said when she shook her head again. "So I thought that while I had my loggers here, I'd cut some of the bigger trees in exchange for the privilege of looking."

Galen turned to her. "Would you excuse us a minute, sis— Peg—while me and Mr. MacKeage have us a little talk?" he asked, nodding for her to leave.

Peg walked between them, ignoring Duncan's surprise in favor of giving him another speaking look on her way by, and headed down the beach to see what her boys and the men were looking at. Only she never reached them because Galen's little talk lasted exactly one minute before he called to his friends and they headed to where Robbie MacBain was standing with some of his crew watching the harvester work.

"Mind telling me why you didn't jump all over him for sending ye off like a good little lass?" Duncan asked as he walked down the beach and stopped in front of her. "He told me you might know a thing or two about construction, but that, and I quote, 'you're too softhearted when it comes to negotiating stuff like prices.'" He snorted. "Did he just come out of a coma or something?"

"Have you ever tried banging your head against a brick wall?" she asked with a derisive smile. "Until you eventually figure out the bricks aren't going to move and that your head hurts?" She shrugged. "Sometimes it's just easier not to bang my head against Galen. Thank you for keeping our business between just us."

"Are ye worried he would want a cut? Is the pit yours outright, or does the family have a stake in it?"

"No, it's all mine. Billy and I bought this property and the double-wide on it when we got married. And I'm not worried Galen is interested in anything other than getting me a fair price. He's a good man, but he can't keep two nickels in his pocket for more than a minute. If he knows how much money I'll be making this spring, he'll be finding ways for me to spend it faster than your wheelers are hauling out of here."

Duncan folded his arms over his chest, his gaze going to the locals talking to Robbie MacBain. "Did I make a mistake hiring your brother-in-law, Peg?"

"Absolutely not. Galen's a hard worker and good at what he knows, which is leveling dirt. Put him in the seat of a dozer and you don't even have to rake out a lawn to seed it when he's done." She smiled. "Just don't ever ask him to run electrical wire."

"I wondered why your husband's family wasn't helping you finish your house."

She shook her head. "Galen and his dad tried, but I told them not to bother because I wasn't feeling up to moving into it without Billy."

He lifted a brow. "They're unaware that you've been finishing it yourself? Quit getting defensive on me," he growled when she lifted her chin—even as his eyes crinkled with laughter. "That was an honest question, not a dig."

Peg brushed down the front of her sweatshirt. "Working on

that house is my therapy. You try dealing with four kids under the age of nine all by yourself every day." She shot him another smile. "At least gnomes and fairies don't ask a thous—"

Duncan was gone in a blur before the scream of terror even reached her, and was wading into the water and lifting Jacob into his arms just as the boy burst into tears.

"Jacob!" Peg cried, running to them.

"You're okay," Duncan murmured, hugging Jacob against his chest. "He's okay, Peg. I don't think he swallowed any water. You're okay," he continued, his broad hand holding Jacob's head against his shoulder. "Quiet down now," he whispered as he shot her a wink on his way by. "You're scaring your mom."

Even though Peg was all but shaking with the need to make sure her son was okay, she took hold of her unusually quiet older twin's hand instead and followed, Duncan's soothing words seeming to calm her just as much as they were Jacob.

"And it's been my experience," she heard him continue softly, "that when moms get scared, they make ye play inside for at least a week." He stood Jacob on the picnic table, then shrugged out of his leather jacket and wrapped it around the boy—who was now valiantly sucking up his sobs. "And if you get yourself stuck inside, you're going to miss my bulldozer pushing all the stumps and topsoil off the—"

"Jacob! Peter!" Galen shouted as he ran toward them followed by the other men. He crowded Duncan out of the way and swept Jacob into his arms. "Lord Almighty, boy, what happened? Are you okay?" He turned on Peg, the wild look in his eyes making her take a step back. "You gotta watch them every minute. The boy could have drowned!"

"Peg is well aware of her responsibilities," Duncan said quietly, stepping between them. "Jacob only got a little wet."

Peg shot around him and pulled her son away from Galen and started walking to her house. "Come on, Peter. It's time for your naps."

"*Mommm.*"

"Let Pete stay here with me," Galen called after her. "I'll keep an eye on him."

She turned to see that even though Galen had moved away from Duncan, the look in her brother-in-law's eyes sure as hell didn't match his tone. "If Peter doesn't mind being too tired to cook hot dogs over a campfire tonight," she quickly prevaricated, "then I guess he can stay out here with you."

Peter gasped so hard, he actually stumbled backward just as Duncan folded his arms over his chest with a grin and—did he just wink at her again?

Peg spun away and started for the house, pressing her cheek to Jacob's wet hair as Peter ran up beside her. "We're gonna have a campfire?" he asked excitedly. "Can we make jellyfish soup? And cook the snails?"

"I think we'll save the jellyfish and snails for your birthday, okay? Say good-bye to Uncle Galen." Only Peg suddenly stopped, turned around, and walked toward Duncan, who was heading down the beach with Robbie MacBain. "You need to thank Mr. MacKeage for pulling you out of the water," she whispered to Jacob. "Can you do that, big man? He was just like the Rescue Heroes you watch on TV. And you're always supposed to thank a hero when he saves you."

Robbie spotted her and nudged Duncan, and both men stopped to let her catch up to them. Peg used her shoulder to nudge Jacob upright. "Mr. MacKeage, Jacob has something he wants to say to you."

"Tank you," her son blurted at Duncan's shirt buttons even as he turned and buried his face in her neck again.

Peg sighed through her smile. "Yes, thank you, Mr. MacKeage, for pulling him out of the water."

"Jacob?" Duncan said in question. "Can you tell me what happened? What was that?" he asked with a chuckle when the boy muttered something into her neck. He ran his hand over Jacob's wet hair. "Did you stumble and fall into the water, or did the ground give out underneath you?"

"I saw what happened," Peter chimed in. He pointed at where Duncan had waded in after Jacob. "We seen bubbles coming out of the water when we was standing at the edge." He looked up at Peg, a tad worried yet somehow defiant—just like the father he was too young to remember used to get. "I swear we wasn't in the water, Mom, 'cause you told us to keep our sneakers dry." He craned his head back again, first glancing at Robbie, then at Duncan. "And the sand suddenly sunk. I jumped back just in time, but Repeat wasn't fast enough. See how the water is all up there now?" he said, pointing a dozen yards down the beach.

Peg shifted Jacob to her other hip when she realized her arms were going numb, but then signaled for Galen to take him when her brother-in-law walked up with his posse. "What's going on?" he asked as he settled Jacob against his shoulder.

"We believe the sides of the old pit are caving in," Robbie MacBain said. He looked at Peg. "How steep was the bank on this side before it flooded?"

"Not steep at all," she said, frowning as she tried to picture it in her mind. She pointed to the west. "It was more vertical on that end, but even that's been eroding over the last three years."

"How deep is it?" Duncan asked.

Peg shrugged, looking at Galen. "What, maybe forty feet deep?"

"More like sixty or seventy feet toward the west end." He looked at the shoreline closest to them. "But this side is mostly sand, so it's probably not all that stable, especially with the tides." He gestured to the east where the water came in from the newly formed fiord. "And there's no telling how deep that opening to the lake is."

Peg heard Duncan release a soft sigh and saw Robbie grin. "You do look like ye need a bath," Robbie said.

"I'm really not due for another two weeks," Duncan drawled, returning his grin. "I believe Alec was smelling a little off this morning, though. And he spends enough time on the ski slopes that he's likely permanently numb."

Peg couldn't imagine what they were talking about—that is, until she saw Duncan start unbuttoning his shirt. "Never mind," he said with a snort. "I'm soaked to my thighs already, so I might as well finish it. Hel—heck, maybe it will numb my ribs."

She grabbed his arm. "Wait, you . . . you're not actually going *swimming*?"

"For the love of God, man," Galen said in surprise, hugging Jacob to him. "That water's freezing!"

Duncan gently pulled free of Peg, reached in his back pocket and took out his wallet, then unclipped his cell phone from his belt. "Somebody has to check the slope on this side of the old pit," he said, handing his belongings to Robbie, "before you walk out one morning and find your driveway underwater."

"No," she growled, grabbing him again when he went back to unbuttoning his shirt. But she was ready for him this time when he tried to pull free, and dug her fingers into his arm. "You are not doing this. I don't care if the entire dooryard sinks into that pit; I'm not going to stand here and watch you drown."

The building gleam in his eyes disappeared, and he covered her hands with his own. "I'm not going to drown, lass. I've been swimming in cold mountain ponds since I was Peter and Jacob's age. We all have," he said, gesturing at Robbie. "And I need to see what that slope looks like so we can shore it up with the excavator. It might only be a matter of setting some large rocks in a few strategic places."

"No," she growled again, actually trying to shake him.

"I'm not willing to risk having it cave in," he said, gently prying her hands off, then holding them against her angry tugging. "Not when it could happen while your children are out here playing, like it did just now."

"Wait, what about the scientists?" she said. "The other day Steve told me they have an unmanned rover, so I'll go to Inglenook and ask him to bring it here to look at the slope. He can drive their boat right into the pit."

Duncan shook his head. "It would likely take them an entire day to bring a rover in here, when I can be in and out of the water in ten minutes and have the problem fixed in an hour. Robbie," he said, turning away as he went back to unbuttoning his shirt. "Radio Alec from my pickup and have him bring down the excavator." He glanced over his shoulder when Peg muttered a nasty little curse of her own under her breath, and arched his brow. "Maybe ye should take your boys inside for their naps."

She started to spin away in disgust, but gasped instead when he shed his shirt and she saw the large bruise on his side and several small cuts on his arms and back. "Did you fall down the mountain *naked*?"

He turned in surprise and looked down at himself, then rubbed a tiny cut on his ribs with a grin. "It's a very tall mountain."

"And yet your jacket doesn't seem to have so much as a scuff mark," she said, gesturing at Jacob still wrapped up in his leather jacket in Galen's arms.

Duncan walked over to sit on the picnic table and started taking off his boots. "Just be a good lass and go in the house, Peg," he said as she walked toward him, "and let us men do our work."

"Dammit," she softly hissed in deference to the men standing behind her as mute as fence posts, she assumed because they were trying to decide if their new boss really was as tough as he looked or certifiably insane. Heck, even Peter was speechless for once. "This is crazy. You don't have to prove anything to Galen and the others."

He glanced up in surprise, then took off his socks, stuffed them in one of his boots, and stood up. "Did ye know a person can see the entire length of Bottomless from the top of the mountain, and all the way to Canada in the other direction?" he asked. "If the weather's nice I could take you and your children up to the summit this Sunday if you'd like, and we could bring a lunch."

Peg dropped her gaze to his chest—which was quite naked, she couldn't help but notice—and also tried to decide if he really was as tough as he looked or insane. Not because it appeared he was going swimming with or without her permission, but because she'd swear he'd just invited her on . . . No, he hadn't just asked her and her kids on a picnic, because that really, really was insane.

"I . . . The kids would like that," she heard herself say, deciding *she* was insane.

"Take the boys inside, Peg." He lifted her chin with his finger, either because her staring at his chest unnerved him, or he wanted her to see his smile. "And try not to worry, okay? I really do swim in mountain ponds for sport." His eyes took on a decidedly wicked sparkle. "Although I usually prefer to do it naked."

Peg spun around and was halfway to Galen before she

heard Duncan's quiet chuckle. She snatched Jacob away, settled him on her hip to take hold of Peter's hand and marched to her house, hoping the stupid idiot caught pneumonia!

No, wait; then he couldn't take her and the kids up the mountain Sunday.

Yeah, well, she hoped Duncan MacKeage liked shaved venison sandwiches, because that's was she was packing for their picnic.

Chapter Seven

"I think I've done a really dumb thing," Peg said, sitting with her back against the picnic table as she stared across her newly reconstructed beach at her nearly barren hillside. She looked over at Olivia. "I agreed to let Duncan take me and the kids up the mountain this weekend to see the view and have a picnic."

Olivia's eyes widened in surprise, and Peg flinched when her friend suddenly threw her arms around her with a soft squeal of delight. "Oh, Peggy, that's the smartest thing I've heard come out of your mouth since last Saturday." She leaned away. "Wait; how can going on a picnic possibly be dumb?"

"Give me one good reason it can possibly be smart."

"Well, you'll get to see why we're building the resort up there," Olivia said, letting her go. "And you'll get to spend the day with an adult male you're not actually related to." She leaned closer. "My first outing with Mac was an ice fishing picnic, and look where that led."

Peg jumped to her feet. "I don't want anything to lead anywhere! I swore on my husband's grave three years ago that I was never, ever falling in love again."

"Shh, the kids will hear you," Olivia said, nodding at the beach and pulling Peg back down beside her. "I'm pretty sure Duncan only asked you to go on a picnic, not fall in love with him." She folded her hands on her lap. "But I remember swearing never to fall in love again, myself."

"How's that been working for you, *Mrs*. Oceanus?"

Olivia gave her a sidelong glance and slow smile. "Pretty damned well, actually." She looked at their children building sand castles—Charlotte and Isabel and Sophie building one and the twins and Henry building their own. "It's working pretty well for Sophie, too. I hadn't realized how much a little girl needs a man in her life."

"She had John," Peg reminded her.

"Grampies aren't the same as dads. Sophie's . . . Well, I don't ever remember her going to John with a problem." Olivia turned on the seat to face Peg. "Just the other day I saw her and Mac sitting in the gazebo, just talking. And that night when I asked her what they'd been talking about, she told me she'd asked Mac how she should deal with a boy at school who kept calling her Sexy Sophie."

"Sexy Sophie? I hope he told her to punch the little snot in the nose."

Olivia's eyes crinkled with laughter. "No, my sweet, dear husband told my sweet, innocent daughter to thank the little snot for the lovely compliment and then ask him out on a date."

"Oh, for the love of— I hope you punched *Mac* in the nose."

"Actually, it worked," Olivia said, sounding even more amazed than Peg was. "It appears Mac was eight years old once, too, and obviously remembers how boys that age think. Because despite my warning Sophie that it was probably going to backfire on her, the next day when the little snot called her Sexy Sophie and she thanked him and asked him out, the kid ran away so fast that he knocked over the food scrap bucket in the cafeteria." She smiled smugly. "And his mother had to be called to bring him a change of clothes."

"Mac told Sophie to call his bluff. I never would have thought of that."

"Exactly," Olivia said with a nod. "Now do you understand what I'm saying? Men see the world differently than we do, and kids need both perspectives. So how can your children *and you* spending the day with Duncan be a dumb thing?"

Peg dropped her gaze. "But what if they start liking him?" she whispered, lifting her head again. "He'll be coming around here at least all this spring, and what if they get attached to Duncan?" She stood up, crossing her arms to hug herself as she looked at her children. "It's one thing for me to survive getting my heart broken," she said, looking back at Olivia. "But I don't want my babies' hearts to get broken again by letting them get attached to a man who will eventually leave or . . . die."

"Oh, Peg," Olivia said softly, standing up to take hold of Peg's shoulders. "We can't stop living because something *might* happen, any more than we can protect our children from life itself."

Peg pulled away to look at the hillside where Duncan— apparently none the worse from his swim—was sitting with Robbie and Alec on the track of the excavator, watching the men cut her pine logs into workable lengths. She turned to Olivia. "That doesn't mean I have to go looking for trouble. Because honestly?" she whispered. "I'm not sure I'd survive getting my own heart broken again."

"It's a *picnic*, Peg," Olivia softly growled.

"But what's the point of it, anyway? Why did Duncan even offer? What man in his right mind wants to spend all day with four kids who aren't even his?"

"Gee, I don't know," Olivia drawled, a sparkle coming back into her eyes. "It couldn't possibly be that he might actually like children, or that he simply wants to spend the day with a beautiful woman he's not related to."

"But I'm not—"

Olivia stepped toward her. "I swear to God, you finish that sentence and I'm shoving you in the water."

Peg lifted her chin. "I was going to say that I'm not . . . that I don't . . . Oh, okay; but besides my *beauty*, and the fact that we beat him up and I nearly ran him over with my van, why is he being so nice to—" Peg suddenly took a step back and pointed at Olivia. "Dammit, are you putting him up to this?"

"What? No!"

"I swear to God, if I find out the picnic was your idea, I'll—"

Olivia burst out laughing and sat back down, pulling Peg down with her. "I swear I didn't put him up to it." Her eyes filled with laughter again. "But only because I didn't think of it. And Mac swears that Duncan's a good man, Peg," she said, turning serious. "A bit old-fashioned apparently, according to a conversation I overheard at the wedding reception, but the consensus is that all the MacKeages and MacBains are noble men." She nudged Peg with her shoulder. "But then, Simon Maher is available now that I'm off the market."

Peg reared away in horror. "He's old enough to be my father!" But then she smiled. "And yours, not that that seemed to matter to him."

They shuddered in unison and both burst out laughing.

"Mom?" Peter called out. "It looks like the men are bringing wood for our campfire. Can me and Repeat and Henry go help them?" he asked, pointing at Duncan and Robbie and Alec walking toward them with their arms full of wood.

Peg looked around, then nodded. "Okay, as long as you stay beside them."

"Come on, guys," Peter said excitedly. "Let's go help them find more wood so we can have a really big fire to cook our hot dogs."

Jacob stood up, looked at Peg, then at the men, then walked over and knelt down beside the girls and started working on their sand castle.

Henry started after Peter, but suddenly stopped and turned back. "Mother? Is it okay if I go, too?"

"Sure thing, Henry; go on," Olivia said, waving him away.

"'Mother'?" Peg said even as she sighed at Jacob's reluctance to go with them.

"That's who I am today," Olivia muttered. "Yesterday I was 'ma'am,' and for three days before that I was 'Mater'—which apparently is Latin for *mother*. Ever since the wedding Henry's been trying to decide what to call me, because he claims 'Miss Olivia' is too formal."

"No offense," Peg said, deadpan, leaning closer. "But have you ever wanted to push Henry in a mud puddle just to see his reaction?" Olivia blinked at her in surprise, and Peg snorted. "Oh, come on, I know you've at least thought about it. The kid's a little . . . stiff. I mean, seriously, *Latin*? What's wrong with calling you plain old Olivia?"

"Too ill-mannered," Olivia said with a sigh. "But hopefully he'll have it figured out by the time we reach California, because I swear if he shouts 'Mater' or 'ma'am' at me in the middle of Disney World, I'm going to pretend I don't know him."

"Jacob," Duncan called out just as Peg saw him accidentally drop a piece of wood on purpose. "Could you come get that for me, please?"

Peg held her breath when Jacob stood up and looked at Duncan, then at her, then at the piece of wood Duncan was stopped beside, and she didn't start breathing again until the boy started running toward him.

"And that," Olivia said, "is why going on a picnic is not a dumb thing."

Duncan dumped his load of neatly cut branches on the dead grass just above the beach. "You said ye planned to cook hot dogs over a campfire tonight."

Peg felt her shoulders slump. "I guess I did, didn't I?"

"Oh, are we invited?" Olivia asked, her eyes lighting up again. "You know how much I like campfires."

"Sorry, I don't have any wine," Peg drawled.

"That's okay," Olivia said, pulling her cell phone out of her pocket. "I'll call Mac and have him bring a couple of bottles as well as everything for s'mores."

Peg glanced at Alec and Robbie and Duncan—who also appeared as interested in the campfire as Olivia was—and smiled sheepishly. "I only have a dozen hot dogs."

"You must have some . . . other meat in your freezer, don't you?" Duncan asked, his eyes dancing. "We could have kebabs."

"I'll make a store run," Robbie interjected, "when I take my crew to Inglenook to bed them down for the night." He looked at Olivia. "We appreciate your letting us use your dormitory until Duncan gets his camp set up, since I couldn't find any cabins to rent within fifty miles of the new Bottomless Sea."

"Yeah, there's actual traffic in town now," Olivia said, looking down at what Peg recognized as a smartphone.

"Wait," she said, touching her arm. "There's no signal here, Olivia."

"My phone works," Duncan said.

"And mine," Alec and Robbie said almost in unison.

Olivia smiled at her. "It appears we have cell phone service in Spellbound ever since the earthquake. You need to get yourself one, Peg, so I can text you a picture of me pushing Mac into the Grand Canyon."

"Speaking of my dad, Mr. MacBain," Henry said, stepping in front of Robbie. "He told me that you were only a few years older than me when your father married your stepmother, and I was wondering how you address her," he asked as Robbie squatted down to be eye level. "Dad said your mama died when you were born, but I was wondering what you call your new mom."

Peg saw Robbie's startled gaze snap to Duncan, then slide to Olivia before it softened with his smile as he looked back to Henry. "Well, Mr. Oceanus, I had quite a time trying to decide what to call her until we both settled on 'Mum,' since I usually referred to my birth mother as my mama." He tapped Henry's chest. "And I call her mother Gram Katie, which she seems to like quite well."

Henry beamed him a bright smile, then turned to Olivia. "What do you think of 'Mum'? And since I have two grandfathers, I could call your father Grampy Sam, and his father Great-Grampy."

"Works for me," Olivia said with obvious relief, giving Robbie a nod of thanks.

"And you can call me 'darling,'" Isabel said, rushing over to grasp Henry's arm. "Come on, sweetheart; let's go finish building our dream castle together."

Peg jumped up. "Sorry, darling," she said with a laugh, grabbing her daughter by the hood of her jacket. "We womenfolk have to go throw together a cookout. Come on, Charlotte, I need your help, too." She turned and started walking backward to see Olivia and Sophie following. "You boys come, too. Jacob, why don't you show Henry your new book about ocean creatures? And you menfolk can build the campfire and cut some sticks for the hot dogs and . . . and the kebabs," she finished lamely, spinning away from Duncan's quiet laughter.

Peg shooed the kids into the bathroom as soon as they got in the house, telling them to wash up and then go play in their respective bedrooms, promising to call them when it was time to start lugging stuff outside. She then waited until Olivia was done giving Mac instructions on what to bring, and pulled her friend into the kitchen as soon as Olivia slipped her cell phone in her pocket.

"I've changed my mind again," she said, opening the pantry door. "I'm back to thinking the picnic is a dumb idea."

Olivia sighed behind her. "For the love of God, *why*?"

"That's why," she said, turning to point at the kitchen table. "Jacob woke up from his nap and decided Duncan needed a hero's badge for saving him this morning."

Olivia went over and picked up the badge that Jacob and Peter had worked on for over an hour. "What a great idea." She turned, holding it against her chest. "Duncan MacKeage, our hero," she said dramatically before suddenly sobering. "Don't you see, Peg? Instead of being scared of Duncan for pulling him off the excavator the other day, now Jacob sees him as a hero."

Peg snorted and turned back to the pantry to hunt for the hot dog rolls. "Yes, everyone loves a hero." She turned back to Olivia. "Aren't we lucky to have both been married to such fine, upstanding men?"

Olivia went perfectly still. "You're angry at Billy? Oh, Peg, I had no idea you felt that way," she whispered, tossing the badge on the table and rushing to her. She took hold of Peg's shoulders and smiled sadly. "But I do know what it's like to feel guilty for being angry at someone who's dead."

"Keith died a war hero, but would you please tell me what's so heroic about saving a bunch of stupid *buildings* in some stupid town? Billy broke his little girls' hearts. And mine," she said, thumping her chest. "And now I'm going to have to spend the rest of my life sleeping in an empty bed and go to every school play and graduation alone, and Billy's brother will be the one taking the girls to father-daughter dances."

Olivia gently pulled the crushed rolls away from Peg, led her to the sink, and grabbed a cup towel. "Wipe your eyes," she instructed, handing it to her. "Nobody but Mac knows this, but my marriage to Keith died two years before he did."

Peg lowered the towel in surprise. "It did?"

Olivia nodded. "But that doesn't negate the fact that he broke his daughter's heart," she said softly. "So I understand your anger. But what I don't understand is why you've decided Billy's dying means that your life is over, too."

Peg turned and braced her hands on the sink to look out the window. "Because it *is* over—at least my love life is—because I'm cursed." She looked past her shoulder at Olivia's snort, and turned and folded her arms under her breasts. "Nobody but my mom and my aunt know this, but all the women in my family became widows before their husbands reached their thirtieth birthdays. And when my mom and aunt waited until they were in their forties to remarry, both of their second husbands died within a few years in freak accidents."

"Are you serious?" Olivia said in surprise. She suddenly shook her head. "Those are coincidences, Peggy. There's no such thing as curses."

"Yeah, well, they're damn freaky coincidences." She glanced toward the bedroom, then glared at her friend. "And I'm not about to risk my children getting their hearts broken again just to prove you wrong. Or is it right? Hell, I don't know anything anymore," she muttered, burying her face in the towel again.

Olivia pulled her hands down and held them. "Are you saying you shouldn't go on a simple picnic because you're afraid if you . . . what . . . that if you happen to fall in love with Duncan that your family's curse is going to kill him?"

"Five generations of women descended from Gretchen Robinson, Olivia; all widowed the first time before their thirtieth birthdays for a sum total of twelve dead men, including second husbands. If that's not a curse, then what in hell is it?" She pulled her hands free and used the towel to point out the window as she arched a brow. "Should we see if Duncan can make it a nice baker's dozen?"

Olivia's mouth opened but nothing came out, and she closed it and walked to the table and sat down. She frowned at Peg, then started fingering the badge on the table.

Peg went to the fridge and took out the hot dogs and set them on the counter, then started dragging out condiments. She opened a cupboard and took down her dinner plates because she didn't have any paper ones, then opened a drawer and gathered up fistfuls of forks and knives.

"I'm pretty sure it's going to take more than a curse to kill Duncan MacKeage," Olivia said into the silence, making Peg stop and stare down at the open drawer. "From what I understand, his entire family is . . . well . . . let's go with *charmed*. And Duncan told me his father is eighty-two years old but looks and acts like he's barely sixty."

"Billy was big and strong, too."

Peg heard Olivia walk over, then felt a hand press onto her shoulder. "You can't love a person to death, Peggy," Olivia said quietly, turning her around. "And you can't—ohmigod," she gasped, her eyes widening. "You think you're responsible for Billy dying. Peggy, that's crazy because it's *impossible*."

"Okay, then," she growled, taking a swipe at her eyes with her sleeve. "Does that mean you wouldn't have any problem with Isabel marrying Henry when they grow up?" She smiled tightly when Olivia dropped her hands in surprise. "Or your father, Sam, falling madly in love with my mother and marrying her even though she's already killed off two husbands?"

"Peggy Thompson, you're outrageous." Olivia made a crisscross over her chest. "And scout's honor, I absolutely wouldn't have a problem with Henry marrying Isabel." She snorted. "Henry might, though." She held up her hand when Peg tried to speak. "As for your mom and Sam . . . well, I'd be more worried about Jeanine than Dad."

Peg felt her mouth twitch. "Yeah, so would I." She blew out a sigh and went to the pantry. "Okay then, let's forget the Robinson curse and focus on my kids getting attached to Duncan—or any other man, for that matter." She grabbed a small plastic bin, threw in a roll of paper towels, and carried it over to the counter and set everything inside it before turning to Olivia. "Weren't you afraid Sophie would get attached to Mac, but that she'd be crushed if things hadn't worked out between you?"

"Of course I was. But *Sophie's* the one who kept pushing me to get a boyfriend—other than Simon Maher," she said with a small shudder. "That's when I realized I wasn't setting a very good example for her. Think about it, Peg; our kids don't do what we say, they do what we *do*. And all Sophie saw me doing was running out the back door of the Drunken Moose or hiding in *your* van to avoid talking to a man."

"It's not only men you hid from," Peg said. "Okay, okay," she conceded, raising her hand. "I'll go on that stupid picnic Sunday. But," she growled when Olivia broke into a way too smug smile, "I am not going on a real date if he asks me."

"He scares you, doesn't he?" Olivia whispered. "He just has to look at you with those piercing eyes and your insides clench and your mouth goes dry and your heart starts pounding, and you think you're going to pass out the moment he touches you and miss something really important."

Peg blinked at her. "Are we talking about me and Duncan or you and Mac?"

That certainly wiped away her smugness. Olivia brushed down the front of her jacket. "Yes. Well." This time her smile was sheepish. "Honestly? I'm still afraid I'm going to pass out and miss some of the best parts. Oh, Peg," she said, grasping her shoulders again. "Promise me that you'll have a good time Sunday."

"I promise I'll *try*."

Olivia's hands tightened. "And promise me you'll get over this crazy notion that you're some sort of black widow, and that you'll at least give Duncan a fighting chance." She let go with a laugh. "Although I did notice he's looking a tad beat-up today—rather like my dear sweet husband."

"Are you saying Mac fell down the mountain, too?"

Olivia frowned in confusion, then suddenly snorted. "They didn't fall down the mountain; they beat the hell out of each other."

"What? For God's sake, why?"

"Because they're idiots," Olivia said with a dismissive wave. "When I asked Mac why he couldn't stop groaning this morning, he told me he and Duncan had engaged in a bit of sport up on the mountain. And then he said that if I thought he looked bad, I should see Duncan."

"What kind of sport? No, wait; I know! Duncan had a sword in his truck this morning, and he told us that his family goes to some games down on the coast every summer. They must have been fencing. But I thought that involved skinny rapiers or foils or something with *rubber tips*. Duncan has little cuts all over him."

Olivia nodded. "I only saw one cut on Mac, but he's got several nasty bruises and he's walking with a bit of a limp."

"Why would two grown men beat themselves up for no good reason?"

"Because they're idiots," Olivia repeated. "And I guess because they feel it's more macho than going to a gym and running on a treadmill."

"And you're hoping I'll date one of those idiots?"

"Hey, I *married* one of them," Olivia muttered, grabbing the plastic bin and heading for the door. "And just so you know, Mac told me they're meeting up on the mountain again tomorrow afternoon to have another go at each other. So try to keep your little tribe of heathens from beating Duncan up too badly this week, okay?" She stopped and looked back, her smile smug again. "You, however, have my permission to attack him in any way you see fit."

Chapter Eight

Not an hour in to the hastily thrown together campfire, Duncan was coming to realize several things about Peg and her children, which taken separately appeared benign, but as a whole were somewhat disconcerting and maybe even sad.

Disconcertingly, the little tribe of heathens—which is how he'd heard Peg refer to them more than once this evening—were meticulously polite, considerate of both the adults and one another, and surprisingly quiet for children on their home turf. Even Pete was subdued, seemingly overwhelmed to have his dooryard invaded by a small band of strange men, and he'd spent the better part of supper sitting on a log scrunched up against his mother while his twin monopolized her other side. Peg's oldest daughter, Charlotte—who was eight, Duncan had learned—and her sister, Isabel—who was six—sat quietly at the picnic table with Mac and Olivia's two children, using a flashlight to pore over an atlas of the United States as they talked about the Oceanuses' upcoming trip while basically ignoring everyone else.

The sad part, to Duncan's thinking, was how self-contained the Thompson tribe appeared to be, as if it were the five of them against the big scary world. But then, what was to say he wouldn't have pulled his family into a defensive hug if he had suddenly found himself raising four children all by himself?

Peg was unusually quiet as well, apparently also trying to come to terms with having her secure little kingdom invaded by men and machinery. He'd caught her staring up at her barren hillside more than once this evening, then releasing a soft sigh. He'd also caught her giving him sidelong glances only to look down at her hands, but not quickly enough for him to miss the hint of panic in her eyes. He didn't know what to make of that exactly, but he did like the idea that she might be seeing him as something other than all that was standing between her and prostitution.

Duncan figured he must have taken a blow to the head during his little exercise with Mac yesterday, because he still couldn't believe he'd asked Peg if she'd let him take her and her children up the mountain Sunday. For a picnic? Really? People his parents' age went on picnics, not thirty-five-year-old red-blooded males—unless they were attracted to a certain contrary, over-proud woman, apparently.

The amazing thing was she'd said yes.

Duncan took a swig of the kick-in-the-ass ale Mac had thoughtfully brought to the impromptu outing, and watched Peg whisper to Jacob—he'd already figured out how to tell them apart—as she handed the boy something before giving him a nudge to get him moving. Jacob took exactly two steps before he stopped and looked back at her, the firelight reflecting the hint of panic in eyes the spitting image of his mother's.

"Peter, why don't you go with him?" he heard Peg say softly, peeling her other son off her side and also giving him a nudge. "Because it could just as easily have been you in that water. And if it wasn't for Mr. MacKeage, we probably wouldn't have a beach to be having our campfire on tonight."

"Come with us, Mom," he heard Jacob whisper tightly.

Her encouraging smile turned into what Duncan was coming to recognize as Peg's I-mean-business scowl when they still didn't move. Pete finally grabbed his brother's hand and, taking a fortifying breath that squared his little shoulders, started dragging Jacob around the fire to where Duncan was sitting with Robbie and Alec and Mac, leaning against some spare boulders they'd set into place with the excavator.

"Mr. MacKeage," Pete said, his little chin lifting exactly like his mother's often did. "Jacob and me made you something after our nap." He elbowed his brother. "Give it to him, Repeat."

Jacob thrust out his hand. "This is 'cause you're a rescue hero," he said when his brother elbowed him again. He suddenly lifted his bright blue eyes, making direct contact with Duncan's as he boldly stepped closer. "All heroes have a bemlem . . . a embal . . . a badge to wear on their chests. Mom helped me draw the evascater and cut it out, but I did all the coloring and pasting."

"The bolt of lightning was my idea," Pete added as Duncan took the badge, "because lightning tells everyone you're fast and strong."

Staring down at the paste-stiffened construction paper covered with enough crayon to make the excavator nearly invisible, Duncan tried to say something only to have to clear his throat as he looked into Jacob's apprehensive eyes. "This is really quite an honor, gentlemen," he said thickly, running his thumb over the badge. He smiled, giving Jacob a nod. "I'm glad I could be of service."

"You gotta put it on your chest," Pete instructed. "Mom stuck a pin on the back so you could."

"Wait," Mac said when Duncan turned the badge over. "I do believe the lovely damsel whose child was saved must do the honor of rewarding the brave hero."

Tomorrow afternoon, Duncan decided as he shot Mac a glare, he was going to shove the cocky bastard off the mountain even if he had to go over with him.

"Oh yes, Peggy," Olivia chimed in, waving her tumbler of wine. "Go pin the badge on Duncan." She stood up when Peg didn't move and hauled the scowling damsel up off her log. "Just try to do it without stabbing him, okay?" she said, dragging Peg around the fire.

"Aye," Robbie said with a chuckle, nudging Duncan's arm just as he was taking another swig of ale to hide his scowl at Peg's obvious reluctance. "It would appear the man's lost more than enough blood already this week."

"Yeah, Boss," Alec drawled, nudging his other arm. "I believe if ye spill too much more you're going to find yourself *staggering* back to TarStone. Be gentle with him, fair damsel," he said with a chuckle. "He's had a hard week."

Duncan scrambled to his feet when he saw Peg suddenly break free of Olivia and stride toward him far too eagerly. Dammit, he hadn't done one thing to deserve this. Hell, he'd gone out of his way to be nice to the contrary woman.

"Yes, give me that," she said far too sweetly as she snatched the badge out of his hand. "I would love to do the honors. And don't worry, Alec; I'm sure your boss is still numb from his swim, so he won't feel a thing if I accidentally stab him." She pulled back her hands. "No, wait; shouldn't you be on your knees?"

"In your dreams," he muttered just before gulping down another kick-in-the-ass.

"Excuse me? Did you say something?"

"Mom," Jacob whispered loudly, tugging on her sweatshirt hard enough that she nearly stabbed herself on the pin. "I gotta see 'cause I made it for him."

Duncan sighed and was just about to drop to one knee when Alec scrambled to his knees instead and held open his arms. "How about if I lift you up, Jacob?"

Duncan sensed Peg go as still as a stone, and he used his eyes to motion to Robbie—who immediately pushed away from his boulder and opened his arms to Pete.

"I could also give you a lift," Robbie offered.

Pete immediately walked into his embrace; Jacob stepping into Alec's in the very next heartbeat so that both men stood up with the boys in their arms. And Duncan nearly did drop to his knees when he saw tears welling in Peg's eyes despite her grateful smile. She gently pressed the badge to his shirt and carefully pinned it on him with trembling fingers, then cleared her throat. "Um, this badge is to honor Duncan MacKeage," she said thickly, "for rescuing Jacob Thompson."

Duncan tried to say something but found he had to clear his own throat again, so he patted the badge on his chest, turned to Jacob, and smiled. "I will treasure it always, Mr. Thompson."

"And you gotta *wear* it always," Pete added. "So everybody will know you're a rescue hero, like on TV."

Well, hell; that was going to be a problem.

Peg gave a sputtered laugh and patted her son's leg. "I think Mr. MacKeage should carry it in his wallet just like the policemen do on TV." She turned to Alec to get Jacob's approval. "That way it won't get torn or wrinkled, and he can pull out his wallet and show it to anyone who needs rescuing."

"But I'll probably wait until *after* I rescue them," Duncan offered. "Okay, Jacob? Pete?" he asked, turning to include him.

"Okay," Pete said. He looked down at the ground then at Robbie, his deep blue eyes widening. "You're even higher than Uncle Galen."

"Mom," Isabel said, pushing her way inside the circle of people to tug on the hem of Peg's sweatshirt. "What's the big deal? Jacob swims like a fish, so he wouldn't have drowned. You call all of us your little trout."

"The deal is," Peg said, taking Isabel's hand and leading her away, "Jacob fell in ice-cold seawater, not the warm water of our old swimming hole."

Alec started to lower Jacob to the ground, but stopped when the boy suddenly reached his arms out to Duncan. "I got som'fin else to give you," he whispered, darting a glance at his mother walking away, and then at Pete, who was running after her when Robbie set him down. Jacob wrapped an arm around Duncan's neck when Alec transferred him over before also wisely walking away.

"My mom gave it to me and I want to give it to you," Jacob said, opening his tiny fist to expose a small rock. "It's a worry stone," he explained reverently, the arm around Duncan's neck nudging him. "Go on, take it," he instructed, dropping the rock into Duncan's palm when he held up his hand. "You're s'pose to carry it in your pocket, and when you get worried or scared or sad, you take it out and rub it." He leaned his head closer. "But you gotta remember to *take it out* to rub it, or people will think you're playing pocket pool. And Mama says only unservalized men do that."

Fighting back laughter, Duncan stared down at the tiny rock and nodded gravely. "I will definitely remember to take it out of my pocket first." He ran his thumb across the stone. "Are you sure you want to give this to me, Jacob, seeing how your mama gave it to you? It must be very special."

The boy folded Duncan's finger over the stone. "No, you

keep it. Mom's got a whole bowl on the counter 'cause I keep losing them." He pressed his tiny hand to the badge pinned on Duncan's chest. "Do you think if you didn't catch me this morning I coulda saved myself? Or if Pete was drownding I coulda saved him?"

"I do," Duncan said with a nod, "if you swim like a trout."

"My daddy didn't save hisself and Mama says he was big and strong like I'm going to be when I grow up."

Okay; apparently Jacob was over his shyness. Duncan turned to look behind him and sat down on the nearest boulder, then glanced across the fire to see Peg staring at them, both her hands clutching her throat. "Well, Jacob," he said slowly, trying to find the right words, "sometimes it's impossible to save ourselves, just like sometimes it's impossible to save someone else. And . . . well, the way I understand it, your dad found himself in an icy river that had a very powerful current. It's likely he hit his head and wasn't even . . . awake when he hit the water."

Jacob sat up, his eyes widening. "Nobody never said that before." He looked directly into Duncan's eyes. "When we swimmed in our swimming hole before it got covered up with water, I tried holding my breath a long time like I thought my daddy did, but it always hurt something fierce and . . ." He dropped his gaze with a shudder. "And I don't want him to hurt like that when he drownded." He looked up. "You really think he was asleep?"

Duncan pressed the boy to his shoulder. "I'm willing to bet my bulldozer *and* my excavator that he was, Jacob. Your daddy didn't hurt."

"I'm glad," the boy murmured, relaxing against him. "I'm gonna tell Mama what you said, so she won't worry about it, neither." He tilted his head back to look up. "And Pete and the girls. We gotta tell all of them."

"We can tell them together, if you'd like."

Jacob settled back against him again. "How come you learned I'm not Pete so fast? Everyone always mixes us up."

"Well, I do believe you have your mama's smile and that Pete's got her scowl," Duncan said with a chuckle, shooting Peg a wink across the fire when he saw that though she was listening to what Olivia was saying, her eyes were glued on him and Jacob. "What about your sisters?" he asked. "Do you have any thoughts on how I can tell them apart?"

Jacob sat up and turned to him in surprise. "They're not twins. They wasn't borned together like me and Pete."

"Repeat," Pete called out, running over to them. "Mama said we can only have one more s'more and then we gotta go in and have baths." He looked at Duncan. "You coming back tomorrow? Mr. Alec said you got a giant bulldozer."

"We'll be here when you wake up, and so will the bulldozer."

"Come on, Repeat," Pete said, grabbing his brother's arm and dragging him off Duncan's lap. "You gotta help me sneak the snails in our bath."

Jacob broke free and, after giving Pete a push to keep going, he turned around. "Mr. Ma—Mr. Duncan?"

"Yes, Jacob?"

"You don't forget to take the worry stone out of your pocket to rub it, okay?"

"I won't forget."

He started off again, but as was his mother's habit, he suddenly stopped and turned and walked back to Duncan. "And thank you for telling me about my daddy being asleep when he drownded." He shrugged his tiny shoulders. "I think it's gonna make my belly not hurt so bad when I'm trying to remember him."

Duncan ran a finger over his cheek. "I'm glad, Jacob. And if ye want, we can tell your brother and sisters about it when we go up the mountain on Sunday for our picnic."

His eyes widened. "We're going on a picnic?" he yelped, looking over his shoulder at Peg, then back at him. "On the mountain? Sunday?"

Duncan snapped his head up at Peg's gasp, and then dropped it into his hands with a silent curse. Dammit to hell; he'd thought she'd told them.

"We're going on a picnic?" Peter shouted. "Mom? Are we?"

"I guess so," Duncan heard her say, a decided edge in her voice.

"That's keeping an eye on her, Boss," Alec said, sitting down beside him.

"Is it going to be a company picnic or a private . . . affair?"

Robbie asked, shoving a bottle of ale under Duncan's nose, then sitting down once he took it.

"I do admire a man who backs his word with action," Mac said as he dropped down next to Robbie, his soft grunt of discomfort making Duncan smile into his bottle as he downed half the kick-in-the-ass in one gulp.

Oh yeah; day one on the job and he felt like he'd worked an entire season—and the day still wasn't over.

Chapter Nine

Peg stared out her bedroom window at the moon-bathed hillside and hugged herself on a shiver. If she lived to be a hundred and two, she would never forget turning around to see Jacob in Duncan's arms, then watching him sitting on Duncan's lap having an honest to God, everyday conversation with a virtual stranger who also happened to be a big, strong hero.

She could have killed Mac and Olivia for pushing her to pin that badge on him, but had quickly decided it was her chance to pay Duncan back for worrying her to death by diving into the frigid water of the pit. That is, until she saw him silently signal Robbie to pick up Peter so that Jacob would allow Alec to pick him up. Her heart had risen into her throat then stayed there for Jacob's entire conversation with Duncan afterward, and hadn't fallen back into place until Duncan had mentioned their Sunday picnic.

Peg released a heavy sigh at the realization that Olivia was right; little girls did need a man's perspective of things, and so did little boys. Why hadn't she ever thought to assure her children that their daddy's death hadn't been painful? But worse, why hadn't she known it had been worrying Jacob? And even worse again, why had her youngest son discussed that worry with Duncan instead of her?

When she'd casually asked Jacob while giving the twins their baths what he and Duncan had talked about, the boy had shot his brother a glance and said he'd tell her later. A bit alarmed that he was keeping secrets from her with a virtual stranger, Peg had made later come sooner by drying Peter off and sending him to go put on his pajamas.

That's when Jacob had told her he'd given Duncan one of his worry stones and then asked if he thought he could have saved himself or his brother. Peg's heart rose right back into her throat again when he'd gone on to say that he'd also asked how come his big strong daddy hadn't been able to save himself. Jacob had then told her that on their picnic, Mr. Duncan was going to help him explain to everyone that his dad had bumped his head when his excavator had fallen in the river, and it hadn't hurt him to drown because he'd been asleep.

Jacob had been nineteen months old when Billy had died, but apparently being too young to remember his father hadn't stopped him from worrying about him hurting.

Why hadn't she known that?

Nearly every day that first summer after Billy's death, Peg had taken her children down to the spring-fed, two-acre pond in their pit to teach them to swim, being careful—or maybe foolish, she now realized—not to reveal that their daddy had swam about as well as a rock. By the end of the summer she'd been calling the four of them her little trout, and by the next spring they'd been dragging her down to the swimming hole every day to test the water temperature with their toes, declaring by early June that is was warm enough to resume their daily outdoor baths. Peg had watched from shore until at least the Fourth of July, claiming she was a warm-water bass, not a trout.

Oh yeah, she owed Duncan MacKeage big-time for assuring Jacob that his daddy hadn't hurt. And for saving her from prostitution by giving her a fair price for her gravel. And for helping butcher her deer, making her beach safe, rescuing her son, loaning her his truck, and . . . and for being a good man.

Except she didn't want Duncan to be good, or big and strong and quick, or sexy, dammit, because she really didn't want to start liking him. But mostly she didn't want to ever fall in love with him because she didn't want to kill him.

Peg started to turn away from the window with another sigh, only to catch a flash out of the corner of her eye. She stepped to the edge of the window and strained to see into the woods to the east, holding her breath when she thought she heard something. And there it was again: the distinct sound of tires going slowly on gravel.

She ran out to the living room and opened the front door a crack just in time to see the moonlight reflect off the bumper of a vehicle—without any headlights—pulling up the narrow tote road along the east side of her property, and worried that whoever it was wouldn't realize the road had washed away when the fiord had poured into the pit.

She waited, holding her breath again until she saw a set of brake lights come on then go off just as she heard the engine quit. She stepped out onto the porch, squinting to see through the trees as she hugged her nightgown around her. Dammit, she thought she'd made it clear that the Thompson pit was no longer the local gathering place for teenagers looking to party.

Doors opened and closed, and she frowned when she heard voices whispering, because in her experience teenagers never whispered. Unless it wasn't kids, but— Peg snapped her gaze to the hillside, just barely able to see the excavator and harvester parked inside the back tree line. Diesel fuel, at today's prices, was liquid gold! She didn't know the size of a harvester's tank, but an excavator held over a hundred gallons.

Yeah, well, nobody was siphoning fuel from any equipment on *her* property.

She quietly stepped back in the house and softly closed the door before heading to her bedroom. Oh, she'd love to call the sheriff to come catch the idiots red-handed; only problem was the closest deputy was over fifty miles away—assuming he wasn't answering a call on the other side of the county.

She pulled her jeans on under her nightgown, then pulled off the gown and plucked her sweatshirt out of the laundry, slipping it on over her head before hunting through the basket for some socks. If those yahoos out there hadn't heard she didn't tolerate trespassers, they were about to hear it tonight, she thought as she shoved her socks in her sweatshirt pocket. She walked over and pulled her shotgun out of the closet, then took the small strongbox off the top shelf and carried it to the window. Not wanting to turn on the light, she held it up to the moonlight and worked the combination, then set it on her bureau to take out the shotgun shells and shove them in her pocket.

She walked into the hall and leaned the gun against the wall, then tiptoed into the girls' room and gently shook Charlotte awake. "Come on, Charlie," she whispered next to her ear before pulling her upright. "I need you to come out to the living room. Shh, it's okay, honey, nothing's wrong." She then guided the girl ahead of her, snatching up the gun on her way by, smiling assurance when Charlotte finished rubbing her eyes awake and blinked at the shotgun.

Her daughter sighed. "Trespassers again?" she whispered with a sleepy smile.

"I'm afraid it's not teenagers, but somebody who's after the diesel fuel in the equipment," Peg said, sitting down to slip on her socks and sneakers.

"Then call the sheriff this time," Charlotte said, rushing over to catch the gun Peg had leaned on the arm of the chair when it started to slide.

"They'll be long gone before he can get here." Peg finished tying her sneakers and stood up. "Don't worry, I'm not going to confront them; I'm just going to see what they're up to and get their license plate number."

Charlotte handed her the shotgun. "You got birdshot?"

Peg took the gun from her with a nod. "Same signal as always; you hear a shot, you call 911 first, and then call Grundy Watts and tell him to hightail it over here." She walked to the pantry and pulled the business card off the bulletin board. "And then you call Mr. MacKeage and tell him what's going on," she instructed, handing her the card. "He's staying at Inglenook, so he's actually closer than Grundy." She lifted Charlotte's chin and kissed her forehead. "You're growing up big and strong and smart, Charlie, and I don't know what I'd do without you."

"Does that mean I'm grown-up enough to get my ears pierced?" Charlotte asked as she started pushing Peg toward the door. "Say, for my birthday next month?"

Peg stopped and looked back at her beautiful little girl bathed in moonlight, and her heart rose into her throat again.

"You know, I think that might be exactly what a nine-year-old should get for her birthday."

Charlotte gasped so hard, she had to use both hands to clutch her nightgown. "Really?" she squeaked in a whisper. "You're gonna really let me get them pierced?"

"We'll go down to Bangor to have it done," Peg said with a nod. "Just you and me on a mother-daughter date."

"Oh, Mom, thank you!" Charlotte cried, throwing her arms around her. She leaned her head back to look up, the moonlight revealing her beaming smile. "Can we get our fingernails done?"

"And our toes," Peg promised, kissing the top of her curly brown hair then stepping away. "But first I have to go see who's out there trying to steal Duncan's fuel."

"You're just going to get their license plate number, right?" Charlotte warned more than asked. "You're not gonna confront anyone."

"Not unless I recognize them and know they're more stupid than dangerous. Then I'm going to stop them from committing a felony."

"Oh, Mom," Charlotte said with a snort, running to the coffee table and picking up the phone. She climbed up on the couch and knelt facing the window, as was her ritual. "Just let all the air out of their tires so they got no way to lug the diesel fuel off."

Peg stilled with her hand on the doorknob. "What?"

"That way they'll be more worried about getting their truck out of here before sunrise instead of stealing anything, and you can just come back inside and go to bed."

"Ohmigod, Charlie, when did you get so sneaky?"

Charlotte rolled her eyes, shooting Peg another moonbeam smile. "I've been living with you for almost nine years." She waved her away. "Go on now; we both need our beauty sleep."

Peg opened the door with a snort, slipping outside before her smile disappeared on a shiver of horror. Good Lord, she thought as she headed down the stairs and across her driveway at a dead run. That girl was going to be flat-out scary at sixteen. But Peg smiled again as she ducked behind a tree at the edge of the tote road, figuring she had it coming since she'd turned her own mama's hair prematurely gray.

She quietly loaded the shotgun as she decided it was better to raise two smart and independent young ladies rather than two doormats for some dumb, chest-beating jerks. And if she died making it happen, every last one of her heathens were going to college so they could get the hell out of Spellbound Falls, because so help her God, not one of them was going to earn a living driving a stupid excavator.

Peg double-checked to make sure the gun's safety was on, smiling when she heard several of the thieving idiots cussing in whispers, figuring they'd just discovered they couldn't reach the hillside because the road had been washed away. And that meant they had to go clear across her beach and all the way around the pit, giving them quite a hike for lugging back the heavy fuel—which also meant she'd be able to get a good look at them in the moonlight. And while they were gone, she might as well get their license plate number and let the air out of their tires so they could spread the word that the Thompson pit was no place to rip off the new boys in town.

Gee, maybe Duncan would make *her* a hero's badge for saving his fuel.

Peg stood with her back to the tree, listening to branches snapping and an occasional curse as the men made their way down the steep wooded knoll beside their vehicle. It sounded like three, maybe four of them, but she didn't recognize any of their voices or the SUV—at least not from this distance.

Hearing them reach her beach, she peeked around the tree to make sure they hadn't left anyone behind, then crouched down and quietly scurried toward the truck, guessing they—

Peg's scream never made it past the large hand that pressed over her mouth at the same time an arm pinned her arms to her sides and lifted her off her feet. She kicked out even while trying to bite the hand all but suffocating her, the arm around her middle nearly finishing the job when it tightened against her struggles.

"Lady, you are one second away from feeling the flat of my sword on your backside," he quietly growled into her hair.

Duncan! Peg stopped struggling, but instead of loosening his hold or at least removing his hand so she could breathe, he turned and headed toward the main road like he was lugging off a— Wait, had he just said his *sword*?

Well, of course he had, because everyone knew men said and did stupid things when they were angry. But threaten her with a sword? Seriously?

"Ye try to trip me up with that shotgun or bite me again and I *will* put ye over my knee," Duncan said quietly. He finally stopped when they reached the main road and set her on her feet, ripped the gun out of her hand and tossed it in the woods, and had her spun around and his nose stuck in her face before she even gulped in her first decent breath. "Are you insane or just suicidal? Ye don't go after men all by yourself with a shotgun."

"Well, gee, I don't own a *sword*."

He shook her.

So she kicked him. Or at least she tried to, but he had her spun around and slammed up against his chest so fast, she ended up kicking herself in the ankle.

"Where are your children?" he growled.

"Charlotte's keeping watch in the window," she growled right back at him, "with the phone in her hand."

He muttered what sounded like a curse in some language she didn't recognize and suddenly let her go, only to snag her hand and start dragging her down the main road toward her driveway. "Is there a reason you didn't call your brother-in-law to come check out who was in your pit?" he asked, stopping to give her a jerk when she dug the nails of her free hand into his wrist. "That wasn't an idle threat I gave ye, Peg," he said way too quietly.

Boy, he must be really angry, because she really believed him. "Um, Galen lives twenty miles away," she said, shoving her free hand in her pocket. "Charlotte's supposed to call 911 and then a neighbor if she hears a gunshot. And I gave her your cell phone number," she rushed on when his eyes narrowed, "and told her to tell you what's going on. Wait, my shotgun," she said, trying to pull him to a stop when he started dragging her off again—only to stumble when she saw he really *did* have a sword strapped in some sort of sheath on his back.

"The gun's not going anywhere tonight." He stopped and grabbed hold of her shoulders. "They're almost to the equipment," he said softly. "I'm taking you to your house, and you're to go inside and tell Charlotte not to call anyone, especially not 911. We've got this covered."

We? Come to think of it, what was *he* doing here? "Who in hell died and left you king?" she muttered, only to lean away when she saw the look in his eyes.

"You step a toe outside before sunrise, and I swear to God I'm going to—"

"Oh, give it a rest," she snapped as she stomped down on his foot and jerked away, bolting for the house as she wondered if she might be insane *and* suicidal—although she did have sense to stay in the shadows of the trees lining her driveway.

The man was guarding his excavator with a friggin' sword!

He caught up with her in less than two strides but merely ran beside her, not touching her again until he nudged her toward the end of the deck facing away from the pit, then pulled her to a stop next to the house. "I mean it, Peg," he said tightly. "You go inside and *stay* there."

God, he wasn't even a little winded, while she could barely catch her breath—although that was probably because her heart was pounding so hard it hurt.

He suddenly crushed her against his chest, threading his fingers through her hair to hold her looking at him. "And, lady? I ever catch ye outside after dark again not wearing a bra, you'll have only yourself to blame for the consequences."

He dropped his hands to her waist, had her lifted halfway over the railing before she even got out a gasp, and finished helping her the rest of the way with a less than gentle hand on her backside. She caught herself from falling flat on her face and spun around with a whispered growl of outrage, only to discover he'd vanished.

Peg took a steadying breath as she ran trembling fingers through her hair, and brushed down the front of her sweatshirt as she walked to the door on rubbery legs. Okay, maybe she *would* fall in love with the sword-carrying, chest-beating jerk, so he'd have only himself to blame for the consequences of the Robinson curse.

The door opened just as she was reaching for the knob, and Charlotte pulled her inside. "What's going on? Where's your gun? I thought I saw you walking out the tote road with somebody."

"Did you call 911?" she asked, leading Charlotte into the bedroom.

"No, not yet; I didn't hear your signal."

Peg led her over to the window and unlocked it, then pulled her daughter down on her knees beside her. "Duncan's out there," she said, slowly lifting the window open. "And Robbie and Alec, I think." She snorted. "They must have camped out on the hillside, worried about someone stealing their fuel."

"Then let's call the sheriff," Charlotte whispered, holding up the phone.

Peg took it from her and set it on the floor. "Duncan said not to. And he's right; you don't pull into a town you're trying to do business in and have the locals arrested the very first night. That's why I was only going to give them hell if I recognized them."

"Is that what Duncan's going to do?"

Peg wrapped her arm around the girl. "I guess we're about to find out, aren't we? Let's watch and listen; and that way maybe we'll learn how big strong men deal with trespassers. Um, speaking of which, you might get your very first up-close look at a really angry man tonight, Charlie. So if Duncan comes in here acting like a chest-beating jerk once everything is over, you just smile and nod, okay, no matter what outrageous thing he says. You need to understand that when men get angry, they go a bit crazy." She gave her wide-eyed daughter a squeeze. "But it's usually only to cover up the fact that they're scared we womenfolk might get hurt."

"Was Duncan angry at you just now?"

"Um, maybe just a tad." She sighed. "Which is why my shotgun is now in the woods and we're probably not going on that picnic Sun—" The hillside suddenly flooded with light just as the harvester and excavator engines roared to life, followed almost immediately by shouts of startled men.

"Ohmigod," Charlotte gasped, covering her mouth with her hands. She pointed to the left side of the woods. "Ohmigod, he's chasing them with the excavator!"

Peg gave her daughter a fierce squeeze. "Quit swearing," she muttered as they both watched two men stumbling over branches and bumping into tree stumps as they ran down the hill just feet ahead of the reaching boom of the excavator, its bucket rattling up and down. "Ohmigod," Peg in turn gasped when another man fell over the side of the bank, his panicked shout ending abruptly when he hit the water.

"Um, Mom? Did Duncan have that sword he had in his truck this morning with him tonight?" Charlotte whispered, pointing up the hill. "Or is that a stick he's holding to that man's chest lying in front of the harvester while he's . . . talking to him?"

Peg watched Duncan suddenly step back and the man on the ground jump to his feet and start running, not even slowing down when he reached the bank—jumping off it right into the water. "Ohmigod," she said, hugging Charlotte.

The lights on the harvester suddenly went off, followed almost immediately by the excavator's lights, which was followed by utter silence when their respective engines shut down. Well, it was silent except for the sound of splashing as the two men swam toward the east side of the pit, and one of the other men let loose a string of curses when he ran into one of the boulders on the beach. His buddy hauled him back to his feet and they started running to where the fiord cut into the pit and waded into the water to haul out their two coughing cohorts.

Branches snapped as the four of them scrambled up the wooded knoll to their vehicle. The SUV's engine started with a whining roar and gravel spewed from its tires as backup lights—and this time headlights—arced through the trees as it backed out of sight. Peg felt Charlotte holding her breath just like she was as they listened to the vehicle screech to a halt on the pavement, then go squealing away.

"Ohmigod," Peg heard Charlotte whisper at the same time she did. "Um, Mom? It looks like the men are coming to the house," Charlotte said, a hint of panic in her voice. She suddenly jumped up. "I guess it's time I went to bed."

"Oh, no you don't," Peg muttered, snagging the hem of her nightgown. "You're putting on your bathrobe and slippers and coming out to face them with me."

"What? But I'm too young to smile and nod at angry men."

"Then I guess you're too young to get your ears pierced."

"Mommm."

Peg stood up. "Make sure Isabel doesn't wake up when you

go get your robe; I'll check on the boys. Close your bedroom door behind you, but make sure you're on *this* side of it when you do," she said, pointing a threatening finger.

Charlotte suddenly smiled and actually nodded. "You're figuring they won't dare be angry if I'm there."

Peg turned her around with a nudge. "See, I always knew you were the brightest bulb in the room. Now go on, hurry." Because, hey, what good was having kids if she couldn't hide behind them once in a while? Peg ran to her bureau, grabbed a bra out of the drawer, pulled her arms out of her sleeves and put on the bra, then smoothed her sweatshirt down with a steadying breath. She'd just made it out to the living room after checking on the boys—having to drag Charlotte out with her— when she heard footsteps as soft as church mice on the deck and a soft knock on her front door.

"Could you get that, Charlie?" Peg said, giving her a push.

"I want my birthstone for earrings, not just gold studs," Charlotte muttered, going to the door. She stopped with her hand on the knob, looking eight years old until her deep breath threw her shoulders back and her sudden smile turned her sixteen. She flipped on the porch light and pulled open the door. "Dun—Mr. MacKeage, what are you doing here?"

The man actually stepped back in surprise, bumping into Robbie and Alec, his face turning a dull red. "Is your mother here, Charlotte?"

Her precious, sweet little heathen nodded. "Would you like to speak with her?"

Peg walked over and took hold of her daughter's shoulders. "Can I help you, Mr. MacKeage?" she asked through the missing pane on her storm door.

"Could you come outside a moment, please?"

Peg's eyes widened in horror and she shook her head. "Oh, I'm sorry, but I was told in no uncertain terms not to step foot outside of my house after dark ever again."

Alec turned away, politely covering his mouth when he started coughing—which must have been contagious because Robbie walked to the rail to clear his throat.

Duncan sighed through the missing glass hard enough that Peg actually felt her hair move. "I'm sure whoever set those terms would make an exception," he said way too quietly. He opened the storm door and stepped back, and Peg pushed Charlotte out ahead of her—smiling when she heard him curse under his breath.

"We're both dying to hear what all the commotion was about," Peg said brightly, ignoring Duncan in favor of addressing Alec and Robbie.

Charlotte, however, didn't seem at all concerned about smiling and nodding—although come to think of it, none of the men seemed all that angry. In fact, they appeared downright proud of themselves for having scared the bejeezus out of the trespassers. Well, except for Duncan.

Charlotte pulled away from Peg and turned to him. "Was that your sword I saw you holding to that man's chest?" she asked.

His startled gaze rose to Peg, two flags of red coloring his cheeks again.

"No, Charlie," Peg said quickly, pulling the girl back against her. "I'm sure it was just a stick like we thought. So, were they carrying fuel cans when you caught them?"

"No," Robbie said, drawing her attention as he held out his hand. "They were carrying a couple of these."

"Bags of sugar?" Charlotte said in surprise.

Peg looked at Duncan. "They were going to sugar your fuel? But why?" She looked at Robbie, then Alec, then back at Duncan. "You hired most of the available local men, so why would they try to sabotage your equipment?"

"We doubt they were construction workers," he said, shaking his head. "There's been talk around town of some opposition to having a large resort built here." He gestured at the busted bag of sugar. "This is a game changer, Peg, and reason enough for you to give me your word that ye won't try to take matters into your own hands again like you did tonight." He looked down at Charlotte. "I want your word, too."

Charlotte canted her head up at Peg. "I agree with him, Mom." She looked back at Duncan. "We promise to stay inside at night from now on. Do we call you when something happens, then? Because it takes forever for anyone to get here."

Peg saw Duncan relax. "You won't have to call me, because as long as any of my equipment is on your property there'll be someone guarding it just like we were tonight. And I'm building a temporary camp a mile up the road for my crew to stay at through the week, so there'll be plenty of help close by." He lifted his gaze to Peg, and the softness left his eyes. "I'll hear your promise as well."

Okay, she'd like to think she was at least as bright as her daughter. "You've got it," she said with a nod, nodding at Robbie and Alec before pushing Charlotte ahead of her toward the door. "If you'll excuse us now, I'd like to salvage what I can of a night's sleep. Charlie, go on in to bed; I'll only be a minute," she said, pushing the girl inside, then grabbing the knob. She waited until Charlotte was heading down the hall before she shut the door and turned and walked back to Duncan. "Thank you," she said, "for not treating my daughter like she's eight."

He folded his arms over his chest and rested back on his hips. "I hope ye know you have trouble coming in another six or seven years with her."

Peg started to beam him a smile but turned when she realized Alec and Robbie were leaving. "And thank you guys for . . . tonight's entertainment."

"It was our pleasure, lass," Robbie said with a wave over his shoulder.

Peg turned back and stepped right up to Duncan, and even stood on her tiptoes to make sure he didn't miss her scowl. "You ever manhandle me like that again," she softly growled, "or even mention putting me over your knee, I'm going to make your little sport up on the mountain with Mac seem like child's play. Speaking of which," she said, dropping back to her heels and stepping away, "Sunday's picnic is off."

"No, it's not."

"Give me one good reason why I should go, after your threatening me tonight."

"Because ye might be the most contrary woman I've ever met, but you're not a coward." He stepped closer. "Don't make me pull out my hero's badge, Peg."

"You're using my *children*?"

He nodded; the porch light exposing the gleam in his eyes. "We MacKeages can be real bastards like that sometimes." He pressed a finger to her shoulder, snagged the strap of her bra right through the material, and let it go with a soft *snap*. "I see you're also as smart as ye are contrary," he murmured, palming her face in his warm broad hands and kissing her right on her startled mouth. He lingered just long enough for Peg to realize *he honest to God was kissing her*, then straightened away and was gone before she could sputter in protest. "Ye manage to stay out of trouble the rest of the night, and ye just might find some cinnamon buns on your doorstep in the morning," he said over his shoulder as he descended the stairs in one leap and strode off toward the hillside—leaving Peg staring after him with her hands balled into fists at her sides.

She ran her tongue over her lips and suddenly pressed her hands over the sharp ache in her chest as she tried to remember the last time she'd felt a man's mouth on hers. Dammit, she didn't want to like Duncan MacKeage.

Chapter Ten

Duncan lay sprawled spread-eagle on the cold granite ledge, his chest heaving painfully as he tried to catch his breath. He turned his gaze away from the gathering storm clouds to glare at Mac. "I thought we agreed no magic."

Considering that last blow should have rendered the bastard unconscious, Duncan didn't know where Mac got the strength even to shrug. "I guess I forgot."

"Ye forgot you were only supposed to use *mortal* brain and brawn?"

"And skill."

"Speaking of the magic," Duncan said in a winded growl. He rubbed an itch on his belly, only to sigh at the feel of blood on his fingers. "I don't suppose ye could bottle up some of your energy to leave with me?" He used his next growl to propel himself into a sitting position. "Say, enough to put a protective bubble around my operation and Peg's property until ye get back?"

Mac also attempted to sit up but fell back with a groan. "Sorry, my friend, but I'm not even certain I could call forth enough energy to walk home right now. Or slow that storm's arrival until after we get off this mountain," he muttered, making a halfhearted attempt to gesture at the sky.

Duncan rubbed his face to hide his smile.

"You're a quick study," the wizard continued. "One afternoon of swordplay and you're already anticipating my next move."

Duncan reached over to snag his shirt and balled it up under his head as he lay back down. "Enough that you had to resort to trickery, apparently."

"I did not conjure up that rabbit."

"You mean the one that appeared out of nowhere just as I was about to cut you off at the knees?"

"More like the one now hopping home with a fantastical tale to tell its buddies, along with some missing fur to prove it."

"So about that protective bubble," Duncan said, smiling up at the sky. "If ye can't bottle it up, could you at least put something in place before ye leave?"

"Why don't you ask de Gairn?"

He turned his head in surprise. "Matt? Why would I ask a drùidh to work the magic for me when I can go straight to his boss? It's *your* road I'm building and your wife's friend I'm keeping an eye on."

"Or you could ask Ian," Mac continued as if he hadn't even spoken. He arched a brow when Duncan shot him a scowl. "What; are you not pleased your nephew found the seat of his power on TarStone, as does that not free *you* of the mountain's hold?"

Duncan looked up at the roiling clouds. "I've never had a problem with taking my place running the resort when the time comes."

He heard Mac chuckle. "Are you honestly trying to lie to me, MacKeage? Or yourself?"

"Well, fine then. If ye don't want to help me protect your resort road, I'll simply buy new equipment when they sabotage mine and send you the bill." Duncan looked over at him. "And you can keep digging into your bottomless satchel of money every time I have to rebuild one of the bridges when the bastards start blowing them up."

"This can't be the first time you've faced opposition to a project you were working on," Mac said. "And since you claim you have no magic of your own, what did you do to protect your equipment and ensure your crew's safety in the past?"

"I didn't price security into this job because I figured you had my back."

He heard Mac chuckle again. "It appears to me you need only hire Peg and her eldest daughter. May I ask why you didn't tell her you were camping on the hillside?"

"I didn't want her worried that I was expecting trouble."

"Your heritage is showing, my friend. Did it never occur to you the lady might be smart enough to realize all the activity in her pit was going to draw no-good opportunists from miles around?"

Duncan rolled onto his side and propped his head on his hand. "I guess I forgot," he drawled, grinning when Mac's eyes narrowed. "Speaking of which, ye wouldn't have something in your bag of tricks to make a mere mortal forget, would you?"

"Now what did Peg do? Or do you wish for her to forget something you did?"

Duncan rolled onto his back, closing his eyes on a sigh. "I'm afraid I threatened to take the flat of my sword to her backside," he muttered, "then added insult to injury by throwing her shotgun in the woods and telling her that if I ever caught her outside after dark again I was putting her over my knee."

"By the gods, you're an idiot."

Duncan rolled onto his elbow. "She was going after those men *all by herself.* And she had Charlotte keeping watch in the window with the phone in her hand, waiting to call the sheriff and a neighbor if she heard a gunshot. The kid's eight!"

Mac also rolled onto his side. "What would you have had Peg do, then, since she didn't know you were guarding your own equipment because *you never told her?*"

"She should have called the sheriff the moment she heard the vehicle drive in."

Mac made a dismissive gesture. "There appears to be a strong reluctance to call the authorities around here—especially from the women. The first time I saw Olivia, she was being attacked by one of her male employees, and when I routed the bastard she refused to report the crime, claiming he was just a dumb kid. Your own self-reliance is a matter of pride, MacKeage, and yet you're angry that Peg was doing nothing more than you were." The wizard rolled onto his back with a snort. "If that's not living in your father's world, then what is?"

Duncan also rolled onto his back just as he felt a raindrop land on his chest. "So I guess getting something to make her forget I'm an idiot is out?"

"Exactly how attracted are you to Peg?" Mac asked quietly.

Duncan snapped his head around, then bolted upright when he saw the look in the wizard's eyes. "Why?"

Mac also sat up. "Because if you are seriously attracted to her, I'm afraid making Peg forget you're an idiot may be the least of your worries."

"Why?" he repeated in a growl just as another raindrop hit his shoulder.

Mac reached under the stunted pine and grabbed his sword's harness. "Last night Olivia told me that Peg believes the women in her family are cursed."

"Cursed how, exactly?" Duncan asked, eyeing him suspiciously.

"It appears the life expectancy of husbands for the last five generations of female descendents of Gretchen Robinson is quite short; the first poor bastards dying before the age of thirty, and ensuing husbands dying—in freak accidents, according to Peg—within a few years of the women remarrying."

Duncan leaned back and grabbed his own harness. "That's plain crazy. It's a fact of life that men are more likely to die in accidents because we're more often in harm's way." He started to slide his sword in its sheath but suddenly stilled. "Are you saying Peg honestly believes she's cursed?"

"William Thompson died on his thirtieth birthday."

"In a construction accident," Duncan said, finishing sheathing his sword. "Curses can't actually kill people because they're not real." He stilled again. "Are they?"

"It doesn't matter if they are or not; what matters is that, according to what she told Olivia, Peg believes she can't ever remarry." Mac shook his head. "She's afraid even to care for another man, much less fall in love with one."

"Love can't kill a person any more than a curse can."

"Nevertheless, I'm afraid your attraction to Peg is going to involve battling more than her pride and contrariness." He suddenly grinned. "But as I said earlier, you're a quick study—assuming you wish to win this particular war. Because if you decide you do, Duncan, then you best be prepared to battle your own demons as well as Peg's."

"What in hell are you talking about? I don't have any demons."

Mac arched an imperial brow. "No? So it's common practice for modern men to threaten to put a woman over their knee just as they did in your father's time?"

"I was angry, dammit."

"I suggest you choose a world, my friend—either this century or Callum's—because if you continue trying to straddle both while taking your perceived lack of magic as a personal affront, I promise that you're going to lose the war . . . and the woman."

Duncan rolled onto his hands and knees and then pushed himself to his feet. "Right now the only war I'm focused on is the opposition to your resort. They fired the first salvo at *me* last night, and I'm damned well taking *that* personally." He bent down and picked up his sword and slipped the harness over his bare shoulders. "And you can take your damned magic to California with you, Oceanus, because I don't need it or Matt's or Ian's to do my job." He swiped his shirt off the ledge and snagged his jacket off the tree and used them to point at Mac just as several more raindrops fell. "And I can damn well get the girl *all by myself*, too."

"MacKeage," Mac said quietly when Duncan started striding away.

He stopped and turned back, saying nothing.

Mac swept his hand in an arc. "Pick a mountain—any mountain—and I will make it yours to command." He grinned, patting the ledge. "Except this one."

"I already have a goddamned mountain."

"TarStone is the source of Ian's power." Mac gestured again. "Pick one."

"I don't *want* one."

The wizard pushed himself to his feet, then stood his sword on its tip and crossed his hands over the hilt. "The energy has been building inside you for thirty-five years, and if you don't find a way to ground it, Duncan, it's going to destroy you. Pick a new mountain or I'll pick for you." He arched a brow. "In the *century* of my choice."

Sweet Christ, the bastard was serious. "That one," Duncan said, pointing to his right without even looking just as several fat raindrops hit him hard enough to sting.

Mac sighed. "I believe you could teach Peg something about contrariness," he muttered. "It's done, then; all that the mountain has to offer is yours to command." He suddenly grinned. "Enjoy your walk home . . . neighbor," he finished just as the sky released a deluge of numbingly cold rain—except on Mac, Duncan noticed as he turned away and walked into the woods to the sound of the wizard's quiet laughter.

God dammit; he hadn't done one thing to deserve this.

And what in hell had he been thinking, anyway, picking a mountain on the other side of Bottomless? It was going to cost him a goddamn fortune to build a road around that damned fiord just to reach it.

Peg blinked at all the strange vehicles lining both sides of the road the entire length of town; most of them cars instead of pickups, mostly wearing out-of-state plates. Which is why she ended up having to drive all the way past where the old train tracks crossed the road before she found a place to park, after she had to stop no fewer than four times to let people cross in front of her. Spellbound had actual pedestrian traffic—most of them gray-haired tourists wearing cameras around their necks. By summer when school was out, Peg guessed as her van's engine rattled backward before finally shutting off, the town was going to be bursting at the seams.

"Okay, gentlemen," she said, turning in her seat to give the twins her I-mean-business scowl, "your challenge for today is to stick beside me like glue. Hand-holding is an option, but only until one of you gets more than five feet away, and then it becomes a requirement. Got that?" Peg turned her scowl into a smile when they both vigorously nodded. "And after we pick up the mail and stop into the Trading Post to find out what I owe on last month's bill, if the three of us are still stuck together like glue I guess you'll have no choice but to follow me into the Drunken Moose for a grilled cheese sandwich."

"Can't we have a cimminin bun instead?" Peter asked.

Peg immediately turned her scowl back on. "Considering there were a dozen buns on our porch this morning, I would say you've had your month's quota."

"How come your shotgun was on the porch, too?" Jacob asked. "It's usually in your closet with the rifle."

"I had loaned it to the bun fairy, and she returned it with the buns."

"What's the bun fairy need a shotgun for?" Peter asked.

Peg stood up, hunched over, and started unbuckling them out of their booster seats—that were looking more tired than her van. So she made an executive decision to get new ones with her very first check from Duncan. "Well, you know, fairies are very sneaky and secretive, so this one never really told me why she needed the shotgun."

"I bet she needed it to shoot cimminins," Peter said, jumping out of his seat. "To put in her buns."

"Cinnamon is a spice—a plant," Peg explained, turning to grab her purse before sliding open the passenger side door. She stepped out and straightened, looking eye level at the boys. "And last I knew, you don't need to shoot a plant to eat it."

"I think she borrowed it 'cause everyone wants them buns, and someone might try to steal them instead of going to the Moose," Jacob declared with great authority.

Peter frowned. "Then why she'd give it back if she's gotta protect the buns?"

Peg swung Jacob out of the van with a laugh, deciding she'd lied herself into a corner. "Forget the shotgun," she said, swinging Peter out next. "And focus on today's challenge."

She slid the door closed and headed along the side of the road to the old railroad bed without bothering to lock the van—because honestly, if someone was desperate enough to steal the heap of scrap, they were welcome to it. Oh yeah, the second thing she was buying was new transportation, she decided as she started down the old rail bed the Grange ladies had turned into a nature trail ten years ago.

"Mom, who are all them people?" Peter asked as he skipped

up to her left side, Jacob falling into step on her right. "What are they doing there?"

"They're tourists who have come to check out the new Bottomless Sea. And you know why that's such a big deal?"

"Because we got whales and sharks and jellyfish now?" Peter asked.

"Well, partly. But mostly because Bottomless isn't supposed to be a sea because it's so far from the ocean."

"The earthquake made it salty and tidy," Jacob declared with great authority. "And it pushed them two mountains apart and made that ford flood our pit."

"That's right, the earthquake created the *fiord*." She stopped and stepped back to have both boys face her. "And you two," she said, "witnessed history being made."

"What's history?" Peter asked.

Peg laughed and started walking again. "History is what happened yesterday and last year and a hundred years ago. History is in the *past*, today is the *present*, and tomorrow is the *future*. And forty years from now you'll be able to tell your children and grandchildren that you felt the earth tremble and saw Bottomless go from being a freshwater lake to an inland sea. What happened is called an historic event, and you were privileged to witness it."

"But all these people missed it," Peter said, pointing at the old train trestle that crossed the Spellbound Stream just below the falls. "So why are they here now?"

"So they can take pictures and go home and tell everyone they saw the new Bottomless Sea, because there isn't another place like this in the whole wide world."

"There ain't no other seas?" Peter asked.

Peg gave him a nudge. "Don't say *ain't*; it's not polite. Yes, there are other seas, but none that were formed in recent *history*, and none that have a massive underground river that allow whales to travel hundreds of miles inland."

"Wow, that means Spellbound Falls is unic," Peter said with his own authority.

"Yes, it's definitely *unique*," she corrected with a laugh.

"Peg!"

She stopped and looked across the road to see her neighbor,

Evan Dearborn, waving at her. He looked both ways and bolted between oncoming traffic. Well, he bolted at a grandfatherly speed.

"Hey there, Pete and Repeat," he said when he reached them, nodding at one boy then the other without knowing which was which. He looked at Peg. "Me and Carl been meaning to mosey over to find out what's going on at your place."

"I'm expanding my pit to sell gravel to the outfit building a road up the mountain. Or haven't you heard that Olivia and her new husband are building a resort?"

"We heard." Evan's eyes suddenly widened in alarm. "They ain't setting that road up behind *our* land, are they?" He glanced at the boys, then stepped toward her, and it was all Peg could do not to lean away when she got a strong whiff of eau de skunk. "I mean, jeeze-louise, Peg," he whispered, "we ain't exactly sure where our back boundary line is, and we might of . . . it's possible we . . ." He sighed, thankfully stepping back as he scratched his beard. "I guess we're gonna have to forget about expanding our garden this year." He suddenly grinned. "Well, good for you then, girl. A road up that mountain's gonna take a passel of gravel, so you'll be rolling in dough."

"Why would Mom want to roll in dough?" Peter asked. "It's sticky."

Evan looked startled, then reached out and ruffled Peter's hair with a chuckle. "Well, Repeat, I guess she wouldn't wanna then, would she?"

"I'm Peter."

"I knowed that. I was just checking if you did." He looked at Peg again. "I thought that horseback of yours ran in our direction."

"It apparently runs north, up the hillside."

"Well, okay then," he said as he started backing away. "If'n you hear that they're gonna set the road anywhere near our back border, you give us a heads-up, okay?"

"I've been led to understand they're going in off the main road about a mile up from us, so I think you're clear."

"Good enough," he said with a nod. He stopped just in time to avoid backing into traffic. "Hey, what'n was all that commotion over to your place last night? Me and Carl snuck through the woods to see, but it was over by the time we got there."

Peg shrugged. "Just some idiots looking for free diesel fuel, but Mr. MacKeage, the owner of the equipment, sent them away empty-handed."

He stepped back over to the path, looking both ways to see who was nearby. "I heared talk that some folks ain't happy about that resort being built. It appears they're forming some sort of committee to try and stop it."

"Locals, or people from away?" Peg asked.

Evan snorted. "Out-of-staters who own land up here and think they know what's good for us locals is more like it." He stepped closer. "I heared they're gonna try to get some big nature group to back them," he said in a whisper, "by claiming it's gonna ruin the wilderness." He looked around at the people and traffic and snorted again. "They're too late, I'd say. That earthquake already turned this place into a tourist trap. And me and Carl was down to Turtleback yesterday, and it was standing room only. They're gonna have to put in a gosh-dang stoplight at the intersection." He suddenly grinned. "You run out of dirt to sell, Peg, you can always turn your pit into a campground now that you got lakefront property."

"A campground?" Peter asked, tugging on her jacket. "What's that, Mom?"

"It's sort of like Inglenook, only people sleep in tents instead of cabins." She looked at Evan and arched her brow. "Wouldn't you worry my campers might go roaming through your woods looking for wildlife and trample your . . . garden?"

That wiped away his enthusiasm. "Gosh-dang it, I hadn't thought of that." He sighed and started backing away again. "I'll be seeing you, then. You hear that road's going near our property, you give us a holler, okay?"

"You'll be the first ones I tell," she said, starting down the path again.

"Are we gonna make a campground, Mom?" Jacob asked, walking backward in front of her. "And have campfires every night?"

"Nope. Because we're not going to run out of gravel for a long, long time if the amount of land Mr. Duncan is clearing is any indication."

Jacob realized they'd reached the trestle and immediately scurried back and took hold of her hand. Peter refused when she held out her hand to him, but he did grab the hem of her jacket as they walked across. And even though Peg would have liked to stop and watch the sixty-foot falls cascading down in a thundering roar just a stone's throw away, she knew neither of the twins were comfortable lingering on the bridge. She often wondered if maybe they'd heard her talking to someone about Billy having been working near a bridge when he died. It's not like it was a secret or anything, but maybe she should have a conversation with all four of her children about exactly what happened—since it appeared they obviously thought about it, judging by Jacob's talk with Duncan last night.

They finally reached the post office, and Peg handed the key to Peter since it was his turn, making him read the number on their box before he opened it. "Mom, look! We got another special delivery," he whooped, pulling out two lollipops and handing one to Jacob. "They're grape ones this time, Repeat. We're gonna have purple tongues."

"What is all the caterwauling out here?" Thelma Banzhoff asked as she came through the door from out back. "Oh, it's Pete and Repeat," she said in mock surprise, only to suddenly frown and bend down to peek in the open box. "Did that mail fairy sneak in here again and leave you two little heathens another special delivery?" She shook her head, making a *tsk*-ing sound. "I warned the little imp that it's illegal to mess with a United States post office box, but it seems she's powerfully determined to make her deliveries. And sneaky, too, because I made sure all the doors and windows were locked when I left here yesterday."

"Locked windows and doors ai—isn't gonna stop no fairy," Peter said. He held his thumb and finger almost together. "'Cause she can fit through a crack this big."

Thelma pointed at the prize in his other hand. "Then how does she get the lollipops through a crack that small?"

"By magic," Jacob piped up around the pop already in his mouth. He pulled it out and grinned up at her. "Just like the tooth fairy. See, I lost my tooth this morning and tonight she's gonna bring me a quarter. But only if I'm asleep, right, Mom?"

he asked, looking up at Peg. "You told Pete when he lost his tooth that if he tries to stay awake all night she won't come."

"That's right." Peg reached in the box and pulled out the few envelopes and several sale fliers. "Now thank Mrs. Banzhoff for not having the mail fairy arrested for delivering your special deliveries."

"Thank you, Mrs. Banzhoff," they said in unison.

"Peg, could I speak with you a minute?" Thelma asked, nodding for her to move away from the boys.

"Okay, new challenge," Peg said, herding the twins over to the bench under the window. "Unglue yourselves from me and work on turning your tongues purple, okay, while I go over there."

"Can we kneel on the bench and watch all the terrists?" Jacob asked.

"The what?" Thelma yelped.

"The *tour*ists," Peg said to Jacob after shooting Thelma a smile. "You may watch the tourists, but keep your sticky fingers off the window. What's up?" she asked softly as she walked to the other side of the vestibule with Thelma.

"Land sakes, my kid-talk is rusty," Thelma said with a laugh. She suddenly turned serious, touching Peg's sleeve. "You've heard there's talk in town about forming a committee to fight the new resort, haven't you?" she whispered.

"Evan just said something about it, but that was the first I heard."

Thelma glanced over her shoulder at the boys, then turned and bent her head next to Peg's. "Well, I've overheard more than one conversation in the last few days where your name's come up." She touched her sleeve again. "Please don't ask me who was doing the talking, Peg, because I need to be discreet about gossiping. But it appears some people feel that you're . . . Well, I just want to warn you that some folks aren't too happy that the gravel for the resort road is coming out of your pit." Thelma clutched her sweater closed at her throat. "I heard them saying that you're just letting that outfit from away come in here and . . . and rape your land," she whispered, "for no good reason other than to make a truckload of money."

"Are you serious?" Peg growled, clutching her own throat

in a futile attempt to tamp down her anger. "I've owned that pit for nearly ten years, and nobody had any problem with it existing before now. They're really calling it *rape*?"

Thelma touched Peg's sleeve again, this time giving her arm a squeeze. "I'm just repeating what I heard. And you need to know it's only a small minority that doesn't want the resort. Most of the people in town are for it because of the jobs it's going to bring to the area, and the shops and restaurants and cottage industries that will follow. Some of the folks are already planning to expand their own businesses. And Bunky Watts intends to open a craft co-op in that empty storefront across from the church."

Peg was smiling and nodding despite trying to get past the idea that she was raping her land. "Those opposed to the resort should go visit Pine Creek," she said. "The TarStone Mountain Ski Resort made that town what it is today, which is an inviting, thriving community. I can't believe they're saying I'm raping my land."

Thelma snorted. "It only takes a few extremists to turn something wonderful into a big ugly fight. I will tell you this much; it's mostly people from away who are raising the stink. But they're the ones who have the money and clout to bring in the big guns." She glanced at the boys, then patted Peg's arm again. "I just wanted you to be aware that, like it or not, you and Livy Bald—I mean Livy Oceanus have made a few enemies."

Peg was incredulous. "Because I'm selling gravel? Dammit, that pit is all I have."

"I know that, honey," Thelma said. "And if I were in your shoes, I'd sell every damn last rock and grain of sand out of it that I could." Her eyes narrowed. "You know, the people who are complaining the loudest don't seem to have a problem buying your gravel to repair the roads to their summer camps. They want to own their little piece of heaven, but they don't want to share it with anyone."

Peg took a deep breath to help throw back her shoulders, and shot Thelma a smile. "Yeah, well, they can just live with the potholes from now on. Even if I wasn't in the gravel business, I'd still be on the front line to get this resort built. It's going to be beautiful when it's done and great for the economy for our children and grandchildren. That earthquake put Spellbound Falls on the worldwide map, and as far as I'm concerned it was the best thing to happen to this town. And another thing," Peg growled, trying but failing to tamp down her anger. "Mac already bought up most of the land around the lake precisely to keep the wilderness wild. Olivia told me they're planning to cater to every walk of life; that if someone wants five-star accommodations they can stay at the resort on top of the mountain, but if they want back-country hiking there's going to be a trail system with rustic campsites, and everything in between."

"I know," Thelma said, her features relaxing into a smile. "Olivia was in here just yesterday and mentioned some of what they're planning. The Grange women are already raising funds to redo the town park, and if they raise enough they want to include a trail up to the top of the falls and a viewing platform."

"Wonderful," Peg growled. "It sure beats raising money for their widow's fund."

Thelma's face reddened. "They came in about a month ago wanting to put a collection jar here at the post office, and they told me it was going to have a picture of your children on it." She snorted. "I told them that one, it was illegal to solicit in a federal building, and two, I hoped you sued them if they did that to you and your kids."

"Thank you for that," Peg said. "I swear I was tempted to brain Janice and Christine with the loaf of bread I was holding when they cornered me in the Trading Post. You know, Thelma, maybe we should form our own *pro*-resort committee, if for no other reason than to show our support to Olivia and Mac." She shook her head. "It would crush Olivia to be accused of ruining the wilderness." Peg gave Thelma as bright as smile as she could muster, considering she was still angry as hell. "She and Mac are taking the kids on a cross-country trip for two months, and we could be fully organized by the time they get back. Heck, we might even have the anti-resort group on the run by then, if we get enough people together to outshout the extremists."

"Mom!" Jacob called, frantically waving her over. "We just seen Mr. Alec and the other man go into the Moose. Can we go have our cheese sandwich with them?"

Peg's anger turned to horror in half a heartbeat. The last person she wanted to run into today was Mr. Kiss-stealing MacKeage. "Was Duncan with them?" she asked, rushing to the window to look out.

"Nope," Peter said around what was left of his lollipop. "Just Mr. Robbie and Mr. Alec. Can we hurry, Mom?"

Peg leaned forward to look up and down the road, trying to spot Duncan's truck, sighing in relief when all she saw was Robbie MacBain's pickup parked in the church dooryard. "We still have to go see Ezra first," she said, straightening away. "And if the men look like they're talking business, we can't bother them, okay? We'll just say hi and sit on the stools at the counter."

"Gosh-dang it, Mom," Peter muttered, making Peg rear back with a gasp. "I don't see why we can't talk business with them."

"Peter Thompson!" she snapped over Thelma's laughter as the postmistress slipped through the door leading out back. Peg gave him a nudge. "You do not say that word. Ever. You hear me?"

Peter gave Peg his worried yet defiant look. "Mr. Evan says it all the time, so what's wrong with *gosh-dang*?" he asked, using the word again just to push her buttons.

She nudged him again, a little less gently this time. "Because it's one step away from cussing, is why. And people will put up with cussing from adults, but not from ill-mannered children. It makes you appear uncivilized."

"I told Mr. Duncan he's gotta remember to take his worry stone outta his pocket to rub it," Jacob chimed in, smiling smugly, "so people won't think he's unsevralized by playing pocket pool."

Peg clutched her chest on a gasp. "You told Duncan that? You actually said *pocket pool*?"

Jacob nodded. "And he promised he wouldn't forget to take it out to rub it."

Oh God, the man must still be laughing. Peg stuffed her mail in her purse and headed for the door. "We're back to being glue," she growled, leading them outside.

Chapter Eleven

Not wanting Peter and Jacob to think they could just walk out into traffic, it took Peg two full minutes to find an opening to cross the road, and they were just reaching Ezra's store when Alec and Robbie came out of the Drunken Moose carrying boxes. They spotted her and the boys and headed over.

"Hello, Thompson tribe," Alec said. "Pete, Jacob," he added with a slight bow, addressing each boy correctly. "What are you gentlemen up to today?"

"We was gonna have cheese sandwiches at the Moose," Peter informed him, "and eat with you if you weren't talking business, 'cause we seen you go inside when we was at the post office."

"It's standing room only in there, so we decided to eat on the tailgate of my truck," Robbie said. "And we'd be delighted if you would join us."

"But we gotta go see how much money to give Mr. Ezra this month."

"Or, your mom could go talk with Mr. Ezra while you boys sit with us," Robbie said. He held out his box. "I bought a bit more than I can eat, so we could share."

Peg pulled in a breath and held it, uncertain what to do,

especially when she saw both boys' eyes light with excitement as they looked up at her.

"Can we, Mom?" Peter asked. "We promise we'll stick to them like glue."

"We'll take good care of them, Peg," Robbie said, his warm gray eyes obviously reading her concern. "We're in no rush, as we're waiting on a special delivery," he added, that warmth turning amused—although she had no idea why.

"You're getting a special delivery, too?" Peter cried. He stuck out his tongue. "See, ows wus gwape."

Peg gave him a nudge. "Don't talk with your tongue out," she said with a laugh. She looked from Robbie to Alec, then down at her boys. Oh God, she'd never left them with virtual strangers before. "Um, do you want to go sit on the tailgate of the pickup with the men?"

Both boys vigorously nodded, and Peg didn't know if she was excited that Jacob wasn't even hesitating or worried that she was hesitating instead.

"And just as soon as you're done with your business," Robbie continued to her, "you could also join us while we wait for our delivery."

Jacob tugged on Robbie's pant leg. "The fairies don't deliver in the daylight," he said with great authority, adding a nod for effect. "'Cause you're not supposed to see her, or she won't leave nothing in the mailbox or under your pillow."

Robbie smiled. "This fairy is a *he*, and his name is Gunter. And I don't believe his delivery will fit in a mailbox or under your pillow." His eyes crinkled with his smile. "Because we're waiting on a trailer of draft horses."

Both boys gasped. "You got the fairy to bring you horses?" Peter cried, immediately turning to Peg. "*Mommm*, we gotta get a boy fairy, 'cause they bring better stuff." He turned back to Robbie, having to crane his neck to see him. "How do we call your fairy? Or can we write him a letter like we do Santa Claus? Hey, Santa's a he, too, and he always brings us good stuff, not just suckers and quarters." He turned to glare up at Peg. "Girl fairies ain't as good as boy ones."

Apparently seeing Peg winding up a good scowl, Alec squatted down with a chuckle and opened his free arm. "I beg to differ, Pete," he said, standing up with Peter on his arm and looking him level in the eyes. "Some of the nicest stuff I've gotten came from girls." He shot Peg a wink. "If you'll excuse us, I do believe it's time for a tactical retreat and a small discussion on genders." He waited for her nod, then walked toward the church dooryard.

"Jacob?" Robbie asked, also squatting down and opening his free arm. "Would you care for a lift, or do you prefer to walk?"

"I like being tall," Jacob said, walking into his embrace. The boy looked at Peg when his chauffeur straightened. "I still like girl fairies, Mom, 'cause I like that they're sneaky just like you."

Peg felt her cheeks turn three shades of red. "You think I'm sneaky?" she asked, keeping her eyes on her son for fear of the laughter she'd see in Robbie's. "Why?"

"'Cause you been finishing Daddy's house without nobody knowing."

Peg relaxed, figuring that was innocent enough.

"And I seen you sneaking them cuton pages out of the newspapers last week when Mr. Ezra wasn't looking."

Peg stepped back with a gasp. "Jacob! I . . . I—"

"Come on, Mr. Thompson," Robbie said with a chuckle as he strode away with the little snitch. "I do believe it's time we retreated as well."

Peg turned to the building and covered her blistering face with her hands. Jacob had seen her stealing coupons out of the newspaper? "Ohmigod, I'm going to burn in hell," she muttered, "and my babies are going to end up there with me."

"What was that, Peggy? Who are you talking to?"

Peg spun around to find Christine Richie eyeing her quizzically. "Oh, I was just talking to myself, Christine," she said, hiking her purse up on her shoulder, then pulling down the hem of her jacket. "I was trying to remember what I'd written on my shopping list because I forgot it at home."

Christine's eye lit up. "Did you hear about our new fundraiser? We're going to redo the park this summer, so the town will look as grand as that resort Livy and her new husband are building."

"I heard," Peg said with a nod.

Christine's smile turned pained. "I know we talked about

a widow's fund and all, but . . ." She suddenly brightened again. "But I heard you're expanding your gravel pit, and word is you're going to be a rich woman by the end of the summer. Oh, Peggy, we're all so happy for you."

"Thank you for that. Well, I guess I better get go—"

The octogenarian grabbed Peg's arm in a surprisingly strong grip. "Wait, there's something you have to know. Phyllis Jenkins told Janice after our Grange meeting that her husband and Chris Dubois have gotten themselves all worked into a thither over that resort being built, and she's worried they're going to cause trouble."

"But they're locals," Peg said in surprise. "Aaron Jenkins was born in Spellbound Falls, and Chris moved here from Turtleback over twenty years ago. What's their gripe?"

"They don't like that Livy's new husband came in here and bought up all the land for miles around, and Aaron and Chris are going around telling everyone that he's going to shut down the forest to logging to keep it pristine for the resort guests."

Peg snorted. "More like they're afraid he's going to shut down their night-hunting instead of their day jobs. Chris was a year ahead of me in school, and even back then all he did was brag about the ten-point buck he'd bagged the night before."

Christine sighed. "I can't believe he's been able to stay one step ahead of the game wardens all these years with that big mouth of his. Everyone knows he's a poacher, but nobody seems to be able to catch him."

"That's because he never keeps the meat or the mounts; he sells them to some buyer out of state." Peg shook her head. "It seems if there's a dollar to be made, Chris finds the quickest and most illicit way to make it. Everyone knows he's the one who found that bird's-eye maple worth thousands of dollars on state park land and had it cut down and dragged off before anyone realized it was missing."

Christine nodded up the road. "He and Aaron were just in the Drunken Moose, and they started in about how that resort's going to change our entire way of life."

"For the better," Peg growled.

"Yes," Christine said. She leaned closer. "But I'm telling you this because I heard your name come up in their conversation."

"My name? Why?"

"Chris said . . . well, he said if Billy were alive, he wouldn't be selling his gravel to build that road up the mountain."

"He sure as hell would!"

Christine pursed her lips and looked around. "Chris is just angry because his mother sold you that land instead of signing it over to him, and he claims you all but stole it from Annabelle for what you paid. And," Christine continued, squeezing Peg's arm again when she tried to defend herself, "he's saying that just as soon as you're done stripping that land bare, you're probably going to build a fancy marina to service the resort because you're right on the fiord now."

"Oh, for the love of— They're only hauling out of my pit until they open their own on the mountain. I'm not going to be rich even by Spellbound standards."

"I know, honey," Christine said, patting the arm she'd just been squeezing. "I just wanted to give you a heads-up, is all. Most of the people here and in Turtleback Station want the resort, but it only takes a few to make a lot of noise." She went back to squeezing Peg's arm, and Peg hoped she was that strong when she was eighty. "But I think you should start locking your doors, what with you and your babies being way out there all alone." She suddenly frowned. "Speaking of babies, where's Pete and Repeat? I'm not used to seeing you without them glued to your side."

"They're having lunch with some of the men who are working at my pit," Peg said, gesturing toward the church. "They're sitting on the tailgate of a truck over there."

Christine shook her head. "It's too bad they have to grow up without a daddy. Little boys need a man in their lives." She patted Peg's sorely abused arm again and gave her a smile. "But everyone sees what a wonderful job you're doing with them, and with those beautiful girls of yours. I raised my Robert up alone from the time he was twelve, you know. It's a sad truth that the only work we have up here is logging and trucking, and that they're dangerous jobs. That is, if our men don't go off to war and get killed; either way, they're dead and we're left to go it alone." She patted Peg's arm again. "But you're young and pretty, Peggy; don't wait too long to find yourself another good man. Billy would want you to be happy."

"I've been keeping my eyes peeled for my next victim," Peg said with a laugh, capturing Christine's hand and giving it a gentle squeeze before slowly backing away. "Thanks for the heads-up. I'll be seeing you," she said, spinning away and all but running into the Bottomless Mercantile & Trading Post.

Peg lost her smile the moment she got inside. Dammit to hell, she didn't need to be the brunt of Chris Dubois's anger, and that pompous ass Aaron Jenkins had better not show his face anywhere near her pit, either. Because to hell with Duncan's dictate; if she spotted those two chest-beating jerks on her property—especially after dark—she was peppering them with birdshot.

"Well, now," Ezra said when he rounded a corner and nearly bumped into her. "Who stuck a bee in your bonnet?" Ezra—who Peg had learned just ten days ago was actually Olivia's grandfather—looked around and even behind her. "Where are the little heathens?"

"Having lunch with Alec MacKeage and Robbie MacBain on the tailgate of Robbie's truck."

"Jacob is?" Ezra said in surprise.

Peg nodded and finally smiled. "Those men Mac hired are miracle workers. Jacob didn't even hesitate to go with them today." She winced. "I did instead."

"Aw, Peg, you don't need to cut the apron strings clean through yet, but it can't hurt to stretch them a little. I've met all those men, and your boys couldn't be in safer hands." He pulled her down an empty aisle when several gray-headed tourists walked in and started *ohh*ing and *ahh*ing over the assortment of just about anything a person needed crammed into every nook and cranny in the store. "There's something I have to tell you. There's talk—"

Peg held up her hand with a laugh. "Get in line, Ezra. It's taken me half an hour just to get from the post office here because everyone has had to tell me about the talk in town." She turned serious, and just barely stopped herself from patting his arm. "It's okay; anybody can say anything they want about my aiding and abetting the new resort, I don't care. I'm just so happy that my gravel ran north and not west that I'm one second away from running down the center of the road yelling *whoopee!*"

Instead of laughing with her, Ezra's clouded blue eyes turned pained and he shook his head. "But I'm worried it's not going to stop at just talk. Sam and I have moved into Inglenook while Olivia and Mac are gone so we can keep an eye on things. Sam's afraid the few naysayers are going to try to get their point across in a newsworthy way." He touched her sleeve. "There's plenty of room in the main lodge, Peg. Why don't you and the kids come and stay with us until they're done hauling out of your pit?"

"Duncan said he's going to post guards to protect the equipment, and through the week he and his men will be camped just down the road. I'm fine, Ezra, and I don't want my children to think anything's wrong or that we have to run away and hide at the first *talk* of trouble."

"Last I knew, sugaring a fuel tank to seize up an engine is a tad more than just talking about doing something." He shook his head. "I don't know what Mac had to promise Olivia to get her to leave this Saturday with all the hoopla going on here, but I have to say I'm glad she's going."

"It's just because the idea of the resort is new, Ezra, and everyone's still trying to reconcile that we have an inland sea instead of a lake now. And all these scientists and tourists are making people think this is what it's going to be like from now on. But once everything settles down, so will the naysayers. In fact, we're going to start our own pro-resort committee, and I think it's better that Olivia and Mac won't be around for the next two months. With no actual target, people will get over it faster. And once we keep pointing out that the resort is a good twenty miles away and up on a mountain, they'll all calm down."

He blew out a sigh and suddenly smiled. "I agree. Okay, girl, what can I sell you today?" he asked, rubbing his hands together.

"Just some paper plates," she said with a laugh. "And since you're so busy, just put it on my tab and the first gravel check I get I'm coming in and cleaning up my bill. And," she growled, "the total better match the slips I've been keeping."

He looked so affronted that Peg waggled her finger in the air as she sauntered away, smiling secretly as she remembered Olivia saying Ezra kept *under*charging all the locals accidentally on purpose, and that it would break his heart if he knew they knew. And Olivia had told Peg to actually give him grief for *over*charging. "And don't forget you agreed to double my coupons."

"Sure thing, missy," he called after her with a harrumph. "Right after I double the price on those paper plates."

Peg sidled past a gathering of tourists checking out the fishing supplies—that she noticed Ezra had already changed to more saltwater rigging—and snatched a package of plates off the shelf and headed right back for the door. Because honestly, she was feeling a tad naked without Peter and Jacob glued to her side.

Peg waved the plates at Ezra talking to customers on her way outside and, being afraid that she'd run into someone else just dying to tell her what was going on, she kept her head down as she rushed toward the church. She stopped at the end of the last building to peek around the corner, and her heart rose into her throat when she saw Jacob perched on Robbie's shoulders as Robbie sat on his tailgate eating his lunch. Her younger twin was pointing out at Bottomless, talking a mile a minute. Peter was sitting beside Alec, half of a man-sized sandwich in his hand, eating and talking and gesturing with the sandwich.

God help her, she had to swipe at her eyes when everything went blurry.

Not wanting the little miracle to end just yet, Peg slowly turned away and headed for her van parked at the other end of town. She'd drive back to the church and pick up the boys—making sure they thanked Robbie and Alec for sharing their lunch with them—and reach the Inglenook turnoff in time to meet the bus so it didn't have to drive another six miles one way just to drop off her girls. And if those rain clouds held on to their raindrops until after dark, she was having another campfire with the kids tonight. A private campfire this time, though, because she still wasn't ready to face Duncan—because she'd swear her lips were still tingling from his stolen kiss.

Peg picked up her pace when she saw the tractor-trailer rig idling into town and realized that instead of a logging truck it was actually a large horse carrier. She stopped to gape as it went by—along with every other person around—and saw the nose of a monstrous horse pressed up against the barred window.

Wait; hadn't Robbie said the special delivery they were waiting for was draft horses? Good Lord, was he using them to haul logs out of the woods alongside the harvesters and skidders? Peg started running to her van so she could go get the twins out of the men's way, figuring they must be waiting to lead the truck driver to Inglenook where there was a huge barn that was almost empty now because most of the horses had gone back to the coast since the camp wasn't running this summer.

Peg tossed her purse and the paper plates across the driver's seat onto the floor and jumped in, only to stop with the key half-slid in the ignition when she smelled fumes. She looked in back but everything was its normal messy self and sniffed again, deciding it smelled chemically. She tripped the hood latch and got back out and walked around the front of the van, but stopped in the act of lifting the hood when she noticed something on the front passenger fender.

Peg walked around the side of the van and nearly fell in the ditch when she stumbled backward, clutching her jacket as she read the words spray-painted the entire length of the lower side of her van. She glanced right and left and then turned to face the woods as she slowly backed up onto the road. She looked toward the path and saw people on the trestle, but nobody she recognized.

She started shaking. Oh God, what if the twins had been with her? There was no way she could drive this van home looking like that and . . . saying what it did. She shoved the van's hood closed, rushed around and reached in and got her purse, then ran down the road trying to decide what to do.

Oh God, she couldn't let anyone see that side of her van!

She stopped at the end of the horse trailer parked in front of the church and leaned a hand on the tailgate to catch her breath, deciding to call her mom to come get the boys and go meet the bus while she got rid of the van. Peg took one last deep breath as she straightened. Yeah, she'd hide it on some tote road for now and decide what to do about it tonight when she had more time to think. She walked around the end of the trailer just in time to see Jacob—still on Robbie's shoulders—reaching up to the bars to pat the large nose pressed against them.

"What's wrong?" Alec asked the moment he turned and saw her. He walked over with Peter in his arms. "You've been running," he said, looking over her shoulder, then back at her. "What's wrong?" he repeated softly.

"Nothing," Peg said with a winded smile. "I was just down at the other end of town when I saw the horse trailer, and I ran up here to relieve you of your two little helpers." She shrugged, mostly to loosen the knot in her pounding chest. "I have to get going anyway, to meet the bus at the Inglenook road."

"Mom, the horses are going to Inglenook," Jacob said excitedly as Robbie walked over. "And Mr. Robbie said we can *ride* on them. But only if you say it's okay."

Peg looked at Robbie. "Logging horses don't mind letting people ride them?"

"They're not harness drafts," he said, appearing offended. "They're mounts."

"Why would anyone ride such large horses?" she asked in surprise.

"Because we're large men," Alec said with a chuckle. "If you're meeting the bus at Inglenook, the boys could ride with us if you'd like."

"Yeah," the twins said almost in unison.

"Pleeeze?" Jacob added.

Oh God, leaving them while she was a stone's throw away was one thing, but letting them go with the men? "Um, I have an errand to run." Damn, she'd lied herself into a corner she just realized. "So I was going to have my mother come meet me at the end of the Inglenook road and take the children home." And she still had to figure out how to get herself home.

Alec's eyes narrowed in suspicion. "We can save your mother the trip by watching the boys and then Charlotte and Isabel until you get back. That is, if you're comfortable leaving them with us."

Oh God, was she? "My errand might take me an hour or two to run."

"Olivia's at home," Robbie reminded her, his smile not quite reaching his eyes as his gaze searched hers. "Is the van running okay? Because Gunter's pretty good with engines," he said, waving at the young man standing at the front of the rig.

"No. No, it's running just fine. There's just something . . . personal I have to do without the children." She sighed and shoved her hands in her pockets so he or Alec wouldn't see them shaking.

"Pete was just telling me that he's going to school on the bus this fall," Alec said. "And that he's worried you're going to miss him something fierce. This might be good practice for both of you."

Robbie reached down on his belt, unclipped his cell phone, and held it out to her. "Take this, Peg, and you can call Alec's phone and talk to either of the boys any time ye want during your errand."

Peg pulled a hand out of her pocket, quickly took the phone, and clutched it to her chest. "They . . . they can be a handful sometimes."

Alec chuckled, jouncing Peter. "I think we can handle them. What do you say, Mr. Pete? Are you going to pull any tricks on us?"

Apparently taking the question seriously, Peter vigorously shook his head, then looked at Peg. "Please, Mom? We want to go with the men."

Peg saw Jacob vigorously nodding agreement with Peter, and she blew out a sigh and did her damnedest to smile. "Okay, you can go, and I'll be right there to pick you up in one hour."

"You take as long as ye need on your errand," Robbie said. He nodded at her hand. "And call us every five minutes if ye want. Alec's number is programmed in. And so is Duncan's."

"Where is he?" she asked, unable to believe she'd forgotten about him.

A sparkle came into Robbie's eyes. "Up on the mountain with Mac."

"Oh. Oh!" she repeated when she remembered Olivia telling her what they did up there. "Um, I'm going now."

"Good-bye, then," Alec said with a chuckle when she didn't move.

"Mommm, leave," Peter whispered. "We got important work to do."

Peg was pretty sure she had something important to do,

too. "Oh! Okay, good-bye," she said, turning away only to turn
back and walk up to Robbie and pull on Jacob's sleeve to get
him to bend down. But it was hopeless; she still couldn't reach
Jacob's cheek—that is, until Robbie dropped to one knee.
"Bye, big man. Be good."

She kissed Peter in Alec's arms. "You be extra good, you
got it?"

"I got it," Peter said, wiping her kiss on his shoulder only
to stop when he realized what he was doing. "Good-*bye*,
Mom."

Peg gestured with the cell phone as she turned and headed
back to her van. "They can call me if they want, too. It won't
interrupt my errand." She started walking backward. "And
thank you."

She turned and started running, once again focusing on
what she needed to do. But at least now she had a cell phone
to call someone for a ride. So other than being the owner of a
heap of scrap covered with vile words that she needed to get
rid of, at least things were looking up in the little boys being
around big strong men department.

Now, if she could just figure out how to actually use the
phone, because honest to God, this was the first time she'd
ever even held one.

Chapter Twelve

Duncan stared down at the cell phone in his hand, tempted to throw it against one of the stall doors. What in hell was Peg doing—other than lying through her teeth?

"So what did she say?" Alec asked.

"She said she's just coming in the Inglenook road." He glanced at Peg's four children brushing two of the horses tied in the aisle and frowned at Robbie. "Ye have no idea what was bothering her earlier, or what her personal errand was?"

"She had the look of someone being hunted at first," Robbie said. "But then her worry turned to leaving the boys with us."

"Which itself shows how cornered she obviously felt," Alec added, "to agree to let us bring them here and also watch the girls."

Duncan looked out the barn door and noticed the rain had finally slowed to a drizzle. "She sounded cold. And she—" He strode to the end of the aisle when he saw the car crest the knoll and watched it turn a circle into the parking lot and stop.

Peg got out and bent down to thank the driver, then closed the door and started toward the barn as the car drove off, shoving her hands in her jacket pockets as she hunched her shoulders. Christ, her pants were muddied all the way to her knees, and if he wasn't mistaken she was limping slightly. She suddenly stopped halfway to the barn when she spotted him just as Alec and Robbie came up to flank his sides.

"She's been walking a muddy road for several miles," Robbie also observed quietly. "And she looks soaked through and chilled to the bone."

She started running toward them, which apparently hurt enough that she slowed back to a hurried walk. "Are the kids in the barn?" she asked as she approached, not making eye contact as she tried to veer past them.

Duncan stepped into her path, making her stop—although she didn't lift her gaze to his. "Where's your van?"

"I sold it to a junk dealer." She tried to move past him. "Charlie, are you in there?"

He stepped in front of her again. "Who brought ye here?"

She finally looked up, and it was all he could do to hold his ground against the desperation in her eyes. "Somebody heading in the same direction I was. Charlie?" she called. "Get out here, please. Could you go see if Olivia can give us a ride home?" she asked when all four children came running out of the barn.

"Never mind, Charlotte," Duncan said, giving Peg a look that dared her to argue. "I'll take ye home."

"Mom, we've been brushing the horses," Pete said, rushing to her. "You gotta come see them. They're huge!"

"Tomorrow, Peter." She reached out to take Jacob's hand. "Come on, guys, we need to go home."

"I'll get our book bags," Charlotte said, heading back into the barn at the same time Peg turned away and headed toward Duncan's truck.

"Where's our van?" he heard Peter ask as he and Isabel ran to catch up to her.

"I sold it. We'll get a new one next week," Peg said, her voice trailing off as she rounded the front of his truck and opened the back door to let the kids in.

Isabel suddenly ran back with something in her hand. "Mom said to tell you thank you for letting her use your cell phone," the girl said, handing it to Robbie and then rushing away just as Charlotte ran by with their book bags.

"Any idea what's going on?" Duncan asked, watching Peg

climb in the passenger's seat as Charlotte got in the back. He heard the engine start and saw Peg fiddling with the buttons on the dash—he assumed to start the heater. He looked first at Alec, then Robbie. "Because I agree with that hunted look."

"She told us her van was parked at the other end of town," Robbie said, "but that it was running fine." He shrugged. "It's possible she did sell it."

"Before she had a replacement?" Duncan whispered so he wouldn't roar. Dammit to hell, what was she hiding? He shook his head. "I'm guessing she ditched it on some old tote road for some reason, and that's why she's soaked and covered in mud." He looked at Robbie. "I need to go back to Pine Creek tonight, so could you look into the missing van for me tomorrow . . . doing whatever in your power it takes to find it?"

Robbie nodded. "I'll find it."

Duncan turned to Alec. "I'm going to drive the wheeler back and leave my pickup for Peg." He smiled tightly. "But I'll let you wait until tomorrow to tell her, because I doubt she's open to hearing it from me right now. You keep an eye on her while I'm gone, and see if ye can find out in town what may have happened."

"People have a tendency to shut up when someone from away walks in," Alec said. "Why don't we just ask Mac to help?"

Duncan snorted. "Because the bastard's too busy not interfering in people's lives." He started toward his truck, but stopped and looked back. "Oh, and Alec, while you're in town tomorrow, see if ye can't find us a camp cook. The one I had lined up called me this morning and said he couldn't make it for family reasons."

His nephew nodded. "I'll do what I can on both counts."

Duncan jogged to the truck and climbed in to dead silence but for the blast of the heater fan. He looked in back to see the twins sharing a seat belt in the middle between the girls, then silently put the truck in gear and headed out of the parking lot. The ride to Peg's house was just as silent, making him wonder what she'd said to the children. Christ, she was visibly shivering.

He pulled in to her empty driveway, and Peg had her door open before he even shut off the truck. "Thank you for the ride," she said before softly closing the door. She opened the back door. "I'll start supper once I get out of the shower, and you all wash up at the kitchen sink. Charlie, help the boys put on their pajamas."

"No bath tonight?" Peter asked as he slid out.

"Not tonight. But take a washcloth to your face and hands, because you've been handling horses. Go," she said, giving Jacob a nudge when he tried to say something.

Duncan got out, watching the kids troop onto the deck and into the house like good little soldiers as he followed Peg up the stairs and pulled her to a stop. "You need to tell me what's going on."

"No, I don't."

"I can help you."

"Yes, I'm sure you can. But I can't get in the habit of letting someone else solve my problems." She made a valiant effort to smile past her chattering teeth. "No matter how broad . . . well, because I can't," she finished on a growl, spinning away.

He caught her sleeve and turned her back around, wrapping her up in his arms—partly to keep her warm but mostly just to piss her off. "I'll find that van if I have to drive down every tote road between here and Turtleback Station."

"No, actually, you won't, because despite some people's opinions, I'm a lot tougher and smarter than I look." She patted his chest. "Just worry about guarding your equipment, Duncan, because honestly, I really don't feel up to the task toni—"

He kissed her just to shut her up, and he didn't stop until he felt her start to tremble—and not from the cold, either. He lifted his head and smiled at her glare.

"Stop doing that," she whispered in a shaky growl.

"I feel I should warn ye that I'm also a lot tougher and smarter than I look. And, I've just recently been told, a quick study when it comes to anticipating a person's next move." He lowered his head until his nose was nearly touching hers. "By the same bastard who also pointed out that I'm really quite contrary."

He kissed her again when she tried to protest, partly to piss her off but mostly to let her know he wasn't ever going to stop. He did cut this particular kiss short, however, when he felt her trembling again and realized she was nearing the end of her control.

"It's okay, Peg," he whispered against her wet hair when she hid her face in his jacket. "I'll eventually find out what happened today, because whether ye like it or not, I have no intention of letting you deal with whatever's going on all by yourself."

"You need to leave me alone," she said into his jacket, "because this isn't going anywhere, Duncan." She looked up, and the sadness in her eyes twisted his gut into a knot. "It's not that I wouldn't like it to, but that I . . . can't." She squirmed for him to let her go, and when he did she took a deep breath and smoothed down her jacket. "So please quit trying."

"No."

She snapped her head up. "It's nothing personal, okay? I just don't want . . . I can't . . . dammit, I need to stay focused on my kids." She waved at nothing. "Maybe in another twenty years I'll think about having a love life."

"You'll have forgotten how by then, lass," he said just to piss her off—because it was a hell of a lot better than letting her come up with any more crazy excuses.

Her eyes widened, and within the next heartbeat she had her I-mean-business scowl in place. "It's like riding a bike," she snapped. "But if *you* need the practice, I suggest you try Angie's Bar in Turtleback on the first Friday night of every month, when they have strippers come in from Canada." That said, she stomped away—causing the entire deck to shake precariously.

"Peg."

She stopped with her hand on the storm door, but didn't turn to look at him.

"I have to go home for a couple of days to pull my crew together, so if ye need anything, don't hesitate to ask Alec or Robbie. I'll be back on Saturday to see Mac and Olivia off, and I'll pick you and the children up Sunday morning at ten for our picnic."

"No," she said, still not looking at him.

"Dress them warmly and in mud boots, and ye might want to bring them each a change of clothes."

He watched her lean her forehead on the door. "Please don't make me go."

"Ten o'clock; and I'll have ye all home by sunset," he said quietly, the knot in his gut making the walk to his truck nearly impossible.

By four o'clock Friday afternoon, Peg had decided that Duncan's idea of help was foisting her off on Alec and Robbie. Oh, and leaving her his truck to use—which she hadn't because she was more stubborn than he was. She didn't dare give the man an inch, knowing damned well he'd take a mile before she even knew what he was up to—including stealing more heartbreaking kisses.

How in the name of God had she gotten herself into this mess? She'd really just been minding her business—trying to make ends meet by poaching deer and stealing coupons and keeping her van running on duct tape and prayers—when the earth had shaken and mountains had moved, and Duncan MacKeage had shown up and started making her tremble worse than the earthquake had.

Peg watched the boys building an elaborate road system up from the beach to the driveway using the convoy of toy construction equipment they'd found lined up on the deck yesterday morning when they'd gone outside. She'd tried to thank Robbie, but the man had gotten a sparkle in his laughing gray eyes as he'd shaken his head, saying he had no idea how those trucks had gotten there, as he and Alec had been guarding the property all night. He'd then pronounced in front of the boys that it must have been a sneaky *girl* fairy, since all the boy fairies he knew always made a lot of noise while making their special deliveries.

It hadn't been until that afternoon when the girls had gotten off the bus that Alec had jumped off the excavator and come down and opened the door of Duncan's pickup to show Peg the fairy had also left Charlotte and Isabel a little something—which she would have discovered that morning if she'd *used the truck*. Her daughters were now the proud owners of some pretty fancy L.L.Bean backpacks.

Charlotte, being the bright bulb that she was, had quietly thanked Alec for the special delivery, and Peg had watched her daughter tug on his sleeve to get him to bend over to give him a shy kiss on his cheek—which she'd noticed had darkened as he'd straightened.

Oh yeah, little girls and little boys needed big strong men in their lives. And dammit, so did she. But *desire* was a four-letter word as far as Peg was concerned.

It was also painful as hell.

Duncan MacKeage had walked into her life less than a week ago, big and strong and handsome and unbelievably appealing, and here the man had been gone less than forty-eight hours and she already painfully missed him.

Her desire for Billy had been a subtle blossoming inside her over their junior year of high school; Billy being a bit slow on the uptake, but quickly getting with the program once she'd finally managed to catch his eye. They'd been inseparable their senior year, and had gotten married the September after graduation—Charlotte being born nine months and three weeks later.

There was nothing subtle about her desire for Mr. Kiss-stealing MacKeage, however; in fact, Peg felt somewhat blindsided by the intensity of her attraction to him.

How was that even possible? How could she meet a man on Saturday—by attacking him, no less—and already have her heart aching from knowing she couldn't act on their obviously mutual desire? She really didn't want to go on that picnic Sunday, because she really liked Duncan too much to lead him on. But telling a big strong man that pursuing her would be detrimental to his health . . . Well, once the guy quit laughing, he'd probably steal another kiss just to shut her up. And then he'd set about proving her wrong, because he really was contrary.

So basically the question was, how did a woman go about discouraging a man she desperately desired? Because just saying no didn't seem to be working.

Come to think of it, why was Duncan even attracted to her, anyway? The guy was sexy as all get-out, and obviously successful judging by the fancy equipment he was running; he could have any woman he wanted. So why was he even bothering with a widow who had four little heathens? Which, now that she thought about it, was almost as disconcerting as her desire for him.

"Grammy's here!" Peter shouted, abandoning his road to run to the edge of the driveway and stop. Jacob was two steps behind him, making Peg smile when he also halted with his toes on the edge of the gravel until the car came to a stop and they heard the engine shut off. Then both boys bolted for the driver's door.

"Gram, come on," Peter said, grabbing Jeanine's hand before she even got her seat belt unfastened. "You gotta come see all our new trucks!"

"A special delivery fairy brung them," Jacob said, grabbing her other hand the moment she got out. "Gram-auntie, you come, too," he added with a wave at Peg's aunt Bea as she got out the passenger side.

"I'll be right along," Bea said as she walked over and sat down beside Peg at the picnic table. "I thought you swore they'd never play with toy trucks because you didn't want them playing with big ones when they grew up," she said softly.

"I guess I forgot to tell the truck fairy." Peg followed Bea's gaze from the boys to the neatly stacked pine logs sitting next to the tote road, then up the hillside where Alec was digging stumps while the bulldozer pushed them into piles. Alec had introduced her to Duncan's foreman, Sam Dalton, just that morning when Sam had arrived in another shiny wheeler towing the front-end loader that would stay at the pit to bucket the gravel into the trucks. Oh yeah, Duncan was settling in for the long haul.

"Who is the truck fairy?" Bea asked.

Peg waved at the hillside. "The crew. I suspect they figured if the twins had their own construction toys to play with that they wouldn't try to play with the big ones." She looked at Bea. "What brings you ladies here this afternoon?"

Bea's face lit up. "We're auditioning."

Peg's mom walked over, her own face bright with laughter. "I told you that you'd give in, didn't I?" she said, waving at the twins. "Boys and trucks belong together." She sat down beside Peg. "Land sakes, I can't remember the last time we've been able to sit outside in the middle of April like this. We're usually still knee-deep in snow, and there they are digging dirt already." She wrapped an arm around Peg and gave her a squeeze. "And here you are, finally on your way to financial independence. You should be all moved in to your new house before the snow flies again."

Peg saw Alec get out of the excavator and start jogging down the road they'd built along the west side of her old pit, and she stood up and faced the women. "What did you mean, you're here to audition?" she asked. "Audition for what?"

"We're hoping to get a job cooking for MacKeage Construction," her mom said, also standing up when she spotted Alec. She pointed toward him. "We overheard Alec talking to Ezra this morning, saying he was looking for a cook for the camp they're building for their crew and MacBain Logging to stay at through the week."

It took all of Peg's willpower to keep her composure, even as her stomach tightened in dread. "No," she whispered, her gaze darting between her mom and aunt. "I don't . . . You can't . . ."

Bea also stood up. "We butted right in to the conversation," she said excitedly, "and told Mr. MacKeage that feeding thirty men required *two* people in the kitchen, and that we just happened to be wonderful cooks."

"But—"

"We told him we also happened to be looking for jobs," her mom said, cutting Peg off. "And that we have experience running a camp kitchen."

Peg gasped. "No, you don't." She glanced over her shoulder to see Alec was almost to them, then narrowed her eyes on her mother. "Serving pancakes one day every year on Maine Maple Sunday at a sugarhouse is *not* camp cooking experience," she softly growled.

"Hush," Jeanine growled back, turning to smile at Alec. "Mr. MacKeage," she said with a nod. "We've brought you a sample of the meals we plan to serve if you give us the job." She gestured toward the picnic table. "We thought we'd cook you and your crew and Peg and the heathens supper tonight right here over an open campfire." She beamed him a bold smile. "I promise no one will leave the table hungry."

The smile Alec gave Jeanine disappeared when he looked

at Peg and she didn't turn her scowl off quickly enough. "Is there a problem?" he asked.

"No, there's not," Jeanine said at the same time Peg said, "Yes."

"Mom," she softly hissed, darting a glance at Bea. "They're going to be here for *two* years; five days a week times three meals a day."

Jeanine also lost her smile. "I can read a calendar," she said, striding to the car.

"But you don't understand," Peg whispered tightly, following her. "There are people in town who don't want the resort to be built, and anyone who works for anyone building it is going to become a target."

Her mother opened the trunk and blinked at her. "What are you talking about?" she asked, not bothering to whisper. "Everyone is excited about the resort. It's going to create a lot of good paying jobs."

"Not everyone," Peg hissed. "There are some who are violently opposed to it."

Jeanine reached in the trunk, picked up a box of food, and shoved it at Peg. "They'll change their minds soon enough," she said with a dismissive wave. "And Sister and I intend to be the first in line for those jobs." She touched Peg's arm. "We're so excited about this, honey. You know how much Bea and I love to cook, and we . . . well, we need to feel needed."

"But you both already have jobs."

Her mother picked up another box and handed it to Bea when she and Alec walked over. "I can do the bit of freelance bookkeeping I have on weekends."

"And I already told Sylvia Pinkham I wasn't coming back to housekeep at her resort this summer," Bea chimed in. "With the cost of gas now, I was losing money driving all the way to Turtleback for five hours of work every day, and she wasn't willing to give me a raise." She smiled, nodding at Alec when he also picked up a box from the trunk. "And even including the tips I made at the Pine Point Resort, I'll still be earning twice as much working for Mr. MacKeage."

"Please, ladies, call me Alec," he said. He looked at Peg and arched a brow. "Mind telling me what seems to have you worried?"

Jeanine made a dismissive sound before Peg could answer and grabbed the last box out of the trunk. "My overprotective daughter is afraid we're going to get the cold shoulder from the *few* people in town who are opposed to Olivia's new resort if we work for you." She balanced the box on the bumper and closed the trunk with a snort. "But it'll be a cold day in hell—pardon my French—before I'll let a bunch of idiots tell me who I can or can't work for. Now," she said, carrying the box to the picnic table. "You just go back to whatever you were doing, Alec, and we'll ring the dinner bell."

He stepped in front of Peg when she started to follow them. "Where's your van?"

"It's taking a really long, well-deserved nap."

He sighed. "We're going to find it, ye know. And personally, I'd rather not be standing in your shoes when we do." He canted his head, studying her as she glared at him, and smiled. "I've never actually seen anyone stand up to Duncan and . . . survive. Are ye not even a little bit afraid of pushing him too far?"

"What's he going to do," she drawled, stepping around him, "use the flat of his sword on my backside?"

"Nay, lass," he said with a chuckle as he followed. "I'd be more worried about seeing him with a short length of rope in his hands if I were you."

Having absolutely no idea what he was talking about, Peg stopped and turned, making him nearly bump into her. "The moment I so much as hear anyone in town has threatened my mother or aunt," she whispered tightly, "I swear I'm ripping up my agreement with MacKeage Construction and chaining off the pit."

Alec's usually warm eyes turned deadly, and he stepped closer. "Where's your van, Peg? Did someone run you off the road?"

"And you can tell Duncan that I don't make idle threats, either," she said, turning and walking away on rubbery legs.

Dammit, she had to figure out how to stop them from hiring her mom and aunt, even if she had to dump a whole shaker of salt in tonight's supper when no one was looking—especially her little tattletale son.

Chapter Thirteen

Duncan showed Jacob and Pete how to buckle themselves into the booster seats he'd set in the second row bucket seats, and handed them each the books on heavy equipment he'd brought them. He then stepped to the side to usher Charlotte and Isabel into the third row seat and handed them the magazines he'd brought—that he'd had his mother pick out because what in hell did he know about little girls? He finally climbed in behind the steering wheel, hiding his smile when he saw Peg studying the dashboard that looked like it belonged in a Black Hawk helicopter.

He'd driven the full-sized SUV back from Pine Creek in the wee hours of this morning, leading his convoy of equipment through a gauntlet of moose out licking the salt that had pooled in the potholes from this winter's sanding. At the rate this spring was going, he wouldn't have many more nights of below-freezing temperatures, which was the only time he could run his trucks until the road postings were removed—which didn't happen until the frost heaves settled back into place and the roadbed dried up.

"Do ye like the truck?" he asked conversationally.

"I don't think I've ever seen so many accessories," she said, fingering the buttons on her door handle. He saw her glance over her shoulder. "Or one with bucket seats instead of a bench in back." She tapped the built-in navigation screen and shot him a sassy smile. "You get lost a lot, do you?"

"No, but my mother does, apparently. This is her truck, not mine."

"Then why are you driving it?"

"Because she's wanting to sell it, and I told her that I happened to know someone who might be interested in buying it."

"Who? Olivia?" She leaned back in her seat with a chuckle. "That way she and Mac would have twin SUVs, only his is pearl white, not gold like this one."

"Actually, I was thinking *you* might be interested in buying the truck, since you . . . sold your van."

She half laughed, half snorted in surprise. "Yeah, right; I might be able to afford the *down payment* if I were getting two *fifty* a yard for my gravel."

"The truck's six years old, Peg, and has close to eighty thousand miles on it, making it very affordable at two *twenty-five* a yard. It's also considerably safer than what you were driving. It's four-wheel drive and has a full frame underneath it, which gives you and your tribe a fighting chance against logging trucks in an accident."

"Affording the truck and affording the gas for it is another matter," she said, even as Duncan saw her studying the dash a bit more discerningly.

But he was ready for her arguments. "Actually, I believe it gets the same gas mileage as your van did. The rear end is geared for economy rather than towing because it was Mom's vehicle."

"Really?" she said in surprise, glancing at the children in back before he felt her eyes narrowing on him. "How much commission is she paying you to lie to a nearly *destitute* widow about the gas mileage?"

Hearing the laughter in her voice, Duncan started to relax. "Well, she did promise to bring me an apple crisp and large bowl of whipped cream when she and Dad come to visit my work site next week." He smiled over at her. "If I have her truck sold so she can go buy the shiny red sports car she has her eye on."

Peg settled into her seat again with a sigh. "I don't think the bank will give me a loan based on future income."

"But I have faith in your future income, which is why on my drive back this morning I thought of a deal we might work out."

He felt her eyes narrowing on him again. "What kind of deal?"

"What if we took one day of wheeler loads out of your weekly check for . . . say, the next twelve weeks?"

He could almost hear the gears turning in her brain just before he heard her gasp. "That's less than ten thousand dollars! This truck is worth at least three times that."

"Not in today's economy. That's why Mom is selling it instead of trading it in at the dealership, because their offer was an insult. And," he said when she tried to say something, "I've recalculated after walking Mac's mountain a couple of times, and I've put on two extra trucks so that I'll be hauling at least forty loads a day out of your pit for the next four months. So that's closer to thirteen thousand dollars for twelve weeks."

He stifled a smile when her brain started grinding away again. "But that would mean—wait. I don't *have* that much gravel."

"Oh, but ye do. That vein is deeper than even I estimated. I dug test holes nearly up to your northern line, and the farther I went, the nicer the gravel was."

He saw her glancing around the interior a bit longer this time before she turned and gave the dash another scan—all while rubbing her hand over the leather arm on her seat. Oh yeah; was he a quick study or what? He had Peg pretty much figured out—except for where and *why* she'd ditched her van.

"Ten weeks," she suddenly said. "One day's worth of wheeler loads for *ten* weeks and we might have a deal."

"What! That's not even eleven thousand dollars. Are ye trying to steal the truck from my mother? Do you have any idea what it cost new?"

"And the booster seats stay with it," she said, her eyes filled with laughter. "I get the title signed over with my first gravel check so I can register it, and we put the deal in writing. But only after I talk to your mother on the phone, which I intend to do the minute we get back from sending Olivia and Mac on their way this morning."

And right then, in less than a heartbeat, Duncan realized

he could live to be a hundred and ten and never have the woman figured out. He turned to glance out the side mirror to hide his smile, wondering why instead of scaring the hell out of him that actually turned him on. "Eleven weeks," he said into the pregnant silence. "And you have to bake me an apple crisp drizzled with maple syrup and topped with real whipped cream each one of those weeks."

"Are you serious?"

"I'm always serious when it comes to apple crisp." He smiled over at her. "But I can be persuaded to share." He held out his hand. "Deal?"

She hesitated, biting her lower lip as she looked around the interior again. "It's awful . . . showy," she whispered, mostly to herself, he realized.

"It's more about safety than luxury, Peg." He put his un-shaken hand back on the wheel when she continued to hesitate, and arched a brow to disguise the black thought she'd just triggered. "Would looking showy prove to be a problem for you?"

"Some people might feel I'm ra—that I'm stripping my land bare just for money, and seeing me driving around in something this fancy would only fuel the . . . gossip."

Duncan glanced in his side mirror again, this time to hide his scowl as he shrugged a deceptively negligent shoulder. "Buying this truck was just an idea I had, Peg, because it's safe for your children and reasonably priced. And I know its history, so I know it won't be breaking down every time ye go to town." He smiled over at her. "But if what some people might say is more than you want to deal with, I'll understand if you pass on the offer."

He saw her frown as she looked around again, absently toying with the buttons on the door before she suddenly thrust her hand toward him. "Okay, we have a deal. Eleven days of gravel for the truck."

He started to reach out but stopped. "And eleven apple crisps."

"It's your waistline," she said with a laugh, reaching more than halfway to grab his hand and shake it. She squirmed in her seat. "So pull over."

"What?"

"I want to drive it."

"You're supposed to test drive a vehicle before you shake on it," he said with a laugh, turning onto the Inglenook road and bringing the truck to a halt.

"Mom, why are we stopping?" Pete asked when Duncan undid his seat belt and opened his door at the same time Peg did.

"Because I'm going to drive our brand-new truck," she said excitedly as Duncan glanced in the rearview mirror and saw all four children gaping at her, only to look over and see her I-mean-business scowl make an appearance. "So today's challenge of no muddy feet continues indefinitely."

"What's *infiniditly* mean?" Pete asked.

"It means *forever,*" Duncan answered before she could. "You're a bit of a tyrant, ye know that," he muttered as he got out.

"Oh, yeah?" she said when they crossed paths in front of the truck. "Then maybe I'll let you be the boss of them on the picnic tomorrow, and see how long you last before you're either barking orders or throwing yourself off a cliff."

"Not a problem," he said across the hood when she reached the driver's door. "I'll just make sure to wear my sword."

Peg sat with Olivia on the steps of the main lodge, watching their children down at the paddock trying to coax the huge draft horses over to the fence with carrots. "Where are Ezra and Sam?" she asked. "I thought they'd be here to see you guys off."

"We said our good-byes this morning," Olivia said with a sad smile. "And I swear it turned into a tear-fest, with me doing most of the crying." She sighed and looked around. "I guess I'm excited about going, but I really don't want to leave Inglenook for two whole months, especially with everything that's going on in town." Olivia gave her a sidelong glance. "What happened the other day, Peg? Henry and Sophie weren't too happy I made them help pack the RV instead of letting them stay at the barn with your tribe, but the truth is I was surprised that Alec and Robbie were watching your children. And then I saw you get out of a car and climb into Duncan's truck, and you looked wet and cold and . . . angry." She touched Peg's knee. "Where's your van? Did you have to take it in for repairs again?"

"No, it's definitely dead this time." Peg shot her a smile and waved toward the parking lot where Duncan and Mac were studying what appeared to be a site map spread out on the hood of Duncan's—no, of *her* shiny gold SUV. "And that's why I am now the proud owner of that fancy truck down there."

"That's yours?" Olivia said with a gasp, looking from it to Peg. "You bought it from Duncan?"

"No, I bought it from his mom, but it was Duncan's idea that I pay for it by taking one day's worth of gravel off the check he's going to give me every Friday."

"Oh, that's wonderful, Peg. And smart. I know you're going to love driving it, since I can't keep my hands off Mac's. I told him he's going to have to buy himself an old pickup when we get back, because he's not driving that beautiful SUV up a half-constructed muddy road to see his work site."

Peg snorted. "I guess that's one way to take over his truck." She looked down at the men again and pulled in a shuddering breath. "I'm in really big trouble, Olivia."

"Now what did Duncan do?" Olivia asked with a laugh.

"He keeps stealing kisses."

Peg flinched when her friend suddenly hugged her. "Oh, Peg, that's wonderful." Olivia leaned away. "Wait, how is that big trouble?"

"Every time I tell him to stop doing it, he kisses me again. Sometimes I think he does it just to shut me up, then sometimes I swear he's just trying to make me angry. And sometimes," she continued in a growl when Olivia started laughing again, "I think he does it just to get a reaction out of me."

Olivia folded her hands on her lap and tried to quit smiling. "Men do like to push our buttons." She nudged Peg with her shoulder. "So how do you react? Do you kiss him back or punch him in the belly?"

"I just stand there like an idiot fighting not to cry, because . . ." Peg hid her face in her hands. "Because it feels so damned good."

"Oh, Peggy," Olivia said, wrapping an arm around her. "Being kissed by a big strong man is supposed to feel damn good." She gave her a squeeze. "And the only reason you want to cry is because you're scared." She brushed Peg's hair back to see her face. "And maybe feeling guilty that you're alive and Billy isn't?" she said softly.

Peg sucked in a shuddering sob. "I loved him."

"Good," Olivia said, straightening away. "Then you know what love feels like. But what you don't seem to know is the difference between a broken heart and a dead one. Yours took quite a blow, but it's still beating strong enough to fall in love again."

"It . . . I wouldn't survive another heartbreak."

"Of course you would, because you're stronger than your fears." Olivia leaned into her again. "I was scared to death to fall in love with Mac, but I was more scared of dying a lonely old widow without ever having experienced honest to God passion. Do you really want to hide in your safe little prison for the rest of your life just to protect yourself from something that *might* happen? Or do you want to shock the pants right off of Duncan the next time he steals a kiss by kissing him back?" She ducked down to look Peg in the eyes. "Because I'm here to tell you that experiencing honest to God passion with a man who makes your insides clench and your mouth go dry and your heart pound so hard you think you're going to pass out is definitely worth the risk."

Peg felt her lips twitch. "Oh man, you've got it bad, haven't you?" She looked at the parking lot again. "But what if my passion kills him? I don't think you can even understand what I mean, Olivia," she said, looking at her. "You can't imagine anything killing Mac because he's so big and scary, just like that mythical god . . . what was his name? Hercules or Atlas or whichever one of them was holding up the world."

Olivia suddenly paled and went very still, but then shook her head with a laugh. "Duncan MacKeage is big and scary, too. And he's got shoulders that appear broad enough to hold up *your* world. Do you honestly believe that he's going to die if you fall in love with him? Honestly and truly?"

"I wrote my family's curse off as nothing more than freaky coincidences just like you did the other day, until I found myself standing in the middle of my kitchen listening to Billy's boss tell me he was dead."

Olivia darted what appeared to be an uncertain glance toward the men, then took hold of Peg's hands. "Do you believe in magic?" she whispered. "I'm not talking about special delivery fairies," she rushed on, giving Peg's hands a squeeze. "I'm talking about earth-shaking, mountain-moving magic that can't be explained. Have you ever thought about *that* kind of magic?"

Peg felt her lips twitch again. "Not since I found out Mom was Santa Claus."

"Then if you don't believe in magic, how can you believe in curses?"

Peg blinked in surprise.

"If one is real," Olivia continued, "then wouldn't they both have to be real?"

"I hadn't thought about that," Peg murmured, looking toward the Bottomless Sea. She looked back at Olivia. "Are you saying you think the earthquake last month was . . . magic? Not just some freaky act of nature?"

"I'm not saying anything," Olivia muttered. "I'm just asking that if curses are real enough to actually kill people, then why wouldn't magic—the good, benevolent kind—be just as real?" She squeezed her hands again. "That wasn't a rhetorical question; tell me why you choose to believe you're cursed but you can't seem to believe Duncan could be . . . what was that word I used the other day? Charmed," she said with a nod. "Why can't Duncan be strong and powerful and charmed enough to beat your family curse?"

Peg was back to blinking at her.

Olivia nodded again. "I thought so; you can't come up with one good reason, can you? That's because if your family curse really does exist, then something with the power to break it must also exist." Olivia folded her hands on her lap again and looked down at the men. "You want to know what real magic is, Peg? It's finding love when you didn't even know you were looking for it. It's honest to God passion. And it's joy and peace and contentment. It's lying in bed with a big strong man, waiting to kiss him awake the moment dawn cracks so you can make him think you command the sun." She lowered her voice to a whisper. "But mostly, real magic is realizing you have the power to overcome anything, even the fear of having your heart broken again."

Olivia stood up when she saw the kids running across the parking lot and looked down at Peg with a warm smile. "You're made of the same stern stuff I am, Peg; which means there isn't a man walking this earth who's big and strong and scary enough to send either of us running." She bent down to get her face right in Peg's. "So the next time Duncan Mac-Keage steals a kiss, you either kiss the pants off him or punch him in the belly. And when I get back in two months," she growled, the look in her eyes making Peg lean away, "if I find you still lying in Billy's casket instead of Duncan's bed, I swear I'm going to show you a whole other kind of magic that's going to make your family curse look like a blessing."

Peg ran trembling fingers through her hair when Olivia turned and headed to intercept the children as they ran toward the huge RV parked next to the lodge. Okay, then; she guessed she knew how her friend felt, now didn't she? Peg looked at Duncan standing with his arms folded over his chest glaring at Mac, and damn if her insides didn't suddenly clench and her mouth go dry and her heart start pounding so hard she thought she just might pass out.

"What do ye mean you can't help me find out what's going on?" Duncan asked as he glared at Mac. "You're a damned 'divine agent of human affairs'; it's your job to help us poor, struggling mortals."

"I gave my word not to use the magic for a while."

"Gave it to whom?"

"My wife."

Duncan snorted. "Tell Olivia her friend is in danger. I'm sure she remembers Peg Thompson, the woman whose problem she commanded me to fix—which I did."

Mac shoved his hands in his pockets. "I also vowed to Providence that I would give the good people of Maine time to recover from my little . . . event."

"So you turn an entire state upside down and then just disappear for a couple of months while the dust settles? Tell me, Oceanus; if you protect the drùidhs who protect the Trees of Life, then who in hell protects us from you?"

The wizard shot him a grin. "Whoever has the brain and brawn and skill—and courage—to take me on."

"I believe you left out one important requirement, because whoever that idiot is would also need some powerful magic."

"Have you even gone to visit your mountain?"

"How? Swim? Somebody shoved it on the other side of a damned fiord."

Mac arched a brow. "I thought at the time you were making an unwise choice, but then I assumed there was a reason you wished to be off the beaten path." He grinned again. "I guess you're going to need a boat. I do believe my grandfather-in-law has boats to rent. Though come to think of it," he said, his grin disappearing, "you could probably buy a yacht with what you're charging me to build fourteen miles of road and five *timber* bridges."

Duncan looked in the direction of Mac's glance and saw Olivia herding Henry and Sophie up the stairs of the RV as Peg's children stood waving at them, and Peg—Duncan frowned to see her sitting on the lodge steps, hugging herself as she stared at him. He looked back at Mac. "Talk to your wife about what I'm charging, as she's the one insisting the road looks as if it's been there since the beginning of time and that I seed its edges with wildflowers. And building timber bridges is an *art*."

The wizard placed a hand on his shoulder. "Go visit your mountain, Duncan, and sit in silence and feel the power it wants to give you." He shook his head. "There is one small thing standing in your way of claiming it, though. Well, maybe two things. First is your refusal to accept that you even have a calling, much less your willingness to own it." Mac's hand on his shoulder tightened when Duncan snorted. "And two," the wizard continued, the look in his eyes making Duncan go very still, "the . . . instrument of that power is hidden somewhere on your mountain, but when you do find it I'm afraid you may not actually be able to reach it."

"Christ, is there a reason ye can't just come out and say what you're trying to say and not speak in riddles?"

Mac shoved his hands in his pockets again. "Even I must follow the rules, MacKeage." His grin returned. "But that doesn't mean I can't bend them to give a couple of contrary mortals a nudge in the right direction. So back to your mountain; if you wish to claim your power, you're going to have to bring along someone to help you. Say, someone with less broad shoulders and much smaller hands," he said, looking toward the lodge steps.

Duncan stiffened again. "If she doesn't think I'm crazy now, she sure as hell will when I ask her to please help me get . . . what? A staff? Amulet? Gemstone?" He snorted. "A bottomless satchel of bunny rabbits?"

"Your father found a way to ease your mother into the magic. Maybe you should ask Callum to help you with Peg."

"Or maybe I'll just ask *your* father to help me protect your resort while you're off on vacation. I believe your buddies in Midnight Bay know how to reach Titus."

"Good luck with that, my friend," Mac said with a chuckle. "It was Dad's idea to send you on this quest, claiming the kind of power you're about to receive must be fought for to be appreciated." He placed his hand on Duncan's shoulder again. "It was my idea, however, that you not be able to do it *all by yourself*, by requiring you to ask a mere slip of a woman to help you claim your . . . prize."

Duncan's chest tightened to the point that all he could do was glare.

Mac gave his shoulder a hearty slap. "I'll be back in two months, eager to drive my wife up our road so we can wave across the fiord at our new neighbors," he said with a laugh, sprinting to the RV. "Godspeed, MacKeage."

Duncan stood staring after him, wondering if he shouldn't just climb in his pickup and run a gauntlet of road-stupid moose back to Pine Creek and stay there.

God dammit, he hadn't done one thing to deserve this.

And dammit again, neither had Peg.

Duncan reclined on his elbow in front of the small campfire as he frowned down the hillside at Peg's house, undecided if he liked what Alec was telling him or not. "Ye hired Peg's mother and aunt to cook for us?" he repeated, sliding his gaze to Alec. "Before I gave my approval?"

"I tell ye, those two women can cook," Alec said, looking to Robbie for support. "Tell him how I caught you licking your plate clean."

Robbie shot Duncan a grin. "They definitely can cook. And they both seem to understand the number of calories a working man needs at the end of a day. I swear the steaks they served us were a pound and a half each. Sam Dalton ate two."

Duncan snorted. "More like they understand how much butter to spread around a job interview to get hired. So," he said, looking from one man to the other. "Is Peg's mother anything like she is?"

"Ye mean smart and capable," Alec drawled, "or sassy-mouthed trouble?"

"I mean, am I going to have to put mittens and blinders on my crew three times a day?" He shook his head. "I hadn't planned on having females in camp."

"I'm certain Jeanine and Bea can handle our crews," Robbie said with a chuckle. "I wouldn't be surprised to find a shotgun standing in the corner of your camp kitchen, along with a bottle of liquid gold."

Alec sat up. "I thought I saw Bea dosing the beans with something, and I swear I tasted a hint of Scotch." He looked at Duncan and grinned. "Ye suppose Peg told them you like a little nip in the morning?" He suddenly sobered. "I'm afraid there's a bit of a problem with my hiring them, though. It seems Peg's not all that pleased."

It was Duncan's turn to sit up. "Why?"

"I overheard her telling her mother that some people in town are targeting anyone who's working on the resort road."

"What else?" he asked when he saw Alec's face darken. "Did Peg tell you what happened to her van?"

"She said it was taking a long, well-deserved nap. And she told me to tell you that if anyone gives her mom or aunt any trouble, she's ripping up your agreement and chaining off the pit."

"So she *was* threatened." Duncan looked at Robbie. "Did ye find the van?"

Robbie shook his head. "Nay, I even drove several tote roads between here and Turtleback Station, and quietly asked around in both towns while keeping an eye out for the car that brought her to Inglenook, but I couldn't find any trace of the van using conventional methods."

Duncan gazed into the fire. "And unconventional methods?" he asked quietly.

"Apparently this is a no-magic zone," Robbie said just as quietly.

Duncan lifted his head in surprise. "Is that even possible?"

"I hadn't thought so. But no matter what I tried, I couldn't do a damned thing. Hell, I had to use a lighter to start our campfire tonight." He canted his head. "It's as if the energy I kept trying to call forth was—and apparently still is—sleeping. It's here; I can definitely feel it, but I can't seem to roust it."

Duncan stiffened. "Do you think it's just in this area, or everywhere?"

"I finally grew frustrated enough to call both Ian and Winter yesterday, and they're not having any problems." Robbie gestured toward the fiord. "It only seems to be around Bottomless." He shrugged. "Maybe Mac turned it dormant."

"But you're a Guardian; you're immune to a drùidh's magic because it's your job to protect us from them."

"Mac's a theurgist, not a drùidh," Robbie thought to explain. "With Providence's blessing thousands of years ago, Titus Oceanus built Atlantis on which to cultivate his Trees of Life to protect mankind from the warring gods. He then trained a handful of men to be drùidhs to protect the Trees he eventually scattered all over the world, only to realize he needed to install Guardians to safeguard the people from the drùidhs. Titus and Maximilian—and eventually Henry—are at the top of the hierarchy." He shook his head. "Even de Gairn would be powerless here."

"For Christ's sakes, why would Mac turn off the magic and then walk away?"

Robbie's deep gray eyes looked directly into Duncan's. "I doubt he walked away without leaving some means to awaken it. Mind explaining to me why he suggested I tell you to go see your mountain *before* all hell breaks loose? And that you remember to bring along someone with less broad shoulders and smaller hands?"

"You have a mountain?" Alec asked in surprise. "Like Ian has TarStone now?"

Duncan dropped his head in his hands. "It appears so."

"Which one?" Alec asked.

He gestured toward the fiord without lifting his head. "That one over there." He finally looked up, his gaze going from Alec to Robbie. "The other day when we were up the mountain, Mac told me to pick one and its power would be mine to command." He gestured across the fiord again. "And being an angry idiot at the time, I pointed over there when Mac threatened to choose one for me—in whatever *century* he decided."

"Sweet Christ," Alec murmured, looking at the dark shadow looming into the night sky across the fiord. "He just up and gave you a mountain?"

Robbie turned his fire-lit gaze to Duncan. "Did he say why?"

"I didn't exactly dare ask at the time, but he was muttering something about my refusal to acknowledge my calling eventually destroying me."

"What calling?" Alec asked.

Duncan snorted. "Hell if I know."

"What do you suppose Mac meant about your needing to take along someone with less broad shoulders and smaller hands?" Robbie asked, even as he looked down the hillside at Peg's house. He looked back at Duncan and smiled. "Does our resident wizard have a matchmaker's heart?"

"Doesn't every newly married bastard want every bachelor he knows to join him in wedded bliss?"

"But if you do claim your calling, how are you going to explain the magic to Peg?" Alec asked. He suddenly grinned. "Ye might want to have a length of rope with you when ye do. I believe Hamish has one that he no longer needs."

"You should at least make sure she's not armed," Robbie said with a chuckle, only to sit up when Duncan eyed him speculatively. "Nay, ye will not."

"Didn't you tell me that when ye took old Uncle Ian back to his original time and spent several weeks trying to steal the taproot of de Gairn's Tree of Life, that you were only gone overnight in *this* time?" Duncan asked. "Sunset to sunrise, right, which is what . . . a little less than eleven hours this time of year?"

Robbie suddenly relaxed, folding his arms over his chest to

lean back against the log. "You're forgetting that Mac put the magic to sleep."

"But what if I can wake it back up? Ian told us that he was able to take Jessie back to the night she was nearly murdered; what if I find my power and then use it to buy myself several days alone with Peg? That would give me time to work some of my own magic on her," he said with a grin. "And she'd only be away from her kids overnight."

"But she would feel as if she were away from them for *several days*," Robbie growled. "And it was all she could do last Wednesday to be separated from Pete and Jacob for a couple of hours." He shook his head. "Ye can't manipulate the magic like that, Duncan—assuming you *can* get hold of it."

Duncan lay back on his sleeping bag with a heavy sigh. "Well, gentlemen, it appears I need a boat." He folded his hands behind his head and stared toward the looming shadow of his mountain. "I came here to build a road and five timber bridges, not go to war with a bunch of village idiots, so would one of you please tell me what in hell I did to deserve this?"

Chapter Fourteen

Just because she had every intention of discouraging Duncan from desiring her didn't mean she didn't want to be as pretty as possible doing it. But it appeared the best she could do was look like a dowdy old widow, since her entire wardrobe consisted of jeans and sweatshirts except for a couple of funeral and wedding outfits. And although the funeral dress might be appropriate for how she was feeling, it wouldn't be all that practical for a picnic on a mountain in Maine in mid-April. Come to think of it, she hadn't even bought herself a new jacket in four years.

Hell, instead of discouraging Duncan, she was depressing herself.

"Mom, it's almost ten," Charlotte said from the bedroom door. "You spent all morning getting us ready and now you're not even dressed."

"I don't have anything to wear."

"Of course you do," Charlotte said, rushing to the bureau. She pulled out a navy sweatshirt and soft pink turtleneck and thrust them at Peg. "The dark blue makes your eyes look big, and the pink looks soft and feminine." She shrugged. "And jeans go with everything. And here," she said, opening the jewelry box on the bureau. "Wear your small gold hoops and leave your hair down so it wisps around your face."

Peg clutched the tops to her chest and spun away when she felt her eyes start to sting. "You don't wear earrings to a stupid picnic," she muttered, dropping the sweatshirt to pull the turtleneck on over her head.

"It's not a stupid picnic," her daughter said softly, touching her back. "It's the closest thing you've had to a date since Daddy died."

Peg stilled with the shirt covering her face. "It's not a date. It's not even close. It's just . . . a picnic."

Charlotte finished pulling the turtleneck down from behind, then picked up the sweatshirt and handed it to her. "Can't we just pretend it's sort of a date?" the girl whispered. "Just between you and me?"

Peg pulled the sweatshirt on over her head, pressing it to her face to wipe the tears spilling free. "Damn, Charlie, no. I don't want you . . . Look, you can't get your hopes up, okay? I'm not going . . . Nothing's going to come of Duncan and me, baby."

The sweatshirt was pulled down from behind. "Okay, I won't get my hopes up. But will you wear the earrings anyway? For yourself?" Charlotte walked around and smiled up at her, one corner of her mouth higher than the other as she held out the earrings. "Just so Dun—Mr. Duncan will see what he's gonna be missing when nothing comes of the two of you?"

Peg took the earrings and tried her damnedest for an I-mean-business scowl. "I'm locking you in your room until you're twenty for even thinking that way at eight."

"I'm nearly nine," the girl said, walking to the door. She stopped and looked back. "And if you think I'm bad now, you just wait until I'm sixteen. Grammy's already told me all the tricks you used to pull on her, and she promised to help me come up with new ones. Wear the earrings." She made a face. "But no perfume, okay? Everything you got is so old, it probably smells like skunk pee."

That said, the girl was gone before Peg could even get her scowl back in place, so she walked to her bureau and started to drop the earrings in the box, only to close her fist around them instead. She pulled her hair out of her collar with a sigh as she stared at herself in the mirror, remembering Olivia saying that kids did what they were shown, not what they were told. So what was she showing Charlie today? That she should look like a frumpy old sexless widow so Duncan wouldn't mistake her for a woman?

Wear them for yourself, the nearly-nine-year-old had said. So when in hell had Charlie gotten smarter than her? Because damn if the dark blue didn't make her eyes look bigger and the pink look feminine. And just when, Peg wondered, was she going to crawl out of Billy's casket?

It took her several tries to slip the tiny hoops on because her fingers were trembling, and when she took a deep breath and tugged on the hem of her sweatshirt, she didn't know what in hell she looked like because the image in the mirror was all blurry. Damn; desiring Duncan was messing with her hormones.

"Um, Mom?" Charlotte called out at the same time the twins started whooping. "You better get out here."

Frowning at the eight-year-old excitement she heard in Charlotte's voice, Peg ran into the living room to find all four of her children kneeling on the couch, staring out the window. Well, the girls were kneeling; the twins were jumping up and down, whooping louder with each jump.

"Horses!" Jacob cried. "He brung the horses!"

"We're riding up the mountain!" Peter shouted. "Mom. Mom! We're gonna ride the horses to our picnic!"

Over her dead body. Peg ran to the door and threw it open to see Duncan riding one of the monstrous horses she'd seen in the trailer, leading two more monstrous horses wearing saddles. She ran down the steps, stopping and spinning back around at the bottom and pointing a finger. "You stay on the deck," she growled to the children following her. "And stop that noise before you scare the horses."

"It's going to take more than hollering to scare these gentle beasts," Duncan said from right behind her.

Peg turned, came nose to nose with a horse, and scrambled backward up the steps, having to grab Jacob when she bumped into him—all while shaking her head. "We're not riding those . . . monsters," she said, glaring at Duncan when he dismounted.

"It's the only way up the mountain, Peg, unless ye want to walk. But it would take so long we'd have to turn around and start back down just as soon as we reached the top. The old tote road ends a good four miles short of the summit."

"But . . . but . . ." She waved at the horses that had all crowded up to the deck to stretch their heads over the railing trying to reach the children—which Peg protectively pulled back with her. "How . . . Who's going to . . ."

Duncan laughed. "The girls can ride old Forget-me-not, you and Pete can ride Lilac, and Jacob can ride with me on Daisy."

Peg pulled her daughters against her sides, squishing the boys. "The girls can't ride a horse all by themselves," she said, hearing her voice rise with her panic.

Duncan turned serious. "They're completely safe on Forget-me-not, as she's a veteran heathen mount. All three of them are, which is why I asked Robbie to bring these particular ones. They're his, actually."

"You had him trailer horses all the way here just for our picnic?"

He nodded. "Aye, but also for myself." His grin returned. "I was getting tired of hiking the mountain every time I needed to work on the road layout. Robbie and Alec will use them this summer, too." He sobered again. "They're perfectly safe, Peg. And Charlotte told me she rode horses when she visited Sophie during Inglenook's summer sessions. She can handle Forget-me-not."

"But . . ." Peg took a deep breath. "But I've been on a horse maybe twice in my entire life—a *normal-sized* horse."

"Please, Mom," Jacob said, craning his neck to look up at her. "They're really nice. And they like us 'cause we brushed them."

"They liked it when I got under and brushed their bellies," Peter added, making Peg squeeze him in horror.

She heard Duncan sigh. "Will ye at least give the horses and your children a chance to prove themselves? I would never do anything to endanger your kids, Peg. We're almost legendary in the state for our gentle mares, and the children of our clan start riding before they even walk."

"I know how to ride, Mom," Charlotte said. "And you'll catch on real quick."

Jacob tugged on her sweatshirt. "I'll ride with you if you want, Mom," he whispered. "And I'll sit in front and you can hold on to me if you're afraid of falling off."

Oh God, *Jacob* was reassuring *her*? When had he gotten so brave?

Oh, that's right; when he'd started hanging around big strong men.

Peg blew out a sigh. "Okay, I guess we can give it a try."

"Whoopee!" Jacob and Peter shouted, jumping up and down.

And to Peg's surprise, none of the horses flinched. In fact, one of them reached its big nose toward Jacob, and it was all Peg could do not to pull him back when she saw his tiny hand inches from its mouth. "Um, how are we going to carry all our stuff?"

Duncan gestured at the sacks tied on all three saddles even as his eyes lit with humor. "If it doesn't fit, then we don't need it. We're going for the day, not a week."

"I know that," she said, turning away. "Come on, guys, help me get our things."

"This is going to be the best day ever," Isabel said, running ahead of her. "The only way it could be better was if Henry was going so I could ride with him."

Peg ushered the others on ahead, but stopped when Duncan called her name.

"Where's your new truck?" he asked, looking around, his eyes turning serious again when he looked back at her. "Please tell me it's not taking a long nap."

She'd called Duncan's mother the minute they'd returned from Inglenook yesterday, and Peg had discovered that Charlotte MacKeage could be just as strong-minded as her son. The woman had persuaded Peg to use the truck until she and Callum got there later this week and signed the title over, assuring her it was fully insured and that she preferred Peg drove it instead of Duncan because . . . well, had she seen the man's pickup? "The kids and I cleaned out a spot in the garage for it yesterday afternoon, so it doesn't get covered in all the dust you're stirring up in the pit."

"I'll keep the road watered when we're hauling. And Peg? Thank you."

"For?"

He lifted the reins he was holding. "For not making us walk those last four miles." His eyes lit with something she couldn't quite identify. "And for not making me have to hunt you down this morning," he said quietly.

Not really sure if he was joking or not, Peg mutely nodded and turned away, walking inside to the sound of his soft laughter.

"How about if for today we forget the 'mister' and you all call me Duncan?"

"Mom's not going to like that," Isabel said, giving him a pretty impressive scowl.

"Your mom's taking today off and she left me in charge, so I guess that means I get to make the rules."

"So when the day's all done we gotta go back to Mom's rules and call you Mr. Duncan again?" Jacob asked.

"That's the plan."

"What other rules you got?" Pete asked, eyeing him suspiciously.

"Well, when my tribe back in Pine Creek goes on a picnic, all the little heathens have to catch their own dinner."

Isabel gasped. "You got a tribe of kids just like us?"

"No, not of my own," Duncan said with a chuckle. "I was referring to my cousin's children. And we call ourselves a clan, which is the same thing as a tribe. So, are you all up for a little fishing?"

"I'm not sticking no slimy worm on no hook," Isabel said, back to scowling—until she suddenly beamed him a big smile and damn if she didn't bat her lashes. "But if you baited the hook for me, M—Duncan, then I could catch my dinner. I love trout."

"Sorry, but it's every man and woman for themselves when it comes to fishing," he said, making sure to hide his smile when she went back to scowling. "So I hope you're not real hungry."

"I ain't afraid of no worms," Pete said. He suddenly gasped. "Hey, can I say *ain't* today if you're making the rules?"

Aw, hell; he hadn't really anticipated that particular problem. "I suppose you can," he said with a nod, "if you don't mind sounding like you're only four years old."

"He is four years old," Isabel said, still scowling. "And so is Jacob."

Lord, that one was going to be trouble for her future husband. "Really?" He looked from Jacob to Pete and shook his head. "I'd swear they were older, because they usually talk and act like they're at least six."

"*I'm* six," Isabel growled. But then she smiled smugly. "And I don't say *ain't*."

"We're gonna be five in . . ." Jacob looked at his oldest sister. "How many months until our birthday?"

"Three," Charlotte said. She glanced up at the ledge where Peg was reading, then looked at Duncan with the same serious blue eyes as her mother. "Are all the men in your clan big like you and Alec and Robbie? And strong swimmers who can go in ice-cold water like you did the other day?"

Figuring where this was headed, Duncan nodded. "We all started swimming in cold mountain ponds around your ages."

"Girls, too?" Isabel asked.

"Well, the girls like to wait until the water warms up a bit."

"They must be bass, not trout."

"Do the men in your clan live long enough to get . . . old?" Charlotte asked.

Duncan stilled, just now realizing that instead of heading where he thought, the conversation for Charlotte was more about . . . Sweet Christ, had Peg *told* the girl about her family curse? "Yes," he said quietly, "we have many clansmen well into their seventies and eighties, including the women. In fact," he said, standing up, "when you meet my parents later this week, I think you'll be surprised to know Dad's eighty-two and my mom—whose name also happens to be Charlotte—is seventy-nine, because they look and act a lot younger." He touched a finger to his lips and gave Charlotte a wink. "But let's not tell Mom that I mentioned her age, okay?"

Still utterly serious, Charlotte nodded.

"We don't got no fishing poles," Pete said, jumping to his feet. "So how we gonna fish?"

Somewhat relieved to be off the subject of longevity, Duncan gestured around them. "We have an entire forest of fishing poles, so I guess all we need is some string and a couple of hooks." He bent down and dug through the sack he'd brought and pulled out a small tin box. "Good thing I brought some gear along on the off chance we didn't care for whatever your mom packed for our picnic."

"But where we gonna fish?" Isabel asked. "We're on top of the mountain."

"We seen a bunch of brooks on the ride here," Jacob said. "Trout live in brooks. We can go fish in one of them."

"The last one we crossed was pretty far away," Charlotte said, glancing toward her mother, then back at Duncan. "It's the first time I've seen Mom reading a book in months, and she looks real comfortable."

This one, Duncan decided, was going to cause a different kind of trouble for her husband, and he hoped the poor bastard was as astute as he was lucky. "I happen to know there's a high-mountain pond just a quarter mile from here," he said, nodding over his shoulder. "So how about you go ask your mom if she's okay with us doing a little fishing while she reads? Or," he said when the girl hesitated, "you can stay here if you're uncomfortable leaving her alone."

"Mom's not afraid to be alone," Charlotte said as she turned and started up the ledge. "But I'll ask her if it's okay if we go fishing."

"Tell her we'll share our trout," Pete said, "so she don't got to go hungry if she don't catch her own." He looked up at Duncan. "You ai—is—aren't gonna make Mom follow your clan rules, are you?"

"Not *today*, I won't," Duncan said with a chuckle. "Now, about those fishing poles; we'll make them the same height as each of you, so if you see a perfect stick on our hike, you tell me and I'll cut it."

Charlotte came running back. "Mom said okay, but that you might want to take your sword," the girl said deadpan, although her eyes were aglow with laughter.

"That might be wise," he agreed, going over to the horses

and pulling off his sword. He slid it on over his shoulders and turned and smiled at the gaping children. Well, everyone was gaping but Charlotte; she just looked . . . Now why should wearing his sword make her appear relieved? "Okay, Thompson tribe," he said, heading toward the trees. "Let's go catch us some dinner."

Peg bit her lower lip watching Duncan disappear into the woods with his band of merry young men and women, and wondered if he honestly didn't realize there was a reason she called them little heathens. She wasn't worried about anything happening to them because she was pretty sure Duncan was carrying his hero's badge—and his sword, for crying out loud. She couldn't believe he'd really taken it with him; she'd told Charlie to tell him that as a joke. But now she was feeling guilty about lounging here in peaceful bliss; because really, what had the poor unsuspecting chump done to deserve her foisting the children off on him for the afternoon?

Oh, wait, that's right; he kept stealing kisses even after she told him to stop. And worse, he kept making her lay in her lonely bed at night *desiring* him.

Speaking of kisses, it had been years since she'd felt as alive as she had the night those idiots had tried to sabotage the equipment. Lord, she'd missed having a rousing fight with a man. There was nothing that made her heart thump like a good argument if she happened to know she was safe to say and do just about anything. Like . . . well, like stomp on a guy's foot and hightail it into the dark even though she knew he was going to catch her.

Honest to God, she'd felt seventeen years old again.

Peg closed her book, lay down, and laced her fingers over her belly with a sigh. She figured the only reason she'd dared stomp on Duncan's foot—considering he'd just threatened to put her over his knee—was that on some deep, intuitive level, she trusted him. Just like she was trusting him with her children today. Maybe it was the way he'd reacted when they'd all attacked him the morning of Olivia's wedding. Duncan might growl and posture and threaten like a grouchy old bear, but the guy was all bluster; a softhearted, protective cupcake disguised as a big scary man—which, dammit, only made her desire him more.

Peg rolled onto her side, tucked an arm under her head, and closed her eyes on another sigh. Apparently she had a thing for big men, since that's what had attracted her to Billy initially. It's almost like she enjoyed flirting with danger.

Nope, she just liked men, period; big, strong, broad-shouldered men.

And maybe one overconfident, contrary man in particular.

Yeah, well, she'd see how confident the kissing fool was by the time her little heathens were through with him. And on that note, Peg gave a yawn that ended in a smile and decided since this was her first day off in three years that she'd have herself a little nap.

Duncan pulled plastic bins the size of shoe boxes out of the rucksack he'd taken off one of the horses and silently apologized to all the women of his clan for all they'd had to put up with over the years during family picnics, considering he'd just barely survived the fishing trip from hell. "These are the treasure boxes I was telling you about," he said, whispering to emphasize that he didn't want to wake up Peg as he handed them each one of the boxes. "Ye empty your pockets into them, and then add anything else you find that catches your fancy."

"Like what?" Isabel asked in a whisper.

"Pretty rocks, odd-shaped twigs, pinecones . . ." He shot her a grin. "That poor angleworm ye refused to feed to the fishes."

"I heard him squeal when he saw the hook, I swear," she whispered, her little chin rising defensively. "I'm not hungry, anyway."

"I'm gonna fill my box with moss, then find me a samalander," Pete said. "And bring him home as a pet."

"Mr. Duncan?" Jacob said as he dug no less than ten small rocks out of his pocket and dropped them in his bin. Duncan sighed, figuring *mister* was forever etched in the children's brains, because only Charlotte had successfully dropped it today. "You gonna tell Mom that I cried?" the boy asked, his big blue eyes pleading.

"No," Duncan said, ruffling his hair, "because then I'd have to tell her that I cried, too. And your brother and sisters aren't going to tell, either, are you," he said rather than asked, giving them each a meaningful look.

All three of them shook their heads, and Charlotte added a shrug as she gave Jacob a motherly smile. "Fish that big are tough to eat anyway, so it's good that you wanted to throw him back."

"You can tell Mom that I baited my own hook," Isabel interjected. "With a grub, 'cause grubs don't wiggle and scream."

"We don't gotta tell her I fell in, do we?" Pete asked, his big blue eyes also pleading yet somehow defiant. "'Cause I saved myself *and* got that gosh-dang fish."

Yes, and the kid had taken ten years off Duncan's life. He'd had to wrap Pete up in his jacket and build a quick fire to dry out his pants and shirt and jacket, because he'd forgotten to bring their changes of clothes and he hadn't wanted to leave them alone to run back and get them. "I'll let each of you decide what your mother needs to know about today's little . . . adventure."

"But I don't think we should tell her you cussed, okay?" Jacob said. "'Cause she might think you're unsevralized and not let you be the boss of us again."

Duncan nodded gravely. "That might be wise. Okay, ye have your boxes and a little while before we have our picnic lunch, so see what treasures this grand mountain is wanting you to bring home—all while being as quiet as church mice." *While I go watch your mother nap and calm my nerves,* he silently added, *and never, ever underestimate her again.*

Jacob and Pete took off, actually tiptoeing as they went in search of treasure. Isabel looked to Charlotte for direction and followed her big sister up the ledge where the two girls started collecting pinecones from under the lone stunted pine.

Duncan walked over to where Peg was sleeping and settled down beside her with a silent sigh as he gazed across the fiord at his mountain. Once he dropped the Thompson tribe back home, he decided, he was going to go find a boat.

He looked down at Peg when he heard her stir and reclined back on his elbow beside her. "Thank you," he said as she stretched like a lazy kitten.

"For?" she asked, blinking herself awake.

"For trusting me with your children enough to actually fall asleep."

"Only my eyes were closed; my ears haven't slept since Charlotte was born."

"Have ye noticed that when ye see her as eight she's Charlotte, but when you need her to be older ye call her Charlie? And that she responds in kind, I believe without even realizing she's doing so? Quit your scowling," he said with a chuckle. "That was a compliment to the both of you. She's going to grow up to be a remarkable woman—just like her mother." He propped his head on his hand with a snort. "And may God have mercy on the poor bastard who eventually captures her heart."

"He's going to have to get past me first," she said around her scowl. "And thank you for recognizing that she's a lot tougher and smarter than she appears—just like her mother." She rolled onto her back and smiled up at the sky. "And also for insisting we come up here today. I hadn't realized how much I needed to . . . just get away."

"I admit to being surprised at how much ye seem to be enjoying yourself."

She turned her smile on him. "There's something about sitting—and napping—on top of a mountain that puts things in perspective. I think it's being able to see so far and also to feel how big the world is from up here. It reminds me how insignificant most problems are in the grand scheme of things."

"Aye," he said, sitting up to rest his arms on his bent knees as he stared across the fiord. "Mountains have a magical way of calming the soul." He turned his head when she also sat up and found her eyes widened in surprise. "What?" he asked.

Those beautiful eyes suddenly narrowed. "Have you been talking to Olivia?"

"About . . ."

"Magic."

It was Duncan's turn to be surprised, although he made sure not to show it as he wondered what in hell Mac's wife was doing mentioning the magic to Peg. Then again, maybe this was the opening he needed to start easing her into it. "Olivia's been talking to you about magic?" He grinned. "As in special delivery fairies?"

"No, she was talking about . . ." She gestured at Bottomless. "She called it earth-shaking, mountain-moving magic that can't be explained." Duncan saw her cheeks darken as she wrapped her arms around her knees and watched her children foraging at the edge of the trees below them. "The kind of magic that makes anything possible." She looked at him again. "Olivia asked me if I believe it exists."

"And your answer was?"

She lowered her gaze. "I told her that I hadn't really given it much thought."

"I've thought about it," he said, which lifted her beautiful blue eyes back to his. "And I've decided magic definitely exists."

"Why?"

"Because not believing is an exercise in futility, as the magic goes about its business whether ye think it exists or not. And if ye don't believe, then why even get out of bed in the morning? Or make plans for tomorrow? Or want, or hope, or dream, or even *try*? Magic is what powers life, Peg. Without it, we wouldn't be able to take our next breaths."

"Olivia called your family . . . charmed. She said all you MacKeage men live to ripe old ages but that you look and act years younger."

"Aye, to our women's dismay, we can be real bastards like that sometimes."

That got him a tentative smile, and then she looked away. "Olivia called the magic benevolent, with the power to overcome . . . bad things."

"That would be the business part of it, lass; the power of right over might." He grinned. "Although might does come in handy on occasion."

"Olivia also said you MacKeages are rather old-fashioned."

"Olivia seems to be saying a lot of things to you about my family; any particular reason why?"

"Because friends look out for each other." She gave him a sad smile. "And because she's worried that I'm going to die a lonely old widow like she thought she was going to before she met Mac." She shook her head. "Are you aware they knew each other only a few weeks before they got married? Olivia was just going along, minding her business, waiting for her in-laws to sell Inglenook so she could buy it when Mac suddenly appeared as if out of thin air, and the next thing I know she's asking me to be a bridesmaid in her wedding—that Mac gave her only six days to plan."

"The man does seem to make things happen whenever he appears out of thin air," Duncan said, wondering what Peg would think if she knew how true that was. He gestured at the mountain they were sitting on. "He certainly didn't waste any time getting the resort started. He called me on the Wednesday before his wedding and asked if I could start the road the following Monday."

"Why you?"

Yes, why him? "Well, I believe there's a distant . . . ancestry between the husband of one of my cousins and the Oceanuses." He shrugged. "I guess Mac wanted to keep it in the family. So we're good on the magic? You've decided ye believe it exists?"

Her pretty little nose lifted just enough that she had to look down it to see him—although he noticed she was also fighting a smile. "I've decided I'll believe it exists when I see this powerful, benevolent magic in action."

He straightened in surprise. "But ye just did, lass."

"When?"

"When I returned *four* children back to ye safe and sound." He scrubbed his face with his hands, then peeked through his fingers at her. "Because I hope ye know that herding chickens is easier than keeping track of your tribe when they're focused on catching fish."

Her eyes widened in mock horror even as her lips twitched again. "Did you end up having to draw your sword?"

He dropped his hands to show her his scowl. "Eventually."

The *mock* went out of her horror. "You threatened my babies?"

"I never said a word. I merely drew my sword when they continued to wander in different directions and proceeded to slice a couple of small fir trees off at their stumps with single blows." He let his smile finally escape with his chuckle. "Ye should have seen your *babies*, Peg. The bloodthirsty little heathens came running so fast that Isabel didn't even realize she was clutching her angleworm to her chest."

He saw Peg blow out a sigh, and her lips finally made it to a full-blown smile. "Maybe the real magic is that they brought *you* back safe and sound. You do have a tendency to limp down the mountain every time you come up here with Mac."

He arched a brow. "Is there anything you and Olivia don't tell each other?"

Peg batted her eyelashes at him, and Duncan saw exactly where Isabel had learned that little trick. "She didn't tell me which of you won the manly duels."

Duncan snorted and rubbed his face again to hide his smile. "I did."

"You did not," she said with a gasp.

He dropped his hands to glare at her. "Feeling pretty brave, are ye, thinking I won't kiss you in front of your children? What makes you so certain I didn't win?"

Her face flushed and she scrambled to her feet. "It's time to eat."

"Peg," he said quietly as she headed down the ledge, making her stop and look at him. "The day will come that ye don't have them to hide behind."

"No, actually, it won't, because the twins and I are stuck together like glue."

He canted his head, studying her. "Ye forgot I told you the magic goes about its business whether ye believe in it or not. And Peg?"

Up went that pretty nose in the air again.

"Someone who believes holds the advantage over anyone who doesn't."

"And . . . and you believe?"

"I was born believing, lass."

Whereas figuring out how to make Peg believe was probably going to be the death of him, Duncan realized as he watched her silently turn and walk away, her hands balling into fists as she shoved them in her pockets. Only problem being that in doing so, he'd likely be damning himself to hell for manipulating the magic for no other reason than to prove that he was bigger and stronger than a curse, and a hell of a lot harder to kill than William Thompson.

Chapter Fifteen

Duncan had just reached the mouth of the fiord when the mother of all whales suddenly breached in front of the small boat he'd rented from Ezra. He grabbed the gunwale and cut the motor as the whale slapped back into the water, the force of the splash creating a wave that nearly capsized him. It resurfaced close enough that he could have touched the behemoth as it began swimming alongside the boat, keeping pace even when he opened the motor to full throttle again.

Duncan cut diagonally toward land when he was halfway up the twelve-mile-long waterway and started looking for a place to go ashore. The whale disappeared only to resurface on the other side of him and gently bump the bow. Not wanting to argue with the beast, he continued down the fiord another few miles before the whale surfaced on his left side and nudged the bow toward land.

Guessing it didn't get any plainer than that, Duncan slowed back to an idle and scanned the shore until the moonlight revealed the small beach spilling out of the dense evergreens growing all the way down to the high tide line. He turned toward it and shut off the engine to let the boat drift in eerie silence until it scraped onto the gravel, and glanced over his shoulder in time to see the whale slip back below the surface.

"Thanks for scaring ten years off my life, you big bastard," he muttered as he walked to the front of the boat and stepped onto the beach—only to have a surge of energy shoot through him with enough force to knock him on his ass, causing him to hit his head on the bow on his way down.

Go sit on your mountain, Mac had said, *and feel the power it wants to give you.* Hell, he'd *have* to sit, as he couldn't seem to stand on it. He grabbed the bow and pulled himself back to his feet with a curse, fingering the bump on his temple as he wondered if the energy still humming through him might leave him permanently sunburned.

The whale breached again not a hundred yards offshore, and if Duncan wasn't mistaken, he'd swear he heard laughter. He turned his back to it and set his hands on his hips as he gazed up at the black shadow looming into the night sky. "And you, you big bastard, nap time's over, so wake the hell up."

The gravel beneath his feet shifted and Duncan tried to catch the boat even as he lunged toward the trees, only to miss on both counts; the boat surged into the fiord as he sunk into frigid water clear up to his waist. "For the love of Christ," he growled, slogging up into the woods, "you could at least have a goddamned sense of humor."

He dropped down on a bed of moss and unclipped his cell phone off his belt, then pulled it out of the leather pouch and poured out the water as he eyed his boat now sitting forty yards offshore. He unlaced his boots, pulled them off, then poured out the water, and unzipped his jacket and shrugged it off. He then started unbuttoning his shirt with a sigh—only to stop midbutton when the boat suddenly lifted on the back of the whale and shot farther out to sea. He set his elbows on his knees and dropped his head in his hands with a muttered curse. For the love of God, he hadn't grabbed his backpack and sword. He snapped his head up and jumped to his feet. "You dump that boat and I'm coming after you with a harpoon!"

The behemoth sunk below the surface to leave the boat floating in the middle of the fiord, the moonlight glistening off the motor as it rocked on the gentle swells. He heard quiet laughter again, this time coming from the woods behind him, and sat down on the moss then flopped back spread-eagle with a groan. He must have really pissed off the magic sometime in his youth, because he still couldn't come up with one good reason why he deserved this.

What in hell was so all-fired important about accepting a calling he didn't even want, anyway? Like he'd told Mac, there were enough magic-makers running around Maine already; what did Providence care if he remained a mere mortal making his way through life one day at a time? Duncan snapped his eyes open when he realized the ground beneath him was slowly moving up and down even as he heard what sounded like . . . snoring. Well, hell; the mountain really was sleeping.

Then who—or what—had been laughing in the woods behind him?

Okay, he had two choices: He could build a fire to dry out his pants and boots and go find his *calling*, or he could lie here until he rotted. Neither choice held all that much appeal, but apparently just giving up wasn't programmed into his DNA. He used a heartfelt groan to propel himself into a sitting position, pulled off his socks and wrung them out, then put them back on and reached for his boots—only to find just one. The cell phone was there along with its pouch, and one boot. And he was far enough away from the water that it couldn't have fallen in.

Duncan quietly undid the sheath on his belt and slowly pulled out his knife as he stopped breathing to listen. Other than the soft snore of the mountain, he didn't—

There, just over the knoll to his right, he heard what sounded like slobbering. He rolled to his hands and knees and silently crawled across the carpet of moss, lowering to his belly when he reached the tangled roots of a large cedar.

He slowly peeked over the top, then blinked to make sure the blow to his head hadn't messed with his vision, because that sure as hell looked like a dog chewing on his missing boot. A puppy, actually; a gangly blond pup that definitely had some lab in the mix, about seven or eight months old. Which meant one of two things: Either Mac had given him a mountain that was already occupied, or the pup had become stranded here when the earthquake had created the fiord.

Then again, maybe his fall had knocked him out and the puppy fairy had paid him a visit while he'd been asleep. "Psst," he whispered, causing the young dog to stop midchew, every muscle in its scrawny body freezing except for its ears, which slid back to listen. "Hey, mutt, that boot's only a month old."

The pup reared up so fast, it somersaulted over backward with a yip of surprise, then bolted into the woods up the mountain, its tail tucked protectively between its legs. Duncan sighed and stood up to walk over and pick up his boot, brushing his hand over the teeth marks in the leather. The damn dog appeared to have been trying to eat it. He looked in the direction it had run off, wondering if it really might be stranded and nearly starved. He went back to his mossy spot above the sunken beach and dropped down to dress his feet, and then just sat staring at his boat. Dammit to hell; he had a change of clothes in his pack, and he really wanted his sword—although not enough to spend the night playing keep-away with a whale.

Duncan lay back on the moss again and closed his eyes and slowed his breathing, trying to bring the mountain's heartbeat into rhythm with his—just like Ian had told him TarStone had done the night he'd claimed his own calling. Except his nephew had been given a tall, gnarly staff to control TarStone's power, where he had . . . nothing. What in the name of God had Mac hidden over here? Hell, did his mountain even have a name? He wasn't sure it had even existed before the earthquake, despite being covered with some pretty impressive old-growth timber. But then, Mac could have merely folded the existing earth when he'd split the land to form the fiord.

"Focus, MacKeage," he muttered, closing his eyes again. "Feel where the energy is coming from."

Wait. Ian had also had a mentor; a thieving, cantankerous old hermit by the name of Roger AuClair de Keage—who also happened to be the original MacKeage.

Then why was he stuck with zilch? No gnarly staff and no mentor—because Mac needed a little vacation to recover from turning an entire state on its ear—no instruction manual or treasure map or sage animal familiar to guide him, no . . . nothing. Just a goddamned sleeping mountain with no sense of humor. Didn't Providence realize he could blow himself and half of Spellbound Falls to kingdom come messing with something he didn't know anything about?

Duncan bolted upright. The pup. If it had been living here since the earthquake almost a month ago, it must know the

mountain pretty well by now. All he had to do was follow it
around until it led him . . . someplace. And it was obviously
hungry, so befriending it shouldn't be any harder than feeding
it. But feed it what? The snack he'd brought was in his backpack, which was in the boat in the middle of the fiord being
guarded by the mother of all whales.

Duncan stood up with a smile and pulled his knife out of
its sheath again. He had a mountain, didn't he, which would
be home to all manner of furred and finned and feathered
food? And roasting partridge or trout could be smelled for
miles if the nose doing the smelling happened to be canine.

He unscrewed the cap on the hilt of his knife and turned it
upside down to shake the contents into his hand: a small coil
of fishing line with a hook, a magnesium flint, a really small
medical kit, a sandwich bag, and a length of fine wire. He'd
taken out the salt tablets and replaced them with aspirin the
day he'd bought the knife, since sweating vital minerals wasn't
a worry in Maine because, hell, he just had to lick a pothole.
He'd also tossed the compass cap and replaced it with something solid enough to pound with, and wrapped the hilt with
rough black tape for a better grip. So he was basically good to
go for his hike around the goddamned fiord—or indefinitely,
actually—assuming he didn't mind being cold and miserable
until he built a fire and dried out.

Duncan stuffed the fishing line in his jacket pocket, carefully worked everything else back into the knife, and screwed
on the cap. He blew out a sigh and headed up the mountain at
a diagonal in the direction the pup had run, figuring he'd eventually come across a stream. Damn, he'd like to have the huge
trout Jacob had caught and insisted they throw back when its
watery eye had stared up at the kid, its mouth gaping open as it
gasped for breath. That particular twin, he decided, was going
to make some lucky woman a really good husband—whereas
Pete was probably going to see the inside of an emergency
room and juvenile detention hall a couple of times before he
pulled his act together.

Duncan heard the gushing stream long before the moonlight revealed its glistening water cascading down over a long
series of weatherworn boulders, ending in a pool spanning a

hundred yards across. It wasn't a vertical waterfall like the one in Spellbound, but it was still a rather impressive sight.

He shed his jacket and rolled up his sleeves as he knelt beside the pool and dipped his hands to splash some water on his face, only to jerk back in surprise. He stuck his hand in the water again and swirled it around, and yup, it was the temperature of bathwater. He sat back on his heels and gazed up at the stream rolling down over the boulders, wondering why it was warm. He cupped his hand in the water and lifted it to his nose and sniffed, then dipped his tongue into it. It smelled and tasted fine; it was just warm.

He pulled his fishing line out of his pocket and tied the end of it to a small rock, then got up and walked over to a bed of moss and knelt down again. Using his knife, he cut a patch out of the moss and folded it back, then dug through the dirt until he found a fat grub. He returned and baited the hook and threw it out into the pool, setting the rock on the edge of the bank despite having little hope he'd find trout in water that warm.

He had just started to get up when the rock suddenly slid a good six inches, and he grabbed it just in time to feel the line tighten again with a rather impressive tug. He tugged back, then stood up and pulled in the line, stepping away when an equally impressive trout flopped out of the water to land beside his feet.

"Son of a bitch," he muttered, pouncing on the flopping fish that had to weigh at least three pounds. "Okay then. I take back every dark thought I had about ye," he said out loud to the sleeping mountain.

He returned to the moss and tossed down the fish and found another grub, baited the hook again and tossed it in the water, but held on to the line this time. The hook couldn't even have reached bottom before he felt the line go taught, and he yanked out another fish half again bigger than the first one. He caught two more before he took his catch down to where the pool spilled into the forest below and quickly cleaned them, then set about gathering fallen branches and had a fire going in less than ten minutes. While it built up a bed of coals, he cut several forked branches and whittled off the bark before carefully skewering the fish. He propped the sticks across two rocks so the fish hung over the coals he'd raked between them, and finally unlaced his boots with a sigh. He may not be making any headway finding the *instrument* of his power, but he was going to have a full belly when he walked home empty-handed.

And if the pup had half a brain, it would get its belly filled tonight, too.

Duncan slipped off his pants, laid them out on a tree branch near the fire along with his socks, and then propped his boots as close to the flames as he dared. He pulled his cell phone out of his jacket pocket, then spread the jacket on the ground and sat down, only to realize the tails of his shirt were also wet. So he took it off and tossed it up on an overhead branch, sidled closer to the fire and added some wood, then tapped a few buttons on his phone to see if it was ruined.

To his surprise the screen lit up, and to his consternation he saw he didn't have any reception. He started to mutter a curse, but stopped. "Sorry. I forgot you're *trying* to be benevolent. But is being able to call Alec to come pick me up in the morning really too much to ask?"

He was answered only by the gushing stream. He shoved the cell phone in its pouch, then carefully turned over the fish before settling onto his side and propping his head on his hand. He couldn't wait to bring the Thompson tribe here, he decided as he gazed across the fire at the pool and watched its ripples sparkle in the moonlight. Isabel would go nuts when she pulled out one of those beautiful trout, Jacob would cry for her to throw it back, Pete would jump in after it, and Charlotte would get a crooked smile on her beautiful face and merely shrug her delicate shoulders.

Peg was doing one hell of a job raising those four kids all by herself. But damn, didn't she get lonely for male companionship? All that beauty and grace and fierce determination, that sexy, sassy mouth perfectly shaped for kissing, that athletic body built to cradle a man; how in hell did a woman simply turn off desire? How had she gone from sharing a bed with a husband for . . . what, at least six years, only to crawl into an empty bed every night with no hope of feeling a warm body beside her ever again? Because if Peg truly did believe William Thompson had died from her family's curse, she wouldn't dare risk killing off another man.

And what about Charlotte and Isabel? They were female descendents of the first black widow; what did Peg plan to tell them when they fell in love and wanted to marry? Had Peg's mother warned *her* what could happen before she'd married?

He might not have children of his own, but if he did Duncan figured he'd do everything in his power to make sure they got to live life on *their* terms, not pay for the sins of some long-dead ancestor. He rolled onto his back and stared up at the summit of his moon-bathed mountain peeking through the trees, a bit surprised at how angry the idea of Peg and Charlotte and Isabel living under such an obscene curse made him. But even more alarming was how much he cared, not only for the women, but for Pete and Jacob.

When in hell had that happened? He'd met Peg and her tribe only a little over a week ago—by being attacked by them, no less—yet he'd felt almost naked the two days he'd gone back to Pine Creek. He gave a derisive snort, realizing he was literally naked right now and missing the hell out of them again. As for Peg, he—

Duncan turned to stone at the realization he was being watched.

Making sure not to make eye contact with the blond body of fur creeping along the perimeter of the clearing, he slowly sat up and reached for the skewered trout, smiling when he saw the pup freeze in place. He laid all four fish on a flat rock and used his knife to peel back the sizzling skin on one of them, then flicked the blade to send the skin flying into the woods in the general direction of his visitor. Using the knife and his fingers, Duncan began eating the succulent trout, making soft slurping noises as he watched the pup slowly creeping through the shadows as quiet as a church mouse.

He continued eating, again making slurping sounds interspersed with hums of pleasure. The pup crept out of the shadows on its belly, then reached out a dog-sized paw, snagged the skin and pulled it back, snatched it in its mouth, and darted back into the shadows. Duncan used his knife to peel another trout and flicked the skin a little farther out into the clearing. "I don't mind sharing my dinner with a fellow traveler," he said conversationally, keeping his tone light, "and my camp-fire. I believe it's going to turn chilly tonight by the looks of that moon."

The pup came creeping back, taking two steps into the clearing then hesitating before taking another cautious step, which allowed Duncan to finally get a good look at what appeared to be a male dog. "Delicious, isn't it?" he said when the pup scoffed up the skin and swallowed it in one gulp. Only this time, instead of slinking back into the trees, the brave and obviously hungry mutt turned to face Duncan, its head canted expectantly as it wagged its tail ever so slightly. "Would ye care for a little flesh along with the skin this time?" He slipped his knife deeper into the next fish to leave a good deal of the meat attached, and tossed it between him and the pup.

The dog pounced on the prize without hesitation, and once again swallowed it in one gulp. It stepped closer, its gaze darting from Duncan to the fish to the knife in Duncan's hand, then back to him. Then another step, its thick yellow tail wagging a bit more robustly as its pink tongue made a swipe around its mouth and over its nose.

"It looks like I'm going to have to throw a line in the water again," Duncan said with a chuckle. He used his fingers to pull off a large piece of meat, then held his hand toward the pup. "Come on, fella. Come eat your fill."

The pup sat down and ducked its head with a soft whine, its tail thumping the moss like a drumming partridge as it trembled with indecision.

"Be a brave lad and come to me," Duncan crooned. "Come on, now."

The young dog slowly slinked closer, crouching submissively with its tail tucked between its legs, until its nose was only inches from Duncan's hand. Duncan stretched the rest of the way and turned his hand palm up so it could get the food.

Again the fish was gone in one gulp, and the pup started licking Duncan's fingers with such delicate care that he chuckled again. "That's a good boy. Come on and have some more," he said, reaching for another fish. "So, do ye live around here or are ye just passing through?" he asked as he ran his knife along the backbone and peeled away the entire side of the trout. "Because I was wondering if ye happened to know of any special areas." He handed the dog the large filet, which required three gulps to get down this time. "Like a cave maybe, or a grotto, or an unusually large tree. Anyplace ye might have felt an unusual amount of energy."

The pup's tail thumped as it canted its head to listen, even as its large brown eyes remained trained on the fish on the rock.

"All right," Duncan said with a chuckle. "I know it's hard to focus when your belly's rumbling and there's food around." He started cleaning all the meat off the bones only to watch it disappear down the pup's throat as fast as he could hand it over. "I have the same problem when a pan of apple crisp is in the vicinity. Sorry, pal, but that's the last of it," he said, holding his empty hands out—which the pup immediately started licking. Once it had licked off all but Duncan's fingerprints, the young dog stepped back to eye him. It then ducked its head and slinked up onto the edge of the jacket, flopped down against his side, and rested its chin on Duncan's thigh with a doggy sigh. And just like that, with only a brace of trout and a warm body to lean on, Duncan realized he and the pup had just formed a bond that God himself wouldn't be able to break.

And when he found himself wondering what he'd done to deserve this, this time he decided it must have been one hell of a good deed.

Duncan felt his foothold giving way and made a desperate lunge for the other side of the gaping hole he was trying to cross, but only managed to slam into the ledge with enough force to bounce him into nothing but heated air rising up from only God knew how far below. His muttered curse ended in a grunt of surprise when he landed a hell of a lot sooner than he'd expected, the sharp pain jerking him awake with another shouted curse.

The pup pushed off his side with a startled yelp, making Duncan protectively grab his ribs as he opened his eyes and immediately closed them against the bright sunshine pouring into the clearing. Shaking and sweating and breathing heavily, he replayed the terror of his dream—which felt so real that every muscle in his body started screaming at just the thought of moving.

Christ, he hurt. He slowly cracked open his eyes again and looked around until he saw the pup standing a few feet away, staring at him in concern. He slowly reached out a hand only to turn it back toward himself when he realized it was covered with bloody scrapes. And then he noticed it also happened to be sticking out of his shirtsleeve; the only problem was he couldn't remember getting dressed last night.

The pup came slinking over with its tail wagging hard enough to move its entire rear end and flopped down to rest its head on his belly—only to jump away again when Duncan bolted upright at the realization the sun was at least two hours high in the sky.

"Damn, I'm late," he groaned more than growled, wrapping his arms around his protesting ribs. "I have an entire crew in place to start hauling gravel today," he told the pup, forcing his voice to soften. He sighed and rubbed his hands over his face. "It's okay, though, Dalton knows what—" He stopped in midrub and ran his fingers over the length of stubble covering his jaw. "Son of a bitch!" he snarled, dropping his hands away to look down at himself. His pants and shirt were filthy and definitely looked like he'd been living in them for at least four or five days, and his new boots looked like he'd nearly worn off the treads, the uppers scuffed and cut in places and stained with mud.

He flopped backward with a groan and closed his eyes as he recalled the dream he'd actually lived through, apparently. He remembered hiking up and down and across the mountain with the pup like a man possessed, searching for something he hoped he'd recognize when he found it; making camp every evening wherever they happened to be, and eating whatever he could hunt or catch.

Duncan's breath hitched when he remembered finding the cave three-quarters of the way up the mountain facing the fiord, and how he'd followed the pup when it had run inside as if it had been there before. It had been tight going for the first ten yards before the cave had opened large enough that he could stand, and the first thing Duncan had noticed was that the air had been unusually warm. The second thing being that the walls were glowing, emitting enough light for him to see the tunnel continued at a downward incline farther into the heart of the mountain.

He'd also noticed that the snoring had been more pronounced.

He'd let the pup lead him deeper into the cave, and estimated they were a good quarter mile inside the mountain when the floor had simply stopped. Duncan had tried to look down what appeared to be a chasm, but hadn't been able to tell how deep it was because its walls weren't glowing. However, there had been a noticeably hot column of air whooshing out of it and then suddenly sucking back in, sort of like . . . breathing. He could see the glowing tunnel continued on past the thirty-foot-wide chasm and opted for the route he could see—assuming he could get past the hole. Hence the fall that had awakened him from his dream that had *really happened*.

He remembered how lying at the bottom looking up had allowed him to see the hole was about twenty feet deep. He had then tried to figure out if any bones were broken that would force him to lie there until he rotted, or if he was going to be able to escape a hole he suspected had been carved out of sheer contrariness.

Although he didn't know how someone with less broad shoulders and smaller hands would have helped him out of this particular predicament, he supposed Peg could have at least thrown him a rope if he'd brought her along—whereas the pup had only stared over the edge and whined, dropping an occasional bit of drool on him. Thanks to his never-say-die DNA, it had taken him nearly half a day by his estimation to find the combination of foot- and handholds to climb out, and most of the night to limp back to his original campsite at the pool.

Duncan scratched the thick stubble on his jaw as he stared up at the crystalline blue sky dotted with puffy white clouds shaped like whales. If he believed the length of his beard, he'd been on his mountain at least five days. "So is there a reason the sky's not filled with search helicopters?" he growled. "I've been missing for five goddamned days. Or are ye all forgetting that I sign your paychecks?"

Hell, Peg could have at least been worried enough to send someone looking for him. And what was up with Alec and Robbie? He'd told them he intended to explore his mountain Sunday night. Granted, Robbie had gone home to his wife and own little heathens Sunday morning and wasn't due back until Tuesday, but this was goddamned *Friday*, so where in hell was everyone?

Duncan used his righteous indignation to propel himself upright again, then set his elbows on his bent knees to hold his head in his hands. He was going to have to stop growling at people, he supposed, so they wouldn't all be celebrating the fact the boss had gone AWOL.

"Peg could at least be missing me," he repeated out loud this time, rolling onto his hands and knees. He slowly stood up, then had to grab a nearby tree to keep from falling flat on his face before he finally felt steady enough to limp to the pool and gingerly sit down. He wrapped an arm around the pup when it came over and had to lean away when it tried to lick his face.

"Hey, you're fattening up," he said, running his fingers over its ribs. "Apparently I've managed to put some flesh back on your bones this week." He hugged the dog to him. "You'd rally the troops if I went missing, wouldn't you, because we're buddies now." He snorted. "And I feed you."

He nudged the dog away and rolled onto his side to dunk his head in the water, then rubbed his face with his hands. Slowly beginning to feel human again and really not wanting to rot here, Duncan stood up and looked around. "I guess we walk down to the shoreline and hope the scientists are more interested in studying the fiord than the main body of Bottomless," he told the dog as he started following the stream from where it spilled out of the pool.

Inglenook was on the opposite shore of Bottomless, but Peg's gravel pit was only about two miles up the fiord. "It's at least a mile across if we mosey down the shore in that direction," he told his faithful traveling companion—the one that hadn't abandoned him and had whined encouragement the entire time he'd crawled out of that hole. "But we'd have to swim across whale-infested waters to get there."

Or maybe he could signal whoever was on Peg's hillside

clearing the top off the new pit. It sure beat the hell out of walking the entire way around the fiord. His decision made, Duncan started hiking diagonally toward where he'd come ashore *five goddamned nights ago*, only to have to stop and cut himself a walking stick when his right knee kept threatening to give out.

Oh yeah, he must have really pissed off the magic at some time; probably when he'd been a full-of-himself teenager more interested in nailing every ski bunny that came to the resort instead of buckling down to learn the business he was due to take over with the other first-generation MacKeage males. He finally reached the place where he'd come ashore and stood staring across the waterway at the opposite side and snorted. He wouldn't be taking over anything anytime soon, since Laird Greylen, Grey's brother, Morgan—who was Alec and Ian's father—and his own father, Callum, showed no signs of slowing down even though Callum was in his eighties, Grey in his mid-seventies, and Morgan was turning sixty-nine later this year.

But then, the MacKeage men were *charmed*, apparently, according to their new resident wizard's bride, Miss Talks-a-lot. He couldn't believe the woman had actually told Peg he was old-fashioned.

Christ, he just wanted to fall into a soft bed and stay there until his body quit screaming. And then he was firing his entire crew for not coming to look for—

The pup started barking excitedly, snapping Duncan out of his black mood at the thought it had spotted something. He started down to what was left of the beach only to have his knee finally explode in pain, the rest of his descent made in a tumbling roll that finally ended when he slammed into an unmovable metal object.

A boat. His goddamned boat! It was sitting high and dry on a gravel bar the low tide had exposed, and when he stretched to look over the gunwale he saw his backpack and sword sitting on the floor right where he'd left them. He leaned back with a groaned sigh and didn't even try to stop the pup from licking his face. What were the chances of his boat drifting back to the exact same spot? He snorted. More likely it had been pushed here by a diabolical whale with a warped sense of humor.

"We're okay now," he murmured, finally nudging the pup away. "I'll have ye back in civilization in an hour. I'm buying you a fifty-pound bag of dog food and then I'm taking you to meet a tribe of little heathens you're instantly going to fall in love with." He grabbed the dog's snout to look him in the eye. "Ye can have the children, but I don't want ye making puppy-dog eyes at the lady, understand? If she's going to be fawning over anyone, it's going to be me. And she owes me an apple crisp today, so ye don't get under her fee—"

The sound of a racing engine pushing water made Duncan stretch to look over the top of his boat, and he spotted another small boat heading up the center of the fiord. It suddenly turned toward him, and he recognized Alec at the tiller.

"Ye have my permission to bite the bastard if ye want," he told the pup as he leaned back with another groaned sigh. "Or if that's a little too intimidating for you, ye might at least lift a leg and whiz on his boots."

The engine slowed to an idle, then shut off, and Duncan grabbed the pup when it tried to run off just as the boat scraped to a stop on the gravel bar a few yards away.

"You intend to spend the morning sitting here contemplating life, *Boss*?" Alec said, stepping onto the gravel bar. "You're late to work."

"*I'm* late?" Duncan growled. "I've been gone five god-damned days and you're just now coming to look for me?"

Alec halted in midstep, his expression going from confusion to shock. "What in hell happened to you? Ye look like ye tangled with a bear and lost."

"I fell. So where in hell have you been for the last five days?"

Alec went back to looking confused. "Five? I've been with you up until yesterday morning, when I helped ye saddle the horses for your picnic with Peg." He finished walking over and squatted down, then gave the pup a pat. "Who's your friend?"

It was Duncan's turn to be confused. "I found him when I landed here *five* days ago. So how could you have been with me yesterday morning when I was lying twenty feet down in a hole in the middle of my goddamned mountain?"

Alec shook his head and sat down to lean against the boat

beside him. "It's Monday morning, Duncan." He suddenly
straightened away to look at him. "You believe you've been
here—for Christ's sakes, ye have a *beard*." He scrambled to
his feet and stepped away before turning to look up at the
mountain, and then slowly lowered his gaze to Duncan. "You
did it; you traveled through time just like Robbie did when he
took old Uncle Ian home to the eleventh century. You just
spent five days on your mountain, but were only gone overnight in this time."

"Robbie said the magic was turned off here," Duncan
whispered, hugging the pup as he tried to decide if the notion
thrilled him or filled him with terror. "And I couldn't find
anything that might be considered an instrument of my power,
so I couldn't have turned the magic back on."

"Ye must have found something," Alec said just as softly.
"Because no one grows that kind of beard overnight, and I
swear this is Monday morning."

Duncan snorted. "I found a twenty-foot-deep hole inside
the mountain." He looked up at Alec and grinned. "And a pool
that has brook trout the size of salmon." He lifted the pup.
"And this guy. Or rather, he found me within two minutes of
my coming ashore. I think he's been stranded here since the
earthquake created the fiord."

"Can ye walk?"

Duncan shook his head. "My last fall just blew out my
knee. And if my ribs didn't get cracked when I fell down the
hole, they sure as hell feel like they are now."

Alec folded his arms over his chest and grinned down at
him. "When did you become a walking disaster? Or should I
say a *falling* disaster?"

Duncan rested his chin on his dog. "It started about half an
hour after I landed in Spellbound Falls, right about the time I
was attacked by the Thompson tribe." He snorted. "And it's
been all downhill from there." He lifted narrowed eyes to his
nephew. "It's Mac; I think he's out to get me."

"But why? He wouldn't hand you the contract of a lifetime
and then beat ye to a bloody pulp. He needs you to build his
road and prep the resort site."

"Personally, I think marriage has addled the bastard's

brain," Duncan muttered. "From what Trace Huntsman told me at the wedding, Mac not only was a confirmed bachelor, but a skirt-chaser in just about every century in recorded history."

"Like you, ye mean?" Alec drawled past his grin. "Except for the century part."

"I don't chase skirts."

"No, they chase you." His eyes lit with laughter. "Ye just don't work too hard outrunning them. Or don't you remember Jessie's friend Merissa? And then there was that woman from Greenville who slowly began moving in with you one bra and panty and bottle of shampoo at a time last winter."

"She started getting her mail delivered to my house," Duncan growled, even as he felt heat climbing up the back of his neck. Christ, he hadn't even realized what she was doing until he'd tripped over a litter box one morning despite not owning a cat. "I'm still finding stuff that belongs to her. But what in hell does any of that have to do with any of this?" he asked, waving up at his mountain.

"You said yourself that misery loves company. If Mac is happily married, he's going to make sure any skirt-chasing bachelor he comes across is going to join him in wedded bliss."

Duncan set the pup down with a snort. "He doesn't have to beat the hell out of me to get his point across," he said as he tried to grab the gunwale to pull himself up, only to fall back with a groan just as Alec rushed forward to catch him.

Alec pulled Duncan's arm over his shoulder, then grabbed his belt and lifted him to his feet. But when he couldn't even stand on his good leg, his nephew gave a sigh as he put his shoulder low on Duncan's stomach and slowly hefted him over his back.

"Dammit, my ribs," Duncan hissed, grabbing Alec's belt to hold himself away.

"Then loosen up. Christ, ye weigh a ton," Alec said on a grunt as he strode toward the boat he'd driven here. "Since ye look like you're about to pass out, I'll tow your boat back," he said as he carefully lowered Duncan into the front seat.

"At least get my sword out of it first. Come on, pup," Duncan said, patting the gunwale. The young dog just stared at him, its tail wagging frantically as it looked at the woods then back at him in indecision. "Come on," he repeated, patting the gunwale again. "T-bone steaks, little heathens, a soft bed; come on, pup."

"Maybe all it wants is to be called something other than 'pup,'" Alec said, setting the sword on the seat next to Duncan.

"I'm going to let Peg's kids name him."

"Now doesn't that sound domestic?" Alec said with a chuckle as he walked back to Duncan's boat—only to swerve at the last minute and scoop the dog up in his arms. "Easy now," he crooned, carrying it to the boat. "He's a mite scrawny, but by the look of those paws he's going to be a monster. Besides the obvious lab, what other breed does he have, do ye think?"

"Hell, the way my luck's been running, probably polar bear," Duncan said when Alec set the dog on the seat beside him. He pulled the struggling pup against his side so it wouldn't jump out, then cupped its head to his chest and stroked his thumb over its worried brow. "You're okay," he whispered. "My MacKeage word of honor; as long as there's breath in me, you'll always be safe."

Alec chuckled. "I'm guessing you'll have an easier time getting the dog to believe that vow than ye will Peg."

"Have we left yet?" Duncan snapped. "I've got eighteen men waiting on me."

Alec walked back to Duncan's boat and grabbed the bow to haul it down to the water. "They're going to have to wait a little longer, because our first stop is going to be the closest hospital I can find."

"I just need a bottle of aspirin, a soft bed, and twenty-four hours of sleep."

Alec hooked a rope onto the boat and tied it to the stern of his, then walked to the front and pushed his boat back into the water. "Not until after ye have your knee and ribs x-rayed and get a prescription for something a bit more powerful than aspirin, I'm afraid." He jumped in and lowered the motor and started it. "Dalton already has the crew hauling gravel to build the pad for our camp." He arched a brow. "I do believe you hired the man because he knows what he's doing, so let him." He turned the boat out into the fiord and slowly increased their speed to bring the second boat into line behind them, then grinned at Duncan. "And ye might want to look at how this may be a blessing in disguise."

"Blowing out my knee is a blessing?"

"It is if you're wanting the sympathy of a certain woman."

Duncan stilled. Well hell, he was right. "Works for me," he said past his grin as he gave his pup a squeeze. He looked up at his mountain. "I'll be back, you big bastard," he shouted. "So enjoy what's left of your nap."

Chapter Sixteen

─────⟨≡⟩─────

If working her children and paying them with food was against child labor laws, then she surely was headed for jail, Peg thought with a smile as she noticed Jacob and Peter eyeing their construction toys on the beach. "Okay, here's the deal," she said as she dished generous helpings of apple crisp into all five of their plates on the picnic table. "You give me two more hours at the new house after lunch, and we'll spend the rest of the afternoon playing on the beach."

Peter eyed her suspiciously. "Are you gonna play with us?"

"Yup. I'm getting right down in the dirt and showing you how to build a proper twig bridge for your road."

"Two hours?" Isabel whined. "*Mommm*, that means I'm gonna miss my show. And the only time I can watch it is during school vacation."

"The weather's too nice to be watching television, so even if we weren't working on the house you'd still have to be outside." Peg shrugged. "But if you don't want your very own new bedroom, then I guess you can sit in a chair *outside* and read a book."

"Me and Repeat don't gotta have our own new bedrooms, do we?" Peter asked for the tenth time in as many months. "I don't wanna move to that dumb house."

"Until you start whining for separate rooms, which I figure will be in a couple more years, the two of you can bunk together," Peg told him for the tenth time. She sat down in front of her plate of apple crisp—which she'd drizzled with maple syrup to practice for the one she owed Duncan this Friday. "In fact, I plan to give you each a set of bunk beds, so you can have the new friends you're going to make at school come for sleepovers."

"And Sophie can come have sleepovers with me," Charlotte said, "just as soon as we move into our new house."

"And I can have Henry come spend the night," Isabel quickly added.

"Girls don't have boys sleep over," Charlotte said before Peg could respond.

Isabel turned her questioning baby blues on Peg. "Why not, Mom?"

Yes, why not? Peg was saved from having to come up with an answer when Duncan's pickup pulled into the driveway, only she saw that Alec was driving and that Duncan appeared to be leaning against the passenger door, sleeping.

"Peg, could I speak with you a minute?" Alec asked when he got out and softly closed his door.

Peg walked over to him as she eyed Duncan. "What's up?" She smiled. "Did we wear out your boss on our picnic yesterday?"

Alec's returning smile didn't quite reach his eyes. "I wish. No, he's had a bit of an accident, which is why I have a powerful favor to ask. Don't feel ye have to say yes, though, because I can find . . . something else to do with him."

"What happened?" Peg asked, rushing to the driver's door to look in the window. The first thing she saw was that the right leg of Duncan's pants was split up to his thigh and his knee was sporting a serious-looking brace. His left hand was bandaged, there was an ugly purple bruise on his temple, and he was cradling his ribs in his sleep. She stepped back in surprise when a dog suddenly poked between the seats from in back, gave her the once-over, then crawled onto the console and carefully laid its head on Duncan's arm. She turned to Alex. "What happened to him?" she repeated.

"He fell. His ribs are bruised and he's banged up pretty

mùch all over, but at least he didn't blow out his knee like he suspected. It's only badly wrenched."

Peg clutched her throat in a futile attempt to stop all the blood from draining from her face. "Was someone chasing him? Or was he trying to stop someone from sabotaging his equipment again?"

Alec's eyes narrowed. "Now why would ye immediately jump to that conclusion?" He stepped closer and grasped her shoulders. "Ye need to tell us what happened to your van, Peg. Tell me," he softly growled, giving her a slight shake.

"I . . . I pushed it into a flooded old slate quarry," she said, glancing toward Duncan. She looked back at Alec and pulled in a deep breath. "The day you took the boys for me, I was parked down at the other end of town near the woods and someone spray-painted the passenger side."

His hands tightened. "Spray-painted what?"

She dropped her gaze to his chest, the blood rushing back to her face in a wave of heat. "It . . . it said *land-raping bitch*," she whispered.

He pulled her against him and wrapped his arms around her with a growl. "I'm sorry some coward targeted you instead of us." He clasped her shoulders again to bend down and look her in the eyes. "But I'm even sorrier that you were too . . . what, embarrassed to tell us? Or is too *stubborn* a better word?" he asked, even as he pulled her into a hug again. "Aw, Peg, ye really need to get over the notion ye can't ask for our help."

"I can't get used to asking for help," she muttered into his jacket. She looked up. "And they're just stupid words, and I didn't want . . ." She slipped an arm free and waved at the truck. "We both know Duncan would have gone looking for whoever did it and only added more fuel to the controversy." She smiled, trying to get him to smile. "And you guys are a bigger target than I am." She sighed when he scowled, and since her arm was free she patted his chest. "I'm a local, so the worst they'll do to me is spray-paint a few obscenities. But you guys are from away, so they won't care what it takes to drive you off." She looked at Duncan, then up at Alec. "Did he really just fall?"

He nodded and let her go, and finally smiled clear up to his eyes. "It seems to be an affliction he's only recently acquired."

"So what's the favor?" she asked, even though she was afraid she already knew.

"They shot him up with a powerful pain med at the hospital and sent him home with some pills, and I'm a little concerned about leaving him alone for the next couple of days. So I was hoping ye might be willing to . . . babysit him for me. You can say no," he rushed on. "I'll understand if ye don't want to deal with an invalid." He smiled again. "Although he'll be a happy invalid if you keep feeding him those pills. But staying with you is the only way I can keep him off the job site long enough to heal." He glanced toward the picnic table. "There's no school today?"

"This week is spring break, and we're all working on the new house together."

"Then don't stop." He grinned. "Duncan can watch."

Peg walked over to look in the truck. "I guess he can stay here. I've got a big old recliner at the new house he can sleep in during the day. Is he mobile enough to . . . to . . ." She sighed when she felt her face flush again.

Alec chuckled. "He can take care of himself for the most part. It's keeping him away from heavy equipment that I'm needing. But if he has you and the kids to focus on, then maybe he'll stay out of Sam Dalton's hair long enough to get the camp up and running." He turned Peg around to look at him. "I understand your concern for your mum and aunt now, and we'll keep an eye on them." His hands tightened. "And on you. But ye need to tell us if anyone even *says* anything threatening, you understand? We can't fight an enemy we can't see."

"It's only a few stupid people."

"It only takes a few." His hands tightened again. "You promise?"

She nodded, then turned away to look inside the truck again. "Where did he find the dog? It looks like it's only a pup."

"It found him, actually. He told me he intends to let your kids name it."

"Wonderful," Peg muttered as she walked back to the picnic table. "Go ahead and drive right up to the new house," she said over her shoulder. "I'll meet you there. Okay, gang, a small change in plans," she said to the four pairs of curious eyes watching Alec climb back in the truck. "Duncan fell and hurt his knee and ribs, so all of us are going to be his nurse-maids for the next couple of days while we work on the house."

"Have you noticed he falls a lot, Mom?" Charlotte said, smiling crookedly.

"Yeah, I have. But I've been told he's normally not so clumsy."

"Mom, he's got a dog!" Peter cried.

Peg turned to watch the pickup drive past and saw Alec trying to pull the pup off Duncan as it pressed its nose up to the window, trying to see them. "Yes, he's got a dog," she muttered. "Okay. I want you all to clean up the table and take everything inside. Charlie, you make sure stuff goes in the refrigerator. Isabel, put the dirty dishes in the sink, and Jacob and Peter, you wait to walk to the house with the girls because the trucks are hauling today."

Orders given, Peg picked up her untouched plate of crisp and headed toward the knoll with a sigh, wondering what she possibly could have done to deserve this.

Duncan sat in the large, overstuffed recliner in the middle of the half-constructed house, grinning like the village idiot as he wolfed down a woman-sized helping of extra sweet apple crisp and contemplated replacing Sam with Peg as his fore-man. The woman was one kick-ass delegator, and had even managed to put the pup to work.

Charlotte and Isabel were going through each of the rooms—which were separated by only studs at this point—counting the number of electrical switches and outlets on each wall and writing the number down on a paper attached to a clipboard. Jacob and Pete were sorting all the scrap pieces of lumber into two large trash buckets, agreeing and sometimes arguing over whether a piece was long enough to be used for something else or should be considered kindling for their campfires. The pup's job, apparently, was to run around the open house and lug any two-by-fours it found over to the boys.

Granted, Duncan felt a little funny just sitting there watch-ing everyone work while he stuffed his face with some of the best damned apple crisp he'd ever had—Lord, he hoped it didn't count as one of his eleven crisps—but not so much that he couldn't stop grinning. That is, until he saw Peg climb up a poor excuse for a ladder and disappear into the attic, then poke her head back down through the hole.

"Peter, go stand beside that roll of wire over on the back wall and watch as I pull it up here. If it falls off the stand, you set it back on, okay?"

"Okay," Pete said, running to where she was pointing.

Peg disappeared, and thirty seconds later Duncan saw the roll of electrical wire start to unwind. Ten seconds after that it came off the stand and Pete grabbed the broken broomstick being used as the axle and lifted it back on the stand—having to perform the job four more times before the spool stopped.

"Okay, go back to sorting wood," he heard Peg call from the attic.

Duncan looked down when his fork arrived at his mouth empty and saw it was because his paper plate was empty. After looking around to make sure everyone was busy, he lifted it to his mouth and licked off every last drop of maple syrup, along with some of the paper. He sure as hell wouldn't mind if Peg wanted to move in with him one panty and bra at a time if she made him a weekly apple crisp like this one, and he wouldn't even care if she snuck her kids in with her.

He went back to grinning like the village idiot when he heard muttering drifting down from the hole in the attic, and laced his fingers over his belly with a sigh as he felt his eyelids growing heavy—only to snap them open when something banged overhead, followed immediately by a rather colorful curse.

"Nobody heard that!" Peg hollered through the ceiling insulation. "Keep working."

Duncan ran an unsteady hand over his clean-shaven face, wondering how he was going to survive the next couple of days sitting here waiting for Peg or one of the children to get hurt.

"Mom," Charlotte called out as she started climbing the ladder. "If two wires are coming out of one of the big boxes, does that count as two switches or just one?"

"I made a place on the sheet for multiple switches, Charlie; put a check mark down for every double and triple switch you find. Same for the outlets, but you should find doubles only in the kitchen."

"I see it on the paper, Charlotte," Isabel said. "I think that word is *double*."

Duncan laced his hands over his belly again once Charlotte was safely back down the ladder and tried to think of a way he could persuade Peg to let him have his crew finish her house *before* he went insane with worry. He knew this project had become a matter of pride for her, but surely he could talk her into letting him at least help. Maybe if he told her a couple of his men were crackerjack Sheetrockers who needed a little extra work because . . . Well, he could invent them having a baby or something and needing the money. Hell, he could have her moved in here in three weeks if he dedicated several of his crewmen to the job.

Then again, maybe the house fairies could keep making special deliveries every night until it was done, because who could argue with fairies?

"Mr. Duncan," Jacob whispered from right beside him.

Duncan snapped open his eyes with a flinch, realizing the pain meds were dulling his senses. "Yeah, Jacob?" he whispered back, smiling when he saw the boy holding a fist-sized rock in his open palm.

"I sneaked outside and got this for you to hold. I got a big one 'cause your hurt looks big, so I thought a small rock wouldn't do no good. You want it?" Duncan reached out, but the boy pulled back. "Only you can't put it in your pocket when you're done rubbing it, okay, 'cause it's too big," Jacob continued in a very serious whisper, "and it'll look like your peanut's . . . you know . . . hard."

Duncan rubbed his hands over his face to stifle a bark of laughter, having to love the kid's determination to keep him civilized. He finally took the rock with his bandaged hand. "Then I definitely won't put it in my pocket," he said thickly. He reached into his jeans with his other hand and pulled out the worry stone the boy had given him last week. "I do believe that between the two of these, I should be feeling right as rain in no time. Thanks, Jacob. I appreciate the thought."

"How come you don't got any kids?"

Okay, it appeared somebody intended to take advantage of the fact the boss was out of sight. "Well, I suppose I should find a wife before I get kids, don't you think?"

"So how come you don't got a wife?"

"Because I haven't found a woman willing to put up with me long enough that I can ask her to marry me."

Duncan stifled his smile when Jacob frowned. "What's *put up with you* mean?"

"It means the women can't handle my tendency to be bossy, I guess. And I do get a little grouchy sometimes, and I've been told I'm a little scary when I'm angry."

The boy smiled. "You need to find someone like Mom. She's not afraid of no one." His eyes suddenly widened. "Hey, she could put up with you long enough for you to ask her to marry you. And then you could have your own tribe of kids. No, not tribe," he said, shaking his head. "What did you call your family the other day?"

"A clan." Duncan glanced toward the attic hole, then leaned closer to Jacob. "But just between us men, your mother sort of scares me when she gets angry."

Jacob's eyes widened again. "She does?"

Duncan nodded. "Doesn't she scare you when she gets angry?"

"Naw," the boy scoffed, even as he patted Duncan's arm. "She's just trying to act scary when she gets all scowly, 'cause she's wanting us to be good so people will know we're server-lized. She's really all soft inside." He patted Duncan's arm again. "But you gotta act afraid if she scowls at you, okay, 'cause it makes her feel good."

"I'll do that," Duncan said with a large sigh of relief. "Thanks for telling me."

"So if you ask Mom to marry you, you could come live in our new house with us. You can sleep with Pete and me, 'cause Mom's getting us our own bunk beds. That means we'll have four beds," he thought to explain.

Okay; apparently Jacob didn't have the finer points of marriage pinned down. "That's very generous of you, but usually when people get married they sleep together in the same bed," Duncan told him, figuring Peg was definitely going to get all scowly when the boy gave her that new bit of information.

Jacob's eyes widened again and he giggled. "You won't fit in Mom's bed with her. It's small like Pete and mine are."

"Really?" Duncan asked in surprise.

Jacob nodded. "How come your dog don't got a name yet?"

And that was the end of that discussion, apparently. "Well, the pup and I just met last night, and I haven't been able to think of a name for him yet. Any suggestions?"

Jacob looked at the pup that was trying to carry a piece of two-by-four lengthwise through the wall studs as Pete rushed over to turn the board so it would fit. "I think you should call him something to do with his color, like Yellow or something."

"Or we could come up with a noble name for him," Duncan suggested, just now realizing that leaving this particular job to the children might end with his owning a dog named Sue. "Because he's a really special dog. He took very good care of me when I got hurt until Alec found me. In fact, he was just like a rescue hero, so we should choose a strong, brave name for him, don't you think? I'll tell you what; why don't you and Pete and your sisters start making a list of names and then we'll all take a vote."

"Oh, we can do that," Jacob said. "Charlotte can write and everything." He beamed Duncan a bright smile. "I can write my name, and Pete can, too. And I can count to twenty and I know the whole alphelet. You wanna hear—"

"Jacob," Peg said far too sweetly, causing the boy to whip his head around. "Mr. Duncan is supposed to be having a nap, and you're supposed to be working."

"It's my fault," Duncan said. "I was just asking Jacob to help me find a name for my new pup."

"Oh, we could name him Swiper," Isabel interjected, rushing through the studs from the kitchen area. "Like the fox on *Dora the Explorer.*"

"He's not a fox and he don't steal," Pete said, dropping his piece of wood and also rushing over. "I think we should call him Fetch, 'cause he brings us wood."

Duncan didn't even try to hide his grin when Peg scowled at the sight of her crew abandoning their jobs. "Jacob was just telling me that Charlotte can write and everything," Duncan said, "so we were thinking about making a list of names and voting on them in a day or two."

"But it's gotta be a noble name," Jacob interjected. "'Cause the puppy's like a rescue hero."

"Hey, we can make him a badge just like the one we made you," Pete suggested.

"But dogs don't have wallets to carry it in," Isabel pointed out.

"No, but once we come up with a name," Duncan offered, "I could have a metal badge made for him to wear on his collar."

Peg walked over while reaching in her pocket and pulled out a small prescription bottle. "I think it's time for one of your meds," she said far too sweetly. "Charlie, could you bring Duncan a glass of water, please?"

"You do know there are child labor laws in this country, don't you?" he asked while fighting back a laugh.

"You try to unionize them and I'm going to accidentally misplace your meds," she whispered, giving him another sweet smile as she handed him a pill, making Duncan wonder if the apple crisp had tasted so good because she'd smiled at it.

"How soon before you're ready to Sheetrock?" he asked.

His sudden change of subject made her frown. "Um, just as soon as I finish insulating the exterior walls."

"I don't know if you're aware of it, but most of my men are carpenters," he said. "And when the groundwork side of my business is slow, we keep busy by building houses. In fact, we spent all this winter finishing off a million-dollar camp on Pine Lake."

He saw her cheeks flush. "This place might not be perfect, but it's completely up to state code and it's solid."

"What? No, I'm not implying . . . I didn't mean . . ." He blew out a sigh. "What I'm trying to say is that I have a couple of really good Sheetrockers who wouldn't mind earning some extra money working evenings, since they're going to be stuck here through the week. And I thought you might be interested in hiring them to rock and mud the house so all you'll have to do is paint."

Her cheeks flushed even more. "Oh. Um, yeah," she said with a nod. "That might be a good idea, actually." She smiled somewhat sheepishly. "Because I really wasn't looking forward to handling those large sheets of Sheetrock all . . . by myself," she finished lamely as she shoved his prescription bottle in her pocket and spun away. "Okay, everyone back to work."

"Peg," he said when everyone scrambled back to their assignments—after Charlotte handed him a paper cup of water and also beat a hasty retreat. Peg stopped and turned to face him. "I'm not the enemy," he said quietly. He gestured around him. "And I apologize for that comment the day you shot . . . the day I came to negotiate for your gravel. You've done a hell of a job on the house all by yourself. My crew couldn't have done any better."

"Thank you."

"And thank you for agreeing to let me stay here for the next few nights."

Her eyes widened and her face flushed again. "Nights?" she squeaked.

Duncan frowned, feeling his own cheeks darken. "I thought Alec . . . Didn't he . . . ?" Well, hell. "Never mind, I love sleeping on the ground."

Peg had her four tuckered-out babies all tucked into bed, and now she was trying to put the fifth baby to bed without hitting him over the head with a blunt object to do it. "Oh, for crying out loud, will you pull up your big-boy pants and get over yourself?" she growled, even as she wondered when her bedroom had gotten so small. Oh, that's right; it had only *seemed* larger since the last big strong man had been in it three years ago. "You'll barely fit in this bed as it is, and it won't be the first night I've slept on the couch. And there's an attached bathroom, so I don't have to worry about your shocking my daughters in the middle of the night because you forgot your *pajamas*."

Speaking of which, Peg went into the bathroom and grabbed her gown and bathrobe off the back of the door and headed toward the hallway. "Sleep tight," she said, only to gasp in surprise when a crutch shot up to block her path.

Duncan hobbled over to replace it with his body. "I apologize, Peg. I hadn't considered how difficult it might be for you to have a man in your house again. I can call Alec to come get me."

"Where's all your crew staying?" she whispered, not quite able to lift her gaze above his chest.

"Both Robbie's and my men have filled Inglenook's dormitory, and the rest are camping at the new site up the road to keep an eye on the equipment. Robbie and Alec are up on your hillside. Look at me, lass."

"I . . . I'd rather not."

He lifted her chin with his finger, his smile softening his ruggedly handsome features and making him so damned desirable that if he kissed her right now, she'd probably pass out before she remembered to punch him in his already battered belly.

"My MacKeage word of honor, I won't ever hurt ye, Peg."

"You already are, Duncan. I don't want to want you. I can't." She pulled in a steadying breath. "I meant it the other day when I said I need to stay focused on my children. Maybe in another twenty years I'll be able to think about . . . other stuff."

He leaned his crutches against the wall and pulled her into his arms, sighing into her hair as he used his chin to tuck her head against his chest. "You're forgetting about the magic, lass; the benevolent kind that makes anything possible."

Oh God, a hug was worse than a kiss, and Peg felt her eyes start to sting at how big and strong and solid he felt, and how tempted she was to just lean into him. "I really don't have time to believe in magic right now."

"Will ye at least give me a chance to show you what it's capable of? And if ye decide that you still can't believe, then I give you my word that I'll . . . walk away."

Too late; sometime when she wasn't looking, Duncan MacKeage had snuck into her heart, and just the thought of him walking away already hurt. "How about if I think about it?" she whispered. She patted his chest and leaned back to give him her best smile. "I'll let you know . . . soon."

He eyed her suspiciously. "How soon?"

She wiggled free and stepped back, clutching her gown and robe to her chest. "Well, once I know I can survive having you as a houseguest without wanting to kill you in your sleep, I suppose maybe then we could . . . you and I could . . . that we might . . ."

He grabbed his crutches with a soft laugh and hobbled toward the bathroom. "I agree; maybe we should see how the next few days go before ye finish that thought. Sleep well, lass."

Peg stood in the middle of her once again large bedroom staring at the closed bathroom door and worried that that had been way too easy. She turned and slowly walked out of the room, a little bummed that he hadn't even *tried* to steal a kiss.

Duncan stood in Peg's utterly feminine bathroom, his hands splayed on the counter as he stared into the sink wondering how he was going to explain the magic to her if he couldn't even get it to cooperate with him. He'd told Alec what he'd found on his mountain during their ride to the hospital. The ride to Inglenook to shave and get cleaned up was a bit blurry, and he couldn't even remember the ride from Inglenook to Peg's. Alec had suggested that he and Robbie go with him to the cave once he healed and help him find whatever in hell he was looking for.

Today was Monday, and his parents were coming Friday afternoon to spend the weekend—he hoped like hell the camp trailers waiting to be delivered were in place by then—so he figured he'd better be healed by Thursday night. Too bad he couldn't just go spend a week on the mountain to heal and come back tomorrow morning.

Come to think of it, he seemed to recall making that very suggestion to Alec on the ride back from the hospital. Alec had laughed and said that would ruin their plan of letting Peg fawn all over him—just before his nephew had gotten serious and said that *they* weren't going back to that mountain without Robbie, since their clan Guardian knew more about the magic than either of them did.

Duncan sighed and turned on the faucet and splashed water on his face, trying to wash away the fuzzy sensation the pain meds were causing. He stared at himself in the mirror and frowned, remembering Alec telling him about Peg's van just before she'd met them at her new house. *Land-raping bitch* some bastard had spray-painted. Hell, he didn't blame her for deep-sixing the van, but he still couldn't get past the horror of her pushing it into a flooded old slate quarry all by herself, then walking out a muddy road in a cold, pouring rain and hitching a ride to Inglenook.

Forget contrary; Peg Thompson needed a goddamned keeper.

And why in hell did the woman sleep in a twin bed?

Chapter Seventeen

Duncan expelled all the air in his lungs to unwedge himself from the narrow cave and then ran the beam of his flashlight over the rock above it, looking for signs of weakness in the granite. "Dynamite would probably work." He grinned over at Alec. "So I take back every disparaging thing I said about your going into military demolition. If I get some dynamite off the blasting contractor I hired for the road, can you get me in there," he asked, waving the flashlight at the hole, "*without* bringing the mountain down on top of us?"

"You can't be serious," Robbie said before Alec could respond. "Are ye insane, Duncan? You detonate even a small charge inside this mountain and you're going to wipe northern Maine and half of Quebec off the map. Can ye not feel the strength of the energy pulsing through the rock?"

Duncan sat down and stretched out his throbbing right leg as he leaned against the granite, rubbing his face with a muttered curse. They were so goddamned *close*. It had taken most of the night to get past the chasm, and then all day to explore the labyrinth of tunnels on the other side before they found what Duncan hoped like hell was the instrument of his power. Only they couldn't reach it because they were all too broad-shouldered to fit through the remaining twenty feet of cave.

And they couldn't actually see what they were trying to reach because the tunnel started curving sharply to the right just five feet in.

Something was in there, though, because all three of them could feel it.

"I knew we should have brought the pup," Duncan muttered. "He'd fit in there."

"And once he did, then what?" Robbie asked, sitting down across from him. "Are ye forgetting the other part of Mac's suggestion, that you bring along someone with smaller hands?" He gave a derisive snort. "I'm guessing whoever goes in there will need opposable thumbs. Ye might as well accept the obvious: Mac's determined that you involve Peg in the acquisition of your power."

"But why? Then I'll have to admit I'm a hell of a lot more than just *charmed*, and the rule is we don't expose the magic to anyone other than our spouses. And I don't need that bastard choosing who I marry, or even that I marry at all. He's supposed to be protecting our free will, and yet he's hell-bent on not giving me any choice whatsoever."

"Mac has no say about our mates," Robbie said, shaking his head. "Only Providence does, and then only to make sure the paths of two people destined to be together eventually cross. It's up to us to recognize the gift we're being given." He grinned. "But our resident wizard does have access to the knowledge contained in the Trees of Life, so he must have discovered that Peg and you are meant for each other and he's merely trying to . . . help."

Duncan hung his head in his hands even as he wondered why he wasn't more disturbed by the notion it had been written in the stars that Peg would be his. Because despite having a hard time picturing himself as some poor woman's husband, marrying this particular one meant he also became an instant father. He snorted. "So what in hell do you suppose Peg and her kids did to deserve me?" he muttered to no one in particular. "I'm the last per—"

The ground beneath them suddenly heaved in a rippling shrug just as a distant rumbling came from deep below. "I don't know about you guys," Alec said, scrambling to his feet with a laugh, "but I'm thinking we've overstayed our welcome."

"We're right behind you," Robbie shouted as the rumbling grew louder.

Duncan scrambled to his feet, but stopped to take one last glance at the end of the cave. "I'll be back you contrary bastard, and ye better be on your best behavior for my woman," he growled, turning away from the blinding light that suddenly shot from the narrow passage, the sound of raucous laughter pursuing him up the tunnel.

The three of them reached the chasm and gingerly scrambled across the bridge they'd built out of small logs that morning, and they didn't stop running until they stepped out under a nighttime sky that was actually darker than the cave had been.

"Do ye smell that?" Robbie asked, looking around. "That's smoke."

Duncan also looked around from the vantage point of their being three-quarters of the way up the mountain. "But it's not a campfire."

"There," Alec said, pointing. "Down across the fiord, do ye see that faint glow?"

"Christ, that's the pit!" Duncan snarled, already making his way into the trees. "They must have torched our equipment."

"Nay, that's not diesel fuel," Robbie said from right behind him. "That's the smell of a structure fire."

A chill unlike any he'd ever experienced ran up the length of Duncan's spine, propelling him through the darkness like a man pursued by demons—or rather like a man who suddenly knew the terror of losing all that he loved in an instant.

Peg stood beside her truck on the tote road overlooking her pit, numbed nearly insensate as she watched the flames shooting into the night sky beyond the knoll.

"Please, Mrs. Thompson, won't you at least sit in the truck where it's warm?" Sam Dalton once again petitioned.

"I'm fine, Sam," she murmured as she glanced behind her to see her children also watching the fire—the girls with an arm wrapped around each of the twins and the pup's nose pressed up against the glass between them. She looked back toward the flashing red strobes of the fire engines, hearing the distant shouts of men rising above the heavy whine of pumps pulling water out of the cove.

She'd awakened to pounding on her door a little over an hour ago and opened it to a man she didn't know. Her house in the woods was on fire, he'd told her, and he wanted her and the children out of her home on the chance the fire might spread. He'd also told her they'd already called 911, and that the rest of Duncan's crew was on their way from the campsite up the main road.

Peg had immediately gotten the children dressed and sent them to stand up on the tote road next to the fiord while she had run to the garage with her arms full of blankets. She'd driven the SUV over to the road and parked it out of the way, leaving it running with the heater on and her children safely inside. She'd spent the last hour keeping watch for Duncan, a little bummed that he hadn't come looking for her. But then, she hadn't seen him or Alec or Robbie since they'd climbed in Duncan's truck at four this afternoon—no, yesterday afternoon, as it was already breaking dawn.

"It could be an electrical fire," Sam said hesitantly, obviously at a loss for how to deal with her. "That happens more often than you know on homes under construction."

"There wasn't any power running to the house," Peg said as she continued watching the fire ravage three years of desperately hard work. "I had the temporary service cut off several years ago and used a generator when I needed power."

"Duncan had six men staying on the hillside," Sam said, "and not one of them heard anything. The two guys on watch said they didn't know anything was wrong until they saw the flames because the breeze was blowing away from them." The older man sidled closer and finally just wrapped an arm around her. "With the firemen here now, they'll be able to keep it away from your home," he assured her, his hand patting her arm. "And the fire marshal will find out what started it."

Not that it mattered, Peg thought as she stifled a sigh; because accidental or arson, her nearly finished house would still be burned down to its foundation.

Sam's arm tightened protectively when a boat suddenly came roaring into the cove from the fiord and slammed almost full length up onto the beach before three men scrambled out and started running toward the knoll.

"Duncan!" Peg shouted when she recognized them in the dawn light. She broke away from Sam and ran down the knoll. "We're up here!"

The men stopped and turned and started running toward her, Duncan stopping just in time to catch Peg when she threw herself into his arms.

"Christ, I've never been so scared in my life," he growled, hugging her tightly as he threaded his fingers through her hair to hold her against his chest. He tilted her head back. "Where are the children?" he asked thickly as he gazed up past her. She felt his chest expand and deflate on a sigh, and he squeezed her against him again. "I thought your goddamned house was on fire."

"My new house is," she said into his jacket, his arms tightening when she shuddered. She wiped her eyes and leaned back. "I brought the kids up here in case it spread." She buried her face in his chest again and wrapped her arms around him, only at the last minute remembering his sore ribs. "Can . . . Will you just hold me a minute?"

"Forever, lass." He pressed his face to her hair and squeezed her again. "Promise me everyone's okay; that the children are all okay."

"They're fine. Your men alerted us."

"What in hell happened?" he growled as he lifted his head, although his hug didn't lessen—and Peg realized he wasn't growling at her. "There were supposed to be two men on watch at all times."

"There were, Boss. And the first sign that anything was wrong was when they saw flames shooting out of the new house."

Duncan leaned away to look down at her. "I need to see the children," he said, his voice thick again as he started toward the truck with his arm around her. "They must be scared out of their minds."

Suddenly drunk with relief that he was here, Peg gave a semihysterical laugh. "Peter said he didn't want to move into that dumb old house anyway."

Duncan veered to put a tree between them and the truck and stopped, turning to palm her face and brush his thumbs over her damp cheeks. "I'll build ye a new house." He lowered his lips just shy of touching hers, the flashing lights reflecting his intense gaze. "And have ye all moved in within a month." He kissed her then, she suspected to keep her from protesting, and Peg wrapped her arms around his waist and melted into him to kiss him back—then nearly fell over when he suddenly straightened.

"*Now* ye respond?" he growled, grabbing her hand and heading up to the truck. "Hell, if I'd known that was all it would take, I'd have torched the goddamned house myself." He opened the rear hatch. "Come here, you heathens, and let me see for myself that you're okay," he said, catching Jacob when the boy threw himself at him. He tucked Peter up against his other side and pulled first Isabel then Charlotte closer and gave the four of them a hug that lasted a full minute.

Peg used the sleeve of her sweatshirt to wipe her eyes in time to see the pup trying to squeeze into the group embrace just as another pair of strong arms eased her back against a solid chest. "I'm sorely glad you're all okay, lass," Alec said, giving her a gentle squeeze. "I swear to God that was the longest boat ride I've ever taken."

Peg craned her head around to look up at him. "Where did you all go in a boat?" Alec dropped his arms and stepped away when Duncan turned to lean on the bumper with Peter and Jacob in his arms, so Peg asked him. "What were you guys doing out on the fiord?"

"We climbed a mountain on the other side," Duncan said, "so we could get a look at where we're laying out the resort road from that perspective."

"At night?"

He shrugged, shrugging both boys. "There's enough of a moon to see the contours better than in the daytime, actually. We were three-quarters of the way up one of the mountains when we smelled smoke and saw the glow of flames."

Peg looked toward the fiord, then toward her house that was nothing but billowing smoke now, and then she looked directly at Duncan. "The wind's blowing in the wrong direction for you to have smelled smoke over there."

"It must be blowing in that direction higher up," he said, giving her a wink.

"Your . . . You look like you haven't shaved in a couple of days." Peg turned to Alec. "So do you," she said, even as she realized it couldn't be true, since she'd just had lunch with them yesterday when her mom and aunt had fed both Robbie's and Duncan's crews here at the pit.

"We do go through a lot of razors," Alec drawled, rubbing his grinning jaw.

"Why don't ye shut off the truck, Peg," Duncan said, straightening to stand with the boys in his arms. "And bring those blankets so we can all sit out here together and watch the firemen work."

"Please put the boys down, Duncan," she said when Alec headed to the driver's door to shut off the truck instead. "Your ribs aren't healed enough to hold them."

"I'm right as rain, Peg," he said, his eyes lighting with the first rays of sun peeking over the mountains across the fiord. He gave the boys a jostle. "In fact, I do believe I've never felt better in my life."

Charlotte and Isabel jumped out of the back, dragging the blankets with them, causing the poor pup to tumble out of the truck with a yelp of surprise. Duncan walked over and set the boys down, took one of the blankets and folded it lengthwise on the ground, and then sat down on it. He leaned against the truck and patted the blanket on either side of him. "Come on, people; I need to borrow some of your body heat."

Peg stood blinking at him as Alec walked up to her. "What he's needing is to hold ye all, lass," he said softly, giving her a nudge. "It was a hell of a boat ride."

Robbie came striding up the knoll just as all four children did indeed cuddle up to Duncan, apparently needing him as well. Robbie silently shook his head at Peg to let her know her house was a complete loss, then looked at Duncan. "There's something I think ye might want to see," he said quietly.

"Whatever it is can wait," Duncan said, snagging Peg's hand. He moved Jacob and Peter onto his lap and pulled her down beside him. "Charlotte, hand me that other blanket, would ye, lass?" He then tucked Charlotte up against his side next to Isabel and covered them all with the blanket, wrapped one arm around Peg and one around the girls, and pulled them all together with a sigh—the group hug completed when the pup landed on top of the blanket and flopped down with a doggy sigh of its own.

"Go away, you two," Duncan said to Alec and Robbie, who were both grinning at the picture they must have made. "We'll be right here when Jeanine and Bea have breakfast ready." He sighed again when Peg tucked her head in the crux of his shoulder. "Just have them feed the firemen before they feed our crews."

Oh yeah, Peg thought with a sigh of her own; a hug from a big strong man was exactly what they all needed this morning.

Chapter Eighteen

Since her beachfront was full of men gathered around a campfire, Peg sat on her deck steps waiting for Duncan to get through talking to his newly returned crew before she rode into town with him to attend the hastily scheduled Sunday night meeting. Folks in and around Spellbound Falls had decided it was time to openly discuss the little resort problem that seemed to be growing into a *big* problem, considering the fire marshal had declared her early Friday morning fire had been arson.

There had still been puffs of smoke wafting up from the ruins of her burned-down-to-its-foundation house when Duncan had Peg's property turned into Fort Thompson; complete, she was afraid, with armed guards. Honestly, all that was lacking were cannons, and she wouldn't be surprised if one of those showed up in the back of someone's pickup next week. Three of the ten bunkhouse trailers and Duncan's own private trailer slated for the camp up the road were now parked at her pit instead, all plumbed into her newly expanded septic system—she had no idea how he'd gotten *that* permit in only six hours—and tapped into her well.

Come to think of it, Peg couldn't remember Duncan asking *her* permission, either, but she wasn't complaining because she liked feeling safe when she flopped into her tiny bed, which Duncan had finally vacated Thursday. Except now he was sleeping on the other side of her bedroom wall in his private bunkhouse—that he'd perfectly aligned so their bedroom windows faced each other.

Peg's neighbors to the west weren't very happy with all the activity so close to their . . . garden, although Evan and Carl had come over to say they certainly didn't mind waiting until that gosh-dang arsonist was caught before they put out this year's crop of hardy seedlings.

Her children were taking losing their new house fairly well, with no obvious signs of distress or lingering fear, likely because all the activity had created quite a distraction. Well, that and Duncan's parents had been spoiling them rotten for the last two days.

Callum and Charlotte MacKeage had arrived Friday afternoon, only to have their son introduce them to Peg and the kids then rush back into the chaos issuing orders—after, that is, he wolfed down half a pan of maple-glazed apple crisp smothered in whipped cream. Callum had also eventually moseyed away, and Peg had watched in awe as he'd pulled a virtual town of small buildings out of the back of his truck, carried them down to the beach where Peter and Jacob were playing, and the three of them had gotten really serious about the twins' construction project.

Charlotte had divided up what was left of the crisp among Peg, her girls, and herself, and they'd spent the afternoon ignoring the fortress being built around them as they'd all gotten to know one another. That's why Peg didn't have any problem letting Callum and Charlotte babysit her heathens tonight while she went to the town meeting with Duncan. The meeting that was slated to begin in two hours, she realized as she glanced down at her watch, which meant they needed to leave now if they wanted to stop by the Drunken Moose first.

She fidgeted with the strap of her purse as she watched Duncan in the last rays of the setting sun quietly talking to his men sitting around the campfire. His feet were slightly spread as he stood with his arms folded over his chest in a stance of authority, and Peg felt her insides suddenly clench.

Damn, her desire for him was starting to get out of control, and Peg was worried she was going to act on it one of these days. She sighed, resting her chin on her fists as she continued watching Duncan. He hadn't stolen any more kisses since the morning of the fire, when he'd gotten all growly because she'd finally kissed him back. Granted, her house had been burning down to its foundation at the moment, but he'd felt so solid and strong and invincible, and she'd been so scared and needy. All she'd wanted to do was lose herself in the passion that had been building inside her for the last three nights he'd been sleeping in her bed, while she'd been out on the couch wanting to be in there with him.

Peg stood up when she saw him striding toward her and slipped her purse over her shoulder with a fortifying breath. She walked to her SUV, brushing down the front of her old spring jacket in an attempt to appear nonchalant. The last thing she needed was for him to see how scared and needy she still was, considering this was the first time since their picnic, when Duncan had declared she wouldn't always have the twins stuck to her like glue, that they would actually be alone together.

Peg dropped the truck keys into his outstretched palm without so much as even a scowl and climbed in the passenger side of her SUV when he politely opened the door. Because honestly, not only did she know better than to argue with an old-fashioned man, she kind of wanted to pretend this was a date, even if they were only going to a town meeting. But taking her to the Drunken Moose for a piece of Vanetta's famous blueberry pie first was sort of like a date, wasn't it?

At least it was according to Charlotte, who'd managed to find a pair of actual dress slacks in the back of Peg's closet, and then insisted Peg wear the top from one of her funeral outfits with them along with the small pearl earrings her short-lived stepdad had given Peg for her wedding. So she was dressed like she was going on a date, she decided as she watched Duncan walk around the front of her truck, even though he was wearing jeans, a heavy chambray shirt under his leather jacket, and work boots.

He climbed in behind the wheel with a chuckle when he

caught her glancing toward the house. "Your babies will be fine. They have the movies Mom brought that they can watch together, and if those fail, Dad's one hell of a storyteller."

"Actually, it's your parents I'm worried about," she said with a sigh. "Peter and Jacob like to pretend they're each other just to mess with people, and sometimes Isabel can be . . . well, Isabel."

"I believe they can handle your heathens," he drawled as he turned the truck onto the main road and accelerated.

Peg folded her hands on her lap so he wouldn't see them trembling as she once again reminded herself this was *not* a date. "They really didn't have to stay a day longer than they'd planned. My mother-in-law said she could watch the kids tonight."

"Mom and Dad are in no hurry to leave." He smiled over at her. "When Dad saw my crew returning this evening, he said he wanted to stay and watch the big boys play with the big toys tomorrow."

"I can't believe he got down in the dirt to help the twins expand the town they're building. You said he's eighty-two." Peg shook her head. "I think that's a flat-out lie, because that would mean he was what . . . nearly fifty when you were born?"

"Forty-eight, actually. Dad is Mom's second husband and I'm her second family. In fact, Alec's mom is my half sister, which makes my mom his grandmother and me his uncle. And his dad and my dad are cousins, so Alec and I are also cousins." He grinned at her again. "We're all just one big happy clan. Now, about your new house; have ye decided yet to let me build it?"

"You don't think you'd be spreading yourself too thin, what with building a road and then the resort site itself up on the mountain for Mac?"

He waved the fingers on his hand holding the steering wheel. "I can do it all. Like I said, the men will welcome the extra income. And I agree you should set the new house on the tote road overlooking the fiord. The old site was good, but that was before you had oceanfront property."

Peg leaned back against the headrest with a sigh. "Yeah, I like the idea of building it there so we'll be able to watch the sunrise from our kitchen table." She glanced over at him. "And with the insurance money, I might be able to afford to have you build a house for me. As long as you let me do the electrical wiring," she added, smiling when she saw his jaw go slack.

But then he snorted and shook his head. "Why am I not surprised?" He held his hand toward her. "Okay then, deal? I'll build your house."

She also reached out, but stopped short of actually shaking on it. "It's a deal if the bid you give me is in line with Grundy Watts's."

He snapped his hand away. "You're taking *bids*?"

Peg looked down to hide her smile and brushed absolutely nothing off her jacket. "Is that a problem?"

"No, it's not a problem at—" He stopped in midsentence and frowned into the rearview mirror. "Do ye recognize the truck pulling up behind us?"

Peg craned around in her seat to look out the rear window and also frowned when she saw the old pickup closing in on them rather quickly. "It . . . I'm pretty sure that's Chris Dubois's truck." She spun around with a gasp when Duncan put on the brakes with a muttered curse to avoid hitting another pickup that suddenly pulled out in front of them. It straddled the center of the road, and she saw the brake lights come on as it slowed down enough to make Duncan brake again.

"Check that your seat belt is secure," he growled as he quickly glanced in his rearview mirror before stepping on the gas again. "Christ, it's an actual ambush. Hold on." He pressed the accelerator to the floor and the SUV surged forward.

Peg grabbed the handle above her door with one hand and covered her mouth with the other so she wouldn't scream when Duncan drove the SUV's right front bumper into the left rear fender of the pickup in front of them. With the sickening sound of metal making contact overriding her scream, he then cut the wheel to the right without letting up off the gas until the pickup started to fishtail. He immediately slammed on the brakes only to step on the gas again, pulling around the pickup when it swerved toward the ditch, his eyes going to his rearview mirror with another curse.

Peg looked out her side window as they sped past the now stopped pickup to see Aaron Jenkins's widened eyes staring back at her. She craned around to look between the seats to see Chris Dubois speeding toward their rear bumper, Aaron pulling back onto the road behind him.

"I can't believe they're doing this!" she cried, turning forward and grabbing the handle over her door again as Duncan floored the SUV. "Why on earth are they attacking us? Oh God, Duncan, can we outrun them?"

"Not by the sounds of that motor in the truck behind us; it's obviously been tricked out, and I told ye this one was bought for its economy."

Not that her poor beautiful truck seemed to know it was supposed to be a dog, she thought hysterically as the trees zoomed past her side window. "Why is Chris doing this?" she repeated without really expecting an answer.

"What do ye know about the bastard?"

"Um, he was a year ahead of me in school, and he tried to get me to date him, but I already had my eyes on Billy." She snorted. "Chris was a braggart and a sleaze even back then. He's also Spellbound Falls's most notorious criminal, although he never seems to get caught. But if there's a way to make money, illegal or not, he'll have his hand in it. I heard in town that he and Aaron Jenkins—he's the guy in the other truck— are all fired up over the resort, claiming it's going to end their logging business. I suspect it was one or both of them who spray-painted my van, because I know they were in town that day. Chris has always been pissed that his mother sold Billy and me the pit, because he thought he should get it."

Peg realized she was on the verge of hysteria when she couldn't seem to stop babbling. "Chris started dropping by not six months after Billy died, trying to get me to go out with him. But I knew he was more interested in getting his hands on my land than on me—although that didn't stop him from trying."

Duncan glanced over sharply. "Did he get aggressive with you?"

Peg dropped her gaze and shuddered. "A bit," she whispered. She turned in her seat to look out the rear window again and saw Chris trying to pull around them as Duncan veered to the center of the road. "I never thought he'd do something this bold, or get so fired up over a stupid resort. He and Aaron must be drunk."

"This isn't about the resort, Peg," Duncan said quietly. "It's about you. Not only did you reject him twice, the bastard's seeing you making money off land he thinks should be his." He glanced at her briefly before going back to watching his rearview mirror and the road, and shook his head. "He's likely the one who burned down your house. This has nothing to do with the resort," he repeated.

"Ohmigod, I never—" She snapped her mouth shut when the SUV lurched forward with a violent shudder and fishtailed slightly before Duncan brought it under control, Peg's scream lost in the sound of Chris's pickup slamming into the back of them. "No!" she cried, bracing her hand on the dash when Duncan slammed on the brakes, which made Chris ram into them again.

Tires screeched and she smelled burning rubber as Duncan kept braking despite the deafening rev of the pickup's engine as it continued trying to push them down the road. Duncan finally brought them to a stop and slipped the SUV into reverse, hit a button on the dash, and stepped on the gas. "Face forward," he snapped as he grabbed the back of her seat to look behind him. "And hang on."

"Duncan, no! Just try to outrun them. Please, we're almost to town." But the screeching tires drowned out her petition as the SUV relentlessly backed up, first slowly and then with increasing speed as it pushed against Chris's truck.

"He might have more engine but we're heavier," Duncan growled just as he let up off the gas. "Cover your face with your hands."

He then stepped on the accelerator again as he cut the wheel and rammed into the pickup behind them, the sound of crunching metal slamming through the interior of the truck as its tires continued to grasp for purchase on the pavement. Peg heard what sounded like glass breaking and slouched down in her seat to peek through her fingers at her outside mirror to see the taillights of Chris's truck sticking out past their rear fender, and she realized Duncan was pushing him sideways down the road.

She then saw smoke rolling up over the front fender of the SUV and realized he had it in four-wheel drive. She moved her hands to cover her ears against the deafening screech, but then quickly covered her mouth to catch her scream when they suddenly stopped and she watched in the mirror as Chris's truck rolled into the ditch onto its side.

Duncan hit the button on the dash and pulled the gearshift down and floored the engine again, snapping Peg back against the seat when the truck lurched forward and once again sped toward town. She turned to look back between the seats and just caught a glimpse of Chris jumping out of his truck and hopping into Aaron's before Duncan pushed her back around.

"Face forward," he growled, glancing in the rearview mirror. "It's not over."

Peg buried her face in her hands again and mumbled something.

"What was that?" he asked in another growl.

She dropped her hands, then used the sleeve of her jacket to wipe her eyes. "I . . . I said I'm glad I didn't insist on driving tonight."

He snorted. "Not as glad as I am." He reached over and actually patted her arm. "Now do ye see what I meant about this truck being safe?"

"I . . . It's all but totaled," she whispered, looking at the crumpled front fender as the trees sped past in a blur again.

"I'll buy ye a new one." He blew out a harsh breath and seemed to relax slightly. "The other truck doesn't have the balls to catch us, so we should make it to town okay." He glanced over at her, then back at the road. "I believe I'll park behind the church," he said, apparently voicing his plan as it came to him. "And we'll go for a walk on the docks behind Ezra's store to calm down instead of going to the Drunken Moose."

"Works for me," Peg said, releasing at least some of her tension with her sigh. God, her clothes were soaked with sweat and she was worried she might have peed a little. She sucked in another shuddering breath and covered her face with her hands again even as she wished she kept a diary. Because honestly, as *sort of* first dates went, this one definitely needed to be recorded . . . somewhere.

Duncan pulled her hands down and held on to the one nearest him, giving it a gentle squeeze before rubbing his thumb on her knuckles. "Ye did good, Peg. I only heard one little scream," he said, smiling over at her.

She pulled in another steadying breath and brushed nothing off her jacket with a trembling hand. "You just couldn't hear all of them over the screeching tires and smashing metal." She finally found the nerve to glance over her left shoulder, then quickly looked forward again, but it had been long enough for her to see the back hatch was folded in, the rear and both side back windows were blown out, and the third brake light was flapping in the breeze as it dangled from the top of the mangled back door.

"You do know that even though your mom signed the title over to me Friday, that I haven't had time to register or insure the truck yet, don't you?"

He gave her hand another squeeze. "It'll be covered under her policy, and I was the one driving."

"There's a good chance the sheriff will be at the meeting tonight because of the controversy," she said, "especially since the fire marshal decided my house fire was arson. We can tell him what happened tonight and he can arrest Chris and Aaron. I definitely recognized them. Um, but let's not tell him about my van, okay?"

"Why?" he asked, slowing down because they'd reached the edge of town.

"I don't think it's all that legal to push a vehicle into a flooded quarry pit." She finally felt relaxed enough to smile. "Although they'd probably have to sift through a bunch of other vehicles looking for it, along with all sorts of other stuff people have wanted to disappear. I read where the state sent divers down in a quarry south of here several years back, and they found over twenty cars and trucks, several motorcycles, lawnmowers, tractors, snowmobiles, and even a skidder; anything a person could file an insurance claim on was down there."

Duncan gave her one last squeeze and put both hands on the wheel as he gave the rearview mirror a glance, then slowed to an idle as they came into town. "I'm glad it's dark enough that no one will notice the condition of the truck," he said, pulling into the church parking lot and driving down past it. "We really don't need an audience," he added as he pulled around the back of the church and eased the nose of the truck into the bushes. He shut it off, unfastened his seat belt, and turned to her. "Are your legs steady enough for a short walk, lass?"

Peg unfastened her seat belt. "What, you think that little carnival ride rattled me?" She opened her door and slid out, only to yelp when she kept right on sliding—only to be snatched up and hauled back into her seat.

"Aye, I can see how unrattled ye are," he said with a laugh. "Stay put."

He got out and walked around the truck, his face completely serious when he reached her door. "Do me a favor and just walk away without looking back, okay?"

"It . . . it's that bad?"

He nodded and took hold of her shoulders and slid her out, then pulled her into his embrace. "I'm sorry, Peg. But ye need to give the truck credit for keeping us safe." He turned while slipping his arm around her with his hand grasping her waist, closed her door, and started walking toward Bottomless only a few yards away.

"My purse."

She heard the truck give a mournful beep and realized he'd pressed a button on the key fob in his pocket. "We'll get it later. I was wondering," he said conversationally, "if you've given any more thought to believing in the magic?"

Okay; mundane conversation was good. "Well, I might believe," she said, wrapping her arm around his waist when she realized she really was wobbly, "if a house fairy were to make a special delivery up on that knoll overlooking the fiord."

His arm around her tightened and he steered her toward the path that ran behind the stores. "The magic prefers to be more subtle, I'm afraid, and having a house standing on a lot that was vacant the day before is a bit much. I was thinking more along the lines of the kind of magic a person feels when they realize they're right in the middle of something wonderful happening."

She looked up at him and smiled. "You mean like walking

into a hospital to give birth to your third child and walking out with two babies?"

He looked down in surprise. "Ye didn't know you were having twins?"

"Nope. We were all set to bring Peter home, but when Jacob popped out, Billy shouted, 'Oh God, it's a repeat!' That's how the poor kid got his nickname." She smiled up at him again. "Is that the kind of magic you're talking about? Because personally, I don't think there's anything subtle about having twins when you're not expecting them."

He turned them onto a newly constructed boardwalk stretching across the low tide and continued down to a set of floating docks. "Maybe not subtle," he said with a chuckle, "but ye have to admit it counts as something wonderful." He stopped, turning her to face him. "That's the magic I'm talking about; wonderful . . . surprises." His grip on her shoulders tightened slightly, and there was just enough moonlight for her to see the planes of his face grow more pronounced. "I've a favor to ask ye, lass."

Peg tensed at the seriousness she heard in his voice. "What?"

"I would ask that ye trust me enough to get in a boat and go for a little ride with me." He grinned, but it didn't come anywhere near his eyes, and his grip tightened again when she tried to step away. "I was going to ask you to go after the meeting, but I believe it would be best if we leave right now."

"Go where?"

"To my mountain. Can ye trust me enough to willingly get in the boat, Peg?"

She dropped her eyes because she couldn't quite face the intensity in his any longer. For the love of God, what was he doing? "I . . . I'd rather not. I feel just fine now, Duncan," she rushed on, looking back up at him. "And we need to tell the sheriff what just happened."

He pulled her forward into an unbreakable embrace the moment she tried to pull free, and Peg felt his chest expand on a heavy sigh. "I'm sorry, lass," he murmured as one of his hands slid up her back to her neck. "Christ, I'm sorry," he growled against her forehead just as Peg felt pressure on the base of her neck and her legs buckled and everything went black.

Chapter Nineteen

Duncan was so goddamned sorry he was shaking with anger—
at himself, at his mountain, and at Providence for giving him
such a contrary woman. But mostly he was angry at Mac for
orchestrating this entire mess and then walking away. The bastard better hope he *didn't* find the instrument of his power, because he was going to use it to blow the top off Mac's mountain
and then his own and cave them into that damned fiord. Duncan
gave one last glance around as he sped up the mirror-calm waterway past the pit, then looked down at Peg cradled against his
chest. Christ, she appeared so damned vulnerable, he wanted to
roar for what he was doing to her.

She'd dressed up tonight—more for him than for the meeting, he was afraid. He really wished she hadn't, though; she
needed rugged clothing for their little . . . adventure. He
snorted, wondering if she'd see it as something magical or a
short vacation in hell.

He had clothes for her in the backpack he'd stashed in the
front of the boat this afternoon when he'd rented it off Ezra.
A bigger boat this time, and faster. He'd packed two outfits
for Peg because he didn't know if they'd be gone a day or a
week, but he'd purchased them at a store in Turtleback so Ezra
wouldn't get suspicious of his shopping for women's clothes.

He leaned forward to glance down at her feet, hoping he'd bought the correct size boots. He was thankful he'd thought of them at the last minute, seeing how she was wearing shoes with a slight heel.

She was going to kill him when she woke up, then probably tie a rock around his neck and deep-six him just like she had her van. Hell, he was tempted to save her the trouble and jump in the water right now and hope the whale swallowed him whole. Surely Peg was capable of driving the boat back *all by herself.*

Duncan broke into a cold sweat as he pictured her crawling into that cramped cave—out of his sight, knowing he couldn't get to her if something happened.

Oh yeah, he had already damned himself to hell, but did he really have to take her with him? He had, in fact, decided not to when she'd handed over the keys to her truck and climbed in without so much as a scowl. And his decision had been re-inforced when she'd gotten all sassy about letting him build her new house. But then they'd been ambushed and Duncan had realized Peg was the target, and he'd known deep in his gut that he couldn't keep her safe without the magic. But to get it *before* all hell broke loose, according to Mac, he needed her less broad shoulders and smaller hands.

Dubois and Jenkins were loggers as well as what passed for local hoodlums, and if they decided they didn't want to be arrested, an army of sheriffs wouldn't be able to find them. Duncan was pretty sure the magic could, though, once he got his hands on it and accepted his calling—whatever in hell his calling was.

He'd had a long talk with Ian when he'd gone home last weekend, and his nephew had told him that he hadn't known he'd had a calling, either, until good old Roger de Keage had all but hit him over the head with it. But Ian had assured Duncan that the moment he'd touched the staff Roger had given him, he'd instantly understood the full scope of his power and how to control it.

Christ, he hoped that's how it was going to work for him, because he really needed some clarity about what he was doing. He sighed, wondering if Peg might be willing to watch sunsets instead of sunrises from her kitchen window, because he was pretty sure he needed to build their home on the seat of his power.

Duncan felt her stir and instantly stiffen, obviously so scared that she didn't dare move even a muscle. He slowed the boat to an idle then shut off the engine, and gently cupped her face to look at him. "I'm sorry for putting ye out like that," he said as he brushed his fingers over her forehead, hoping she could see his smile in the moonlight. "I'm guessing ye have one hell of a headache, but I thought it would be less traumatic than a rope and gag."

Okay, that probably wasn't the brightest thing to say, seeing how she shrank away from his touch and stopped breathing, the moonlight showing the terror in her eyes. He sighed again and slowly sat her up on the floor in front of him—ready to grab her if she decided jumping in the water might be preferable to being in the boat with him. "This isn't what it seems, lass. I'm not really kidnapping—well, okay, I am, but not to do ye any harm. I have a powerful favor to ask, but I . . . You're going to have to trust . . . Aw, hell, Peg," he growled, scrubbing his face with his hands. "My word of honor, I'll have ye back home safe and sound an hour after sunrise."

She scrambled away with a gasp until she bumped into the next seat. "I can't be gone all night. My children!"

"They're perfectly safe with Mom and Dad."

"But your parents are expecting us back no later than ten!"

He shook his head. "I told Dad that if we're not home by eleven, then we won't be back until morning."

"Your *father* knows you're doing this to me?" She dropped her gaze to his feet. "Please, Duncan, just take me home."

"I promise I will—in the morning." He reached forward to lift her chin. "But ye need to know that the magic's going to make it seem like we're gone for several days."

She gasped again, clutching her coat closed at her throat as her eyes searched his. "Are you insane or am I?"

"Do you remember the night of the fire when Robbie and Alec and I arrived by boat, and ye noticed we all had the beginnings of beards?"

He saw confusion replace some of her fear as she slowly nodded.

"That was because we'd been on the mountain across the

fiord for two and a half days even though we'd left you just the afternoon before."

"That's not possible."

"It is for the magic, lass. Because remember I told you that even if ye don't believe, the magic goes about its business anyway?"

She dropped her gaze to his feet again, saying nothing— only to suddenly scramble toward him when something gently bumped the boat and surfaced right beside them. "Ohmigod, what is that?"

She was squeezing his neck so tightly, Duncan couldn't help but smile that she was more afraid of things that went bump in the night than of him, apparently. "That would be a big old whale with a warped sense of humor." He pried himself free, then turned Peg to put her back to his chest and wrapped his arms around her. "He's just wanting to meet you, since I've told him all about this amazing woman I've been trying to catch the eye of." He tightened his arms against her trembling. "I'm not sure if this is the same one or not, but a friend of Mac's from Midnight Bay told me about this giant whale named Leviathan. Trace said he actually met Leviathan up close and personal one day, and that the beast is quite . . . friendly. He's not going to hurt us, Peg. He's just wanting to say hello."

"P-please take me home," she softly petitioned.

"In the morning," he repeated, lowering her to sit between his legs. Keeping a hand on her shoulder, he reached back and started the engine. "I promise to have ye home before your children wake up."

So with Peg huddled on the floor in front of him hugging herself and occasionally rubbing her forehead, Duncan resumed his trip at full throttle, not slowing down until he spotted the once again fully formed beach. The whale slipped back from keeping pace with them when Duncan shut off the engine and lifted the motor, and silently sank beneath the surface as they drifted up onto the gravel.

Peg didn't move, and apparently wasn't even willing to look at him. Duncan walked past her and climbed out and dragged the boat farther up onto the beach, then grabbed the rope on the bow and tied it to the closest tree. He took his sword out and slipped it on over his shoulders, then grabbed the backpack and extended his free hand. "Come on, Peg."

She still didn't move except to curl into a tighter ball.

"The sooner we get going, the sooner you'll be home, lass." He sighed when she still refused to move. "And the more cooperative ye are, the less of a bastard I'll be."

She finally lifted her head. "You promised never to hurt me."

"I'm trying to keep that promise by keeping you safe, but I need to get hold of the magic to do that."

"W-what's the favor you want from me?"

He dropped his hand. "There's something I'm needing that's in a cave up on the mountain behind me, but my shoulders are too broad to reach it. Wait; you aren't claustrophobic, are you?" he asked, just now realizing that might be a problem. "Because there's about twenty or thirty feet of the cave that's quite narrow."

She immediately nodded. "Yes. Yes, I'm scared to death of tight places," she blatantly lied. "I just freeze up and can't move." She lowered her gaze and shrugged her shoulders. "So I guess I can't help you, so you might as well take me home." But curiosity apparently getting the best of her, she looked up again. "Um, what is it that you wanted me to get for you?" she asked, her gaze lifting to the mountain behind him. "Gold? Or tourmaline? Did you find a gem mine or something?"

"I doubt it's gems," he said, shaking his head. "I'm not exactly sure what's in there because I can't actually see it, because the cave curves too sharply."

"Then how do you know something's even there?" she snapped.

Duncan ran a hand over his jaw to hide his grin, glad to see she was finally tired of being afraid. "I just know. I can feel its energy."

She snorted and settled back against the side of the boat and hugged her knees to her chest. "Then I guess you're going to have to ask some narrow-shouldered fairy to crawl in there and get it for you."

"Christ, you're contrary," he muttered, dropping the backpack. He walked along the boat, reached in, plucked her out, and stood her on her feet, then bent to get right in her face.

"We can do this the hard way if you insist, just so long as you realize we're not leaving here until I have what I came for— even if it takes a *month*. You really want to be away from your children that long?"

"Fine," she growled, jerking away and striding toward the woods. She waved over her shoulder. "Just so *you* realize that I'm pressing kidnapping charges against you the moment we get back." She stopped and turned and even pointed a finger at him—which he happened to notice was trembling. "And I'm chaining off the pit, and if I ever see you on my land again, I'm digging out my shotgun."

That said, she spun around and strode up into the trees, and Duncan finally let his grin escape as he wondered how long before Peg realized she didn't know where to go. He walked over and snatched up the backpack and followed, only to find her standing in the middle of the bed of moss hugging herself as she looked around.

"The cave's three-quarters of the way up the mountain," he said, dropping to one knee beside her and opening the backpack. "I've brought ye a change of clothes and some sturdy boots that you might want to put on before we start the hike up."

She turned to face him and stepped back. "You've had this *planned*?"

He pulled a pair of jeans and a sweatshirt out and set them on the ground. "For a few days," he said with a nod. He looked up at her. "I came over here twice before; first trying to find what I was looking for, and then with Alec and Robbie. The first trip is when I found the pup and also when I fell into a hole inside the mountain. The last time was the night your house burned. I had hopes of reaching my . . . instrument of power without involving you, but it seems Mac has made that impossible."

She took another step back. "What does Mac have to do with this?"

Duncan sat down and patted the moss beside him. "Come here, Peg, and I'll tell you a fantastical tale that might help make sense of what we're doing."

She did sit down, but on the other side of the backpack. "If you think I'm going to— What is that noise I keep hearing?" she asked suddenly, looking around. "It sounds like breathing or . . . snoring or something. Only it's seems to be coming from everywhere."

Duncan rolled to his knees in front of her. "You can *hear* that?" He grabbed her shoulders. "Truly, Peg, you can hear the mountain?"

She shrank away from him. "The mountain?" she whispered, looking around again. "You think it's *breathing*? You . . . you hear it, too?"

He pulled her into his arms and kissed the top of her head. "Ah, lass, ye have no idea how relieved I am that you can sense the mountain's energy." He tilted her head back, although he couldn't see her that well because they were in the woods. "That's the magic, Peg. That's what I've been talking about." He hugged her to him again. "And you can feel it."

"Mountains don't breathe," she muttered, pushing against his chest. She bent her knees when he let her go and wrapped her arms around them, apparently to keep him from hugging her again. "Mountains are inanimate objects made of rock and dirt and granite."

"Tell the good people of Spellbound Falls they're inanimate," he said with a chuckle, sitting down beside her. "Because I'm pretty sure some of these mountains picked themselves up and *moved* about a month ago." He rested his arms on his knees and looked toward the fiord. "Nothing's inanimate, lass; quantum physics has already proven that much. Everything, even something as solid as granite, is nothing but pure energy." He gestured behind him even though he wasn't certain she could see it. "This mountain is very much alive, but at the moment it's . . . napping."

"Okay," she said with a snort. "Now you're just messing with me." She picked up the clothes he'd set beside the pack and scrambled to her feet. "I have no idea why you're so all-fired determined to make me believe mountains breathe and there's something on this one that you— Um, Duncan?" she suddenly whispered in midsentence. "How did you pick out what size clothes to bring for me?"

He frowned up at her; enough moonlight reflecting off the water for him to see that she'd dropped the shirt and was holding the jeans up by the waist. "I guessed, mostly. I wear a thirty-eight waist, and figured since you're about half my size that you'd wear an eighteen or twenty."

"You got me size *twenty* clothes?" she cried. She stepped up and held the jeans spread open in front of his face. "Do you honest to God think my ass is that wide?" she growled, shaking the pants at him.

Duncan snagged them out of her hands so she would quit hitting him with them. "I *think* that's a loaded question coming from a woman," he growled back, even as he held the pants up and realized they'd likely fall off *him*. "Why in hell are they bigger than mine if the number is less than half my waist size?"

She snatched them back. "Because women don't like wearing big numbers on our asses." She shook the jeans at him again. "Did you even unfold them to see if they at least looked like they'd fit me?"

Duncan dropped his chin to his chest to hide his grin. Christ, she was in a full-blown rage, and all over the size of a pair of jeans. But at least she was through being afraid of him—although she may be planning his death, he realized when she hurled the jeans at his head.

"Did you even look at them?" she repeated.

"Not closely," he muttered, tossing the pants over his shoulder into the trees. "Wait, check out the other pair. I had the salesgirl go get them when I realized I should bring two changes of clothes, and I told her that you were just about her size. Maybe she grabbed smaller ones. Here," he said, opening a side pocket on the pack and handing her a headlamp. "Put this on so you can see what you're doing."

She turned on the light, slid it on her head, and adjusted the straps, then pointed the three LED bulbs directly at him, making Duncan have to lift his hand before he went permanently blind. "Thanks," she said far too cheerily, turning to look down into the top of the pack—which thankfully took the lights off him.

He heard her sigh just before she sat back on her heels holding the other jeans and blinded him again. "The only reason you're not dead right now is because the salesgirl was a size smaller than me." She straightened to her knees and trained the light into the pack again, then reared up with a gasp when her hand came out holding a box.

Duncan closed his eyes when he saw what she was holding. "I . . . ah . . . I had a worry that it might be your time of the month."

"Please tell me you didn't buy this stuff from Ezra," she whispered.

"Nay, I shopped in Turtleback Station."

She dropped the box on the moss with a snort, then pulled two pairs of thick wool socks out of the pack, another sweatshirt—that he was afraid was size twenty—and finally the boots. She peeled back the tongue on one of them and shone the light inside before tossing them down. And then he heard her gasp again as her hand emerged with a pair of panties dangling from her finger.

"These you get in a size *four*?" she growled, blinding him with light as she shoved the scrap of lace in his face.

He snatched the panties away and shoved them in his pocket. "What in hell size do ye wear, then?"

He didn't know how she did it, but her nose lifted in the air even while she still managed to keep the headlamp blaring at him. "Women do not discuss their sizes with men. I can't wait to see what you got me for a bra," she said, training the light down inside the pack again.

Duncan tried to stifle his chuckle but out it came anyway, although he was afraid it sounded more nervous than humorous. "I didn't get ye a bra."

"Because?" she asked far too softly.

"Because last time I checked I was a red-blooded male, and for us bras are just one more confounding obstacle we've got to get past."

That little comment was met by silence as the lamp's beam dropped toward the ground, only to suddenly shoot up into the forest as she scrambled to her feet. "I'd better go change," she said.

Duncan jumped up to cut her off and pulled her into his arms. "You're perfectly safe with me, Peg," he quietly told her as the beam illuminated his chest. "I would never force myself on you."

"Yeah," she muttered. "You've even stopped stealing kisses."

"Did ye ever consider I might be waiting for you to steal one from me?" He pulled the light off her head when its beam hit him smack in the eyes and tossed it on the ground as he took a calming breath. "Sometimes a man needs a little encouragement."

"We can't be together . . . that way, Duncan. It's not that I really don't want to, but that we . . . just can't."

"Because our making love might kill me?" He snorted. "Trust me, Peg; what I'm about to show you will make your family curse look like a parlor trick."

"Olivia *told* you about my curse?"

"No, Mac told me after Olivia told him."

"She told *Mac*?"

Duncan smiled at the horror in her voice. "What, do ye honestly believe that husbands and wives don't share their concerns for a friend with each other? Tell me, did you keep secrets from your husband?"

"Um . . . I guess not."

Duncan prepared himself for a really big gasp this time. "So ye never told him about the kiss from the ski patroller who got you safely down off TarStone eleven years ago? Were ye not dating your future husband at the time?"

Only instead of gasping, she went as still as a stone. "How do you know about that?" she whispered, the horror back in her voice. "Ohmigod. Ohmigod," she repeated louder, suddenly struggling to get free.

Duncan crushed her against him with a laugh. "I guess we know what sort of impression I made on you that day, don't we?" He threaded his fingers through her hair and tilted her head back, turning serious. "Do you have any idea how many nights I lay awake thinking about the bonnie lass I let get away? Ye haunted my dreams for years." He lowered his mouth to hers. "Ye still do," he murmured, capturing another "Ohmigod" when he kissed her.

Not that she participated—as usual. In fact, this time she gave him a punch in the belly and started talking the moment he lifted his head.

"It was *you*," she cried. "Even after I told you I'd gotten separated from my *boyfriend*, you kissed me *again*."

"Ye had such a kissable mouth, lass. Ye still do," he said,

pulling her more firmly against him when she tried to punch him again.

"You gave me a card with your phone number." She snorted. "You actually had cards made up to . . . What? To hand out to every female you rescued?"

"I saw ye slip it inside your bra when you thought I wasn't looking," he said, struggling to hold back his laughter.

"Only so I could show my friends what an arrogant, no-good, rotten—"

He kissed her again, partly to shut her up but mostly to taste her fire. She might not remember their kiss all that fondly, but he sure as hell did. Because even being the skirt-chasing idiot he had been at the time, he'd recognized that the young girl was different; her taste and smell and contrariness at not kissing him back, her not agreeing to meet him that evening because she had a boyfriend, and refusing even to give him her name.

Christ, talk about Providence having two people's paths cross; he'd searched every damn square inch of the resort for a week after finding her lost and hurt and crying in the woods several hundred yards from the trail, even chasing down every female he saw wearing a bright pink knit hat. But a damn lot of women wore pink hats, he'd quickly discovered to his frustration.

Duncan's attention suddenly snapped back to the woman he was kissing right now when he realized she'd wrapped her arms around his waist and was kissing him back. Lord, she tasted as good as he remembered when her lips parted and her tongue tentatively touched his. And that's when he knew why her apple crisps were so sweet, because he caught himself wanting to lick every square inch of her.

"Ohmigod," she said in a winded whisper, breaking it off and burying her face in—did she just lick his neck? "We can't do this, Duncan."

"Okay, we won't," he said, grinning over the top of her head.

He was surprised she even knew the cuss word she muttered under her breath, and decided he better not kiss her again, afraid he wouldn't stop until they were both naked and sweaty and too exhausted to move. Speaking of which, he noticed she didn't seem in any hurry to move right now, and in fact actually snuggled into him.

"Is this cave very far from here?"

"Nay, it's only about five miles to the entrance."

Her head reared back. "Five *miles*? All uphill? It's going to take all night to get there. Wait, how far from the entrance to whatever the thing is I'm supposed to get?"

He shrugged. "A little over a mile down."

She scrambled away with a small shriek. "Down? *Inside the mountain?*" She started backing away, and Duncan could see in the beam of the headlamp lying on the moss that she was shaking her head. "I'm not going a mile underground. Ohmigod, if I wasn't claustrophobic before, I certainly am now just thinking about it."

"It's a really big cave most of the way; only the last twenty or so feet are tight. There is one area we had to build a bridge across, but other than that the going is easy and not all that steep."

"Can't you just get a long, flexible stick to reach whatever you're trying to get?"

"Sorry. I thought about sending the pup in, but Robbie believes it's going to require someone with opposable thumbs," he said, smiling when she stepped into a beam of moonlight and he saw her scowl. "I told ye that Mac made it impossible for me to reach *all by myself.*"

"Again, what does Mac have to do with any of this?"

Duncan walked over and picked up the jeans and sweat-shirt and handed them to her. "Change your clothes and boots, and on our hike up the mountain I'll tell ye everything I know about Mac."

Apparently not believing him, he saw her chin take on a stubborn tilt. "Tell me one thing about him now."

"Okay. Maximilian Oceanus is a theurgist. Or in laymen terms, a wizard, with the power to move mountains and turn freshwater lakes into inland seas."

Chapter Twenty

Peg was finding it difficult to dress in complete darkness—she wasn't about to use the light with Duncan sitting twenty feet away—what with her hands not wanting to cooperate. The only problem was, she didn't know if she was shaking from being kidnapped, or from realizing the reason the name MacKeage had been familiar is that it had been on the card the kidnapping kiss-thief had given her eleven years ago. Because she really couldn't be this rattled from Duncan's telling her that Mac was a wizard, because that was absolutely impossible.

What had Olivia called it? Earth-shaking, mountain-moving, anything is possible magic—which meant her best friend had knowingly married a *friggin' wizard.*

And Duncan needed her help to find something buried inside a mountain so he could get hold of some of that magic for himself. Magic that Mac had hidden in a place that would force Duncan to kidnap her because she had less broad shoulders and smaller hands—and opposable thumbs—and could climb into a really narrow twenty- or thirty-foot cave a *friggin' mile* underground to get it for him.

Okay. If this wasn't the most bizarre dream she'd ever had, then she was tripping out on plumber's glue or contact cement fumes or something. Yeah, her house hadn't burned to its foundation; she was hallucinating and just imagining all this weird stuff—including, she hoped to God, her beautiful new truck being a mangled wreck.

"Do ye need some help?" Duncan asked way too pleasantly.

Peg gave a snort just as she finally managed to get the one-size-too-small jeans zipped up and fastened. She then slipped the hooded sweatshirt over her head, only to discover it came down to her knees and the sleeves hung six inches past her hands. "Jeesh," she muttered, rolling up the sleeves as she walked over to the backpack and sat down. "Why would anyone think just because a woman might be a size twenty that she has gorilla arms?"

"Ye look like a kid playing dress-up," Duncan said, holding the beam of the headlamp toward her at an angle that didn't shine it in her eyes. "I'm really sorry that I messed up on the sizes, Peg. Are the pants okay?"

"Sure, they fit perfectly as long as I don't breathe. I'm just glad the salesgirl wasn't a size three." She pulled off her knee-highs and slipped on the wool socks, then grabbed the boots and pulled them on and started lacing them. "What did you mean when you were trying to get me out of the boat that you need the magic to keep me safe?"

There was what Peg considered an ominous pause before he answered. "I can't say exactly, as it's just a feeling I have that our little run-in with Dubois tonight won't be the last." He reclined back on an elbow and toyed with the headlamp even while keeping its beam trained on her feet. "I don't like that he's targeting you, and I have a worry that an army of sheriffs won't be able to find him if he doesn't want to be found. Ye said he's a logger, so he knows these woods better than anyone."

She stopped lacing. "And you think if you have whatever's in the mountain that *you* can catch Chris? Duncan, you can't just take the law into your own hands like that."

"No," he said, sitting up. "But I can make damn sure the bastard doesn't get close enough to harm you—or your children. And with the magic, I'm fairly certain I can do it in a way that's . . . well, that's inoffensive to Providence."

"Providence?"

"That would be the power of life, lass, the very heartbeat

of the universe." He grinned. "And ye don't ever want to piss off Providence, so you make sure the magic ye work is always for the benefit of mankind."

"But didn't your father tell me you flew helicopters in Iraq? How do you reconcile the benevolent magic you and Olivia keep talking about with being a soldier?"

He snorted. "War is completely devoid of magic." He grinned again. "But ye may recall I mentioned that a strong arm is sometimes needed to help benevolence along." He started toying with the headlamp again, working the straps and making the beam wobble through the darkness. "I may have been raised a warrior, but I've never relished the fight." He swept the beam through the treetops above them. "I much prefer to battle the elements in God's cathedral. Ye like the outdoors yourself, Peg; I've watched you spend every day at your beach that ye could, and see you teaching your children to embrace nature." He dropped the lamp and rose to his knees in front of her, and clasped her hands in his. "That's why I wasn't worried about bringing ye here to hike a living, breathing, magical mountain with me, and have ye sleep on the ground and drink from its springs and eat the food it willingly provides. You and I are kindred spirits, Peg, and that's a gift I'd given up on ever finding. Will ye give me a chance to prove that together we can be stronger than a curse? If not for yourself, then would ye do it for Charlotte and Isabel?"

"What do they have to do with . . . us?"

"Together we can make sure your girls are given the chance to grow old with the men they love." There was enough light for Peg to see his smile. "And also your mum and your aunt Bea. Wouldn't ye like to see them find love again as well?"

"You're using my *family* to persuade me to have sex with you?"

His smile widened and he nodded, and Peg was sure she saw a sparkle come into his eyes. "We MacKeages can be real bastards like that sometimes, especially with the women we love."

His hands tightened on hers when she flinched on an indrawn breath. He let her go to cup her face.

"Yes, ye heard correctly; I love you, lass."

"You can't," she barely managed to whisper. "We've known each other a week."

"Nay, more than two." He pulled her toward him even as he leaned closer. "But it's been two weeks and eleven years for me," he murmured just before he kissed her.

And Peg was instantly transported to a mountain forest where she'd sat crying in the snow—lost and hurt and scared to death—when this big, strong, and way too handsome man in a TarStone ski patrol jacket had appeared out of nowhere and dried her tears, assured her that her ankle was only sprained, and then pulled her into his arms and kissed her. Oh, she remembered Duncan MacKeage, right down to how he'd made her insides clench and her mouth go dry and her heart pound so hard she'd thought she was going to pass out, only to then wake up to find it had been nothing more than a wonderfully exciting dream—just like she must be dreaming now.

Had he really said he loved her? Out loud?

He was kissing her like he loved her more than just wanting to have sex with her.

She probably should kiss him back. But honestly, she was terrified that loving Duncan would kill him.

His kiss ended with a sigh and he leaned his forehead against hers. "I hope ye consider yourself lucky that I'm a patient man, lass, with a healthy enough ego that your lack of response doesn't send me into a hopeless depression."

"Excuse me. Did you say *patient*?" she whispered against his mouth as she fought a smile—because it was either smile or burst into tears. And hadn't she already learned he would pounce on any sign of weakness? Okay, maybe two weeks *was* long enough to get inside a guy's head. "This from a man who turned my life upside down within minutes of arriving in town," she growled when she felt his thumbs lowered to the pulse on her neck, "and who made me sell him gravel too cheap and go on a picnic I didn't want to go on, threatened to take the flat of his sword to my backside, tricked me into buying a truck for my own good, kidnapped me, bought me size twenty pants and size four panties but no bra, and . . . Should I go on, or are you going to kiss me to shut me up—again?"

"Are ye wearing a bra now?" he asked way too quietly.

"No."

She was flat on her back and he was settled between her legs before she even managed to gasp. "I had every intention of waiting," he said thickly, "but I can see you're quite eager to experience the consequences of my finding you outside after dark missing some important clothing." He brushed the hair back from her face with a gentle hand and kissed her softly on the lips, then lifted his head. "Say ye want me, Peg. Give me permission to make ye mine; right here, right now, in this great cathedral."

"I want you so much it hurts, Duncan, but I'm scared."

"My word of honor, ye can't kill me by loving me. You can only do that by not letting me prove I'm more powerful than a curse."

"How . . . But how can you know that for sure?"

"I was born knowing. Go quiet, lass; can ye not feel the mountain humming through every cell in your body?" Except he apparently mistook her trying to feel the mountain for hesitation, and she heard him sigh again as he dropped his forehead to hers. "I'll tell ye what: It'll take us about two hours to reach a pretty little pool at the base of a gushing waterfall. Ye spend the hike listening to my magical tale, and tell me then if you want to continue on to the cave or . . ." This time *he* hesitated. "Or if ye want to make camp and share the one sleeping bag I brought."

About an hour and forty-five minutes into their hike, Duncan felt like he'd been walking for two weeks and eleven years. He'd spent most of the trek telling Peg how Mac's father, Titus Oceanus, had built Atlantis on which to cultivate his Trees of Life; about the drùidhs—some of whom he was related to—and their role in protecting the Trees, one such species growing right here in Maine; about Robbie MacBain's role as clan Guardian; and his, Robbie's, and Alec's fathers and Laird Greylen actually being eleventh-century highland warriors.

Peg had quietly listened for the most part while asking only the occasional question, but had grabbed his pack and pulled him to a stop when he'd mentioned the time-travelers. Her big blue gaze—looking more fearful than disbelieving—had risen to the hilt of the sword on his back, and she'd asked if he could just disappear one day like the elder MacKeages had from their families eight hundred years ago. He'd assured her it wasn't any more likely to happen to him than it could to her, and suddenly there had been no more questions or any more soft snorts of disbelief, even after ending his long-winded tale with why he needed her help to attain his calling.

With the last fifteen minutes of their trek being made in complete silence, Duncan both assumed and worried that Peg was trying to decide if they would continue up the mountain tonight or bed down together in the sleeping bag—preferably naked—by the pool. He hoped she chose the latter, as it was important to him that she believed that together they could break her family's curse *before* she witnessed the full extent of the power he was about to gain. Because, hell, he was just red-blooded enough to want his woman to want him for himself rather than what he could do.

Had Mac had that same worry with Olivia? He knew Ian had captured Jessie's heart before she'd discovered the truth about him, because Duncan had outright asked his nephew last weekend. Ian had grown amused and in turn had asked Duncan if he wanted to spend the rest of his life wondering if his woman had a believer's heart before he had to hit her over the head with the magic to open her eyes.

But Peg could hear the mountain breathing, which meant she must be a believer deep down inside where it counted, and he was also fairly certain that neither his mountain nor the whale would have so openly welcomed her if they didn't know her heart.

He was the only one who didn't know a goddamned thing, apparently, which was why he needed Peg to willingly give herself to him *before* she saw what was in the cave. Because as he'd told her earlier, a man needed a little encouragement from the woman he was hopelessly in love with.

Christ, why wasn't she saying anything?

"C-can we stop?"

He stopped so quickly she bumped into his back, making him have to catch her even as he stifled a curse at how pale she was. "What's the matter?" he asked as he tried to read her eyes in what stingy moonlight was filtering through the trees.

"I . . . These new jeans are stiff and they're . . . chafing me," she whispered to his chest. "And my feet are starting to blist—"

He dropped a hand behind her knees and swept her into his arms, not even trying to stifle his curse. "Just once could ye simply *ask* for my help instead of being so goddamned stubborn?"

She also didn't stifle a rather impressive curse, or even bother to mutter it under her breath. "I'm too heavy," she growled right back, even as she wrapped an arm around him when he started up the trail again. "You're going to trip and break both our necks. No, wait; I forgot you can see in the dark by magic."

"It's *the* magic," he said softly, this time stifling a smile. "There's only one, lass, and ye seem to be forgetting what I said about offending it."

"I thought it was Providence we're not supposed to offend."

"They're one in the same. So," he said above the sound of the gushing stream as he stepped into the clearing made by the glistening pool, "it appears ye don't get a choice after all whether or not we're spending the night here."

"I don't?"

"It's another mile to the cave, and then another mile inside." He skirted the pool, set her down on one of the boulders at the bottom of the waterfall, shucked off his pack and sword, then knelt at her feet and started unlacing her boots. "So here's the plan: I'm going to build a fire while you strip off and go for a swim to soothe the chafing. Then," he continued despite her gasp, "I'll wash your jeans and give them a good beating on the rocks and set them to dry on a branch by the—"

"That water's got to be freezing!" she cried before he could finish.

He grabbed the hand trying to push him away from her boots and held it in the water, smiling when she gasped again. "It's warm!"

He went back to taking off her boots, being careful when he felt her foot flinch. "Isabel warned me you're a warm-water bass, not a trout. Speaking of which, if ye feel little nibbles on your toes, see if you can't sneak up on the lucky buggers and catch us a couple of trout for supper."

"That water's too warm for trout to live in."

He reached up and gently tapped the tip of her nose, then straightened. "Not for a magical stream, it's not." He stood up. "Just leave your clothes here on the rock and I'll get them as soon as I have a fire going."

"You promise not to peek?"

He turned away with a snort. "No."

A boot hit him square in the back and another one dead center of his chest when he turned. He caught the sweatshirt that came at him next just as he saw Peg roll into the pool wearing her jeans, her laughter stopping when she slipped underwater.

Oh yeah, the woman definitely owned his heart.

And they weren't leaving this mountain until she understood what that meant.

The sting of her chafed legs having eased from lounging at the base of the falls to get the whirlpool effect, Peg lazily floated in the shadow of a towering spruce as she glanced across the moonlit pool at Duncan reclined beside the blazing fire he'd made. Charmed, Olivia had called him. But to Peg he was an old-fashioned, sword-carrying, kiss-stealing, scary-driving knight in leather armor, determined to save her from a five-generation curse she desperately didn't want to pass down to a sixth.

But could she chance it would be different this time, considering how high the stakes were? Then again, maybe it already was too late for Duncan, because she wasn't sure if the curse applied just to husbands or if a man only had to fall in love with a descendent of Gretchen Robinson to meet a quick demise.

But then yet again, if she hadn't personally witnessed an earthquake that had moved several mountains and split Bottomless Lake wide open without cracking a window in Spellbound Falls and Turtleback Station, Peg might think Duncan was at the very least delusional and at worst insane. But she *had* felt the mountains moving and heard the booming thunder, and she *had* arrived home to find saltwater spilling into her gravel pit without so much as a chipped dish in her cupboards. So a good deal of his fantastical tale had to be true, considering the proof was staring her in the face every time she looked out her kitchen window.

Peg smiled up at the moonlight showering the unusually tall trees surrounding the unusually warm pool with soft white light, and decided she liked Duncan's idea of the forest and mountains being God's cathedral. As for his dad and those other men traveling through time, and Mac being from Atlantis, and Trees of Life growing right here in Maine, if Duncan had told her all that stuff hoping to persuade her to have sex with him . . . well, he'd certainly caught her attention. Of all the arguments he could have made, having the power to break her family curse was the most potent. Because not only would he be saving her daughters' futures, Duncan would also be saving hers. And honestly, she didn't know how much longer she'd survive sleeping in a small empty bed every night before the part of her heart not filled up by her children finally atrophied.

Peg glanced over at Duncan again, looking big and strong and unkillable as he reclined on the mat and sleeping bag he'd unrolled on the moss next to the fire. After, that is, he'd beat the jeans she'd tossed to shore against a rock before spreading them on a branch—after she'd watched him secretly peek at the label to see their size. Now he was lying with his head propped in his hand, pretending to be gazing at the fire like the patient man he was even though she knew he was secretly peeking past the flames in hopes of seeing something interesting.

When in the name of God had she fallen in love with him?

She'd caught herself being attracted to Duncan the day he'd helped her butcher the deer, which to her dismay had turned into desiring him when he'd stolen a kiss the night his equipment was being sabotaged—which had then turned into her desperately needing him sometime when she hadn't been paying attention, apparently. And if she had to wait much longer to feel him inside her, Peg was afraid she was going to be the first *female* to die of the Robinson curse.

She'd thought, much to her delight, he was taking the decision away from her down by the beach when she'd lied and said she wasn't wearing a bra. But the contrary man had suddenly backed off, and then made her spend two friggin' hours watching the moonlight play over his broad shoulders as he'd carried a sword that had to weigh at least twenty pounds, and the heavy backpack, and eventually *her* up the mountain.

Damn, big strong men turned her on.

And really, it's not like he hadn't been forewarned that making love to her might kill him. So what was she doing here in this magical place with this magical man—with no danger of being interrupted and all the time in the world, apparently—acting like some seventeen-year-old virgin planning to give herself to her boyfriend on Valentine's Day? God, she'd been a romantic idiot when she was seventeen.

Yeah, well, she was twenty-eight now, a full-grown woman with four children, an empty bed, and a hole in her heart the size of a house. And if she had to go through the worry of letting a man see her naked for the first time again, she really couldn't have devised a better setting. She might not have a seventeen-year-old's body thanks to three pregnancies, and her boobs may be heading south and she might have a few stretch marks, but moonlight and water were great disguisers of imperfections.

Peg rolled onto her stomach, quietly swam toward a rock embedded in the sandy gravel shore, and folded her arms on it to rest her chin on her hands. "I still have that card, you know. The one you gave me eleven years ago."

He sat up. "Ye do?"

She nodded on her hands. "I'd forgotten about it, actually. But your telling me that it was you on TarStone that day, I remembered slipping it inside the torn lining of my jewelry box when I got home from the ski trip." She smiled, knowing the fire was casting enough light for him to see it. "And your kiss did leave quite an impression on me. I had some pretty erotic dreams for a virgin that winter."

God, she'd swear his chest actually puffed up.

"Are you going to make me try to catch these trout all by myself," she asked, "or come in here and help?"

The fire certainly cast enough light for her to see him go still but for the sudden flare in his eyes. "I didn't bring a swimsuit with me, lass," he said thickly.

She shrugged. "Last I knew, red-blooded females consider swimsuits just one more obstacle to get past." She reared up slightly and pushed off the rock to glide on her back to the center of the pool. "Come swim in this magical pool in God's cathedral with me, Duncan."

Why weren't men the least bit modest? This one had his boots and socks off in three seconds flat, unbuttoning his shirt as he stood up, dropping his pants—boxers included—and stepping out of them all without taking his eyes off her. Peg's breath caught when he skirted the fire with an unhurried but deliberate stride and walked into the pool, not stopping until the water was up to his waist and there was only about ten feet separating them. Knowing that if she gave him too much time to think through his plan of attack that he might not attack at all, Peg dove under the surface and swam directly toward him, knowing he'd assume she was swimming away.

His muted bark of surprise confirmed her guess when she popped up in front of him. "Shh, you'll wake the squirrels," she whispered as she wrapped her arms around him and pressed the full length of her body to his, making him suck in his breath. She touched her lips to his chest and pulled in his wonderfully male scent. "And I'm not into having an audience."

He cupped her face and tilted her head to look at him. "You're sure, Peg?"

"About what I'm doing? No. But about doing it with you? Oh, yes." She searched his eyes searching hers. "I loved my husband with the heart of a young girl wanting nothing more than to be a wife and mother. And now with a woman's heart, I've fallen in love with you. I really didn't want to, since you're a little more than scary sometimes, but I think that's precisely why it's safe for me to love you." She gave him a tentative smile. "Because I definitely believe a woman needs a big, strong, scary man to keep life . . . interesting. For instance, I can't wait to find out what that is poking my belly."

Peg dropped her hands from his waist when he still didn't move and wrapped her fingers intimately around him as she cupped his scrotum with her other hand. Only he caught her shoulders when she started to slip underwater and hauled her back up against his chest with a warning growl. And since she was finally the right height, and before he could say whatever he intended to say, she wrapped her legs around his waist and her arms around his neck and stuck her tongue in his mouth.

Because really, the man never should have admitted he loved her.

She leaned away. "Well, are you going to kiss me back or not?"

"What, ye find yourself needing a little encouragement?"

"No, I need cooperation." She leaned her forehead on his and sighed. "Okay, if you really were serious about wanting me to start asking for help, there is something I've been having a hard time doing . . . all by myself."

"And that would be?"

"Well, I've tried . . . um, pleasuring myself, but it's just not the sa—"

Peg couldn't tell if his roar meant she'd better shut up and prepare herself for his cooperation or if she'd just unleashed the really scary man who'd been driving her SUV earlier. But her first clue arrived when his mouth came down on hers in anything but cooperation; harsh, demanding, and so full of promise that Peg felt her insides clench in anticipation. The next clue that she'd unleashed more red-blooded male than she might be able to handle was when she felt herself falling backward into the water, the weight of his body pushing her all the way down to the sandy bottom of the pool.

She was pretty sure warm-water bass could hold their breaths as long as trout could—that is, until Duncan broke the kiss and slid down and cupped both her breasts, sucking first one nipple and then the other right there at the bottom of the pool in four feet of water. Peg's shout of surprise released a good amount of air from her lungs, and her moan ended with a frantic struggle to find a way to replace it.

His hands spanned her waist and pushed her to the surface, where she gave another shout of surprise when his mouth pressed intimately between her thighs and his tongue pushed into the folds of her sex. She went boneless on a moan of pleasure, and would have slipped beneath the surface again if he hadn't been holding her. One of his hands lowered to her hip so he could control her movements and one arm slid between her thighs to lift one leg, allowing him better access as he splayed a hand across her lower back to keep her from falling over.

Peg clung to his shoulders to brace herself when he found

her sensitive bud and suckled, gently at first then quite eagerly, making her insides clench again and her mouth go dry in response. He was going to drown. She was drowning in desire. His tongue drove into her and then he suckled again.

She heard whimpering, raw and needy and ragged, and Peg tugged at his head so he'd come up and breathe with her. But just like the man in her SUV, he was relentless, pushing wave after building wave of searing heat through every cell in her body, until the world receded but for his demanding mouth as it drove her closer and closer toward release. His hand slid between her thighs again and Peg cried out when he slipped two fingers deep inside her. Her muscles clamped around them and she bucked forward, climaxing with a cry of unbelievable pleasure.

She was nothing but a trembling, jerking, convulsing, boneless mess when he finally surfaced, his hands spanning her waist as he pushed her backward towards shore. God, he wasn't even winded, and she was still trying to catch her breath. Her back had barely touched the sandy bank when he was pressing into her; no hesitation, no request for permission, no testing her readiness.

His penetration wasn't careful, but neither was it rushed; his mouth capturing her startled cry as he pushed deeper. Peg clutched his shoulders bunched with undeniable strength and turned her mouth away to suck in ragged breaths as she tried to adjust to his invasion.

He moved his arms next to her head to hold her looking at him, his eyes dark and intense and locked on hers as he eased back and she relaxed, and he pushed into her again. Her nipples hardened as his chest hair brushed over them with each stroke of his body, pushing, then retreating, then pushing deeper into her with each thrust.

"Again," he commanded. "So I can watch ye this time."

Peg forgot all about breathing, admittedly a little scared by his intensity.

"Again," he repeated, obviously fighting to soften his . . . request.

He leaned away—somehow without breaking his slow, maddening rhythm—and slid one hand under one of her legs to settle it over his arm, effectively changing his angle of penetration. "Oh God, don't stop," she groaned, throwing her head back, which in turn lifted her aching breasts into his chest, each of his thrusts pulling her closer to that spiraling vortex of shattering pleasure.

She cried out when his other hand lowered, his palm scorching her stomach as his thumb pressed into her folds and found her bud. He worked her intimately against the slick length of his shaft moving in and out, and within the next heartbeat Peg crested again, her fingers digging into his arms in a futile attempt to keep from flying in a thousand different directions.

His thrusts stopped with him buried deep inside her even as his thumb continued stroking her through the storm of her climax, his gaze locked on hers as she convulsed around him two, five, eight pounding heartbeats. Ten. Twelve.

And then he exploded in motion, placing his elbows on either side of her head as he drove into her again, his lips brushing her forehead and his chest hair roughening her supersensitive nipples. And all Peg could do was cling to him through his own climax, knowing with blinding clarity that she was in really big trouble.

With the both of them lying mostly in the warm water of the pool, Duncan kept as much of his weight off Peg as he could while remaining embedded deeply inside her, considering every muscle in his body felt like lead as he lay his forehead on the ground beside hers and sucked in ragged breaths.

Her ancestor's curse wasn't going to kill him, but she might.

Christ, he'd lost it completely when she'd asked for his help with a little problem she was having; the picture of Peg lying in her feminine room in a small bed in the dark touching herself igniting a firestorm in him that Duncan was afraid wouldn't be brought under control, much less extinguished, in his lifetime. He'd taken her boldly when she'd unwittingly brought forth his need to claim her in a way that would leave no question in her mind that she belonged to him.

He smiled at the sand, wondering if she recognized yet that they'd only just begun. He slowly lifted his head to find her big, unblinking eyes staring up at him, her soft, lush chest heaving into his as her trembling hands pressed against his shoulders on the misguided notion she could hold him at bay. He pressed his hips forward, her eyes widening with a gasped moan of surprise.

"I would have ye come again," he said quietly.

"Are . . . are you serious?"

He slid an arm under her shoulders, which canted her head back. "Again," he growled, setting his mouth on her throat and pressing his tongue to her pulse.

She shifted restlessly beneath him, her soft shriek of alarm making him smile as he moved his mouth lower, leaving a trail of quivering flesh in its wake as he pressed his hips forward. Her second shriek ended on a moan as he felt her dig her heels into the sand to lever herself into his slow thrusts, and he heard her whisper, "Ohmigod, you're serious," just as he felt her clenching around him with her building climax.

Aye, if the lass had only suspected it before, before this night was through she would definitely know she had fallen in love with a demanding, never-say-die, very possessive man.

Chapter Twenty-one

Peg opened her eyes to see the sun just peeking over the top of the mountain, although its rays weren't reaching this far down yet, and she decided it was a good thing she didn't want to move because she couldn't. Partly because every muscle in her body had given up the ghost two love-makings ago—she'd lost count of her orgasms—but mostly because Duncan had her so tightly wrapped in his arms that it was a wonder she could even breathe.

The man wasn't scary; he was flat-out terrifying.

Relentless was too benign for what he'd been last night, Peg decided now that her brain wasn't suffering from passion over-load and she could think. Well, think at least semiclearly, because she *was* emotionally as well as physically exhausted. No, Duncan had been driven by something she couldn't quite put her finger on. Intense. Determined. Frighteningly focused. Really, really driven to prove . . . something.

For the love of God, she hadn't known a man could keep making love after he came, much less that he could come that many times in one night. She was chafed in more places than just her legs now, and a little worried her skin was so super-sensitized from being in a constant state of arousal that she was going to have another orgasm just getting dressed.

Assuming she could ever move again.

He nuzzled her shoulder and Peg stiffened, and he chuckled softly as she nevertheless moaned when his thumb lazily brushed over her nipple.

"I swear to God," she softly growled, "you say 'again' and I'm going to hit you over the head with your own sword, and not with the flat of it, either."

"I doubt ye can even lift it, lass," he said with another chuckle, turning her around in his arms so that now her naked backside was sticking out of the sleeping bag. He kissed her forehead. "Did ye sleep well?"

She snorted, pressing her cold nose into the crux of his neck, making him chuckle again as he palmed her exposed backside and pulled her up against his wide-awake front side. "Insatiable," she muttered under her breath, adding another word to her growing list of his finer qualities.

"Excuse me?"

She patted his chest, a bit surprised that she could even lift her hand. "I was just mentioning it was sunrise, so I guess that means you have an hour to get me home like you promised." *So I can send the boys to my mother-in-law's and collapse into bed and sleep all day,* she silently added.

"This sunrise doesn't count, Peg," he said, the humor having left his voice as he tilted her head back. "We could see a hundred sunrises from this mountain, but when we cross the fiord it will only be the morning after we left. Monday morning."

"But that's really not possible, Duncan. Really. I need to be home when my children wake up or they'll be worried sick."

He folded her into his embrace with a heavy sigh. "I told ye it's only going to *seem* like you're gone days." He tucked a finger between them to nudge her chin up. "My word of honor, Peg; you'll be away from them for less than twelve hours."

He sat up, sitting her up with him, and chuckled again when Peg scrambled to grab his shirt beside the dead fire and immediately slipped it on.

He lifted her chin to look at him again, his expression gone back to serious but his eyes still showing a hint of amusement. "I'd have thought we put any shyness ye might have with me to rest last night, but I can see it's still something we're going to have to work on."

He stood up, as naked and immodest as the day he'd been born, walked to the pool, and dove in. Peg flopped back on the bedroll and pulled the sleeping bag up to her nose with a sigh of relief—followed by a smile at the treetops finally catching the first rays of a magical sunrise.

Oh yeah, based on last night's experience, nothing could kill Duncan MacKeage.

"The way I see it, ye have two choices," Duncan said as he dripped water from his fingers onto Peg's forehead, causing her to pull the sleeping bag up over her face with a groan. "You can get up and get dressed so we can get on with the day, or I can crawl back into bed with you and work on that little shyness problem."

It wasn't her cute, well-perfected scowl she was wearing when she pushed the sleeping bag down to her chest; it was an outright threatening glare. "Here's a third choice: After *you get dressed*, you can hike up the mountain and then a mile down inside it and make sure your . . . whatever," she said with a negligent wave, "is still there. If it is, maybe I'll hobble up the mountain and a mile down inside it, and then cram myself into the last twenty feet of cave and get it for you." That said, she pulled the sleeping bag back up over her face. "Go away, Duncan. Go catch us a trout for breakfast or something."

"I can't," he said with a chuckle. "The poor scandalized buggers all jumped over the small dam of the pool last night when they heard ye carrying on like that, and Leviathan is probably having them for breakfast. What was that?" he asked when he heard her muttering something.

Duncan knew Peg was wanting an apology this morning, or at the very least expecting him to inquire as to how she was feeling. But he hadn't been lying when he'd told her he could be a real bastard sometimes, so he figured he might as well begin as he intended to go on. Hell, half the reason he loved her was that Peg was the first woman he'd met who could handle a lifetime of living with him.

He grabbed the edge of the bag and simply rolled her out of it, then picked up the growling woman and stood her on her feet, pointed her toward the pool, and gave her a nudge to get her moving. "Five minutes for a refreshing swim, five to dress, and then we're headed up the mountain even if you're barefooted."

"What about breakfast?" she grouched as she hobbled to the pool. "I haven't had anything since supper last night."

"I'll have something ready when you're ready."

She stopped with her toes in the water and looked over her shoulder, saw him blatantly watching her, then waded into the pool without bothering to take off her shirt.

Duncan turned to hide his smile, squatting down to straighten their bed. Christ, the contrary woman turned him on. He packed up anything he intended to leave here at the campsite—which was just about everything—then went about gathering firewood to save himself from having to do it in the dark when they got back. Satisfied he'd done his manly duty of providing heat and shelter for his woman's comfort tonight, Duncan dropped a fistful of granola bars beside his sword, then took the wrapper off one and moseyed over to a rock near the waterfall. He sat down to munch away as he watched Peg sitting under the gushing waterfall, letting it pummel the muscles in her back.

Oh yeah, he could be a real bastard sometimes. "Ye have two minutes before we're walking up the mountain. Can you really get dressed in that amount of time?"

"Look, I'm a little tender this morning, okay?" she muttered, not even bothering to open her eyes. "The mountain's not going anywhere."

"You know, ye could have simply asked me to stop last night."

That opened her eyes. "I just had to say *stop*?" she said in a strangled whisper.

He nodded. "But the truth is ye never asked, and you seemed to be having so much fun, I didn't *dare* stop for fear of disappointing ye."

He saw a blush creep into her beautiful face even as he noticed her hands braced on the rocks balling into fists. Granted, he'd pushed her beyond what Peg may have thought *she* was capable of last night, but even if it had killed him, he would have stopped at the first sign she was in distress. But he hadn't wanted to stop because he'd wanted to make damn sure lovemaking wasn't something she'd even think about doing *all by herself* ever again.

"One minute."

"Fine," she snapped, standing up and wading out of the water. "Oh, here, let me give you your shirt," she said far too sweetly, pulling it off over her head and slapping it against his bare chest.

She then turned on her heel and, apparently over her shyness, walked toward the sleeping bag where he'd left her clothes. Duncan decided she looked damn fine for a mother of four children. He took another bite of his granola bar and watched her dress right there in plain sight beside the sleeping bag, noticing she started to put on her bra only to immediately pull it down off her breasts and toss it on the bag.

He'd have to remember those two lovely ladies were obviously a little tender and find himself a new favorite spot on her body to explore tonight. He took another bite and slowly chewed, remembering that her backside had fit his hands quite nicely.

She pulled her sweatshirt down over her head, then glanced toward the pool—specifically the lower end—before looking at him. "I . . . um, I lost my panties in the current of the falls last night when I slid out of my jeans. Is the pair you shoved in your pocket the only pair you brought?"

He took another bite of his bar and nodded.

"Did *you* bring a change of underwear?"

He nodded again, chewing to hide his smile when her face darkened, then used what was left of his bar to point at the backpack—even as he felt himself growing hard at the idea of her wearing his boxers. "They're in the bottom pouch." Only he jumped up and strode over to her when he remembered what else was in that pouch, realizing she was going to get that apology after all. "I'll get them."

"Too late," she said, pulling out the box of condoms. Except instead of throwing them at him like he expected, she tossed the box on the ground with a snort and stood up holding his boxers. "You in the habit of making love to a woman without a condom?" she asked as she slipped first one leg and then the other into the shorts and pulled them up under her sweatshirt.

He took hold of her shoulders when she started to bend down to get the jeans. "I swear to God, Peg, I had every intention of protecting you last night." He ran a hand through his hair, then rubbed the heat creeping up the back of his neck. "My only excuse is that I went . . . I was a little . . ." He blew out a sigh. "I'm sorry. It won't happen again."

She must have read his sincerity, because her face softened and she patted his chest. "Don't worry; I'm not going to get pregnant. I had my tubes tied after the twins." He saw her cheeks flush with heat. "So I can't ever have any more babies," she whispered, her gaze dropping to his chest. "If I ever wanted to . . . remarry, the man would never be able to have children of . . . his own."

Duncan pulled her into his arms. "Ah, lass; any man would be privileged to share the four ye have now. But there's something ye need to know, Peg. Providence decides when a soul's needing to be born, and if it decides *you* should be its mother, you will get pregnant." He lifted her chin to smile down at her. "The only foolproof way to prevent a baby is abstinence."

"Then why did you even bother to bring condoms?" she asked softly. "They're less reliable than what I had done."

"We can't stop the inevitable, but we can postpone it sometimes. Ye remember my telling you about Laird Greylen MacKeage? Well, he had seven daughters," he continued when she nodded. "And although I'm fairly certain some of them had lovers before they married, I do happen to know that each of Grey's girls got pregnant the very first time they made love to the men they were destined to marry despite using contraceptives." He gave her astonished lips a quick kiss, then bobbed his eyebrows. "You're not the only one living under a family curse—although I do believe all seven girls eventually saw it as a blessing."

Her cheeks flamed red and she went back to looking at his chest. "Um, what if Providence decides I should get pregnant?" she asked in a barely audible whisper.

He lifted her chin and brushed a thumb over her hot cheek. "We pray it's not triplets." She gasped so hard, he had to catch her when she nearly tripped over the sleeping bag, and Duncan hugged her to him again. "Together we can handle anything life throws at us, Peg, including three or four or five more little heathens."

He grunted when she poked him in the belly. "You're not the one carrying them inside you for nine months."

"Nay, but I'll carry them the rest of their lives." He gave her a squeeze. "As well as you." He set her away, bent down and picked up her jeans, then tossed them at her. "Now, if ye don't want to go meet my mountain up close and personal barefoot and half naked, I suggest you speed things up a bit."

He turned and dug a dry shirt out of his pack and slipped it on, then settled his sword over his shoulders while she sat down and pulled on her boots. "You're not wearing your jacket?" she asked as she laced them up.

"The cave gets warmer the farther down we go. We'll sit outside it for a bit to make sure ye haven't worked up a sweat on the hike before we go inside."

"Do you have a second headlamp and extra batteries?" she asked, standing up and taking a deep breath as she glanced at the top half of the mountain.

He grabbed her hand and led her toward the falls to follow the stream up. "Trust me," he drawled, "we'll have plenty of light to see where we're going."

Chapter Twenty-two

Duncan wiped the sweat from his forehead with his shirt that he'd had to take off before he died of heatstroke—which had nothing to do with the temperature in the cave. He'd broken into a sweat the moment Peg had crawled into the narrow passage, and now that she was out of sight his heart was pounding so hard that he was in danger of being passed out cold if she needed him.

She'd called back that the tunnel actually opened up slightly after the curve, the proof being that she'd turned around and crawled back out just enough to blind him with her headlamp before disappearing back around the curve.

He wiped his forehead again. "Well?" he quietly called into the tunnel when he noticed the beam of her light had gone steady thirty seconds ago. "What did ye find?"

"The cave just stops. All that's here is a hole the size of my fist about three feet up from the ground."

"When ye shine the light in it, what do you see?"

"Nothing. It curves to the right so I can only see about a foot in."

Duncan scrubbed the sweat off the back of his neck, wanting to roar. "Whatever ye do, don't stick your hand in there, okay? Let me think for a minute."

"Too late."

"Goddamn it, get back out here. Now!"

He was answered by silence, and if he wasn't mistaken, even the mountain seemed to be holding its breath.

"Peg!" he roared. "Answer me, dammit!"

"I . . . um, I'm stuck."

He closed his eyes to lean his forehead on the granite above the tunnel. "Stuck as in ye just need to relax and you'll get free," he asked softly, "or *stuck* stuck?"

"As in 'the mountain closed around my wrist' stuck. Um, Duncan, why can't I hear it breathing anymore?"

Christ, she sounded scared. Calm, but scared. "I don't know, lass." He sat back on his heels and studied the granite to the right of the cave again. "Ye said the tunnel curved back on itself, so that means you're only . . . what? A few feet from me?"

"I'd say that's about right."

"And the hole your hand is stuck in, is it coming toward me?"

"Yup."

"Is the mountain hurting ye, Peg?"

"No, it's just holding me. I can feel something, though. My fingers are touching . . . metal, I think. Large hoops, like bracelets or something. Two of them; both thick and wide, but one feels slightly smaller."

"Stop touching them and see if the mountain releases you."

"Nope; still stuck." He heard a nervous laugh. "Have we offended Providence?"

"Nay, Peg. It takes a lot to offend such a benevolent force." He sat down to rest his arms on his knees, blowing out a heavy sigh when he realized the truth of his words. They hadn't pissed off Providence; it was just wanting something more from them before it released its prize—which as far as he was concerned was Peg. "Do ye believe in the magic yet, lass?" he asked softly.

He heard a muffled snort. "Pretty much. Um, do you?"

Duncan stilled. Did he?

He certainly didn't doubt it existed, having seen it in action more times than he cared to remember. But did he believe he had the magic *in him*? Because if he did, he sure as hell didn't need anything to work it other than belief itself; the magic didn't come from an instrument of power, it came from the heart of the person needing the miracle. The object—be it a staff or sword or *bracelet*—was just a symbol of potential, a tangible means to turn that potential outward from the heart into the physical world.

"A-are you still there?"

Duncan scrambled to his knees and slowly ran his hands over the granite where he estimated she was trapped. "I'm still here, Peg. And in about one minute you're going to be here with me. Close your eyes, lass, and turn your head away."

"What are you going to do?" she asked, the calm having left her voice.

"Hush. Listen. Do ye hear that soft thumping?" he asked conversationally as he pressed his palms against the granite and felt it begin to pulse in rhythm with his own thumping heart. "I'm waking the mountain up from its nap, Peg." He pressed harder, feeling his hands heating up as the granite slowly softened to the consistency of putty.

Duncan closed his eyes against the brilliant swirls of white energy that suddenly pulsed around him, but not before realizing it was coming from *him* instead of the walls of the cave. He put the backs of his hands together and slipped them inside the yielding granite, then spread the wall with no more effort than opening a curtain.

Peg slammed into him with the force of her entire weight, sending him sprawling onto his back as he wrapped his arms around her with a laugh.

"Ohmigod. Ohmigod," she muttered. "How did you do that?"

He kissed the top of her head, squeezing her so hard she squeaked. "By magic."

She looked at him, then reared away as far as his embrace would allow. "You . . . Your eyes are . . . they're . . . ohmigod, they're *green*."

He gave a chuckle. "I'm fairly certain they've always been green."

"No, *green* green. A brighter . . . scarier green."

He pulled her down and kissed her, not stopping until he

felt her soften against him, only to sigh when he realized she wasn't returning the kiss.

She was back to being contrary, he guessed.

She sat up straddling him the moment he stopped and held out her hand. "Here; I believe these are what you were after?"

Duncan lifted his head just enough to see the two dark cuffs she was holding, then dropped back with another sigh. "You can keep them, as I just realized I don't need them after all."

She slapped them down on his chest hard enough to make him grunt, then leaned forward until her face was right over his—he assumed so he could better see her scowl. "I just risked dying a slow, gruesome death to get your *instrument of power*, and you're telling me you don't need it?" she said far too softly.

He shook his head, fighting back a grin. "Nay, I wouldn't have let ye rot in there, Peg. It's just not in me to give up." He finally let his grin escape. "I would have kept bringing ye food and water until Mac got back and freed you if I couldn't jack-hammer the granite to get ye out."

"Two months?" she whispered, her own eyes growing a bit scary. "You expected me to sit there with my hand stuck in a hole for *two months*?" She picked up the cuffs and shook them in front of his face. "I have no idea what in hell these are, but you're going to wear them if I have to hit you over the head with a blunt object and put them on you myself."

He took them from her and sat up, only allowing her to scramble back as far as his thighs. He grabbed her left wrist and, ignoring her gasp, slipped the smaller cuff on over her hand—watching with satisfaction as it immediately molded itself to her arm just above her wrist.

She gasped again when she tried to get it off but couldn't. "Ohmigod," she whispered, lifting huge worried eyes to his. "What did you just do?"

He started to slip his own cuff down over his right hand, but then quickly switched it to his dominant left hand and felt it gently close over his arm. "I believe I just sealed our fates together—forever." He took hold of her face to lift her gaze to his. "Ye know a man who works around heavy machinery can't wear a wedding band."

"A . . . a . . . wed . . . a wedding band?" She tried to look at his wrist only to lift her arm to see her own cuff when he wouldn't let go of her face. "Aren't you supposed to . . . Do you honestly expect me to believe . . ."

Duncan nodded when she fell silent, and he brushed his thumbs over her pale cheeks. "We'll have a ceremony for the sake of the children, of course, but ye need to know it's only a formality."

"You're supposed to *ask*," she snapped.

"Will ye marry me, Peg?"

"No."

"Christ, you're contrary—which is exactly why I didn't ask," he said, watching a flush of red spread across her cheeks. He leaned down until his nose was touching hers. "Too late, lass; you became mine last night."

She went back to scowling at him as she lifted her arm to see the cuff again, and her eyes suddenly widened and she snapped her gaze to his. "Hey, does that mean this is *my* instrument of power? Can I . . . do stuff, too?"

Duncan pulled her into his embrace to hide his horror even as he gave a bark of laughter. "Absolutely not. Ye have to be *born* a magic-maker," he blatantly lied. Holy hell, just the idea of Peg being able to *do stuff* sent chills down his spine—just like it had Ian's, his nephew had said, when he'd realized Roger de Keage had given Jessie a small staff.

"Then why do I have to wear a bracelet?" Peg muttered against his chest.

"For the same reason you'd wear a wedding band; to know who ye belong to."

He felt more than heard her sigh. "You are so old-fashioned."

"And charmed," he whispered against her hair, giving her another squeeze. "Let's not forget what a bastard I'm going to be growing old with you. Are ye ready to go home now, Peg?"

She tilted her head back to look up at him. "You can't . . . um, *act* like a husband or anything," she said, her cheeks flushing again, "until after we're married in a church in front of the children. Wait; how am I going to explain to them that I just up and decided to marry you out of the blue? We haven't even gone on a real date."

Well, if she wasn't quite reconciled to the fact they already were married in the eyes of Providence, at least she was acknowledging they *were* getting married. "Jacob already gave me permission to ask you," he said past his grin. "And he even offered to let me sleep in one of the bunk beds you were going to buy him."

· "When did he say that?"

"The first day I was in that recliner in your new house. He told me I didn't have to be afraid when you *get all scowly*, because you're really all soft inside." He pulled her toward him, stopping just shy of their lips touching. "So I guess ye better go talk with your preacher when we get back this morning and see if he can marry us this evening," he finished, just before kissing her.

And damn if she didn't kiss him back—until his words apparently sank in and she reared away. "This evening!" She must have seen he was serious because she went perfectly still. "But Mac gave Olivia at least a week to put a wedding together."

"Do I look like Mac?" he asked quietly.

"You . . . You're big and scary like he is. How about this coming Saturday?"

"I'm sleeping with my wife tonight, with or without a formal wedding."

"We need a license."

"I believe you'll find it's already on file at the county courthouse."

"How?" she asked on a gasp.

"By magic." He pulled her against him and held her head to his chest, preparing for a really big gasp. "And your new house—that *I'm* building—will be over here, Peg, and you'll be watching sunsets from our kitchen window instead of sunrises."

She didn't gasp, she snorted. "Are you forgetting I have four children who'll be riding on a school bus this fall?"

"I'll build a road around the fiord."

That got him his gasp. "It would have to be at least twenty miles to reach here, and that's only one way! The bus isn't going to drive that far for four children."

"Then you can take them into town by boat to meet it."

"And in the spring and fall, when the ice is rotten?"

"Bottomless is saltwater, Peg," he said, smiling over the top of her head when he realized she needed to voice all her concerns out loud—or at least let him know what he was getting himself into. "It's not going to freeze."

This time he both heard and felt her heavy sigh. "The kids are never going to get their friends to come for sleepovers. First their parents wouldn't let them stay over because I live in a falling-down doublewide, and now they're not going to let them because I'll be living in the middle of nowhere."

"I'll make sure they come."

She tilted her head back. "You can't fix everything, Duncan."

"Watch me," he said, giving her a wink just before setting her beside him. He stood up, then held out his hand. "Come on, wife," he said just to piss her off. "The sooner we get home, the sooner you can start planning *today's* wedding."

Except instead of taking his hand, she started tugging on the cuff above her wrist, and Duncan reached down and lifted her to her feet. "Are ye deliberately trying to offend Providence after it gave ye such a wonderful gift?"

She stopped tugging and scowled at him. "Providence gave me this bracelet?"

"Nay, it gave you *me*," he said, grabbing her hand just as a soft rumbling laugh echoed through the tunnel. "Did your mother warn ye about your family curse before you married William Thompson, Peg?" he asked as he led her toward the entrance.

"Yes. But I was eighteen, and all eighteen-year-olds believe bad stuff only happens to other people."

"Did ye tell *him* about the curse before ye married?"

She gave a soft snort. "Billy said it was going to take a lot more than some dead old biddy to scare him off. One night we even went to the cemetery where Gretchen Robinson is buried and he peed on her grave." She pulled him to a stop. "I'll marry you today if you *promise* you're not going to die."

"I'm not going to die for a long, long time, Peg, I promise."

"But how can you be so sure?" she whispered.

"Because last night when we were making love—the fourth time, I think—I saw ye lying beneath me all beautiful and filled with passion. You were . . . oh, eighty years old, I'm guessing." He caught her shoulders when she reared away with a gasp. "It was the magic's way of letting me know everything will be okay."

"You saw me at *eighty*? *Naked?*"

He took her hand and started walking again to hide his grin. "Ye looked damned good, too, lass, all flushed with pleasure. But ye might want to hold on to that other pair of jeans I bought ye, because I do believe they're eventually going to fit."

This time she gasped loud enough that the whale probably heard it down in the fiord. Duncan knew his mountain certainly did when Peg shot past him with a yelp of surprise.

"Ohmigod, something just patted me on the ass!"

Chapter Twenty=three

If she lived to be a hundred and two—which Peg was beginning to worry might be a real possibility—she couldn't imagine herself being any honest to God happier. She was six weeks pregnant according to Robbie's mum, Libby, who besides being a surgeon also was a less technical . . . healer. That's why a feather could have knocked Peg over when Libby had said she was having a son, considering she'd been less than a week pregnant at the time.

She'd met Libby and Michael MacBain when Duncan had taken his new little clan of heathens to Pine Creek the weekend after their rushed Monday evening wedding so his big clan could throw them an old-fashioned wedding reception. That's when Libby had told Peg that not only was she having a boy, but that she was carrying only one. "Guaranteed," Libby had said, a smile curving her lips as she'd added, "This time."

With the gentle rock of the boat making her drowsy, Peg closed her eyes and tilted her head back to feel the sun's rays on her face. She sighed contentedly at how wonderful it felt to be a wife again—even if she was married to the most contrary, scariest, never-give-up-or-give-in man on the planet.

Oh yeah, Gretchen Robinson's bones were rattling in her grave.

Peg lifted her head to see Jacob and Peter leaning over the side when something gently bumped the boat. They were wearing matching life vests with their names embroidered on them—that she happened to know they'd switched—trying to coax Leviathan closer with gummy worms so they could pat him.

"Mom, he came!" Jacob softly whispered.

The whale always did. Peg guessed Leviathan knew the sound of their particular motor, because none of the scientists had been able to get a picture of him despite having spent two months trying. "But I don't think he's into gummy worms," she warned. "And stop feeding them to Hero before you make him sick."

"Yuck, Levi's got stinky breath," Peter said, scrambling away when a misty spurt came out of the whale's blowhole.

"You would, too, if all you ate was fish and you couldn't brush your teeth."

"I can't wait to show all them scientists my pictures," Jacob said, resting his chin on his hands on the gunwale as Hero rested his doggy chin beside him, both of them eyeing Leviathan eyeing them back. "I can't believe Mr. Steve's gonna give us ten whole dollars just for a picture of a whale."

"There's the camera on the console," Peg said, nodding toward it because she was too lazy and contented and pregnant to move. Lord, she'd forgotten how all she'd wanted to do was sleep through the first trimesters of her pregnancies. "Duncan showed you how to use it, so go on and take a bunch of pictures. Ten bucks will buy quite a few cinnamon buns."

"No, Mom, remember we said we're gonna buy Nerf swords," Peter reminded her for the tenth time that afternoon.

Peg had lost that particular battle, seeing how the twins had Duncan on their side. Damn if she didn't lose more arguments to her husband than she won—although she won the really, really important ones, so she guessed that made them even. Like this boat; Duncan had gotten her a pontoon boat so he could have the fast and way-too-sexy boat for himself. But the reason she could lounge around in the sun for another half hour before she had to meet the school bus in town was because *her* fast and way-too-sexy boat would get them to Ezra's dock in ten minutes.

Yup, there was nothing like having rousing arguments with a big strong man and winning the ones that counted. Life was good. Everyone was happy, including her mom and Aunt Bea, who were both enjoying the attention of several eligible men from Robbie's and Duncan's crews. At Duncan's suggestion, Peg had told her mom and aunt that she was pretty sure only men born in the Bottomless Lake area were susceptible to the curse. The women had looked through their family history, and sure enough, all the husbands who had met an early demise had been locals—which meant any male from away was fair game.

Chris Dubois and Aaron Jenkins had disappeared off the face of the earth just like Duncan had said they would, but everyone knew the lowlifes were still around because there had been several hit-and-run attacks on the resort site. It was virtually impossible to guard fourteen miles of road up through the wilderness, and sometimes a bridge under construction got blown up, grade stakes got relocated, and equipment tires got shot out with a high-power rifle. Occasionally notes were left saying it had been the work of one or another radical conservation group, but everyone in town knew Chris and Aaron were the culprits, since most of the protests against the resort had died down. Aaron's poor wife, Phyllis, was so embarrassed that she'd filed for divorce and gone to live with her sister in Indiana.

There'd only been one attack on the site where Duncan was building their new home on the fiord at the base of his mountain, and then it appeared to have been interrupted by . . . something. Peg suspected Duncan had had a little talk with his mountain about napping on the job after he'd found the slightly scorched pile of lumber, because he'd taken a hike up to the cave and there hadn't been any incidents since. In fact, despite every board and nail having to be hauled over on a small barge, Peg guessed they'd be moved into their new home before school started in the fall.

Oh yeah, she was married to a very relentless man.

Mac and Olivia would be home in a few days, which meant Olivia hadn't followed through on her threat to push Mac into the Grand Canyon—probably afraid her husband might decide to rearrange the national landmark. And according to the letter Olivia had sent Peg, the bone marrow transplant had gone well for both little Riley and Sophie, and Riley's prognosis was very promising. But then, why shouldn't it be if the stepdaughter of a *friggin' wizard* was involved?

"Here, give me the camera," Peg said, dropping her feet to the floor of the boat and holding out her hand. "I'll take a picture of you two patting Leviathan just to make Mr. Steve really jealous."

"I bet he'd be really jealous if you took a picture of us *riding* on Levi," Peter said, one of his legs already halfway over the gunwale.

"Oh, no you don't," Peg yelped, jumping up and pulling him back with a laugh. "The water's too cold and Leviathan might accidentally squish you."

"No, he wouldn't," Jacob said, immediately jumping to the whale's defense. "Duncan told us Levi's a rescue hero." He pointed toward the whale's tail. "See, he's even got a badge. Duncan called it a tattoo and said it means he's from Alantus. It's a tide . . . a trilide . . ."

"A trident," Peter said. "It looks like a fork you eat with, but Duncan called it a trident just like Pesidon carries. He's the boss of the ocean," her son added with great authority, his little chest puffing out against his life vest.

Peg smiled, remembering how it had taken Duncan nearly a week of subtle corrections before he'd finally gotten all the children to drop the "mister." He'd introduced them to Leviathan the day he'd taken the kids to see where he intended to build their new home, and he explained the whale was from a faraway magical island by the name of Atlantis—which was, Peg had finally realized, why Henry Oceanus was so well versed on mythological gods. So when the twins told people in town about their pet whale, everyone thought her boys had quite the imaginations.

"Okay, stand just a little bit apart," Peg said, looking at the screen on the camera, "so I can get Leviathan between you. You get in the picture, too, Hero. Smile. Smile, Leviathan!" she called out, which effectively put huge grins on the boys. Only the whale slipped below the surface just before she could snap the picture, and Peg looked up when she heard the sound of a fast-moving boat coming from the far end of the fiord.

"Oh, shoot," Peter said, also looking toward the boat. "I bet it's them scientists and they scared off Levi before we got our picture."

"I already got some of him," Jacob said. "Look in the camera, Mom."

Peg took one last glance at the fast approaching boat, then turned to put the camera in the shade of her body and scrolled through the last few pictures. "Sorry, big man," she said, showing Jacob the screen when he came over to see. "But . . . no, wait; you got part of his tail in this one." She kept scrolling. "And I think that's his blowhole." She sighed as she shut off the camera, set it on the steering console, and ruffled Jacob's hair. "You must have hit the zoom button, so none of the shots show him well enough for ten dollars, I'm afraid. But don't worry; we'll get more pictures tomorrow."

"It ain't Mr. Steve anyway," Peter said just as the boat slowed down at the very last minute and pulled up beside them.

Too late, Peg recognized Chris Dubois. "Boys, lie down on the floor!" she snapped as she lunged to start her engine—only to cry out when Chris rammed his boat into the side of theirs.

He leapt onboard, his beefy fist catching Peg on the shoulder with enough force to shove her against the opposite gunwale, making her glad she'd worn her life vest when it knocked the wind out of her. She scrambled after her screaming boys, only to have Chris slap her hard enough to knock her off her feet again.

He then gave Hero a swift kick in the ribs, the dog's snarl turning into a yelp of pain as it went skidding into one of the rear fishing chairs. Chris grabbed the dog before it could scramble to its feet, picked it up, and threw it over the side of the boat, only to swing around and backhand Peg when she tried to stop him.

She got to her feet when she saw him make a grab for Peter, then watched the boy leap away so quickly that he slammed against the console with a shriek. "Leave them alone!" she shouted, going for Chris's face even as she tried to knee him in the groin.

Only he twisted at the last minute and pulled her off balance, spinning her to clamp a hand around her throat. "Call them off, Peggy," he growled, kicking Jacob when he tried to ram into him. "Get back, you little shit!" The blow sent Jacob sprawling to the floor, the momentum slamming him into the stern. "Both you little shits climb in my boat," he shouted. "Now!"

"No!" Peg twisted free but Chris shoved her hard enough that she fell to her knees again. "No! You're not taking them!"

He grabbed Peter and tossed him into his boat, then went after Jacob. Peg looked around for something to fight with and grabbed the fire extinguisher. But Chris kicked it out of her hands, and she heard it plop into the water just as he grabbed Jacob by the vest and flung the kid toward his boat. Realizing it had drifted away from theirs, Peg ran to the gunwale to jump in after him, only to have Chris yank her to the floor—but not before she saw her son climbing onboard with Peter's help. Hero was barking and treading water between the two boats, apparently uncertain which one to swim to.

"Mom! Mom!" Peter and Jacob cried as their boat drifted farther away.

"No, you can't just leave them! They're only babies!" Peg screamed, lunging for Chris's arm when he turned the key and started her motor.

He grabbed her by her vest and dragged her kicking and screaming to the front of the boat, then punched her in the head hard enough that Peg nearly passed out. He unhooked the bow rope and used it to tie her hands to the post of the front fishing chair.

"You leave Mom alone!" Peter shouted over Jacob's screams.

Peg struggled to sit up as Chris walked back to the console and pushed the throttle forward. "Boys! Just sit still and someone will find you!" she shouted over the roar of the motor, not knowing if they could even hear her as Chris sped toward the end of the fiord. Shaking with both rage and terror, Peg could only helplessly watch the twins clinging to each other while screaming something she couldn't hear as Hero clawed at the side of their boat.

She touched her throbbing cheek with her shoulder as she glared at Chris. "God *damn* you. How can you leave two little boys adrift like that!"

"You're lucky I didn't just toss them overboard like the dog," he said with a laugh that sounded more sick than sane. "Or maybe you wanted me to bring them along." He suddenly jerked the wheel sharply then straightened back out, making Peg slam against the seat and fall on the floor. "So they could watch what I'm going to do to their stuck-up bitch of a mother."

He jerked the wheel again just as she sat up trying to see the building sight at the base of Duncan's mountain, making her cry out when she slid sideways and the rope tightened against her wrists. But she knew her husband wasn't there because he'd taken the pontoon boat when she and the boys had left in the speedboat half an hour ago; Duncan going down to the pit to meet the blasting contractor while she'd only gone a little ways down the fiord in search of Leviathan.

Peg looked back over the stern trying to spot the twins, just barely able to see Chris's boat now. Dammit, the boys were only maybe two miles from the pit; would their screams and Hero's barks carry that far over water, even with machinery running? Or maybe the scientists would come into the fiord. Surely *someone* would find them.

She turned her attention to Chris. "Are you insane? Why are you doing this?"

He just smiled.

"Is getting even with me for buying your mother's land worth going to jail for years and years?" she shouted over the roar of the powerful engine going full throttle. "You're a woodsman, Chris; getting locked up would kill you. It's not worth it. Just beach the boat and walk away, and I promise I won't press charges."

All that petition got her was a laugh.

"Look, there's a marine radio. At least call someone. Ezra; he's got a radio in his store now. Call and tell him to send someone after my boys. They're four years old, Chris! If anything happens to them, that's *murder*."

He eased back on the throttle, and Peg looked around to realize they were already nearing the end of the fiord. "They can't lock me up if they can't catch me," he said past a smug grin. "And by this time next week, we'll be far enough into Canada that nobody will find us." He slowly guided the boat up a small stream until it became too shallow, running it up onto the bank around a bend so it couldn't be seen from the fiord.

For the love of God, he was taking her to Canada? "Um, I don't know if you've heard, but I got married several weeks ago," she said as he walked to her.

He squatted down and clasped her jaw in his grimy hand. "I heard you married that MacKeage bastard." She tried to pull free when he leaned in, and his hand tightened painfully. "So is that why I never appealed to you, Peggy? You like your men *big*?" His fingers dug into her jaw, his thumb pressing her flesh against her teeth as he leaned closer. "Only this time I see you went for rich as well." He licked his tongue across her lips, then reared back with a laugh when she tried to bite him.

"He's going to kill you. And I swear to God, if anything happens to Jacob and Peter, I'm going to help him."

"Yeah, him and you and what army?" Chris said, untying her from the post of the seat. He shoved her down when she tried to scramble away, then grabbed her hands and quickly retied them, leaving a length of rope to pull her to her feet. "Like I said, Peggy darlin', he's going to have to catch me first. Come on," he growled, giving the rope a yank as he stepped onto the bank. "It's a long walk to Canada."

Peg fell onto the ground, then scrambled to her feet when he started dragging her after him. Dammit, she needed to do something! Had he taken the keys out of the boat? Where in hell was Aaron? He gave another jerk when she apparently wasn't moving fast enough, the rope chafing against the cuff on her left wrist. Yes, the magic! Surely it could help her get away. Or maybe she could at least use it to rattle Chris enough to get him to make a mistake.

"Um, do you believe in the magic, Chris?" she asked, only to bump into him when he suddenly stopped and turned to her.

"What in hell are you talking about?" he growled, looking as if *she* were insane.

So Peg gave him the best insane smile she could muster. "You know, magic; the kind that moves mountains and turns lakes into inland seas like what happened here a few months ago? The scientists still haven't been able to explain it, so people are starting to think this entire area might be . . . cursed," she whispered. "You believe someone can put a curse on a place or a . . . person?"

"What in Jesus kind of question is that?"

Peg dropped her gaze and shrugged. "I was just wondering if you believe in stuff like magic and curses and bad karma."

He turned and started walking again, giving the rope another violent snap.

Peg let out a loud, exaggerated sigh. "It doesn't matter," she said, adding an insane little laugh, "because I've been told the magic goes about its business whether you believe in it or not, and that it especially likes to sneak up and surprise a person."

Chris glanced over his shoulder at her, and yup, he was definitely looking a little rattled. *Okay, husband,* Peg silently petitioned; *it's time to use your mountain's magic to save me like you promised—after you save Peter and Jacob.*

Duncan stopped in midsentence and turned away from the blasting contractor he was talking to and opened the door on his truck. He reached in for the radio mike and ordered all the men driving machinery in and around the pit to shut off their engines, then tossed down the mike and walked toward the beach. But he changed direction and started running up the knoll to the tote road when he heard barking and screaming coming from the fiord, and spotted Pete and Jacob and Hero in the strange boat heading into the cove.

Realizing the boat was going too fast for the engine only being at an idle, Duncan ran into the water and caught it just as he saw Leviathan back away from the far side and slip under the surface—only to have to catch the twins when they threw themselves at him, sobbing loudly and both talking at once.

"You gotta save Mom!" Jacob cried as he hugged Duncan's neck.

"A bad man stole her!" Pete added in a wail, also clinging to his neck.

Duncan waded out of the water onto the road, Hero jumping out of the boat and following. He shook his head at Paul when the contractor tried to take one of the boys from him just as several of his crew ran up to them. "Slow down and tell me what happened," he said calmly, kneeling to stand the boys on their feet and hug them so they wouldn't see his own terror. "Where's your Mom?"

"A man smashed right into our boat and jumped in with us," Jacob said. He leaned back to look at Duncan. "H-he hit Mom really hard, and he throwed Hero in the water when he tried to bite him. Then he tried to grab Pete and he kicked me."

"Then he threw me in his boat," Pete added.

"And he hit Mom again," Jacob continued with a shudder that racked his whole body. "And he threw me at his boat, too. But I fell in the water 'cause it was too far, but Pete pulled me inside."

"And he tied up Mom to the seat and left in our boat," Pete said as he started crying again. "And she hollered to us to sit down, 'cause someone would find us."

"But no one was f-finding us," Jacob said with huge sobs. "And we pulled and pulled but we couldn't get Hero in the boat."

Duncan rubbed their tear-splotched cheeks with his thumbs, saying nothing so they could get it all out.

"But then Leviathan helped," Pete said. "He just floated beside the boat so Hero crawled right up his back and got in with us."

"And we pulled the handle on the rope like we seen you do on the old boat," Jacob continued in a rush, "and the motor started and . . . and we started going."

"In circles," Pete added, swiping his puffy eyes with a trembling hand. "But Levi bumped us and we started going straight."

"W-we tried to go after Mom," Jacob said, valiantly trying to suck up his sobs. "But Levi kept pushing us this way. And when we got close, Hero started barking so we started screaming."

"I heard you," Duncan said, pulling them against him and kissing each of their foreheads. He held all three of their heads together with Hero having pushed between his thighs. "You did good, boys, and so did your pup. You're all rescue heroes for staying calm and brave and coming to get me. So ye don't worry now, because I'm going to go save your mom." He kissed them again, then leaned away to pat his hind pocket with a reassuring smile. "I've still got my badge in my wallet to show the bad man." He folded the twins back against him and looked up at his crew. "Jason, get on the radio and have Robbie and Alec get down here, but tell them to pick up Jeanine and Bea on their way out the road." He looked back at Pete and Jacob. "Can ye tell me where the man took your mom? Did he go toward Bottomless or farther up the fiord?"

"U-up it," Jacob said, pointing north.

"He went so far we couldn't see them no more," Pete added in a whisper.

Duncan scooped them up in his arms and started toward the house. "Jon, you and David catch that boat and pull it onto the beach." He stopped and looked at the other men. "Do Charlotte and Isabel know any of you on sight?" he asked, only to start walking again when several of them shook their heads. "Jim, call the Trading Post and have Ezra meet the girls when they get off the school bus. Then I want you to drive Bea into town to get them and bring them home."

"We need to call the sheriff," Paul said, walking beside him. "And the warden and forest services; they can have a plane and chopper in the sky in an hour."

Duncan sat the boys in the front passenger seat of his truck after motioning for Paul to open the door, then let Hero jump in on the floor in front of them. "Jacob, Pete, did you recognize the man who took your mom?" he asked softly. "Or did she call him by name?" he added when they shook their heads.

"Yeah," Jacob said even as Pete nodded. "Mom called him Chris."

Duncan gave them each another kiss, then turned to the contractor. "You call the sheriff and let him know that Chris Dubois has my wife, Peg MacKeage. But you tell him I don't want anything in the air as long as she's still with Dubois. After I get her away from him, then they can go after him with everything they've got."

Paul's jaw slackened. "How in hell . . . You expect to go after him all by yourself?"

Duncan turned at the sound of a truck racing down the road and into the yard and watched Robbie pull to a stop directly behind his pickup. All four doors opened; Alec and Robbie jumped out of the front and Jeanine and Bea out of the rear doors.

"Peter, Jacob!" Jeanine cried. Duncan stepped away so she could lean inside to pull both boys into her arms. "Ohmigod, you poor babies, are you okay?"

Duncan walked over to Robbie and Alec when he saw Bea open the driver's door and slide in to hug the boys along with Jeanine. "Can ye get to Peg?" he asked Robbie.

Robbie shook his head. "I'm still powerless. Only you have any authority over the magic in this area, as your mountain is the sole source of energy at the moment."

"But I woke it up, so why in hell can't you use it?"

Robbie shook his head again. "It's tuned only to you, Duncan, and will remain so until Mac chooses to release all the magic again."

Duncan glanced back at the truck to see the women still hugging the boys, then looked toward the fiord and rubbed his hands over his face. "Christ, I can't imagine the hell he's putting her through." He turned beseeching eyes on Robbie and Alec. "What if the bastard's already killed her?"

"Nay," Robbie said quietly. "He wouldn't have bothered taking her if he merely wanted her dead." He gestured at Duncan's right arm. "Go quiet and focus on your cuff. It's connected to Peg's. Listen to what it's telling you."

Duncan faced the fiord again and took a calming breath, focusing inward until he felt his cuff softly tighten against his pulse and vague snapshots started flashing through his mind. Only instead of seeing Peg, he *felt* her emotions hit him with enough force to nearly drop him to his knees.

"Sweet Christ," he whispered, closing his eyes when her calm yet utterly lethal anger resonated through every cell in his body. "She's toying with Dubois, trying to scare him with the magic so he'll panic and make a mistake." He turned to Robbie and Alec. "She's in pain; I can feel every bruise the bastard put on her."

"The connection to your wife runs in both directions," Robbie said. "Send her your strength, Duncan. Have Peg feel you the same way you're feeling her, and let her know you're coming for her." He grinned tightly. "Ye may also want to convey that anyone who tries to manipulate the magic in anger

could find themselves with more power than they can handle."
He set a hand on Duncan's shoulder. "And I suggest *you* remember that as well when ye come face-to-face with Dubois."
He dropped his hand away with a shrug, his smile turning
genuine. "Then again, if ye happened to accidentally . . . say,
send the bastard back a few centuries, I believe Providence
would understand you're still getting used to the magic."

"The sheriff's on his way," Paul said, walking over to them.
"We're in luck; dispatch said he's nearby. She's sending the
state police and game wardens, too."

"Thanks," Duncan said, striding to the pickup. He gently
moved Jeanine out of the way and clasped both twins' trembling shoulders as they clung to each other with Hero's head
squeezed between them. "Ye have my word, boys, I'll have
your mom home by sunrise tomorrow. Your gram and gram-
auntie will stay right here with you and the girls until I get
back, and so will Alec." He gave them each a kiss on their
foreheads, then wrapped his arms around them in a careful
hug. "Ye just continue to be the brave heroes ye are," he whispered. "I love you."

He gave them a reassuring squeeze, then turned to Jeanine.
"One of my men will drive you or Bea to Ezra's to pick up the
girls. Then I would ask that ye keep the children here until I
get back. Ye don't worry about my crew; they can cook their
own supper. I'll be back with Peg by daybreak."

"Wait," Jeanine said, grabbing his arm when he turned
away. "You can't mean to go after her all by yourself. Is the
bad man the boys are talking about Chris Dubois? Then he
knows the backcountry better than anyone," she continued
when Duncan nodded. "How are you even going to know
where to look?"

He pulled his frantic mother-in-law into his arms. "Ye need
to trust me, Jeanine," he whispered. "Because I have a secret
weapon that's going to make Dubois sorry he was ever born."

"W-what weapon?" she asked against his shoulder.

Duncan gave her one last squeeze and stepped away. "Your
daughter," he said with a wink, just before he turned and
headed toward the beach. "I already know how to manipulate
time," he said as Robbie and Alec fell into step beside him. He
stopped at the front of his pontoon boat pulled up on shore and

looked from one man to the other. "So once I decide where he's taking her, I'll get ahead of them and be waiting."

"There's a lot of wilderness out there," Robbie said, even as his deep gray eyes suddenly lit with amusement. "But then, your mountain did have the foresight to give ye a tracking device to put on your wife, didn't it?"

"Aye, apparently the magic took pity when it realized it had given me such a contrary woman," Duncan said, leaping onto the deck of his boat and walking back to the steering console. "Keep an eye on things here, as we don't know if this might also be a diversion for Aaron Jenkins to take another shot at the resort road." He started the engine, letting the powerful motor warm up at a quiet idle. "And try to stall the sheriff from mounting a search until morning, if ye can do it without drawing suspicion."

Robbie and Alec nodded, then both grabbed the front deck of the boat and pushed it off the beach when Duncan slid the engine into reverse.

"Where's your sword?" Alec softly called after glancing over his shoulder to make sure no one was in the immediate area.

Duncan put the motor in forward. "In my cave. I need to stop there first, anyway, and have a little talk with my mountain." He looked at Robbie. "I'll see if I can't persuade it to share its power with ye before I go after Dubois, on the off chance I end up sending myself to hell with him."

Robbie chuckled. "I've a fear ye may have to go through Peg to get there. Godspeed, Duncan." Robbie gave a wave and turned away just as the sound of a fast-approaching siren echoed up the main road.

Alec jogged down the beach to keep pace as Duncan idled toward the fiord. "Are ye sure you don't want to take the pup?" Alec asked.

"He's too young to know the art of stalking yet," Duncan said with a shake of his head. "And the children need him now." He slid the engine out of gear when he reached the narrow channel in the old tote road and let the boat glide toward shore. "Alec," he said as his nephew waded into the water and grabbed the side of the deck. "You'll look after the children?" he asked quietly, leaving the full request unsaid.

"Aye," Alec said with a nod. "They'll never want for love and family." He tapped the side of the boat with a chuckle. "Not that I'm worried," he said, giving it a shove toward the fiord. "Since we both know contrary always triumphs over stupidity."

Duncan gave him a nod and pushed the throttle all the way down, the powerful engine making the boat surge into the fiord with surprising speed as he headed toward his mountain. Aye, and if the stupid bastard Dubois didn't already know it, he was going to be living that very truth before the day was through.

Chapter Twenty-four

Peg was growing more exhausted from trying to slow Chris down than from trying to keep up with him, and she wasn't sure how much longer she could go before she collapsed. One of her eyes was swollen nearly shut from one of the blows she'd taken, and her wrists were bleeding and her hands were swelling up like balloons. Her shoulders felt ready to fall out of their sockets from Chris's constantly jerking on the rope, and she was afraid she was getting hypothermia because all she had on was a thin shirt under her life vest.

Peg grasped the rope in preparation for the jerk she knew was coming. "Please, Chris, we need to stop," she pleaded, falling to her knees the moment he did and then collapsing onto her side with a groan. "I need water. And if you don't untie my hands, they're going to fall off."

He stood with his fists on his hips and stared down at her. "Ain't so prissy now, are you, Peggy?" He squatted down and grabbed her chin, his fingers biting into her jaw. "You want water, you're gonna have to earn it." He pressed his thumb into the corner of her mouth. "Say, the longer the kiss, the longer the drink."

She jerked away and turned her face into the ground, only to cry out when he pulled her upright by her hair and smashed his mouth down on hers. Fighting not to gag, Peg forced herself to open her lips and push her tongue inside his mouth, even making a soft moaning sound as she pressed toward him.

Chris reared back, giving her hair another painful yank. "What in hell are you doing?" he growled, the last of the sun's rays catching the surprise in his eyes.

Peg smiled. "I'm really thirsty, Chris." She shrugged one shoulder. "And if you don't seem to care about my family curse, then why should I?"

"What curse?" he hissed, shoving her away.

Peg fell back, but then held up her bound hands. "Untie me and I'll tell you why I didn't dare go out with you after Billy died. Or didn't you notice I haven't gone out with anyone since I became a widow? I wasn't rejecting you, Chris; I was saving your life."

"What? How?"

She lifted her hands again. "Untie me and I'll tell you about my curse. Because if I don't," she continued when he hesitated, "then you can't blame me if something happens to you."

Peg gritted her teeth when he jerked the knots on the rope trying to loosen them, his fingers becoming slick with her blood. "What in Jesus are you talking about?" he snarled, backing away when he had them loosened enough that Peg could finish the job herself. "What curse? What's going to happen?"

Peg slowly flexed her fingers, refusing to cry out at the pain shooting through her hands with the renewed circulation, and took a slow, fortifying breath. "You know my mom and aunt are widows, right? Well, my father died when I was five, and my stepdad died within a few years of Mom marrying him. It was the same with my aunt Bea; she lost both of her husbands in freak accidents just like I lost Billy."

Chris scurried back even more. "You're all black widows or something?"

Peg nodded, stretching her throbbing legs out in front of her. "Yeah, it appears all the women in my family for the last five generations have been deadly to men. Our first husbands never make it past the age of thirty, and if we remarry or if any man even has sex with us," she added for extra insurance, "the curse kills them off."

His eyes narrowed. "You just married MacKeage." He snorted. "You hoping he'll last long enough to change his will and leave you a *rich* widow?"

"No," she said, shaking her head. "I'm not worried about Duncan dying, because he has the power to break my family curse."

"How?"

"By the magic I was talking about. Remember I said there's something around here that's powerful enough to move mountains? Well, Duncan's tapped into it."

Chris snorted again. "You're fucking crazy."

But Peg could see his doubt. "Yeah, crazy enough to believe what I see with my own eyes," she said, looking directly into his. She suddenly had a thought. "I know you and Aaron tried to burn the building supplies at our house site across the fiord. So what stopped you right in the middle of setting that lumber on fire?"

Peg saw his doubt turn to outright fear, and he suddenly stood up to move even farther away. "We don't know what the hell happened," he said, nervously rubbing the back of his neck as he stared down at her. "Aaron swears something tapped him hard on the shoulder, but when he turned around nothing was there. And he swears to God when he started running that something tripped him—*three times*—as he made his way across the building site to me."

Peg gave a soft snort. "I don't think it was God; more like a pissed-off mountain. So what put out the fire you started?"

Chris took another step back, shaking his head. "I swear to—A deluge of water came out of nowhere and nearly drowned me when it landed on the lumber."

Peg widened her eyes with appropriate horror. "Oh, Chris," she whispered. "Forget my stupid curse; I'd be more worried about Duncan's magic if I were you."

"What!" Sweat broke out on his forehead as he suddenly looked around, his widened gaze stopping on their back trail before dropping to her.

Peg nodded, coiling onto her side on the ground when she felt herself getting dizzy, disguising her moan by snorting again. "Sometimes Duncan scares the hell out of me, too. But like you said, he is rich. So if his magic can't break my family curse, then I guess I'll be widowed again, only not so poor this time."

Chris stepped closer to stare down at her, then pulled a metal canteen bottle out of the pack he'd had stashed in the woods not far from where he'd hidden the boat. He squatted down again and held it out to her. "You're looking pale. But don't drink too much or you'll puke. We still got a couple of miles to go to reach my campsite."

"You sure you wouldn't be better off just leaving me here?" she asked, slowly pushing herself into a sitting position to take the water from him. "You'd make better time getting to Canada." It took some doing to get the cover off the bottle because her hands were shaking and more than useless, but she finally took a long, blessedly wet drink. She wiped her mouth on her sleeve, then canted her head at Chris. "I'm pretty sure Duncan's magic gets weaker the farther away you get from his mountain."

"There ain't no such thing as magic," he growled—apparently trying to bluster away his fear. "And MacKeage wasn't even around here when the earthquake hit." He snorted and stood up, then reached down and grabbed her life vest and pulled her to her feet. But then he had to hold her when she swayed toward him. "Jesus, don't touch me!" he yelped, stepping away.

"You're touching me!" she snapped, jerking free, only to have to grab a tree to keep from falling. "Just leave me here. I'll find my own way back. Run, Chris; run as fast and as far as you can."

He eyed her with indecision for several heartbeats, then suddenly bent to snatch up the rope before he grabbed her vest and pulled her away from the tree. "Oh, I'm running all right, but not without insurance," he snarled, wrapping the rope around her neck. He slapped her hand away when Peg tried to stop him from tying it into a slipknot. "Take one more drink," he said, lifting her arm holding the canteen.

Peg took another long drink and handed the canteen to him, looking him directly in the eyes. "You made your first mistake when you boarded my boat," she said with utter calm, "your second mistake when you hit me, and your third when you left Peter and Jacob in the middle of the fiord. But trying to take me to Canada with you is as good as signing your own death warrant, Chris. Doubt me or the magic or whatever you want, but I'm actually trying to save your life."

He turned away with a snort and started walking—although he didn't jerk the rope this time. "Just shut the hell up and make sure to keep up with me if you don't want your neck looking like your wrists."

Peg stumbled after him with a stifled curse, having to grab trees to keep from falling, as her legs felt like rubber and she was so dizzy that she could barely see straight. Dammit, she'd nearly had him convinced to leave her behind.

And where in hell was Duncan, anyway? He'd promised to keep her safe once he got hold of the magic, so where in hell was the relentless man?

Duncan stood in the darkness of the night with his back against a large pine tree, undecided if he wanted to kiss Peg for her genius or shake her until she apologized for scaring ten years off his life by pushing Dubois nearly past the point of reason. Didn't she realize the bastard could have simply killed her to be rid of the stone she'd become around his neck? Hell, according to what his mountain had told him, even Aaron Jenkins had realized his partner in crime was losing his grip on reality and had run off to Canada over a week ago—right after their botched attack on Duncan's house site.

And Peg was wrong; Dubois's first mistake had been spray-painting her van, his second burning her house, his third trying to run them off the road. And the bastard had signed his death warrant the moment he'd boarded her boat. As for striking Peg and leaving the twins alone in the middle of the fiord . . . well, that had guaranteed his death would be slow and painful. Duncan was so goddamned angry, he wasn't going to need his mountain's help, either.

He was about a hundred yards up the trail ahead of them, but he'd mastered the magic enough that he might as well be walking beside them, he was so attuned to Peg. Her every thought, every emotion, every twinge of pain she felt was like he was inside her skin.

Christ, she was brave. And scary smart. And so goddamned

contrary she hadn't heard one thing he'd been trying to convey to her because she'd been too focused on rattling Dubois. Hell, he could openly hear her now as they approached, still pushing the man to the edge of reason even as Duncan felt she was on the verge of collapsing.

"Did you know Livy Baldwin's new husband is an honest to God wizard?" he heard her ask as they drew nearer. "Mac's the one who caused the earthquake. He's also the boss of all the drùidhs who guard all the Trees of Life. One of those Trees is growing right here in Maine, someplace around Pine Creek, I think." She snorted. "Gee, Chris, maybe you should cut it down so you could buy a new truck and *drive* to Canada."

"Shut up!" Dubois shouted just as they passed Duncan, the bastard jerking the rope around Peg's neck—making her cry out as she stumbled.

To hell with just shaking her, Duncan decided; he was putting the reckless woman over his knee. After, that is, he kissed every scratch and bruise on her body.

He silently drew his sword and stepped into the trail, creeping up behind Peg to cover her mouth with his hand as he sliced the rope with his blade—only to have her go boneless in his arms with a silent sigh of relief. He lowered her to the ground and continued on, snatching up the dangling rope and giving it a hard jerk.

Dubois turned with a snarl, but stopped in midstep when the tip of Duncan's sword pressed into his chest. "Fuck," the man hissed, going perfectly still.

Duncan lifted the bastard's chin with the tip of his sword. "For the record," he said quietly, "your very first mistake was getting aggressive with Peg two and a half years ago." He lowered the tip to Dubois's windpipe just above his collarbone. "Your last and ultimately fatal mistake, however, was not walking away just now when *my wife* was sincerely trying to save your life."

"Um, Duncan?" Peg rasped from the darkness behind him. "I really wish you wouldn't do anything when you're this angry, because I really don't think I can deal with more magic than we can handle right now."

"You *heard* everything I was conveying to you?" he

growled without taking his eyes off of Dubois. "And yet ye still continued to goad the bastard?"

"I . . . I liked your idea of turning him into a dung beetle, even if it was just a fleeting thought. But I don't think you should turn him into anything Leviathan could eat, because that might give the poor whale belly cramps or something."

Christ, she was going to be the death of him—or else his salvation. Not knowing if he wanted to laugh or roar, Duncan dropped the tip of his sword to the ground between his feet and crossed his wrists over the hilt with a sigh, watching Dubois slowly raise his hand to his throat. "Then what do you suggest I do with him?"

"I . . . I don't care, just as long as you don't offend Providence."

"Ye like the wilderness, do you, Dubois?" Duncan asked as he watched the wide-eyed man inching backward.

"Y-yes."

"Then enjoy the rest of your life, you stupid bastard," Duncan growled as he finally released the magic.

The light of a thousand suns shattered the air with a thunderous boom, the powerful percussion shaking the ground in echoing rumbles. Commanding the whorls of vibrant colors to gather in a howling tempest of tightly focused energy, Duncan smiled in satisfaction when Dubois simply vanished, the man's scream of terror fading into the nighttime sky with the retreating vortex. The light dissipated as suddenly as it appeared but for the few sparkles he commanded to illuminate the immediate area, and the forest fell silent but for the whispered litany of "ohmigods" coming from behind him.

Duncan slid his sword into its sheath as he turned and walked to Peg, shedding his backpack to kneel on the ground beside her. Christ, he almost wished he hadn't kept any of the light when he saw the bruises and scratches on her face. He drew in a shuddering breath at the sight of her raw and bleeding wrists when she raised her hand to cover her swollen eye as if she were embarrassed.

"Aw hell, Peg," he whispered thickly, carefully lifting her into his arms. He turned to sit leaning against a tree and set her on his thighs to cradle her against him. "I'm so sorry I wasn't able to bend time enough to stop this from ever happening."

"P-please tell me Peter and Jacob are okay."

"They're better than okay," he said as he slowly unbuckled her life vest. "Your sons are brave, strong young men, lass." He sat her upright just enough to carefully slide the vest off her shoulders, hesitating when he heard her soft hiss of pain, then finally got it off and tossed it away. "They managed to get the motor started," he continued conversationally as he unbuttoned her blouse, "right after Leviathan helped them get Hero into the boat. Then the whale steered them toward home despite their determination to go after you themselves."

He slipped off her blouse, being extra careful as he pulled the sleeves over her bloody wrists, his gut knotting when he heard her try to stifle another hiss. "All your little heathens are safe at home with your mom and aunt," he quietly continued as he tossed the blouse into the woods. He raised a hand to the back clasp on her bra, only to break into a sweat when he saw the angry bruise covering a good portion of her right shoulder. "You'll be back with them by sunrise, I promise."

"I don't want them to see me like this," she whispered, holding the unfastened bra against her breasts.

"They won't, lass. I'll have ye right as rain before we leave here. But I'm going to need your cooperation, wife, to let me heal you."

She lifted her head to finally look at him. "H-how?"

He smiled. "By kissing away your boo-boos," he said, partly to piss her off but mostly because he was serious about touching every inch of her trembling body.

She looked down at her lap, but not before he saw a slight scowl tug at one corner of her swollen mouth, and Duncan took his first full breath since he'd heard Peter and Jacob shouting from the boat out on the fiord.

"Where . . . where's Chris?" she asked, glancing at where he'd been standing.

"Right here, actually, only four hundred years in the past."

She looked up, this time with a hint of a smile as she pressed a trembling hand to his cheek and sighed. "You can be a real bastard like that sometimes," she said, dropping her hand and snuggling against him with another sigh. "Okay, husband, you may start kissing away."

Epilogue

———

Peg stood at the end of the Inglenook road, undecided who was going to burst into tears first, her or Duncan or Mac. Well okay, the men might not actually cry, but they definitely weren't looking all that big and strong and unkillable at the moment. But having barely survived this ordeal twice already and knowing this time would be even worse, Peg had all her pockets stuffed with tissues.

Hell, even Hero knew something was afoot.

Olivia seemed to be the only one who didn't look as if she were attending a funeral, instead appearing eager to have the whole matter over with so she could get to the Drunken Moose for some cinnamon buns. Yeah, well, the woman would be wearing a different expression six years from now. But then, Peg thought with a sigh, she'd be wearing the same expression herself for the *fourth* time.

She really, really needed to have a little talk with Providence, because she really didn't think she could go through this a fifth or sixth time.

"Mom," Jacob whispered, tugging on Peg's sleeve. He held up his other hand to her. "Maybe you should keep this in your pocket today, 'cause you look like you need it more than me."

Peg dropped down to one knee and closed Jacob's fingers

over the small, smooth stone Duncan had given him last night when he'd tucked the boys into bed, which was identical to the one he'd handed Peter. "Thanks, sweetie, but I think you better take it with you. And if you get even a little bit scared today, you reach in your pocket and close your fist around your very own piece of home." She pulled the straps of his backpack together to press them against his chest and smiled. "Remember Duncan said that rock is filled with very powerful magic because it came from deep inside our mountain, and that all you have to do is close your eyes and picture swimming in the warm water pool when you're holding it, and you'll start feeling right as rain in no time."

"But don't forget to take it out of your pocket first," Duncan said thickly, having also dropped to one knee. He brushed a hand—that Peg noticed was shaking slightly—over Jacob's hair. "You're going to be fine," he murmured, even as Peg wondered if he was trying to reassure the boy or himself.

She saw her husband suddenly stiffen then quickly stand up, his gaze shooting down the main road. He scooped Peter up in one arm, then reached down and helped her stand before he scooped Jacob up in his other arm. Mac was also holding Henry, Peg noticed just as she heard the rumble of the school bus climbing the long grade that crested a quarter of a mile down the road.

"Quick, everyone," Olivia said, pulling a camera out of her pocket. "All of you stand together and I'll get the bus in the picture with you when it stops."

Everyone dutifully moved to the opposite side of the Inglenook road as directed. Peg pulled Charlotte and Isabel in front of her as she tucked herself up against Duncan's chest between the twins. Sophie held Mac's hand as he held Henry in his other arm, and Hero trotted over and sat down in front of everyone—only facing the main road instead of the lens.

"Wait. You need to be in the picture, too," Peg said. "Trip the timer and set the camera on the hood of your truck."

Olivia snapped one quick shot, then rushed around the front fender of Mac's SUV. She set the camera on the hood, then leaned down to align it, pushed a button, and ran over to tuck herself behind her daughter against Mac's side. "Smile, everyone," she said just as the school bus ground to a halt on the main road, sending a billowing cloud of dust toward them.

"Duncan," Jacob said. "You got to let us down 'cause we got to get on the bus."

Peg took a fortifying breath and turned, reaching up to take Peter away from him. Only Duncan stepped back, his grip on the boys tightening. "I've got them," he growled thickly. "You're not supposed to be lifting anything heavy."

Peg looked down to hide her consternation as he turned and very slowly walked to the school bus, still carrying the twins. And then she took another deep breath when Charlotte slid her hand into hers.

"You'll be okay, Mom," her daughter said as she started leading Peg toward the bus. She gave her a squeeze as she tilted her head up with a smile. "I'm not real sure about Duncan, though."

Peg pulled her to a stop, then grabbed Isabel's sleeve to stop her, also. "What am I going to do all day without the boys stuck to me like glue? And you two," she said, smoothing down each girl's pretty new jacket. She tucked a strand of hair behind Charlotte's ear to expose one of her shiny birthstone earrings. "We had so much fun together this summer out on Bottomless and hiking the mountain."

Charlotte patted Peg's arm, smiling crookedly. "We'll be back this afternoon, Mom. And don't worry; Isabel and I will keep an eye on Pete and Repeat."

Peg bunched Charlotte's jacket in her fist. "You don't let anyone at school call him Repeat, you understand? If you hear them, you go tell the principal."

"Mommm," Isabel said, pulling Peg along. "Duncan's waiting at the door for you to kiss the boys good-bye."

"Oh. Oh! Peter, Jacob," she said, rushing to them. She pulled each one down and gave them each several loud kisses. "You both be good, you hear?" she said, gripping their arms as she valiantly held her tears inside. "I promise I'll be right there at Ezra's store waiting to pick you up off the bus this afternoon."

"Mommm, good-bye," Peter whispered tightly, eyeing the children on the bus eyeing them.

Only instead of setting them down, Duncan walked right up into the bus behind Sophie and Isabel and Charlotte, followed by Mac carrying Henry.

Olivia slid her arm through Peg's with a laugh. "Wouldn't it be nice if there were a bus that took the men away all day, too?"

Peg found her first real smile of the morning as she patted her slightly bulging belly. "I swear Duncan spends more time watching me than he does working." She sighed. "Apparently pregnant women can't even lift something as heavy as a paintbrush, much less hang curtains. And God forbid I should want to go for a walk in the woods *all by myself*," she said with a laugh.

Olivia snorted, patting her own protruding belly. "Mac flew into a panic the other day when I said I was taking Sophie to Bangor to have a mother-daughter day before school started. I swear no fewer than two dozen seagulls followed us all the way down to Bangor and back, the little spies." She gestured toward the bus—which the men were *still* on. "Honestly, you'd think Henry was going to Siberia the way my dear sweet husband has been acting all morning."

Peg shook her head. "I would like to have been a fly on the wall after you took Henry in to be tested for his grade level. I bet no one at school knew what to do with him." She gave Olivia's arm a squeeze. "I'm glad you only let them put him ahead two grades. He might be the smartest kid on the planet, but he's still only six years old. Isabel's pretty miffed Henry's starting school in the third grade with Sophie instead of in her class."

"She can't be any more upset than Mac is," Olivia said. "When Sophie showed him some of her schoolwork from last year, he threatened to open a private school for all our children right here at Inglenook." She leaned closer. "He wanted to bring in a couple of teachers from Atlantis, claiming he was fluent in six languages and doing algebra by the time he was Sophie's age."

"He's a friggin' wizard," Peg said on a laugh. "He was probably doing algebra in the womb." She glanced down at Olivia's belly, figuring they'd have their babies within a few weeks of each other. "So, when are you going to tell me if you're having a boy or a girl?"

"When it's born," Olivia said. "Mac wants to be surprised, so he's not peeking."

They both looked up at the sound of the bus finally leaving, and Peg had to grab Duncan as Olivia grabbed Mac, and the women pulled them over to the side of the road. Duncan had brought his little clan over on the pontoon boat this morning to join the Oceanuses so all the children could meet the bus together for the thirty-mile ride to Turtleback Station on this first day of school.

"The bus turns here," Olivia explained when Mac frowned at her, "because this is its last stop now that Peg lives across the fiord."

The men wrapped their arms around their respective wives, Duncan resting his chin on Peg's head. She smiled when she felt the tension in him as the school bus backed into the Inglenook road then turned and headed toward town, and Peg felt her first tear slip free when she saw Peter and Jacob's excited little faces looking out the window as they waved to her.

Duncan dropped his arms from around her when the bus suddenly stopped not a hundred yards down the road and the driver's head popped out a window. "Somebody want to come get this dog off the bus?" he hollered back with a grin.

Duncan took off with a muttered curse, running down the road and disappearing up the ditch side of the bus, only to reappear a minute later carrying Hero as the dog kept whining and frantically struggling to get down.

Mac suddenly ushered Peg and Olivia toward the SUV. "We should probably hurry to the Drunken Moose before all the buns are gone," he said, opening the back door for Peg before leading Olivia around to the front passenger side.

Duncan tossed Hero in the back, then got in the seat next to Peg. "Let's go," he said, his attention on the bus rumbling out of sight down over the hill.

Mac pulled onto the main road without even looking for traffic, and Olivia glanced over her shoulder at Peg, her eyes dancing with amusement. But instead of going around the bus when it pulled over to let them pass, Mac patiently made every stop it did to pick up more children before reaching town. And then, instead of pulling into one of the open parking slots, he stopped right in the middle of the road.

"Why don't you ladies go in and visit with Ezra," Mac suggested to Olivia. "There's a store in Turtleback that Duncan says has the exact pair of work boots I need for the construction site, so I believe we might as well run down and get them right now. We'll be back in no time, and then we'll all go over to the Drunken Moose for breakfast."

Peg figured Olivia didn't move quite fast enough when she saw Mac unclip his wife's seat belt, then lean over and give her a quick kiss on the cheek just as her door suddenly opened on its own. "See you soon, honey."

Duncan pulled Peg out his side of the truck with him, gave her a quick kiss on her forehead, then hugged her. "Ye don't fret over the boys," he whispered. "They'll be just fine," he said, again making Peg wonder who he was trying to reassure when he jumped in the front seat and Mac took off before he even had his door closed.

Olivia slid her arm through Peg's and started walking toward the path leading down to the newly reconstructed park at the foot of the falls. "How much do you want to bet they get halfway back here before they remember they went to buy boots?" she asked, pulling Peg down beside her on one of the benches.

Mimicking Olivia, Peg also leaned back, folded her hands over her belly, and shook her head with a laugh that still had a lingering trace of tears. "Aren't we lucky to have both fallen in love with big, strong, invincible men?"

"And charmed," Olivia whispered, nudging Peg's shoulder with her own. "Let's not forget how charmed they both are."

LETTER FROM LAKEWATCH

Spring 2012

Dear Readers,

Mother Nature absolutely has no modesty. I can personally attest to this, as for the last several days there's been a lot of sex going on just outside my writing studio. I've stormed out onto my deck and shouted that I'm trying to write a book here, so could everyone please go get a room, only to be answered by such raucous laughter that I had to slink back inside and close my windows and pull the shades.

Honestly, I swear they shouted right back at me to get a life, lady.

It's not just those horny mallard drakes all vying for the attention of a single harried hen, either. It's my dear sweet crows renewing their vows of monogamy while directing maiden aunts and bachelor uncles on building a new nest. It's a pair of bald eagles trying to get this year's family started while putting up with last year's offspring complaining that they're bored and can't find anything to eat. And it's loons showing up with the first crack in the ice large enough to be a landing strip and immediately starting in with their haunting, tremulous calls day and night. It's male woodpeckers incessantly tapping a metal chimney, hoping there's a cute little female within earshot. Muskrats, robins, squirrels, skunks, fox, osprey, Canada geese; you name it and LakeWatch has it—all having sex (or trying damned hard to) right there in broad daylight, in plain sight of children walking home from school. Heck, even the frogs and peepers are calling from the bogs before the ice is completely gone from the lake.

I'm beginning to think one of the most powerful forces in the universe is the need to reproduce. Pacific salmon die swimming upstream to lay their eggs. A mama octopus starves tending her brood and is too weak to save herself once her little octopi set off to explore the deep blue sea. Even plants are more concerned with furthering their species than saving themselves, putting their energies into propagation at the first signs of stress. (I believe I've mentioned before that I'm addicted to the Discovery Channel.)

Speaking of energy; I must be getting old, because I look at young people and wonder where they get the energy to deal with all the drama involved in pairing up while trying to get their own lives in order. I feel even older still seeing them having babies, when my husband and I need naps after our grandkids come visit for just a few hours.

I digress. Sorry. Back to Mother Nature's immodesty and how that inspires my writing. I get a lot of raised eyebrows when I say I'm a romance author—usually from the men. The women usually just ask for titles. (When my husband gets one of those raised eyebrows, he just says he does all my research. Honestly, he says that with a perfectly straight face! But it effectively forestalls any more questions, and is quite often met with envy from the men.)

From the prudes I immediately get, "Oh, you write those kinds of books."

Yes, I do, and I'm damned proud of it. Can somebody please tell me how to tell a story involving two people falling in love and not have sex be part of their journey? Sure, I could have the hero sweep the heroine into his arms and carry her into the bedroom, then have him kick the door closed with his foot to keep the reader out. But honestly, I want to go in there with them, because I've discovered you find out an awful lot about people when they're naked. Stuff you would never find out when they're all dressed up in their designer-label armor. A sassy-mouthed vixen sud-

denly becomes self-conscious; a powerful warrior hesitates; a wallflower awakens.

It's not about the sex; it's about the love. It's discovering who is really hiding behind the masks people hold up to the big scary world, and about the truly most powerful force in the universe—that of love rippling with passion and desire.

Birds do it, bees do it; and if those noisy ducks can do it with wild abandon right there on my beachfront, then by God my hero and heroine had better let me—and my readers—sneak into the bedroom while they do it.

We promise we won't giggle . . . too loudly.

Until later from a raucous LakeWatch, you keep reading and I'll keep writing.

Janet

Keep reading for an excerpt
from the next Spellbound Falls romance
by Janet Chapman

Courting Carolina

Available September 2012 from Jove Books

Alec heard the distinct rumble of thunder over the gush of the cascading falls and tossed his shovel onto the stream bank with a muttered curse before vaulting up behind it. He picked up his shirt and used it to wipe the sweat off his face, then turned to glare at the dark clouds rolling across the fiord toward him. "Go around!" he shouted, pointing north with his free hand as he wiped down his chest. But the storm gods didn't have any sense of humor, apparently, and the hairs on his arms stirred just as lightning flashed on a sharp crack of thunder. "Well, fine, then!" he shouted with a laugh as he bolted toward camp. "Take your best shot, you noisy bastards!"

Alec slipped into his shirt when the wind pushing ahead of the storm took on an ominous chill, and lengthened his stride when he realized he was losing the footrace to the sheet of rain sweeping up the mountain. How in hell had he been caught by surprise? There hadn't been a cold front forecast to come through or even any clouds in the crisp September sky ten minutes ago. Another crack sounded to his right just as the wind-driven rain hit with enough force to make him stagger, and Alec scrambled to catch himself with another laugh.

But he came to an abrupt halt at the sound of an unmistakably feminine scream, followed almost immediately by an enraged shout that was also human—and male. He held his breath through several heartbeats, trying to discern its direction in the downpour, then took off at a run again, leaving the trail at a diagonal down the mountain. He weaved through the old-growth forest even as he wondered who was out here, as this section of the resort's wilderness trail was closed to guests until he had all the footbridges and lean-tos in place.

Alec came to a halt again next to a large tree and lifted his hand against the rain as he quickly calculated his odds of saving the woman without getting himself killed in the process. The two brutes attacking her weren't much of a worry, whereas the large dog racing up the mountain toward them might be a problem.

The woman gave another bloodcurdling scream as she bucked against the man straddling her, and twisted to clamp her teeth over the wrist of the guy kneeling at her head pinning down her hands. His ensuing shout of pain was drowned out by a vicious growl as the dog lunged at the man on top of her, the animal's momentum sending them both tumbling to the ground.

Okay then, the dog was on her side. Hoping it realized he was also on the woman's side, Alec drove his boot into the ribs of the man she'd bitten, sending him sprawling into a tree just as lightning struck so close the percussion knocked Alec to his knees. And since he landed next to the woman, he caught her fist swinging toward him, grasped her waist with his other hand, and lifted her to her feet. "Run! Up!" he shouted as he gave her a push. "God dammit, go! The dog and I will catch up!"

She hesitated only a heartbeat, but it was long enough for him to see the stark terror in her eyes as she glanced at the dog before she turned and ran uphill. The guy he'd kicked lunged at her on the way by, and Alec leapt to his feet when he realized the bastard had a knife.

The woman scrambled sideways, crying out as she grabbed her leg and kept running. The man started after her again but suddenly turned at Alec's roar. Alec caught the wrist holding the knife and drove his boot into the man's ribs again, twisting the guy's arm until he felt it snap before plunging the blade into the bastard's thigh. He then spun around when the dog gave a yelp, only to see it regain its footing and lunge again, this time going after the arm holding a goddamned gun.

Alec slammed into the guy, grabbing his wrist just as the weapon discharged. The dog tumbled back with a yelp, and Alec snapped the bastard's arm over his knee, causing the gun to fall to the ground. He then shoved the screaming man head-first into a tree, watching him crumple into a boneless heap before he turned and rushed to the dog that now had its teeth clamped down on the other man's neck.

"Hey, come on!" he shouted over another sharp crack of thunder. He grabbed the dog by the jowls and pulled it away. "That's enough," he said, holding its head from behind so it couldn't turn on *him*. "I know you'd like to see them both dead, but they're not worth the hassle it's going to cause us. Easy now, calm down," he said loudly over the raging storm, guiding the dog uphill several steps then giving it a nudge with his knee. "Go on. Go find your lady."

The dog hesitated just as the woman had, its eyes narrowed against the rain and its lips rolled back, then suddenly took off in the direction she'd run and disappeared into the storm. Alec looked down at the man cradling his broken arm against the knife in his thigh, knelt to one knee, and drove his fist into his face. "Sleep tight, you son of a bitch," he muttered, glancing over to make sure the other guy was still out before he also headed uphill at a run.

Only he hadn't gone two hundred yards before he found the woman lying facedown on the soaked forest floor, the dog licking her cheek. Alec approached cautiously, crooning calm words loud enough to be heard over the pounding rain, and slowly knelt on the other side of her. He laid a firm hand on the dog's raised hackles when it stiffened on a warning snarl. "You're going to have to trust me, ye big brute. Your lady's hurt, and I need to see how badly."

He felt the dog—he suspected it was a wolf or at least a hybrid—tremble with indecision, and Alec slowly reached out with his other hand and touched the woman's hair, which was plastered to her head. "Easy now," he said when the snarling grew louder, moving his fingers to her neck to feel for a pulse. He breathed a sigh of relief to find it strong and steady, and carefully rolled her over. "There we go," he said, releasing the dog when it lowered its head and started licking her face again. Alec slid an arm behind her shoulders and a hand under her knees, and stood up.

He headed uphill until he came to the trail and turned toward camp. "No, heel!" he snapped when the dog stopped and looked back down the mountain. "They're not going anywhere." The animal fell in step beside him, and Alec repositioned the woman's head into the crook of his neck to keep the driving rain off her face, and blew out a harsh breath to tamp down his own anger. Christ, it had been all he could do to keep from killing the bastards himself when he'd caught them brutalizing her.

What was she doing out here? Had the men brought her into the wilderness to rape and kill her and bury her body? The nearest old logging tote road was six miles to the south, and the resort itself was over ten miles away on top of the mountain. But she'd been running up from the fiord—which was just a mile below his camp—which meant they'd probably come by boat.

Alec scaled the lean-to steps, then dropped to one knee and carefully set the woman on the plank floor beside his sleeping bag, keeping her upper half cradled against his chest. He slid his hand from under her knees, then had to shove the dog away when it started licking her again. "Nay, you let me check her out," he murmured as he smoothed the hair off her face—only to suck in a breath.

She was stunningly beautiful but for the angry welt on her pale cheek and the darkening bump on her forehead that ran into her hairline. Alec looked down at her endlessly long legs and saw the bastard's knife had drawn blood. Realizing she was shivering violently, he started undressing her, but stilled in surprise again when he pulled her soaked blouse out of her pants and saw the dark bruise on her side. It ran over her ribs into her sheer blue bra, and he recognized that it was two or three days old. Filled with renewed rage, he carefully worked the blouse off her shoulders, only to find her arms also covered in small bruises, some of them appearing to be fingerprints.

It was obvious the woman had been struggling against them for several days, and he started rethinking his decision not to kill the bastards as he continued exposing the full extent of her nightmare. Feeling much like the storm raging directly overhead, Alec fought back the darkness that had been his life for eight years when he caught himself thinking there wasn't any reason he couldn't bury the *men* out here; quietly, efficiently, and with the calm detachment he'd once been known for.

The woman had obviously been bound, as evidenced by the raw chafing on her wrists. He found more bruising on her legs when he carefully peeled down her slacks, and she was missing a shoe. Alec pushed the dog out of the way, lifted back the edge of his sleeping bag, and carefully set her inside it.

He pulled over his duffel bag and dug around until he found a T-shirt. "Sorry, sweetheart," he murmured as he sat her up and unhooked her bra, "but I'm afraid getting you completely dry trumps modesty at the moment." He worked the T-shirt over her head, carefully slid her arms into the sleeves, and smoothed it down over her utterly feminine, rose-tipped breasts all the way to her thighs. He pulled her heavy mess of long, wet hair out of the collar and laid her down, then grabbed a towel hanging on the back wall of the lean-to and wrapped it around her head. Setting his jaw determinedly, he slid his hands under the T-shirt and carefully worked off her matching blue panties, but stopped when he reached the knife gash. "Damn," he growled, pulling off the panties and tossing them beside the discarded bra. He tucked the sleeping bag over her upper half and opposite leg, then dug through his duffel for the medical kit.

The dog settled against the woman's side and rested its chin on her shoulder, keeping a guarded eye on him. "You're a good friend," Alec said conversationally as he examined the wound on her thigh. "Ye can guard my back anytime you're wanting."

It wasn't a deep gash that needed stitching, he was relieved to see as he carefully cleaned it with gauze then started placing butterfly bandages along the length of the cut. He dabbed it with salve and covered it with another piece of gauze, taping it into place before tucking the baby-soft leg into the sleeping bag.

"Had ye reached the end of your strength or is that bump on your head making you sleep?" he asked the unconscious woman, carefully lifting first one and then the other of her eyelids. Again relieved to see her pupils appeared normal and even, Alec sat down and took off his boots. He then stood up and started stripping off his own wet clothes as he studied what was definitely a full-bred wolf. A northern timber wolf, he would guess; its long guard hairs muted black over a soft pelt of gray, with piercing eyes of hazel-gold watching him from a broad wet face. "Aye, you're a good partner in a fight," he said as he shoved off his pants and boxers. "And I thank you for not going for *my* throat."

The wolf's brows were all that moved as its gaze followed Alec around the shelter as he dried off with another towel and slipped into clean clothes. He pulled the band off his wet hair, toweled it dry as well, then combed his fingers through the shoulder-length waves before tying them against the nape of his neck again. He crouched down and laid a hand on the woman's forehead, gently smoothing her brow with his thumb. "She's going to be okay," he promised the wolf as he stood up and walked to the front rail of the three-walled lean-to that sat twenty yards up from the trail.

The storm was finally making its way north between the mountain they were on and the one at the end of the fiord, leaving in its wake an almost obscene silence but for the water gently dripping off the leaves. Alec glanced in the direction of the men and blew out a sigh, then walked to the rear wall and pulled down a small backpack. He placed a coil of rope inside, along with the resort's satellite phone and the medical kit, and slipped the pack over his shoulders. He sat down and dug two pairs of socks out of his duffel, putting on one pair followed by his boots, then rolled to his knees and peeled back the bottom of the sleeping bag.

He slid off the woman's socks—one of them shredded from her running in only one shoe—and covered her feet with his hands to take away some of the chill. He then slipped his oversized socks on her and tucked the bag around her legs before moving to her head. Alec reached inside the sleeping bag, pressed his palm just below her collarbone, and felt her steady heartbeat and even breathing.

"Ye stay here and keep warming her up," he told the wolf,

tucking the bag tightly around the woman before standing up, "while I go tie our two sorry friends to a tree and call the sheriff to come get them. And I'll call the resort to come get your lady." He grinned down at the wolf. "I hope ye like riding in a helicopter."

Alec started to leave, but stopped when the woman suddenly moaned, and he turned to see her lift a hand from the confines of the sleeping bag when the wolf licked her face. He crouched down beside her again, laying a steadying hand on her shoulder when she tried to sit up. "Easy, now. You're safe. No one's going to hurt you."

She pressed back into the pillow, confusion clouding the deepest green eyes he'd ever seen. "Wh-who are you? Where am I?" she asked, her gaze darting around the shelter. She started to pull her other hand free, only to gather the over-sized T-shirt she was wearing into her fist, her gaze snapping to his. "You undressed me."

He nodded. "I needed to get you dry to warm ye up," he explained, stifling a grin when her other hand moved inside the bag and she gasped. "Don't worry, I kept my eyes closed," he said with a wink when her emerald gaze narrowed, her indignation assuring him she was well on the road to recovery. "What's your name, lass?"

She blinked up at him, saying nothing.

Alec shrugged and stood up. "If you'll excuse me, then, I have some trash I need to deal with. I'll call the sheriff and then the resort to have their helicopter come pick you up." He nodded toward the wolf. "Does your tenacious protector have a name, at least? Because I'm thinking he deserves a few slobbering kisses in return for the way he ran to your rescue."

She pulled the sleeping bag up to her chin, again saying nothing.

"Okay then, I guess I'll be on my way."

"Wait," she said when he walked down the steps, making him turn back. She rose up on one elbow, causing the towel to fall off her hair. "I don't . . . Could you please not . . ." She took a deep breath. "Please don't call the authorities. I don't want anyone to know I'm here."

"You can't be serious," he said, scaling the steps to crouch

down beside her again. "Your family must be going out of
their minds looking for you." He touched her bruised wrist.
"You've obviously been missing for several days."

"But nobody knows I'm missing," she whispered, clutching
his arm. "Please, could you let me stay here with you for a few
days, just until I get my strength back and can decide what I
need to do?"

Was she serious? "Hell, woman, for all you know I could
be more dangerous than the bastards who had you. You don't
know a damn thing about me."

"I know you didn't hesitate to save me from two armed
men."

"The wolf took care of one of them," he snapped, standing
up. Why in hell was she asking him to stay? Was someone still
after her? Or was that bump on her head making her delirious?
"What's your name?"

Her gaze lowered. "Jane."

"Jane what?"

"Smith," she said, her cheeks darkening with her obvious lie.

"Well, Jane Smith," he muttered, walking off the platform
again. He stopped and looked at her. "We'll discuss your staying when I get back from dealing with the trash before it
crawls away."

"You could just kill them," she said quietly, "and bury their
bodies under a rock."

Okay then, *he* must be delirious, because he'd swear she'd
just asked him to commit murder. "No, I can't," he said just as
quietly, "because then I would have to kill any witnesses."

She didn't even bat an eyelash. "I won't watch."

At a complete loss as to how to respond, Alec strode off—
only to stop when she called him again. "I have a couple of
bags," she said. "But I had to leave them when I realized the
men were gaining on me. Could you get them for me, please?"

"Are they full of gold? Stolen art? *Drugs?*"

"No," she said, startled. "They're full of my clothes." She
reached behind her and gave the wolf a shove. "Kitty knows
where they are."

Alec closed his eyes. "Please tell me ye didn't just call that
noble beast Kitty."

"And could you feed me when you get back from dealing with the . . . trash? I haven't eaten for three days."

She was a rather bossy victim. "I'll see if *Kitty* and I can't hunt down a squirrel or two while we're at it," he said, turning away to hide his grin and jogging down the trail before she thought of something else she'd like him to do—other than commit murder and find her clothes and rush back to feed her.

Oh, but he was tempted to let her stay, if for no other reason than to keep himself entertained for a few days. That is, until he remembered her battered though otherwise flawless body and felt his groin grow heavy. Hell, spending even one night in the same lean-to as the beautiful woman would likely test the noble intentions of a saint, much less a man who'd been alone in the woods all summer.

Alec followed the wolf into the forest from where they'd emerged onto the trail earlier and tried to remember when the last time was that he'd been so immediately captivated by a woman. Especially an obviously high-maintenance princess who'd given him a fictitious name, who didn't want anyone—including her family—to know where she was, and who woke up from a nightmare and started issuing orders.

He found the men right where he'd left them, the only problem being the bastards were dead. Hell, one of them was actually smoldering, as was the exploded tree he was crumpled against. The other guy was riddled with shrapnel, a large piece of wood so forcibly driven into his chest that it was sticking out of his back.

Alec crouched to his heels and rubbed his face in his hands, then stared at the men in dismay. This ought to be interesting to explain to the sheriff: two fried corpses that upon closer examination would show cracked ribs and broken arms and a knife wound, and also a discharged gun nearby. Oh, and a battered, not-missing woman in his sleeping bag going by the name of Jane Smith, who also happened to have an illegal pet wolf named Kitty.

Speaking of which, where was Kitty?

Alec scrubbed his face again, undecided about what to do, then suddenly stilled. Well hell, it wasn't his fault these two idiots had chosen this particular piece of wilderness to settle their differences, was it? In fact, he could think of several scenarios for their being out here, from a drug deal gone bad to a botched smuggling trip to . . . to an execution interrupted by a thunderstorm that had killed both executioner and executee.

As for the beautiful princess in his sleeping bag . . . well, what princess? He could let her stay a few days to get back her strength, then run her down to Spellbound Falls in his boat in the middle of the night, hand her a few dollars, and kiss her saint-tempting mouth good-bye. Hell, he used to make his living orchestrating damage control—on damage he'd caused, usually. In fact, he'd been so good at it that he'd had to leave the game before he'd irrevocably damaged himself.

Alec went over and started carefully rifling through their pockets, only to come up empty-handed. He didn't find a wallet, money or loose change, or even any lint—which meant they weren't going to tell him what was going on any more than the woman was. But just as he started to stand he noticed the odd-looking burn mark on the smoldering bastard's shirt, unbuttoned a couple of buttons, and pulled away the material.

"Bingo," he murmured, taking his knife out of its sheath. He cut the leather cord and peeled the still hot-to-the-touch medallion off the charred skin before buttoning the guy's shirt back up and standing.

Alec studied what appeared to be an ancient coin of some sort as he walked to the other man and crouched down, used the tip of his knife to snag the cord around the bastard's neck, and lifted another medallion out of his shirt. He sliced the cord then held the coins beside each other, frowning at the identical symbols crudely stamped into what he suspected was bronze, before turning them over to see writing in a language he didn't recognize.

Okay then; these weren't telling him anything, either, since he didn't have a clue what the symbol was. Could it be the calling card of some criminal organization? Or judging by the men's plain, almost crude clothes, maybe a cult? Hell, for all he knew these two bastards could be members of an arcane fraternity he'd heard about a few years back that got its jollies pulling elaborate international crimes, and Jane Smith could be nothing more than the innocent victim of a pledge prank that had gone bad when she'd escaped.

Alec shoved the medallions in his pocket as he walked
a short distance away, deciding to keep them his little secret until he got more pieces of the puzzle to put together. He
sat down, slipped off his pack, then reached in past the now-
useless rope and medical kit and pulled out the satellite
phone—because the resort owner and his boss, Olivia Oceanus, had decided *cell* phones ruined the wilderness experience
for her guests and had talked her wizard husband into block-
ing reception in the resort's backcountry. He dialed 911, dutifully reported the *accident* he'd stumbled across—because
he really didn't want to bury the problem under a rock—and
gave the dispatcher the coordinates. He also gave his satellite
phone number, saying the sheriff could give him a call when
he arrived so Alec could lead him to the bodies.

He shoved the phone back in his pack, then started walking
the area looking for wolf and smaller shoe tracks in the scattered patches of mud. He erased them all the way up to where
she'd collapsed before he backtracked through the scene and
headed down to the fiord, again leaving only the tracks the
men had made. He eventually found where they stopped—or
rather had started—at the inland sea's high tide line; the problem was that he didn't find the boat they must have used to get
here. He saw only his boat, which was pulled into the trees and
turned over, its motor stowed beneath it. He looked out at the
fiord, wondering if the storm's waves had set their boat adrift.
But if the men had been chasing Jane, then there should be two
boats floating out on the water instead of none. That is, unless
she'd escaped the moment they'd stepped ashore and the storm
had sunk their boat.

Alec faced the looming mountain at the end of the fiord and
frowned. He knew the water was more than two thousand feet
deep in the unnatural waterway, and that the underground saltwater river ran up from the Gulf of Maine before it continued
north all the way to the St. Lawrence Seaway. The twelve-mile-
long fiord had been added to Bottomless Lake when an earthquake had pushed several mountains apart two and a half years
ago, at the same time turning Maine's second largest freshwater lake into the new Bottomless Sea—all compliments of
Spellbound Falls's resident wizard, Maximilian Oceanus, who
also happened to be Olivia's husband and Alec's other boss.

None of which explained how Jane and Kitty and the two dead men had gotten here. But at the moment he honestly didn't care, as he had damage control to see to, a woman to hide—and feed—and two bags to find. He'd found her missing shoe when he'd followed their trail down, making him realize that she'd traveled over half a mile wearing only one shoe.

Which meant Jane Smith was one hell of a *tough* princess.